Praise for William X. Kienzle and
Marked for Murder

"*Marked for Murder* is so real you
may become suspicious of every
black Ford Escort traveling down
the road, especially if there's a
black-robed priest behind the
wheel....This mystery leaves one
feeling satisfied, an uncommon
ending to many of today's novels."
Dayton Daily News

"Definitely one of his better ones.
Father Koesler's ability to solve
difficult and challenging cases
seems to improve with each story."
Asheville Citizen-Times

"It has the best plot of any of
Kienzle's books since the first
Koesler novels."
The Flint Journal

"Another superb entry in a gritty
series distinguished by its Catholic
slant and grim urban setting."
Booklist

MARKED
FOR
MURDER

WILLIAM X. KIENZLE

BALLANTINE BOOKS • NEW YORK

Library of Congress Catalog Card Number: 87-37353

ISBN 0-345-35397-8

This edition published by arrangement with Andrews and McMeel, a Uni-
versal Press Syndicate Company

Manufactured in the United States of America

First Ballantine Books Edition: April 1989

FOR JAVAN

ACKNOWLEDGMENTS

Gratitude for technical advice to:

Robert Ankeny, Staff Writer, *Detroit News*
Roy Awe, Investigator, Attorneys' Grievance Commission
Olga Bachmann, Ph. D., and Rudy Bachmann, Ph.D.,
Clinical Psychologists
Ramon Betanzos, Professor of Humanities,
Wayne State University
Sister Claudia Carlen, I.H.M., Archivist,
Archdiocese of Detroit
Detroit Police Department:
Robert Hislop, Commander, Major Crimes Division
Sergeant Mary Marcantonio, Office of Executive
Deputy Chief
Thistleton Robertson, P.O., Organized Crime Division
Barbara Weide, Lieutenant, Homicide Section
Jim Grace, Detective, Kalamazoo Police Department
Sister Bernadelle Grimm, R.S.M., Samaritan Health Care
Center, Detroit
Sister Elizabeth Harris, H.V.M., Director, Women ARISE
Margaret Hershey, R.N., Pulmonary Care Unit,
Detroit Receiving Hospital
Timothy Kenny, Deputy Chief, PROB, Wayne County
Prosecuting Attorney's Office
Noreen Rooney, Editor, TV Listings, *Detroit Free Press*
Andrea Solak, Principal Attorney, Grants and Legislation,
Wayne County Prosecuting Attorney's Office
Werner Spitz, U.M.D., Wayne County Medical Examiner

Any technical error is the author's

1

"IT'S ALL RIGHT, YOU KNOW—I MEAN, IF YOU can't . . ."

The young man tried feverishly—as he had for the past fifteen minutes—to stimulate himself. But the longer and more frantically he tried, the less likely it seemed that he would maintain or even attain an erection. And, before he'd begun, she had spent another quarter of an hour trying to help him. She'd used every means she knew. And she knew them all.

Nothing.

"Believe me, honey," Louise Bonner assured him, "it happens to everybody once in a while. It's nothing to get upset about. Tomorrow you'll probably have a hard-on all day."

"I can do it." His teeth were clenched as he thrashed about. "Goddammit, I've done it all my life."

"Yeah, sure, honey. But this is your first time with a woman, right?"

He flushed deeper as he continued his effort.

All his life. Louise suppressed a smile. All seventeen or eighteen years of his brief life. She had a mental image of him in his room, alone. On the walls, photos of females, nude or in various stages of dishabille. And there he would masturbate the night away. Then the fateful day—today. He'd saved his money. Or his father gave him ten bucks, told him to find a whore and become a man.

Well, what can you get for ten bucks these days, Louise mused. Forget the pricey bitches in comfortable hotels. Head for Cass Corridor in the decaying center of Detroit and you're

1

likely to find a Louise Bonner—El to her street friends.

She had plied this, the oldest of professions, for all but sixteen of her fifty-one years. And, as far as she was concerned, she had never achieved her full potential. Even as a kid with tight skin, she'd been on the streets. For that she blamed her early pimps.

Now? Hell, she knew she was much the worse for wear. Oh, she had managed to stay slim. And even if the curves were no longer shapely, the angles were still there. But her legs were a bit flabby, the flesh of her upper arms sagged, and the wrinkles—God, how they betrayed her!

But she was still good enough for this kid. It wasn't her fault he couldn't get it on. Even though she was old enough to be his mother. Forget that; old enough to be his grandmother!

All this she thought as she lay back on the metal bed with its stained sheets and grungy mattress.

"Look, honey, if it's the money. . ."

"It's not the money, dammit! I can do it. I know I can."

She shook her head. Time was money, even on a Sunday afternoon. The longer she spent in the room and off the street, the more potential business was driving away from this tired old neighborhood. By now, she would gladly give back his ten bucks. If she spent countless hours waiting for ten dollars to get used up, she could forget about eating.

She sat up and reached for her pantyhose.

"No, wait!"

She hesitated.

He went to his coat, which he had thrown across a chair. He fumbled in the pocket and brought out what appeared to be some kind of feminine undergarment. He offered it to Louise.

"What the hell!" she exclaimed. "It's a garter belt."

"Put it on."

"Honey, it won't fit. It's way too large."

"Put it on. Please put it on."

"But, why—?"

"It's my mother's."

She shrugged. Why not? It had been a crazy afternoon. Maybe she could get rid of him if she humored him. She

2

slipped the belt on. It was, as she had anticipated, several sizes too large. She looked at him to check his reaction.

He was ready.

"Well," she sighed, "I'll be damned."

It did not take long. In a few seconds he was no longer a virgin.

It was obvious from his demeanor as he dressed, and the jaunty wave he gave as he left the room that, as far as he was concerned, today he had become a man.

She dressed, pulling her coat tightly about her. Early January in Michigan could be cold. Or it might be warm. One never knew what to expect from Michigan's weather.

But this was a cold one. The wind whipped through the parallel streets of Woodward, Cass, Second, and Third— which, for the purposes of work, made up Louise Bonner's world.

She walked briskly, leaning into the wind, up from Cass and Selden, the corner where her apartment was located, toward Third and Willis, the corner she and a few others had staked out for these many years.

As she walked, she pondered. You're never too old to learn, she reflected. Take that kid. She'd heard of the Oedipus complex. Sometimes when she was younger, but even now occasionally, she would entertain a trick who happened to be a psychologist or a psychiatrist. From them, she had learned, among many other things, about the Oedipus complex. Matter of fact, one of her current regulars was a psychologist. She'd have to tell him about the kid. He'd get a kick out of that.

Indeed, she had told that shrink so many things about some of her tricks that she had considered raising her rates for him. He seemed to get a lot out of her information. Sometimes he would get so interested in her experiences he would forget to screw her. After which, he would argue about the money. She always got paid up front. That was one of her first lessons in the trade. But Doc would want his money back if they didn't get it on.

She never gave it back, of course. But, now that she

thought of it, she was performing a double service for him. And dammit, she ought to get paid for it. What did the Bible say? Something about a worker being worthy of his hire. Something like that.

Thinking on it further, this whole business had started with her learning things.

Lord, it was cold!

It wouldn't be so bad if it weren't for the humidity. There was nothing like damp cold along with bitter wind.

Where was she? Oh, yeah: learning things. School.

She'd gotten good marks during the ten years she went to school. Especially considering the turmoil that went on at home day after day, night after night. God, how her parents had fought! She could never figure out what kept them together. Even so, she had been good in school. Except that she'd had to work so hard for those marks. Until the ninth grade. Then that science teacher had showed her how to get great marks without any study at all.

Until he entered her life—and her—she had been unaware that she possessed dispensable favors. And that those favors were worth compensation. Suddenly, she had become a 4.0 student of science without cracking a book. Being naturally bright, she had put two and two together and came up with prostitution.

She was in school to learn how to earn a living. Along the way she discovered how to make what could be a very adequate living whereby school was irrelevant. She could make more money on her back than she ever could as a nine-to-five secretary. And she could start right then at age sixteen. Added boon: She would get out of that wretched house with its perpetual state of war. And where, as the years ripened her, her ox of a father had begun to ogle her.

It hadn't worked out as well as she had anticipated. Oh, the pimps weren't so bad. She was luckier than many of the girls in that she had never had a pimp who deserted, or worse, beat her. Nevertheless, for years now she had been pimpless—in the language of her profession, an outlaw. In fact, she had

4

become adviser and confidante to many of the women, particularly the younger ones.

But like almost all the other women, particularly those on the street, she could do little or nothing about the four plagues that afflicted today's hookers: certain cops, jail, society, and sorry-ass tricks.

Mostly the tricks. Who could depend on a john?

Massage parlors were worse than the streets. In the parlors, the girls had to service whoever came in, with little or no chance to veto anybody whose money the boss had taken. It was better on the streets, but just barely. A girl could turn down anyone she chose to, whether he approached her on the sidewalk or in a car. But the inclination was to accept anybody's money. After all, that's why they were out there. However, too often, indiscriminate acceptance led to a lot of abuse, verbal as well as physical. And murder was all too common.

There were few defenses. Experience, added to some well-honed intuition, was the main protection. But that took time. And while one was gaining that experience, one made mistakes. One hoped none would be fatal.

Another defense was the buddy system. Working in pairs or in groups of three or more, they demonstrated that there could be safety in numbers. Louise recalled a time when she was just getting started on Eighth Avenue in New York City. She was propositioned by a sailor. Before she could accept, an older woman advised against it. She was right: The sailor turned out to be a cop in disguise. Sailors don't offer to bring you to their apartments, the woman told Louise. Sailors live on their ships. Besides, there was just something about that guy...

Experience.

Another benefit of having a buddy was being able to check on one another. When one entered a car, the buddy could take down the license number and note the time. If too much time went by, the buddy could begin checking likely places where they might have gone. In a genuine emergency, at least the buddy would have a license number.

Thinking of buddies, Louise began looking for Arlene. Louise was now at the corner of Third and Willis, but no Arlene. Well, that happened.

El would have to depend even more on her intuition and experience, as she had earlier with the kid. There had been something about his immediate reaction to her. And he hadn't bargained. She had itemized what he could choose from and what each service cost. She perceived he was only waiting for her to mention the ten-dollar service. That's all he had and he was going to spend it all.

He had been unaware that he was expected to pay in advance—indicating this probably was his first time. And his politeness had reinforced that hypothesis.

Once they got to the small apartment she rented for assignations, his ineptness had further betrayed him. To mix a metaphor, this was his maiden voyage. And Louise had foreseen the entire scenario from the first few words they had exchanged.

So her intuition was running well today. She'd go on playing her luck whether or not Arlene got back before Louise got another customer.

She hunched and shivered. This frigid, damp gale cut right through one. The only silver lining Louise could think of was that bundling up hid the telltale signs of age. In the summer it was easy to see she was far from young. On the other hand, johns who cruised streets such as Cass, Second, and Third had no reason to expect Miss America.

This was the third time that particular black '86 Escort had passed by.

It wasn't that difficult to note; late Sunday afternoon there wasn't much traffic. Was the Super Bowl on TV this afternoon?

She didn't pay much attention to football. Only as it affected trade. The crazy thing was on sometime in January, that much she knew. (Actually, it would not be played till next Sunday.) In any case, whether it was football or the lousy weather, there wasn't much traffic. It was easy, especially with her experience, to spot the Escort.

On each pass, the guy had eyed her very carefully. Again, she was grateful she was all bundled up. Whoever the guy was, he wasn't going to get much of a look at her unless he put his money where his eyes were.

She was right. On the fourth pass, the Escort pulled to the curb directly in front of her. The driver lowered the window on the passenger side. She approached the car. "Want to party?" It wasn't much of an invitation, but it did have antiquity going for it.

"I guess so. Are you available?"

"Sure thing, honey. I'd almost pay you just to get out of this cold. Almost!" She emphasized the word, indicating it was only an attempt at humor.

She got in the car and gave directions to her apartment. Directions were followed by an itemized listing of services. ". . . Well, honey, what's your pleasure?"

He was silent. She studied him. One couldn't be too careful.

There was nothing about him to cause anxiety in the casual observer. He was wearing a black coat, hat, trousers, shoes, and gloves.

So he liked black. Not particularly unusual. Lots of people favor dark colors in the winter. Dark doesn't show slush marks as such. Dark helps trap and retain the heat of what little sun there might be.

She got a strong and unmistakable tobacco odor. He wasn't smoking just now, but he had to be a heavy cigarette smoker. And booze—there was the distinct smell of alcohol, though he did not appear to be drunk. He was wearing gloves, but she would bet her last buck that the index and middle fingers of one or both hands bore the telltale yellow nicotine stains.

Half-turned in the passenger seat, she had a clear view of his profile. He looked to be younger than she. But not by much. Maybe in his late forties. He was clean-shaven and, judging from what little hair she could see below his hat, he was either blond or gray-haired.

7

"I don't know," he answered at length, "I kind of thought of spending about twenty-five dollars."

"Sounds fine to me, honey." Most johns specified just what kind of action they wanted. Some, as this one, settled on the amount of money they were willing to invest. Nothing very unusual in that. And twenty-five dollars probably represented the amount he'd been able to squirrel away from his wife. "But I've got to have it up front."

"Huh?"

"I need it now."

"Oh, okay . . . sure." He had stopped at the light on the corner of Third and Selden. They were but two blocks from the apartment. He would turn left and they would be there. He opened his coat and reached into his breast pocket for his wallet. For a brief moment, his coat was open at the throat.

Louise gasped.

He took a twenty-dollar and a five-dollar bill out of his wallet and handed them to her. As he did, he noticed that she was staring at his collar. He smiled. "Something wrong?"

"You a preacher?"

"You might say so. That a problem?"

"Well, I'll say this for you: You don't try to hide it."

"Why should I?"

"I dunno. Most guys at least try some kind of masquerade. They claim they're single . . . but they're wearing a wedding ring. Or they're married but the wife won't give them any. There've been some I knew were preachers, though they wouldn't let on. But you—"

"My money not good enough for you?"

"No, no! It's just that . . . what kind of preacher are you, anyway?"

"Huh?"

"I mean . . . Baptist or what?"

"What do you think?"

"Anglican?"

"Why would you guess Anglican?"

" 'Cause of your collar."

"Oh?"

"I guess it has to be Anglican or Catholic."

"Not necessarily. But you're right: It's Catholic."

"You a priest?"

"Uh-huh."

"A Catholic priest?"

"Uh-huh."

Louise paused. He was parking on the corner of Selden and Cass, in front of her apartment. "I don't believe I've ever screwed a Catholic priest before . . . that I know of."

The car was parked but since she showed no inclination to get out, he let the engine continue to run and pump heat in.

"I mean, I used to be a Catholic . . ."

"Did you?"

"Yeah." Louise sat facing front. "A long time ago. I still go to church once in a great while. But I haven't been to confession or Communion in . . . God, I don't know how long."

"I didn't come here to hear your confession, you know."

"Right. Business before pleasure. Let's go, honey."

She led the way up to the second floor. Her apartment was at the head of the stairs. She unlocked the door and they entered.

It wasn't quite an efficiency. The most prominent article of furniture was the less-than-sanitary bed. There were a couple of chairs and a coat rack, a minuscule kitchenette, and a small table. He correctly concluded that this was only her workplace, not her residence.

She removed her coat and dress and hung them on the rack and sat on the bed. She kicked off her shoes and began removing her pantyhose, then stopped. "Aren't you gonna get comfortable, honey?"

"Sure. I want to watch you first."

"Whatever turns you on."

She continued taking off her pantyhose. Something about him made her nervous. She couldn't put her finger on it, but something . . . For one thing, he hadn't even taken off his gloves. You'd think he'd at least take off his gloves. The room was plenty warm. She fought periodic battles with the landlord over the heat. Today, at least, it was working fine. But he hadn't taken anything off.

There was something about his expression, too. He would not take his eyes off her. And there was something very hard about his expression. She began to have misgivings. But it was too late to call things off now. Best get on and get it over with. At the very least, she promised herself, this would be the last one today. She would gather up Arlene and go someplace nice for a good warm dinner.

But first, she'd have to get through this one.

"Come on, honey." She'd almost said, "Father." "You just got to get into the spirit of things. Why don't you get rid of those clothes?"

"You're right," he said. He removed his hat and coat and placed them on one of the chairs. He took off his jacket, placed it on a hanger and hung it on the rack.

"Oh, it hasn't got any back," she exclaimed.

"Huh?"

"That thing with your collar on it: It hasn't got any back."

"This? It's called a clerical vest." He unsnapped the catch that joined the two bottom edges of the vest at his waist. Then he undid the collar at the nape and removed the vest.

"All this time," she said, "I always wondered who buttoned your shirts up the back."

"Now you know: nobody." He removed the belt from his trousers. "Come on, now; your turn."

She seemed dubious. "What about your gloves?"

"I've got Raynaud's. It's a syndrome. Hands get cold and stay cold. It's not important. Until we get down to it, the gloves are more comfortable. I'll take 'em off in a minute."

She shrugged.

She rose and turned her back to him. Perfect.

She unsnapped her bra and let it drop to the bed. He fitted the end of his belt through the buckle. She slipped down her panties. He noticed that the skin of her buttocks sagged, betraying her age.

It was only a momentary impression. As she stood on one

leg, slipping the other out of her panties, he acted. He let his belt, now formed into a noose, fall over her head. She started, but as it reached her throat, he yanked . . . tight. She tried to suck in air as he pushed her face down onto the bed. He knelt on her back as he pulled the belt as tight as he could. She clawed at it. There was no way she could reach him. She struggled for a few minutes. He had expected that. But he held on implacably, sweating profusely. Then it was over. She was still.

He took a small mirror from her purse and held it before her mouth, her nose. No sign of breath.

He took the belt from around the dead woman's neck, reinserted it through his trouser loops and buckled it at his waist.

He donned his hat and coat and returned to his car, checking to make sure there were no witnesses. He saw none. He expected none. On a cold Sunday in this neighborhood, one could reasonably expect empty corridors and near-deserted streets.

He removed an object from the car, inserted it in his coat pocket, and returned to the apartment. He turned on a stove burner and placed the object on it.

He dragged the body into the adjoining bathroom and placed it in the tub. He then returned to the stove. With tongs he took from his coat pocket, he affixed the now red-hot object to a small wooden handle, and carried it into the bathroom, where he branded the body.

He then took a large knife from his pants pocket. With it, he opened an incision from just above her navel to her crotch.

He turned on the water tap, rinsed the knife and cooled the branding instrument, and returned the items to one coat pocket, stuffing the folded clerical vest in the other.

From beginning to end, he had not removed his gloves.

He surveyed the apartment. All seemed as he wished.

He pulled his coat collar up around his neck and exited.

Once again, he checked the staircase and hallway, then the street. Once again, all seemed deserted. With a sense of resigned satisfaction, he left the scene.

2

IT WAS ABOUT THREE HOURS LATER, JUST a little after eight o'clock that evening, that Arlene found Louise.

Arlene had returned to Third and Willis about thirty minutes after Louise had departed on what turned out to be the final assignation of her life. Arlene sensed that she had just missed her friend. She waited with growing impatience. There were no more tricks for her and it was getting colder by the hour. After giving up the idea there might be more business that day, she adjourned to a small nearby eatery, where she kept vigil for Louise.

At last, perturbed, she walked to the apartment Louise used.

The door was unlocked. It should not have been. She found Louise in the tub. After vomiting, she went in search of a phone and called 911.

In a matter of minutes, two uniformed officers arrived. Neither had a doubt about what to do. One secured the apartment and began questioning Arlene; the other called homicide.

Since it was just after eight o'clock in the evening, only five officers were on duty: a lieutenant, a sergeant, two investigators, and a P.O. (police officer). The sergeant and one of the investigators were out, responding to a call. The lieutenant decided he'd take this one himself, along with the P.O., who was a recent addition to the division. The lieutenant didn't want two relatively inexperienced officers making up a response team.

It took only a few minutes to reach the apartment. After a briefing by the uniforms, the newcomers began their own investigation. They went immediately to the bathroom. Barely bigger than a closet, it was hardly large enough for the two men. P.O. Mangiapane stood in the doorway.

Arlene had mopped up after her nausea; otherwise nothing had been touched.

"Good God, wouldja look at that!" said Mangiapane. "Somebody tore out her guts. Looks like some sicko, eh, Zoo?"

"Yeah, maybe."

Nearly everyone called Alonzo Tully "Zoo." Five-feet-eleven, slim, black, and reflective, Tully had twenty-one years in the department, twelve of them in homicide. He gave little thought to the prospect of retirement in four years.

He pulled off his unshaped Irish tweed hat and stuffed it in a pocket of his overcoat. His close-cropped hair was flecked with gray.

Mangiapane turned and gave the apartment a quick glance. "Don't see any blood around. I guess he cut her in the tub. Considerate of him."

Tully bent closer to the body. "Probably dead already when he cut her."

"Oh?"

"The bruises on her neck. Strangled. If she was alive when he cut her, blood'd be all over. She had to be dead at least a little while. When you're strangled, you quit breathing, but your heart keeps pumping for a bit. Her heart was gone when she was cut."

Mangiapane edged next to Tully at the tub. "What's that on her tit? Looks like a cross."

"Uh-huh."

"Well, I've heard about being religious, but that takes the cake."

"No, it looks fresh. Looks like it was burned into her. Maybe between the strangulation and the gutting. Or, maybe after he cut her. But it looks fresh."

"You mean he branded her!"

13

"Looks like it. Check it out with the M.E. when he gets here. The marks on the neck, the branding, the time frame for the gutting . . . the whole shot. Write it all down . . . everything." Tully had been making notes from the minute he'd entered the apartment. "You're gonna do the SIR . . . the Scene Investigation Report."

"Okay, Zoo."

"And don't write 'tit.'"

"Huh?"

"If we get to court, our report could be an exhibit. So be professional." Tully turned to leave the bathroom. "Take a look at the rest of the place."

Mangiapane found Louise's purse. He gingerly spread it open. "There's some money here, Zoo. Can't tell how much, but I seen a twenty and some tens."

"Uh-huh. But then just a thief wouldn't have any reason to cut and brand her."

"Here's her wallet. Maybe it's got her ID."

"Her name's Louise Bonner."

"Huh?"

"Most called her El."

"You know . . . er . . . knew her?"

"When I was in vice."

Mangiapane paused in his search and stood open-mouthed. "Holy hell, what a fluke! You knew her!"

"More than that. She's been one of my better sources over the years. That's what I've been wondering about. I don't know how far this coincidence is gonna stretch, but . . ."

"But . . . ?"

"El's given me some great leads. There have been times when I got to close cases just 'cause of the inside track she gave me."

"You think that had anything to do with this?"

"Could be. One thing for sure: Whoever did it is telling us something."

"You mean like the Mafia with the dead fish for somebody they've drowned or the privates in the mouth for somebody who broke the *omertà*?"

"Uh-huh. Whenever they catch up with a snitch they usually deal with 'em something like this. There's no way they could know that I'd be on the response team, but it was my source they offed. I gotta find out if there's a connection.

"Now, what I want you to do is start the report. Draw a floor map of the whole place—just approximate distances, but get everything in. Check those things with the M.E. When the techs get here, I want shots of everything. But tell 'em to pay special attention to those marks on El's neck and the brand. Also, take some close-ups of the burners on the stove. He probably used one to heat up the cross. See if you can find the goddam thing. And make sure her hands are bagged before they take her down to the morgue."

Mangiapane was taking notes furiously. He had the three-page investigation form but he knew instinctively, and was learning empirically, that Tully expected much, much more than the information demanded by the form.

"Right, Zoo. What are you going to do?"

"I want to talk to that girl." Tully flipped back a few pages in his notebook. "Arlene—El's buddy. The uniforms are holding her in their car.

"Then the two of us are gonna ring some doorbells."

3

IT WAS BRIGHT AND VERY EARLY THE NEXT morning when Zoo Tully settled in at his desk. At just seven o'clock, he had entered Police Headquarters at 1300 Beaubien. Everyone seemed surprised to see him check in so early. Especially astonished, though concealing it, was Inspector Walter Koznicki, head of homicide. He had no way of knowing that he was the reason for Tully's early appearance.

Koznicki habitually arrived well in advance of nearly everyone else in his division. In addition to his devotion to his job, there was a practical reason for his punctuality. The Scene Investigation Reports of the previous day were routinely arranged on his desk. His job was to review each report and assign the investigations to specific officers.

Tully busied himself at his desk, reviewing cases his squad was working on. But he frequently checked his watch, waiting for the right moment to interrupt his superior.

Now.

Tully knocked at the open door. "Walt, got a minute?"

"Certainly. Come in, Alonzo." Koznicki was one of the few who did not use Tully's nickname. But then Koznicki never used anyone's nickname.

"I want the Bonner investigation."

Koznicki was not surprised at Tully's brusqueness. The lieutenant was a direct person and Koznicki appreciated that fact. He also appreciated, in more than one sense of that word, that Tully was one of the division's best and most successful investigators.

Yet Koznicki hesitated. Only someone with a lieutenant's rank or higher could have made that request expecting that it would be granted. A P.O., investigator, or sergeant would have been forced to go through channels.

The fear was that an officer might want to work on a case in which he had an emotional involvement. The thinking was similar to that which argued against a surgeon's operating on a close relative. In either case, emotions or prior involvement could easily cloud an otherwise sound judgment. So, even though it was a lieutenant making the request, Koznicki was somewhat hesitant to grant it carte blanche without additional information.

With a gesture toward a huge carton labeled "Homicide-Prostitutes," Koznicki asked the logical question. "What is so special about the Bonner case?"

"She was one of my snitches. In fact, one of my better sources."

"So you feel somewhat involved? Responsible, in a sense?"

Tully knew the inspector was testing for an emotional tie. He also knew that though he was emotionally involved he must not let that bit of truth escape or Koznicki might deny him the case.

"Walt, there's a good chance whoever did this hit her because she was my snitch. It could have been retaliation for some lead she gave me.

"And if that's a fact—if she was executed because of some information she gave me—then there's a connection with me. When I come across the perpetrator, I'll know him. Or, put it another way: I know him already. He's gotta be a case I worked on—but one that El gave me a lead on. So, among other leads, I can check my files and my memory for the guy who connected El with me."

This was true enough and it skirted his emotional involvement.

"You are basing this on the modus operandi?"

"Uh-huh. It looks like a mob hit. Somebody kills a prostitute, he kills a prostitute. He doesn't gut and brand her. There's some kind of message in that. But it's different from anything I've ever seen." He pointed at the carton at the foot of Koznicki's desk. "I'll bet in all the cases you've got in that box, there's not one like this one."

Koznicki shook his head. "Not to my knowledge."

"All right, Alonzo, the case is yours. What have you got so far?"

"Besides hunches, not much. El had a buddy. She was too street smart not to. Arlene's the name. But she wasn't much help. She wasn't around when El was picked up. Which means either that our perp was lucky or he knew enough to survey the area until El was alone."

"Had Bonner told her buddy about any especially weird characters she had been with? Any threats?"

"Not really. Hookers service some pretty odd characters as a matter of course. But Arlene wasn't aware of anyone who

17

might be anywhere nearly as violent as our perp. And no threats. Just a day-to-day working schedule."

"Nothing else?"

"Mangiapane and I went door to door in the building last night after the crime scene—by the way, I'm taking Mangiapane with me on this one—anyway Mangiapane came up with one woman, lives in the apartment directly below El's. She thinks she heard the comings and goings. She says they came in about five o'clock in the afternoon. She heard them go up the stairs. But mostly, she heard them go into the room above hers.

"Apparently, the lady spends her time counting El's tricks. There were five yesterday afternoon—one of El's slow days, she said.

"What was interesting was that she can tell when there's action going on upstairs. She can hear the springs squeak. El's final trick—the one who killed her—the springs didn't squeak."

"He had no other purpose than to kill her."

"Uh-huh. And the M.E. is undoubtedly gonna find semen in her. But, if the lady is right, it ain't gonna be the perp's. So we're not gonna get a blood type."

"Prints?"

"All over the room. But maybe none from the perp. He must have touched the tub, but the only prints we could find in or on the tub were El's."

"None other?"

"No. And the perp must have handled the stove to heat whatever it was that he branded her with. Again, just her prints."

"You think he wore gloves?"

"Must have. But how'd he get away with it? How come El didn't insist he take them off? Or how come she didn't tumble to something haywire going on?"

"Interesting."

"That's not all. The lady downstairs, after she heard the couple go up to El's room, heard someone come down later all alone. Then she heard someone go up into the room, and then someone came down and went out."

"Meaning?"

"It had to be the perp. With a trick up there, why would El come downstairs, go out, then come back up? No, I think the perp went out—probably to his car, where he got the instrument he used for branding.

"So," Tully summed up, "what we've got so far: They got to the apartment about five o'clock. They went up. They didn't get anything on. Instead, he killed her. And somehow, she let him get away with leaving his gloves on. And why not? Hookers are used to quirky customers—to johns having all sorts of fetishes.

"But he couldn't bring the branding iron in with him. So, after he strangles her, he goes out to his car, gets the iron, goes back upstairs, drags her to the tub while the iron is heating, guts her, brands her, and gets out. And nobody we've talked to yet saw him."

"And now?"

"Now, I'm going to the autopsy. Then Mangiapane and I will canvass the neighborhood."

Koznicki nodded. He knew he did not need to tell Tully that time was of the essence. In an investigation, hours were important, days critical. The longer it took to run down a case, the less likely it was to ever be closed.

"One more thing, Walt: I want to arrange for her funeral."

Koznicki raised an eyebrow, as if to ask what Louise Bonner's funeral had to do with him.

Tully correctly interpreted the body language. "I'm nothin' —oh, maybe a Baptist once, a long time ago. But El was a Catholic. She used to talk about it every so often. Only she wasn't very active in it . . . not lately, anyway. She'd just go to church once in a while, almost like when no one was looking. So she didn't have any church or—what do you call it?—parish. I'm not so sure the average parish would have her funeral."

Again the raised eyebrow, not quite so elevated this time.

"You're a Catholic, Walt. I thought you could help me."

Koznicki spread his hands on the desk. "Alonzo, I am certain any number of downtown churches would accommodate your wish. All you need to do is explain the situation and the pastor would—"

"How about St. Aloysius?"

Koznicki controlled an apologetic smile. "Be fair, Alonzo. St. Aloysius is on Washington Boulevard serving a basically transient group. People go in and out all day. A funeral of any sort there can become a three-ring circus—especially one like the Bonner woman's is bound to be.

"You might try Old St. Mary's or St. Joseph, or, even better, Sts. Peter and Paul."

"The point is, Walt, I haven't got the time to shop around for a church for El."

"Then—?"

"How about your friend?"

"My friend?"

"Father . . . what's his name . . . Koesler?"

"Father Koesler! But his parish is way out in Dearborn Heights!"

"I know. But he's your friend. He'd do it if you asked him. It would save me a helluva lot of time and it would please El. As a favor, Walt?"

"I will phone him."

"I'll check back with you later. . . . I'm obliged, Walt."

Tully permitted himself a slight smile as he walked the few blocks to the Wayne County Morgue.

It had been late last night as he riffled through his files when the problem of El's funeral had occurred to him. Ordinarily, he felt no responsibility for the final disposition of the bodies in cases he worked on. If he had, with Detroit's homicide rate, most of his waking hours would be spent arranging funerals.

El was different. She had friends. It wasn't that. But none of her friends would be in a position to secure for her what she certainly would have wanted: a Catholic burial. He—Alonzo Tully—was the only one who might be able to pull it off.

But he wanted more than simply a Catholic burial. When

the idea first came to him, he, as had Walt Koznicki, initially thought of one of the core city parishes. He knew he wouldn't have to look far to find one of those dedicated priests who not only would handle the funeral but would do so graciously.

Tully wanted more.

El had lived most of her life well beyond the outer fringe of polite society. He wanted her to have in death what, in life, had been beyond her wildest expectations. He wanted her funeral to be held at a respectable, reasonably well-off suburban parish.

He had liked the idea from the first moment it had occurred to him. But which parish? He had no time, especially with the complex puzzle of her death to solve, to shop around in the 'burbs for a priest brave enough to take on what could easily become a most controversial requiem. He was not acquainted with any priests, in or out of the city.

Then the figurative light bulb had lit over his head: Walt Koznicki's friend.

Tully, as well as everyone else in homicide, was aware that over the recent years, this priest—Koesler—had participated in some investigations. Always there had been something "Catholic" about the case, something that a priest would be familiar with.

Tully had never had any direct dealings with this priest. But it was common knowledge in the department that Koesler and Koznicki had become close friends.

That, then, was the key: Get Koznicki to ask his friend.

He was sure Koesler would not refuse the request. Tully would contact the priest later, when he had time—whenever that might be—to take care of the details. But for the next few days, it would have to be one thing at a time.

He entered the vast, nearly empty lobby of the morgue.

"Hi," Tully greeted the receptionist. "The M.E. start yet?"

"He just went down."

Tully took the stairs to the basement. As he neared the autopsy chamber, that distinctive odor that early on had made him gag became pervasive.

Dr. Wilhelm Moellmann was at work.

Stretched out in long aluminum trays were three corpses. In front of each was a lectern on which was a form with the outline of a human body. Normally, the M.E. moved from one body to another, making notations on each chart, indicating the location of injuries, wounds, and the like.

But today Dr. Moellmann was giving his undivided attention to the body on the middle tray.

Tully and Moellmann knew each other well. The detective attended autopsies on his cases faithfully. And although Moellmann tended to play the flamboyant showman, Tully knew the doctor was one of the most competent medical examiners in the country. Perhaps in the world. Each respected the other's professionalism and expertise, even if the two were locked into role playing.

Though Moellmann became aware of Tully's presence, he did not turn to formally acknowledge it. "Your case, Lieutenant?"

"Uh-huh."

"Interesting. Very interesting. I don't believe we've had one like this before."

At this point, Tully guessed why Moellmann was giving his exclusive attention to the corpse of Louise Bonner. Like a psychotherapist who has treated too many emotionally disturbed people, the M.E. had autopsied so many corpses that the bodies virtually had lost their distinctiveness. There were so many shootings, drownings, asphyxiations; deaths from sharp and blunt instruments; traffic deaths, OD's. The medical examiner reaped the maimed shells of what had been God's most intricate creation. Though it might be noted that Moellmann believed neither in any afterlife nor in God. His incredulity was his peculiar reaction to his work.

Thus, just as the psychotherapist who is sated with manic-depressives, phobics, and the like, so was Moellmann inundated with death pure and simple. The psychotherapist's interest might be whetted by a rare psychological aberration. Moellmann clearly was excited by the challenge offered by this mutilated body.

"Was strangulation the cause of death?" Tully asked.

22

"What?"

It was as if Moellmann had been roused from some private reverie. "Oh . . . yes, it certainly seems so. Yes, asphyxial death. There's a tremendous fullness of blood in the internal organs. But she was not eviscerated until at least—oh, ten minutes after death. Otherwise, the heart would still have been pumping and she would have lost much of this blood."

Moellmann moved back and forth between the body and the lectern. He made many notations on the chart.

Tully next spoke when Moellmann turned his attention to the mark of the cross on Louise's breast. His face was only inches from the body as he studied the branding.

"So . . . ?"

"Mmmm . . ." Moellmann touched the edge of the mark. ". . . unquestionably makes this one unique. Makes it a ritual. A ritual killing."

Ritual. Tully's brain went into quickstep.

He would have to enlist the aid of the news media. This murder, unlike many other killings in Detroit, would make the news—at least the local news. The police as well as the medical examiner's staff would have to keep certain details from the media. At the same time, they would direct the media not to divulge certain other details to the public. This sort of crime could more likely be solved if the authorities alone—besides the killer, of course—knew all the details.

"What do you make of it, Doc?"

"It's a cross, of course. The mark seems to have been made by some metal instrument. Very thin. We'll get exact measurements. Heated. Was there a stove in the room?"

"Uh-huh."

"Then heated over the stove. There may be two parts to this instrument."

"Huh?"

"The vertical mark is more clear, more burned in, than the horizontal mark. Possibly the thing comes apart. Then he would have to put it together—fit one beam into the other, as it were. . . . Wait: This is interesting."

Moellmann was now using a magnifying glass. "There's

some sort of . . . something on this horizontal mark. It looks like letters of some sort. Perhaps just the upper part of letters. It isn't clear because the breast curves just there. It appears he may have wanted to leave a message of some kind, but failed. Maybe because he hadn't counted on the curvature of the breast."

"Can you get me that, Doc?"

"We'll have enlargements made. But I don't know that you'll be able to make heads or tails of it." Moellmann continued to study the marks. "Definitely the top portions of letters. But it's almost impossible to supply the bottoms. I can't make any sense of it. It might be four words. There's one open space on the left side of the vertical bar and one space on the right side."

"Nobody knows anything about this but us," Tully cautioned.

"Of course."

"It's the best we've got so far."

"The belt that was used to strangle her was one inch and seven-eighths wide."

Considerably wider than the average belt. That was unusual—and helpful. Anything unusual was helpful.

From the scrapings taken from under El's fingernails, it was determined that the belt had been of black leather. Evidently she had clawed at it while being garroted.

The remainder of the autopsy reverted to the routine. It was established that the deceased's stomach was nearly empty except for the remains of a hamburger. Tully recalled a greasy spoon near the corner of Third and Willis, El's prime place of business. She had probably stopped sometime yesterday afternoon for a snack. Maybe the proprietor or some of the customers had noticed something.

It was worth a try. Tully returned to headquarters, picked up Mangiapane, and returned to the area in Cass Corridor that belonged to the hookers, their pimps, and their johns.

Meanwhile, eventually, the autopsy on the body of Louise Bonner was completed. One of the attendants put Louise back together and sewed her up.

24

The attendant who ministered to Louise had taken an extraordinary interest in her from the very beginning of work today. In fact, he had almost come to blows with another attendant over custody of Louise's body. The scuffle had to be broken up by the technical assistant who was supervising the attendants. Both men had been warned at this time that they were on probation and could be dismissed summarily. But for a little while, the tussle had been the prime topic of conversation among the technical assistants.

Until that moment, only a few of the assistants had even known the name of Arnold Bush. Now his name would become almost an "in" word and Bush would become the subject of ribald humor, most of it having to do with necrophilia and his willingness to do battle over a dead whore.

But the jokes for the most part were exchanged behind Bush's back. For Arnold Bush had a short fuse and, despite a very commonplace appearance, he was uncommonly strong. He was a loner. And, especially after this morning's brief turmoil, he was left alone.

The attendant Bush had vied with for custody of Bonner's body had bruises on both arms. He showed the bruises readily, hoping for some sympathy. The marks of Bush's fingers were clearly evident. Anyone who could cause such injury simply by grabbing another's arms was given a wide berth.

Thus no one else challenged Arnold Bush's claim to exclusive care for the remains of Louise Bonner.

4 IT WAS NEARLY TEN O'CLOCK WHEN Alonzo Tully approached St. Anselm's rectory. He had phoned earlier to make sure that, first, Walt Koznicki had contacted Father Koesler regarding El's funeral and, second, that this would not be too late to call on the priest.

It had been a busy day. Tully was tired with that peculiar enervation that comes after pursuit down a series of blind alleys.

Which was not to say there hadn't been any progress. The M.E. had been particularly helpful. Now, if only they could determine what words, what message, had been burned into El's breast. That might clarify the entire mess. That could be the key.

Ever since this morning's discovery of the partial lettering, Tully had been certain that his initial premise was correct. This was a mob-sponsored killing in retaliation for El's having given him some tip, some information.

The problem was, what message did the ritual convey? It did not seem manifestly symbolic. What could it symbolize, the garroting, the gutting, the cross? That damned cross! The message was in those words. It had to be.

Tully had checked with the M.E.'s office periodically throughout the day. But, as yet, nothing. All they would tell him was that they were working on it.

Otherwise, it had been a day like so many he had spent in past investigations. A day where you take on the street and the street people. People who knew nothing. People who knew something, but weren't going to help a cop.

The owner of the greasy spoon remembered El. She was a regular, a regular in that restaurant of ill repute and a regular on that corner. He remembered serving her the hamburger, the remains of which Moellmann found partially digested in El's stomach. But he'd read the early Monday papers and knew what happened to El, so he knew nothing more. Whether or not he could have helped, it was obvious he wasn't going to.

Much more disposed to cooperate were the street hookers. On the one hand, one of their number had been murdered and each knew, at all times, that the same could happen to any of them. So the quicker the weirdo john was put away, the safer life would be for all of them. Additionally, many, particularly the older women, knew Tully from his days on the vice squad. They knew him to be eminently fair, even understanding and, more's the miracle, often kind.

Thus, Tully experienced a great deal more cooperation than did, say, Mangiapane. Even so, there just was not all that much information available.

By far, Tully's most significant breakthrough came from a woman who was both a friend of El's and beholden to Tully for past favors.

This woman had been working the street a few blocks from El's corner. Yesterday had been particularly slow, she said, so she had been able to be more aware of details than she ordinarily would.

It had been late afternoon, maybe about five, when she noticed something a little out of the ordinary. A black four-door sedan—a Ford, she thought, though she couldn't come up with the exact model; but it was black and so was the driver—no, wait: He wasn't a black—although she had thought he was the first couple of times she saw him. Yes, she saw him more than once because he seemed to be circling the same several blocks. About the third pass, she could tell he was white, but he was wearing black: black hat, black coat, collar pulled up.

She figured the guy was cruising, looking for a party. She would have pursued him more aggressively, but it was so damned cold she was almost frozen.

What was so peculiar was the number of times he circled. Most tricks go around a couple of times making their selection. This guy kept going around and around—like he was looking for something else.

This meshed with Tully's hypothesis that the perpetrator took care to make sure El's buddy was nowhere in sight.

Intrigued by this somewhat erratic behavior, the woman, against her better judgment—what with the cold and all—walked over to Third to see the man's next pass. There she saw somebody—she was sure it was El—get in the guy's car. But dammit, she didn't get a number. Nonetheless, it was another piece of the puzzle. A puzzle he was going to solve. Of that he was certain.

Tully had no problem finding St. Anselm's. His years on the force had made him familiar with all sections of the metropolitan area. Anselm's was just north of Ford Road, set well back on West Outer Drive. As he saw it now, under a light cover of snow, with the Christmas crèche still up and the facade of the church illuminated by soft floods, it looked like a lovely Christmas card. El would enjoy being buried from this church.

Father Koesler, in cassock, collar, and soft slippers, answered the rectory doorbell. Tully figured the slippers indicated either that the priest had sore feet or hoped their meeting would be brief, as bedtime was calling.

Koesler greeted the officer and led him into the main office, which was none too large. At this hour, and given the identity of his guest, Koesler might have held their meeting in the rectory's more comfortable living room. But in his phone call, Inspector Koznicki had briefly explained what it was Tully wanted. Koznicki had suggested nothing. He asked the priest for no favor, only cleared the way for the appointment.

Although Tully had noticed the priest at Police Headquarters several times over the past few years, he had always been too occupied to take much note of Koesler. Now, one on one, Tully took a closer look.

The priest was taller than he had appeared at a distance—

maybe six-foot-three. His thinning hair was completely gray and the cassock's sash did not conceal a slight midriff bulge. The glasses were bifocals. There were no facial wrinkles, only a hint of laugh lines around the eyes to betray his late fifties age.

Tully sat in one of the two visitors' chairs. "I came to arrange for a funeral, Father. I never did this before." Help me, his expression said.

"That's what Inspector Koznicki said. It's for that woman who was killed yesterday?"

Tully nodded.

"Horrible," Koesler said. "The paper said her body was mutilated."

"Uh-huh." Tully was not about to confide details. In truth, Koesler did not want to know.

"Well, Lieutenant, a couple of questions do come to mind. First, was the woman—Louise Bonner—was she a Catholic?"

"Oh, yeah. I knew her pretty well. Every once in a while she'd talk about growing up Catholic. She even attended a Catholic school. 'Course, she didn't go to church much lately . . . what with her, uh, profession and all. Is that a problem— that she didn't go to church very often?"

Koesler smiled. "It used to be. But not so much any more."

Since the inspector's call this morning, Koesler had been reluctantly awaiting this appointment. Instinctively, he was opposed to holding the rites at St. Anselm's. He feared there would be a lot of publicity, not to mention notoriety, attending such a funeral. St. Anselm's needed neither publicity nor notoriety.

So, off and on through the day, Koesler had been formulating reasons why Louise Bonner could not be buried from his parish. The primary and overwhelming reason her funeral should not be here was, of course, that there was no reason why it should. At least no reason he could think of. Now he began exploring the soft underbelly of the matter.

"These few times Louise attended church," Koesler said, "did she ever come to St. Anselm's?"

"Not to my knowledge."

"I didn't think so. Does she have any relatives in this parish?" If she did, Koesler was not aware of any.

"Not that I know of."

"Then I must assume Louise lived somewhere in Detroit and probably dropped in at some of the central parishes. Or maybe one particular city church."

"If she favored one church over another, I certainly didn't know about it. She was the type who would go in on the spur of the moment. So she probably went to a lot of different parishes . . . is there a problem about that?"

"The central problem I've got, Lieutenant, is: Why St. Anselm's? We don't know that she ever attended this church. She has no relatives here. There's just no connection at all."

"That's a problem?" Tully was being naive, and he knew it.

"The problem, as I see it, Lieutenant, is that there is no reason to have Louise Bonner's funeral from this parish."

Tully shrugged. "She's gotta be buried."

"But why St. Anselm's?"

"Why not? Look, Father, I went over this with Walt Koznicki earlier today. The point is, El was a Catholic. She was even kind of proud of it. She went to church sometimes . . . oh, nothing regular; she was never specific. Not with me. I couldn't put my finger on any one parish, Detroit or the suburbs, and say, 'Yeah, I know she attended there.'

"Point is, it doesn't matter which parish I go to, which Father I talk to, everything comes down to I can't tell any priest, 'Yeah, Father, I know she went to your church sometime or ever.' Point is, I could go to any church and the priest could tell me, 'There is no reason to have El's funeral here.' Just like you just did.

"Point is, I came to you 'cause you're a friend of Walt Koznicki's. I figured I'd get a better than even break here. But . . ." Tully rose halfway out of his chair.

"Wait a minute," Koesler waved him seated again.

Several moments of silence followed.

Tully correctly surmised that the priest was wrestling with his conscience.

Koesler was periodically reminded of a sort of reverse discrimination in the Catholic Church, at least in the Church of Detroit. Catholic churches in the city of Detroit were better able to bend, or even overlook, Church laws, rules, and regulations than suburban churches. And the more rundown the city area happened to be, the less official notice was taken of this freewheeling attitude.

The pertinent law in the burial of Louise Bonner was Canon 1184 of the revised Code of Canon Law, promulgated November 27, 1983. Paragraph three of Canon 1184 stated that ecclesiastical funeral rites are to be denied manifest sinners for whom these rites cannot be granted without public scandal to the faithful. Another paragraph added that if there was any doubt regarding a specific case, the local bishop was to be consulted and his judgment was to be followed.

The basic problem was, of course, did Louise Bonner qualify as a "manifest sinner"? Koesler's conclusion was that she probably did. Not only was she a prostitute, but the local news media, in reporting her murder, had made her profession crystal clear.

But would her church burial cause scandal? This was a more difficult question. There were, after all, varying kinds of scandal. There was a genuine scandal that seldom was recognized as such. Koesler had long considered the church burial of Latin American despots a real scandal. Too often, he thought, the Church refused to face the hard decision and buried the ruthless dictators. The fact that frequently such rulers were responsible for the torture and death of many innocent people, including priests and nuns, could easily identify them as manifest sinners.

Of course white-collar crime seldom was labeled manifest sin—unless it was committed by a Communist.

On the other hand, there was a type known as pharisaical scandal. In that instance, the scandal was in the eye of the hypocritical beholder. If there was any scandal to be had in the Church burial of Louise Bonner, Koesler was certain it would be of the pharisaical type. Was it not Jesus who said that harlots would be welcomed into the kingdom of heaven ahead of the self-righteous Pharisees?

Koesler was sure enough of the law's application that he felt no need to solicit the opinion of Cardinal Mark Boyle, Detroit's archbishop.

Once satisfying himself on the matter of law, Koesler was unconcerned about the possibility of scandal. It was the notoriety that troubled him. And this was where the problem of reverse discrimination reared its ugly head.

It was quite possible that Louise Bonner might be laid to rest from some all-but-deserted core city church with a minimum of publicity. But at a parish such as St. Anselm's, it would be another matter. Koesler could visualize the TV cameras plus the radio and print journalists. He could stand opposed to pharisaical scandal anytime. He wasn't so sure about notoriety.

But when Tully made as if to leave, it all gelled. In actual elapsed time, it took only a few moments to decide, especially since Koesler, earlier in the day, after he'd been alerted by the inspector, had pretty much resolved for himself the interpretation of Church law.

The expression on Tully's face as he explained the futility of shopping for a parish to bury his friend had settled the matter. As Koesler saw it, on one side of the scale was the notoriety that would come to him and his parish. On the other was a police officer trying to do no less than a corporal work of mercy: burying the dead. And the deceased was a poor woman who'd lived a hard life and died a worse death.

So to hell with the notoriety.

"We'll have the funeral, Lieutenant. And we'll try to do our best for Louise—for El." Koesler adopted Tully's term of affection for the deceased.

Tully's expression relaxed into a relieved smile. "Appreciate it, Father."

Koesler opened a pad on the desk and began to take down information. The Mass of Resurrection—a term that had to be explained to Tully—would be Wednesday at 10:00 A.M. The

32

matter of a rosary recitation was left in abeyance since no funeral home had yet been selected. Koesler would take responsibility for all the religious aspects of the funeral. Tully would see to the mortuary, the cemetery, and the pallbearers.

As he bade the officer good-bye, Koesler winced at the prospect of his immediate future now that he had agreed to take on this funeral. There would be notoriety. Of that there could be little doubt. And all he wanted was a quiet ministry among parishioners he'd come to know and love. Then, inevitably, there would be scandal; pharisaical, to be sure, but scandal nonetheless. Something with which he would be forced to deal. Doing what one realized was the right thing, was that really enough?

On top of all this, it was entirely possible that local Church officials would fault his judgment.

Undoubtedly, some priests would argue that Louise Bonner was not a "manifest sinner." Rather, she was more sinned against than sinning. But those priests would not very likely be found in official positions in the Church. That, however, was not the bone of contention. The pivotal question was the matter of scandal. Here, nitpickers would split hairs over genuine versus pharisaical scandal.

When it came right down to it, it was not a matter of law. Koesler's stand had nothing to do with any direct violation of Church law. It was, as with an umpire in some sports, a judgment call. One might argue that a base runner was out or safe. But the umpire's decision would stand—subject, of course, to review.

Review, in the case of this burial, was the province of functionaries in the chancery and, of course, the archbishop, Cardinal Boyle. Koesler's decision to grant ecclesiastical rites was not of a magnitude to spread beyond diocesan boundaries. He had no reason to expect it to be examined by an apostolic delegate in Washington, much less by the Pope.

And that was all to the good. While there was an abundance of unrest, distrust, suspicion, and condemnation in the Church on national and international levels, Cardinal Boyle remained amenable to reason and slow to denounce the judgment of one of his priests unless it was grossly incorrect.

So, while he could and should expect hypocritical scandal, notoriety, and at least some ecclesial flak, Koesler could be reasonably sure that, in the final analysis, he would have at least the tacit support of his archbishop.

Indubitably, he could have avoided the entire controversy and escaped all responsibility had he followed the advice of Canon 1184 and turned the decision over to the archbishop in the first place. But every drop of experience he'd had in more than thirty years as a priest anticipated the outcome in that eventuality. The answer would have been "No." All following the tight-to-the-vest philosophies of "When in doubt, don't." Or, "Better safe than sorry." As far as officialdom was concerned, in a choice between the burial of a marginal Catholic and a public relations mess, there was no contest. Especially since ecclesial burial or the denial of same, by everyone's theology, had nothing to do with a statement on salvation or damnation.

All in all, Father Koesler closed out the day with mixed emotions. He was convinced he'd made the proper decision. He was also convinced it was going to cost him.

Lieutenant "Zoo" Tully, for his part, returned to his northwest Detroit home with the sense that he had, indeed, accomplished one objective today: El's final send-off in the style she would have chosen in her fondest dreams. This achievement he attributed to his lifelong study of human nature.

Without actually knowing him, Tully had figured out Koesler almost perfectly. Koesler had given up and agreed to host El's funeral a bit too easily. That had been Tully's only misjudgment. Reflecting on it now, he attributed Koesler's quick surrender to a sense of guilt more profound than Tully had anticipated. He'd seen it often in clergymen, particularly in those who pastored in suburban churches. Many seemed to experience some sense of guilt when confronted with a poverty problem in the core city. There they were in the comparative comfort of the suburbs while he forced their attention to the city slums.

All in all, as far as Tully was concerned, it was not a bad

34

trait. The evidence of this tendency to be moved by another person's need might almost make a believer out of Tully—if that were possible. But it was not to be.

He parked in the driveway. There was a light in the kitchen. The rest of the house was dark.

It was too big, way too big now that his family was gone. His former wife, now remarried, and their five kids were living in Chicago. He visited them four or five times a year. He would have visited them more often but the situation that had caused the marital breakup still endured: He was married to his job. It came before his wife, even his children, before everything.

His wife had put up with it until she had no further endurance. It had been about as amicable a divorce as possible. He had agreed to the alimony and child support. It had been a "no-fault" divorce, but if there had been any fault needed, he was ready to admit that fault was his. He had agreed to her custody of the kids. He had no time for them while he and his wife were still together; how could he possibly have cared for them alone?

The light in the kitchen? That had to be Alice.

Their relationship was still in the trial stage.

Alice, a social worker assigned to juvenile court, was an extremely attractive woman in her early thirties. They had met only a few weeks ago over lunch at George's Coney Island on Michigan near Livernois. It had not been love at first sight. But it had been the beginning of a fast and easy friendship.

Alice had never married. But she found it quite natural, after a few dates and a tentative compatibility, to move in with him. There had been no strings or promises, just a tacit agreement to try it.

So far so good.

"How'd it go? Did you get a church for El's funeral?"

"Uh-huh."

Alice was seated at the ancient kitchen table. She was wearing her blue down housecoat. The house was too large and there were too few people living in it to heat it all. So no part of the house, even the rooms that were heated, was very warm.

"Which church?" She was doing some paperwork.

"Anselm's." He got a bottle of beer and sat opposite her.

"Just like you figured."

"Uh-huh."

"Any progress?"

"Got a black car—probably a Ford—and a guy dressed in black. Picked El up just before she was killed."

Alice looked up. "That's something."

"Uh-huh. Plus the cooperation of just about all the other working women. El was like a mother to some of them. A friend to the rest. I don't think she had an enemy."

"Except for the killer."

"Not an enemy, I think. At least not hers. Mine."

"Yeah, that's right." Alice pushed her work aside and removed her glasses. "You figure she got it because she was one of your sources. Anything new on that?"

"Maybe." Tully finished the beer and got a replacement from the refrigerator. The first had been to satisfy thirst. This one would be just for enjoyment. "Doc Moellmann is trying to figure out the words that were branded in her skin. That could be the key. Whoever did it is trying to send me some message. If I could figure it out, I'd be a helluva lot further ahead. This way it's like working on a case where the central clue's in a foreign language, and I don't know the language. It's damn frustrating."

"Can I help?"

"Not right now. But I sure as hell will let you know when you can." Tully lifted the lid off the cookie jar and put several brownies on a plate. He hadn't had dinner. Not unusual. "How'd things go with you?"

"The usual. Some kids in their late teens. Adults in everything but years. They know only too well that as long as they're juveniles we can't hold them after their nineteenth birthday." She shook her head. "I don't know how they get so hard so young."

"They teach each other. Older brothers teach younger

36

brothers. They go to detention and learn some more tricks. One of the first lessons is that the straight life is hard. Got to go to school, got to study, got to learn. Or they can hit the streets and with street smarts they can make more before they're twenty-one than they could make in an entire lifetime straight."

"If they live to see twenty-one."

"The final lesson: Life is short. It's short whether they're pushing, using, or just standing on the wrong corner at the wrong time."

Alice rested her head on her folded arms. She was tired and this conversation was discouraging. "There's this one I've been working with for a few months," she murmured. "I thought there was some hope for him. Today, for the first time, he finally shed a tear. I actually saw a tear trickle down his cheek."

"That's good." Tully had difficulty hearing her muffled words.

"The tear was shed because I told him they were going to waive him into adult court. He may spend the rest of his life in Jacktown."

Tully reached out and touched her affectionately. With the other hand he lifted the bottle of beer and took another sip. "Well, that's the way it goes." What was there to say?

Alice snapped upright. "Zoo! This is a *kid* I'm talking about. Just a child. And he's going to be locked up for the rest of his life. Maybe forty, fifty years!"

"Yeah, I know. But he might just last longer in Jacktown than he would on the street. A lot longer."

"But he's just a kid."

"Like you said, a kid in actual years counted. But in everything else, he's an old man. Look in his eyes: He's seen everything."

"I guess you're right." She shook her head. "He has seen everything. Probably more than I have."

"Look at it this way, Al: If he went into detention, he'd be out in what—a year or two? And the court would just be handing him over to us. He'd get some goddam gun, blow

37

somebody away, then we'd get him. And then: Jacktown."

"Good God, it's depressing. Why don't we quit?" She said it half in jest.

"Speak for yourself, Al. As for me, and just about everybody else in homicide, it's the case; it's the game."

"The game?"

"Every once in a while, you get one handed to you on a platter—a platter case. A man kills his wife. There's witnesses all over the place. The husband is guilty and feels guilty. He confesses. The case is handed to you on a silver platter. A rookie just out of the academy could close it.

"But then, you get a puzzler and you start putting the pieces together. A guy's shoes match the tracks outside a window. The guy's prints are lifted from the glass that held the poison. You dig and dig until you find enough reluctant witnesses who can put the guy at the scene of the crime. No one of the clues is enough all by itself. But you keep piling up one bit of circumstantial evidence after another. Pretty soon, you get enough strands of evidence to make a rope that you tie in a hangman's noose."

"Like a whodunit."

"Exactly like a whodunit. Only for real. And that's it, Al: That's the whole thing. The chase, the game, the puzzle. Solving the puzzle. The whole thing."

"Aren't you forgetting something?"

"Huh?"

"Putting the guy away."

"Putting the guy away," Tully repeated scornfully. "No, Al, the game ends when you solve the puzzle. What goes on over in court is something else . . . another world. You go to court and you don't recognize the bum you took off the street. The defense has gotten the guy a haircut and a shave and a three-piece suit. He just sits up straight all during the trial and doesn't take the stand. And the jury asks, 'How could that nice-lookin' man do all those horrible things?' So he walks.

"Or the defense finds a legalistic loophole, and the guy walks. You know—I mean, you *know*—he did it. But he walks.

"Or one of your witnesses doesn't show. And the judge goes out of his way to make you feel like a fool 'cause he was *your* witness and he didn't show.

"No, Al, what happens in court is another world. It might go good, or it might go bad. It might be justice, or it might be a farce. No; the game ends when you catch him, when you solve the puzzle."

"And that's what's going to happen to the guy who got El, eh? You're going to solve the puzzle."

"Damn right! Only this one's not gonna end there. I'm gonna nail him." He was unnaturally truculent. "Nobody does that to one of my people; nobody does that to me and walks."

"Well, Zoo, there's lots of people out there want you to do just that."

Alice got up, walked behind Tully's chair and began kneading his shoulders. He groaned as she found one taut muscle after another.

"You've had a rough day." She continued to dig her fingers into his back. "I've had a rough day. We've had a rough day. What say we go to bed?"

Tully hesitated. He seemed to be weighing the pros and cons. Finally, he shook his head.

"No, Hon; you go ahead. I want to go through my files again. Someplace in there is the guy who did this—or had it done. I gotta find him. And I gotta find him quick. There's a whole day gone and we're not even close."

Alice slowly climbed the stairs—alone. Maybe Zoo's first wife had a point in leaving. The chase, the game, the puzzle. Maybe it was just impossible for a woman to compete with a real-life whodunit. Maybe it wasn't even worth the try. She slid between the cold sheets and curled into a ball.

Tully went into the den. He poured a generous glass of inexpensive Gallo wine and opened the private files of cases he'd worked on. He would stay at it until the early hours of the morning when he could no longer keep his eyes open. Even under the steady pressure of precious elapsing time, there were limits beyond which even he could not push himself.

5

MEANWHILE, IN AN AREA OF DETROIT MUCH closer to the center city, Arnold Bush was awake and alert. He was busy in his efficiency apartment. By anyone's standards, it was not much. A cot, two chairs, a small table, a hot plate, and a sink. The bathroom, shared by everyone on the second floor, was down the hall. It was a poor apartment, in a poor complex, in a poor section of the city. It was all Bush could afford.

With his pay as an autopsy attendant, he could have been a bit more kind to himself. But he needed money for some of his exotic habits and hardware. Such as these pictures he was mounting on one of the apartment's walls. He had paid an exorbitant amount to the morgue technician for enlargements of the exhaustive series of pictures of the late Louise Bonner.

The pictures had been shot at every conceivable angle. There were close-ups of the head, showing clearly the marks a belt had made on her neck. Her torso had been photographed over and over, with particular emphasis on the breast that had been branded.

One by one, Bush affixed them to the wall. After hanging each photo, he would step back to judge the overall effect, the balance of one photo with another. Frequently, he would rearrange them to achieve a more satisfying grouping. He kept returning to the small table where a cigarette smoldered. Taking a deep drag, he would exhale slowly through his nostrils. The table held several ashtrays, all overflowing with the remains of cigarettes that had been smoked as completely as was humanly possible.

These were by no means the only pictures on the walls. But they were the first pictures of their ilk. On two other walls were pictures taken from pornographic magazines. And, while many of the posed photos were sado-masochistic, none approached the brutality of the photos taken at the morgue.

Only one of the four walls in this apartment was not covered with pictures of tortured, nude, or nearly naked women. The wall at the head of Arnold's bed also held pictures. But they were the sort traditional Catholics called "holy" pictures. Mostly individual pictures of Jesus, Mary, and Joseph depicted as blond, blue-eyed Anglo-Saxons in maudlin poses reeking of insincere sincerity. In the midst of these pictures were two crosses and one crucifix.

Arnold Bush was at least nominally a Catholic. In infancy, he had been baptized as a Catholic, and that religious designation had been permanently attached to his record as he was shifted about as a child. He managed to make his First Holy Communion, but was never confirmed—a conjunction of sacrament and nonsacrament that indicated his religious training had been spotty at best. As an adult, his personal brand of Catholicism was superficial and highly superstitious. Thus he saw no incongruity in decorating his room with a mixture of pornography and pietistic art.

Finally! All the Bonner photos were now arranged to his satisfaction. He moved a chair to the opposite wall and sat down to appreciate his handiwork.

Arnold Bush, of moderate height but powerful build, blond, and unmarried, was fifty-three. He looked much younger. Orphaned early in life, he had resided in a series of foster homes, some of them better than others, but none approximating a secure haven with loving parents.

By far his most traumatic experience in growing up occurred when he was twelve. The foster couple he was placed with at that time had to leave the state abruptly; a matter of bouncing checks. They left him with the woman's sister, who happened to be the madam in a house of prostitution.

He watched, he listened, he absorbed. It left an indelible impression.

After two years of this, the state bureaucracy found him again and, after entering this latest misfortune in his record, the state shipped him off to an institution for young men.

Arnold never recovered from his years of residence in the whorehouse. The experience marked him for life. Several times, mostly at the insistence of another man, he tried to strike up a normal relationship with a woman. He was never successful. There were too many memories of the hard, emotionless brief encounters that he'd witnessed. He knew how the women talked about the men they'd been with. He would not let that happen to him.

So Arnold cut himself off from almost all human contact. He worked very hard. He had to. He had no one to help him with anything. He had isolated himself from everyone. He grew physically strong. From time to time, he amazed even himself at how strong he was.

Take this morning, for instance, when his fellow worker had tried to take Louise Bonner away from him. Arnold had grabbed the man roughly. When the man pulled away, angry red marks—Arnold's handprints—appeared on his arms. Arnold had been genuinely surprised. And with surprise came renewed pride. He felt—for at least a little while—that he could do anything.

This was a time of change for Arnold Bush. No longer would anyone take advantage of him. He would be in control. And these pictures on the wall were but a sign of what was to come.

6

"WE'RE DOING BETTER, YOU KNOW," FATher Dick Kramer said. He balanced the phone receiver between his right shoulder and right ear while he lit a fresh cigarette from one that was down to its last millimeter. As he did so, he observed, but was barely aware of, his hand trembling.

"I'm sure you are, Father," replied Mrs. Ginny Quinn, associate director of planning for the parochial school system. "But you must remember, I'm dealing with figures. And figures don't lie."

"But you haven't got all the facts," Kramer asserted. "Figures are not all the facts. Spirit goes into this too. You can't measure the spirit of this parish. And I can tell you without any reservation, Mother of Sorrows wants its school to stay open. Even now our parish is enlisting several fund-raisers to bail the school out. But how can we do that if you insist the school has to close down? How can I motivate my people to work to keep it open if you, in effect, tell them it's a lost cause?"

Ginny Quinn sighed. She had been through all this too often with too many pastors and parish councils. It takes tons of money to run a school. More money, in fact, each year. There just was not that kind of money to be had in the poorer sections of Detroit. But all that so many of the pastors could see was the long history of their schools, which, realistically now, had no future.

"Father," she said, "*I'm* not closing your school; the *arch-*

diocese is not closing your school. The budget simply states that the parish can no longer afford to keep it open. Do you know what your deficit was in the past fiscal year?"

"I . . . I don't have the figures right here." He stubbed out the cigarette, forgetting to light another from the butt. He shook out another unfiltered Camel and lit it.

"It was $82,104, Father."

He was impressed. Not only at the extravagant sum, but that she had it down to the dollar. She undoubtedly had the cents too, but didn't care to grandstand.

"Well," he remarked after a moment, "that's considerable."

"I should say."

"But we can cover it. Even now the parish council is making plans—"

"Father," Mrs. Quinn interrupted, "that's just this fiscal year. I don't doubt that with a maximum effort the parish might be able to cover the debt this year." Actually, she doubted the hell out of it. "But," she pressed, "what about next year? And the year after that? The money just isn't there, Father. Once it was and now it isn't. It would be a mercy for everyone, Father, to face facts and pull the plug."

"But—"

"I'm sorry, Father; this is my considered opinion. Of course, if you want to take it up with my superiors in the school office . . . or with the archbishop . . ."

"That won't be necessary," Kramer said hastily. "Maybe I could talk it over with you again . . . I mean, after we've both had a chance to think it over."

"Certainly, Father. I'll always be happy to talk to you." Another small lie. She devoutly wished he would dry up and blow away.

He hung up, leaving his hand on the receiver as if about to make another call. He took a double drag of the Camel, then crushed it in the ashtray. Even to his seasoned mouth, the smoke was excessively hot.

"No luck, eh?" Sister Mary Therese asked. Although, since she had been party to at least his end of the conversation, she knew.

He smiled grimly. "She said I could appeal to the arch-bishop."

"Are you going to?"

"Are you kidding? I think that's why Boyle insulated him-self behind all these layers of bureaucracy: Underneath it all, he's too much a priest. Oh, I think I could reach him . . . but he'd only tell me he had to follow the informed suggestions of the experts."

"Like Mrs. Quinn."

"Exactly." Kramer lit another Camel.

Both hands were trembling, but only slightly. One would have to be extremely observant to notice. Sister Mary Therese noticed.

Mary Therese Hercher's position was relatively new and, so far, quite rare in the structure of the Catholic Church. For many years she had been a teaching nun. Then, in the wake of renewal and change that swept the Church in the sixties and seventies, she and so many other nuns reevaluated their voca-tional direction.

After much prayer and consultation, she had felt called to an inner city parochial apostolate. With Father Kramer's affir-mation, she assumed the title of pastoral assistant at Mother of Sorrows parish, which was on Grand River Avenue near the boundary of the corporate limits of the city of Detroit. In effect, she became a quasi copastor with Kramer.

While his was the ultimate responsibility, and while he was very definitely the canonical pastor, she was given the care of many parish ministries. She could not offer Mass, absolve or, in fact, administer sacraments. But she could—and did—ad-minister many programs for youth, for families, for the unem-ployed, for the elderly. And, in her own quiet way, she infiltrated some sacramental spheres. She listened patiently to the woes and sins of troubled souls. Then she forgave their sins. And the people felt forgiven.

Asked how she managed to give absolution without any ecclesial power to do so, she would answer, "I give them a little hug."

Her trim little figure, lively sparkling eyes, and ready smile brightened the homes of Mother of Sorrows parishioners and, in no small measure, made the rectory a much more livable place, even though she spent only some of her working hours there.

Of all the parishes that would have welcomed her, Mary Therese had chosen Mother of Sorrows for the sole reason that Father Richard Kramer was pastor. For several years she had been aware of his work around and for the people of this parish. Indeed, by almost any measure, Kramer was one of the hardest working pastors in the archdiocese. However, some would claim his work was largely unproductive, particularly in relation to the time and effort he invested. He seemed driven and in a constant manic state.

Mary Therese's feelings toward Kramer were mixed. She admired and respected his total dedication. Yet she feared— was almost certain—he was pushing himself too hard.

Then there was his smoking! She had no way of counting —and he would not admit to any definite number—but she was sure he was going through three to four packs a day. And unfiltered to boot! The rectory, his car, even his typewriter, reeked of nicotine. But she had long since ceased badgering him about a habit that had been condemned by just about everyone save the tobacco industry.

"Dick," she said, after waiting in vain for the slight tremor to leave his hands, "don't you think it's time to circle the wagons a little closer?"

"What? What are you getting at?"

"Maybe it's time to let things take their course. Maybe it's time to let the school close."

"What? Do you know how many years Mother of Sorrows School has been operating?"

"Sure I do. But what lasts forever? Most of the city's other parochial schools have closed."

Kramer ran a hand through his blond hair. Though in his mid-fifties, he was wrinkle-free, thus he looked much younger. "Have you seen them, Therese? They're ugly! They're shells! The windows are broken. They look like they're haunted. And they are! By their own past. Kids—

thousands of kids—grew up in those schools. Now the buildings just stand there idle, mocking the church, the rectory, the whole damn neighborhood. No, I won't have it!"

"Not all of them are idle, Dick. Some of them—most of them—have been converted into other kinds of service. And God knows that—"

"But they're not *schools*. And they're only partially used. And they're not schools!" Kramer was growing somewhat incoherent. "Mary Therese, you just don't know. You've never been attached to a parish that doesn't have a school. You were a teaching nun. So naturally, any parish you were associated with had to have a functioning school—or you wouldn't have been there. So all you know is the kind of spirit you find in a parish with a school.

"Let me tell you, I was an assistant at St. Norbert's when they built their school. It was like night and day. Before the school, it just didn't seem like anything held the place together. But once the school was there, it was as if somebody poured glue. The parish hung together like never before!"

Mary Therese knew the school was going to close. The handwriting was on the wall. Everyone saw it—everyone except Father Kramer. She wanted to soften the blow for him if at all possible.

"As you say, Dick, I was a teaching nun. So I know better than most that we are an endangered species. And it's not so much that I and many others had opted out of teaching. It's that so very few young women are entering the convent now. There are almost no teaching nuns coming along. And you know as well as I, Dick, that this country could never have begun or built or sustained our vast parochial school system without the nuns to staff them. If the Church had had to pay a realistic wage to these teachers, there would never have been a parochial school system; the Church could never have afforded it.

"And that's where we are now. Oh, maybe the barrel isn't entirely empty . . . but almost. There just aren't enough teaching sisters to come even close to staffing the schools. Some of the suburban Catholic schools are hanging on because they are just barely managing to pay a competitive wage to lay teachers. But that's not going to go on forever. Meanwhile, here we are: How can we possibly afford to pay lay teachers? And lay teachers are what we've got. There are no nuns."

"This parish can rise to the challenge."

"This parish is great, Dick. And its greatness is a direct tribute to you."

"No . . ."

"It is. But it's as Mrs. Quinn said: The school is like a bottomless pit. We're putting almost every penny from every other service we have into the school. And still it isn't enough."

"So that's it! You're jealous 'cause *your* programs are not getting everything they were budgeted for."

"Dick! That's not worthy of you!"

He reddened. "I'm sorry . . . I didn't mean . . ."

"It's all right. It's just that if you could put the school behind you, we could do so many other things. This parish is not going to fall apart just because we can't keep the school open."

He tapped a cigarette on the desktop, tamping the tobacco tightly together. "But I gave my word. I gave the people my word it would stay open."

"For God's sake, Dick, if anybody understands how hard you work for this place, it's the people. They'll know you did everything humanly possible to keep it going. The last thing you ought to be concerned with is how the people will react."

"Maybe. . . . Maybe . . . maybe . . ." Absently, he placed the cigarette between his lips and struck a match.

He resembled a small boy who had just been told there would be no visit from Santa this year. Mary Therese felt an impulse to cradle his head, put her hand on his slumping shoulder, touch him in some way. That she did not was not so much her decision as it was a matter of his character. His

48

entire demeanor seemed to forbid any physical expression of emotion, let alone affection.

There was nothing more for her to do. Silently, she rose and left the room.

He seemed unaware of her departure.

7

FATHER KOESLER PULLED INTO THE PARKING lot of the Burtha M. Fisher Home, better known as the Little Sisters of the Poor, Home for the Aged.

The Little Sisters took excellent care of the elderly and the aging ill. So exceptional was their care, according to the nuns themselves, that there was seldom a vacancy. The residents just lived on and on. The Little Sisters exulted in the fact that while their waiting list was long enough to discourage all but the most determined, there was almost always room for another priest.

Among the four priests presently in residence was Monsignor Lawrence Meehan.

Freshly embarked on his eightieth year, Meehan had been retired, having received "senior priest status," for the past ten years. Though he was arthritic, stooped and shriveled, still his mind remained mercifully alert and his memory sharp, if selective.

Koesler visited the monsignor at least once a month, more often if the occasion presented itself. Almost thirty years before, Koesler had served as an assistant to Meehan in a suburban parish. The two had hit it off then and continued their congenial relationship over the years.

Occasionally now, Koesler might submit a problem for the monsignor's consideration and advice. But not often, since Meehan no longer cared to pontificate or even adjudicate. He had pretty well left behind him with the active ministry most of the decision-making that had been his ordinary role for forty-five years as a functioning priest.

Mostly the two just visited and told each other the same stories over and over. Koesler did not mind; they were good tales, tried and true. Meehan didn't mind; his memory of recent events, such as when and with whom he had lately shared these stories, was fuzzy.

Koesler entered the monsignor's room and the two greeted each other. Koesler breathed a sigh of relief. He feared the day when the accumulation of years would roll over Meehan and he would not recognize his former assistant.

"So, how's it going, Monsignor?" Koesler placed his coat and hat on the bed and sat near the elderly priest.

"Oh, pretty good, Bobby, pretty good." Meehan, seated near the window, listed slightly to the right, the result of his arthritis.

"You're lookin' fine."

"Maybe so . . . but I think I'm in trouble again."

"Oh?"

"See, there's this nurse—physical therapist. She takes me through my paces twice a week. Well, yesterday she said, 'Monsignor, have you been turning your neck to the right and left like I told you to?'"

"And you said . . ."

"'Only when you walk by, Honey.'"

That was a new story.

"Did you follow that up by asking her for a date?"

Meehan's eyes twinkled. "What's a date?"

"If you don't even remember, I can't see that the Pope's going to get sore about this." Koesler had not intended bringing up the topic weighing on his mind, since he tried to keep heavy matters out of their conversations. However, the segue from what Meehan had recounted was irresistible. "But I may be in trouble."

"Oh?" There was hesitancy in Meehan's demeanor; he hoped this would not be a problem in which he was expected to get involved. As always, he would do his best to keep it light.

"I had a rather controversial funeral this morning," Koesler proceeded.

"Controversial?"

"We buried a prostitute."

"Somebody had to."

"She wasn't even from my parish." Somehow, as Koesler started to explain, the whole matter began to seem silly.

"Now, why would you do that?"

"Somebody asked me to."

"Remember that funeral we had back at St. Norbert's?" Meehan, as he frequently did, sought shelter in history. "That Italian family who owned the bar . . . what was their name? . . . Ventimiglia, wasn't it?"

Smiling, Koesler nodded.

"Yes," Meehan continued, "but it wasn't one of them. It was somebody—Uncle Angelo—who died. Hadn't darkened a church door since his confirmation. But the Ventimiglias wanted him buried from the church."

"Uh-huh. And they were the only ones. If Uncle Angelo had been able to express his opinion, he probably wouldn't have given a damn."

"Remember," Meehan said, "you and I spent almost an entire day trying to find somebody who had seen Angelo do anything, absolutely anything, religious."

"Yes, even tip his hat when he passed a front of a church. Notwithstanding that it had been the wind that had blown it off."

"Could have been an act of God," Meehan commented.

"Finally, as I recall, you found someone who claimed that Angelo had attended a relative's First Communion."

"Might have been a lie, but that was on *his* conscience. In any case, it was enough to satisfy the chancery that we could bury him from church. And then, when I told the Ventimiglias the good news, they asked if they could have a solemn high

51

Mass. Imagine: three priests for Uncle Angelo!"

"Yeah, I remember. You almost hit the ceiling and floor simultaneously." Koesler paused. "Church law isn't quite so demanding anymore. It's really quite open about burying somebody who maybe was Catholic in name only."

Meehan reflected. "I'm not so sure whether that's good or bad."

"Right at this minute, neither am I. With the old law, I think maybe I would not have been able to have this woman's funeral this morning—which might have saved me lots of grief."

"What are the requirements now?" Meehan obviously was somewhat tentative. Having retired before the new version of Church law was promulgated, he had not read a single canon of it. There was little or no chance that he would have read it even if he had not retired.

"It mostly has to do with scandal now. Angelo could have sailed right through today's law. It merely mentions *notorious* sinners. And then only when burying them would cause scandal. It gets down to the priest's judgment . . . or, he can consult with the Ordinary."

"Which you wouldn't do."

"Which I wouldn't do."

"So you buried the prostitute."

"This morning."

"Are you worried about the scandal?"

Koesler shook his head. "Not the scandal—although somebody might call me on that. No, I think I'm on pretty firm ground there. But, in a little while, a goodly bit of this morning's funeral is going to hit the fan."

"Oh?"

"One thing even I didn't figure on was that the deceased's colleagues would attend the funeral."

"Colleagues?"

"Other prostitutes."

"They were there?"

"Uh-huh."

"How did you know?"

52

"The way they were dressed, the makeup, the whole thing."

"You could tell?"

"They weren't members of the Rosary Altar Society." He shook his head again. "Do you get the daily papers?"

"Yes."

"It'll probably be on the front page tomorrow. And on TV and radio tonight, for that matter. Didn't you see the news earlier this week about the prostitute who was murdered and mutilated?"

"I don't pay much attention to that sort of stuff. Not anymore."

"Well, it doesn't matter. The news media will have a fresh angle on the story now. They were all there this morning. I'd bet my last buck that they won't bother with any of the circumstances that got her a Christian burial. They'll just do the 'prostitute and the Church' deal. The 'sacred and the profane.'"

Meehan thought for a moment. "That shouldn't be too bad for you, Bobby. You should come off as the good guy in the whole thing. You know, 'Hate the sin; love the sinner.'"

"I don't know about that. But it was a judgment call. And long ago I learned that if you spend your life second-guessing yourself, you'll go nuts."

"I'd have to agree. Just pray that your judgment is sane. Not like the guy . . . do you remember the story, Bobby, about the guy who was about to be ordained a priest, and he was going through his final oral exams?"

Koesler not only knew the story, he had recounted it many times. But he knew there was no way to head the monsignor off . . . nor did he want to; it was a good story and Meehan would get pleasure from telling it. So Koesler remained noncommittal as Meehan proceeded.

"Well, the test was part of the Moral Theology exam," Meehan began. "The question was put to the student by the Moral Theology prof as a hypothetical problem . . . by the way, Bobby, do you happen to know what a sacrarium is?"

Koesler smiled in spite of himself. Odd that Meehan would ask such a question. In his earlier life as a priest, when

Koesler had been a lowly assistant, he'd had many an occasion to use a sacrarium.

Back then, when it came time to wash sacred linens, principally the cloths used at Mass—such as the purificator—none but the consecrated hands of a priest were supposed to handle the initial washing. So priests—all over the world, as far as Koesler knew—rinsed out the cloths in some small container, the water from which was to be poured, not into an ordinary sink, but rather into the sacrarium that resembled a sink. Except that it was usually covered with a metal lid and, most importantly, the drain led not into the sewer, but directly into the ground. Thus, even the water that was used to wash blessed linens would be treated in a special manner.

Yes, Father Koesler well knew what a sacrarium was. All older churches had such utensils in the sacristy. Even many modern churches had them, though now they were used most infrequently. Koesler thought it passing strange that Meehan would ask this question. Perhaps the elderly just assumed that lots of things in their lives would pass into desuetude along with themselves.

Assured by Koesler's smile that he was, indeed, familiar with the sacrarium, Meehan continued, "Well, then, the professor proposes this hypothesis: 'Suppose,' he says, 'that you're saying Mass and you get past the consecration. You've already consecrated the host and the wine. Then, while you're continuing the prayers of the Mass—you have both hands raised in prayer—suppose a mouse runs across the altar table, grabs the consecrated host in its mouth, and runs off. Now, what would you do?'

"Well, sir, the student thinks about this for quite a while. Finally he says, 'I'd burn down the church and throw the ashes in the sacrarium.'"

Koesler chuckled appreciatively.

"Ya know," Meehan continued, "that's a true story."

Koesler doubted that; Meehan had told it so often it had undoubtedly transformed itself for him from fiction into fact.

"And ya know," Meehan concluded, "they ordained that man!"

"Maybe," Koesler said, "the poor fellow had some redeeming qualities. Maybe turned out to be a hard worker."

Meehan thought that over. "I don't believe I've ever considered it from that angle. You may just have something there. Maybe he did have some redeeming features. I wonder what ever became of him."

Koesler wondered how one would trace the lifespan of a fictional character. "Let's just hope he didn't have a series of mice snatching his hosts. Otherwise, this archdiocese would become churchless."

Koesler's comment fell on deaf ears; Meehan seemed lost in some reverie. "Hard worker," Meehan said. "Hard worker. That reminds me: How is Dick Kramer getting along? I wonder about him from time to time."

The association was natural, Koesler admitted. Of all the priests in the Detroit archdiocese, Dick Kramer easily was the hardest working—a distinction on which almost everyone would agree. And such unanimity was rare enough to possibly qualify it as unique.

"I suppose," Koesler answered, "he's working as hard as ever. And I suppose that's why I so seldom hear about him."

Meehan shook his head and shifted in his chair. "Works too hard. Always did. I worry about him."

"That's right; he was with you at St. Norbert's, wasn't he?"

"Indeed he was. I shan't easily forget that."

"You don't easily forget much of anything."

"Oh, yes, too much. Too much! But it would be hard to forget Dick Kramer. Why, he almost singlehandedly kept all those church buildings in repair. And when he wasn't carrying hammers and nails and an acetylene torch, he was taking Communion to the sick, or teaching in school or giving instructions." Meehan sighed. "He was the closest thing I ever saw to perpetual motion."

"Well, I don't know if he's still doing all those things, but I can tell you that, by common consensus, he is still hard at work. And he's got his hands full just keeping Mother of Sorrows parish open . . . word is the school is as good as closed."

"Sad. Sad. That could break his heart."

Koesler thought it appropriate to change the subject. The conversational theme was becoming depressing and he was sure that, with all his aches and pains, Monsignor Meehan didn't need to be depressed.

"It may be academic," Koesler said. "There's such an exodus from that part of town that eventually they may not even need a parish there anymore. In which case Kramer can get his carpenter's license and earn some real money."

"Carpenter's license," Meehan mused. "Say, Bobby, did I ever tell you . . ." Koesler was certain Meehan had.

". . . about St. Mary's Seminary in Baltimore? Back when I was a student there we had the French Sulpicians—actually from France. Most of them had trouble with English. I remember one of them one day mentioning that Jesus was a carPENter. And when we all laughed at that, the professor said, 'Oh, yes, zat is true. Not only was Jesus a carPENter, but he was the *son* of a carPENter.'"

Now that they were on the French Sulpician stories of the early days at St. Mary's in Baltimore, Koesler could almost predict the tales to come. But, why not? They were good stories, tried and true.

8

THERE WERE A FEW PEOPLE ON THE FRONT porch. They were not standing outside in the cold by choice. They were waiting to get inside the crowded house. Inside the house there was considerable commotion that was audible almost half a block away.

Father Richard Kramer heard it as soon as he stepped out

of his car. He shuddered. His task would have been unpleasant under the best of circumstances. This noisy crowd insured his visit would be attended by the worst of circumstances.

It took the people on the porch a little while to figure out who he might be. But they solved the puzzle rather quickly. He was white and he was wearing black trousers, a black hat, and a black coat. He was either a mortician or a preacher. If he had been the mortician, he probably would have been black, so odds were he was the alternative. As he climbed the steps, one of the onlookers spotted his roman collar. So she announced his arrival. "Look out here for the Father."

The crowd, like the waters of the Red Sea, parted.

"The Father's here. Look out. Give him room."

Kramer nodded to the people as they made way. Soon he was in the packed parlor. The focus of all attention was a frail, middle-aged woman seated in the largest chair in the room. She had several tissues in her hands. Her head was bowed and her shoulders trembled as she cried quietly. Her grief was all but silent; it was the others who were making the racket ... although as Kramer neared the grieving room the others reduced their decibels to whispers.

Someone vacated a chair next to the one occupied by the grieving woman.

Kramer had been through similar situations countless times. There was little or nothing that could take away the grief. Silently, he put his hand on her shoulder.

She looked up at him. Tears clouded her eyes. "Oh, Father, why'd it have to happen? Rudy was a good boy. Why him?"

Most mothers would have said the same thing. In this case, Kramer knew it to be true. "Yes, Sarah, Rudy was a good boy."

"Then why'd it have to happen, Father? Why?"

"No answers, Sarah. Rudy was on the wrong corner at the wrong time."

It was one of those tragedies for which Detroit was notorious. Kids marketing, pushing, supplying, selling, using dope. Kids with every kind of gun imaginable. Kids out looking for someone who had double-crossed them. Mistaking

57

young Rudy for the sought-after victim. Several shots fired. Two bystanders wounded. Rudy dead before his body hit the pavement. Rudy, one of Father Kramer's altar boys. Rudy, his mother's only son. Kids killing kids.

"Did they catch the kid, the kid that did it? Did they catch him yet, Father?"

"I don't think so, Sarah. I heard the news on the radio as I came over. But there was no word of it."

Someone handed him a cup of hot coffee. He thanked the person and reflected on how badly he wanted a smoke. But this was neither the time nor the place.

"Sarah, try to forget the kid who shot Rudy. The cops'll get him. They'll get him in time. Probably real soon. But it's not going to do you any good to have vengeance in your heart. Not at a time like this."

"What am I gonna do, Father? Somebody took my Rudy. How can I not think about who did it, Father?"

"It's not easy, I know, Sarah. But it just doesn't do any good."

"Then what am I gonna think about, Father? I got a hole in my heart."

"I know you do, Sarah. And you have all your friends around you to try to heal your heart.

"What are you going to think about? Think about how fine a boy Rudy was. No, how fine a boy Rudy *is*. What good is it for us to talk in church about Jesus coming back from the dead if we don't make that talk live for us?"

"Doctor Jesus?"

"Doctor Jesus. That's right. We believe He came back from the dead. He's alive. And so are we. We live in Him. So we live in this life and in the next life. That's where Rudy is now. He's alive in another life. A better life. A perfect life. Everything we do, even here on earth, is part of our eternal life in Doctor Jesus. Rudy was my altar boy. He is your son. But now he is with God."

During Kramer's exhortation, Sarah kept looking at him intently. The tears ceased to course down her cheeks. She was absorbing his every word as a sponge takes in water. But as he finished speaking, her face clouded once more.

"I want him back, Father. He didn't even have a chance to live." She began sobbing again.

Kramer could do nothing more than sit next to her and give her his presence.

Meanwhile, the crowd resumed its expression of grief. It began gradually and crescendoed. After a while, Kramer was hardly conscious of the noise. He was lost in his thoughts. Only when someone turned on the television was he drawn back to the present. Perhaps it was the movement of the crowd, forming a kind of passageway so everyone could see the set, that brought him back to reality.

"It's six o'clock. The news is on," someone said. "Let's see if it's on the news."

Sarah gazed at the TV set. Her attention was totally taken up by the image on the screen. As yet there was no sound. By the time picture and sound were both functioning, the teasers had been read and one commercial message finished. Now it was the strikingly beautiful Robbie Timmons on the screen

"The funeral for the slain alleged prostitute Louise Bonner was held today. . . ."

The picture switched to the facade of St. Anselm's Church. Kramer recognized it at once. He'd been there a few times at the invitation of its pastor, Father Koesler.

Kramer watched, mouth partly open, as the TV picture showed the funeral cortege approaching the church. He began to feel very warm. It started as a sudden flush and quickly grew more discomfiting. He trembled slightly as he rose from the chair.

"You all right, Father?" one of the bystanders asked.

"Yeah, sure. I'm okay. I've just got to get out of here. TV makes me nervous."

Kramer made his way out of the room and the house as speedily as he could.

"Can you imagine that?" observed the bystander. "TV makes the Father nervous."

"Poor man," said another bystander.

9

"POLICE ARE CONTINUING THEIR INVESTIGA-
tion into the murder of Ms. Bonner." TV reporter Ken Ford
spoke in hushed tones into his hand-held microphone as, in
the background, the simple casket was carried into St. Anselm's. "With me is homicide detective Lieutenant Tully. . . ."
The picture widened to include Tully's impassive face. "Lieutenant," Ford asked, "is there any progress to report in this
case?"

"We're following leads. There's been some progress. But
there's nothing really new to report." Tully looked away from
the camera, creating the true impression that he was uncomfortable being interviewed.

"Look at that," said Sam. "That guy ain't wearin' no hat."
He was referring to reporter Ford.

Sam owned a small bump and paint shop on Second Avenue near Warren. Most of the other buildings in that block
were either boarded up or gutted by long-ago fires.

"It was goddam cold this morning," Sam persisted. "Why
wouldn't he wear a goddam hat? That's what I wanna know."

"I don't know," Arnold Bush said. "Maybe he's trying to
prove something."

"What—that he can catch the goddam flu?" Sam laughed
at his own humor. The laugh disintegrated into a hacking
cough. When he finally got the cough under control, he retrieved the stub of a stale cigar from an overflowing ashtray,
relit the cigar, and coughed some more.

Sam and Arnold had been friends for almost two years.

60

They shared a natural mechanical ability, a love of working with their hands, a respect for tools, and an overpowering addiction to smoking. Sam smoked cigars, Arnold cigarettes.

Although Bush had recently been hired at the Wayne County Medical Examiner's department, he still spent much of his free time with Sam, helping with an occasional auto repair or just doing some fix-up work for someone or for himself. At this moment, he was painstakingly constructing frames for his most recent photos.

"Oh, the hell with the news," Sam said. "Maybe there's a game show on . . . or maybe a basketball game." He moved toward the television set, which was mounted high on the wall.

"No! Leave it!" Arnold almost shouted. "I want to see this."

"Okay, okay." Sam retreated from the TV and delicately balanced the cigar stub atop the pile of butts in the ashtray. "You don't have to bite my ass off."

Bush put down the aluminum strip he had been working on and gave full attention to the report of Louise Bonner's funeral.

The TV camera zoomed in to a close-up of the coffin. It was a simple metal box. Louise Bonner would have been buried in the simplest coffin of all—a wooden box—except that her sister prostitutes had taken up a collection among themselves, raising, by almost anyone's standards, a fairly generous amount. They insured that she would be buried with dignity.

A smile appeared on Arnold Bush's face as he contemplated the casket. It was as if he had X-ray vision. He pictured Louise's body beneath the lid, under the silken lining. He could see in his mind's eye those photos of her mutilated torso—the very same photos for which he was now making frames. He recalled the procedures that had followed the picture-taking and the autopsy. He remembered in great detail personally tucking Louise's organs back inside her body and sewing her up. Painstakingly sewing her up preliminary to the mortician's work.

In his as yet brief time with the medical examiner's office, this was the first body that had been all "his." He had reserved her to himself. He had almost come to blows over possession of her. He would have fought, too, had the other man pushed him further.

Yes, this was "his" first body. It was not likely to be the last.

Meanwhile, he was enjoying the pictures of the funeral.

10

"INSIDE, THE CHURCH WAS FILLED to near capacity." On the six o'clock news, TV reporter Ken Ford continued his muted commentary. "Many in this morning's congregation were the merely curious who came to attend the last rites of a woman almost completely unnoted in life. A woman who might have remained unknown in death had it not been for the bizarre manner of that death."

Father Koesler grimaced as he watched the TV account of the funeral he had celebrated that morning. He had been having second, third, and fourth thoughts all day about what he had done. All that he had told Monsignor Meehan earlier about the funeral had come true. The afternoon *Detroit News* carried two photos with an accompanying story in its first section. Undoubtedly the *Free Press* would feature coverage in its early editions.

Koesler could watch only one TV channel at a time. This happened to be channel 7. Later he would try channels 2 and 4.

He was standing in the doorway between the rectory kitchen and the dining area. He was trying to cook supper, a never-ending adventure in his life. After this morning's funeral, it had been easy for him to convince himself that he deserved a treat. So, on the way back from visiting Monsignor Meehan, Koesler stopped to purchase a succulent porterhouse steak.

Ordinarily, he would flip something like that into a pan and fry it. But not this beauty. It deserved something better. Thus, he had solicited directions from one of his parishioners on the method of broiling. The parishioner had assured him that the process wouldn't take long and that he should check the steak's condition every few minutes, first to turn it, then to finish it.

Several minutes ago he had set the stove's control on "broil" and tenderly placed the steak in the oven. He had just now checked for the progress. Nothing. The oven wasn't even hot. But Koesler was a man of faith. The kind lady had told him how to broil a steak and by God he was going to follow directions to the bitter end.

While waiting for some action from the oven, he had made himself a cup of instant coffee, which he was now sipping. He could not understand why his coffee was so universally disliked. *He* found it quite good. But it was difficult for him to recall anyone who had tasted his coffee ever accepting another cup. Ever.

"In the congregation," reporter Ford continued, "were many of the slain woman's friends and former associates. . . ." Ford put a peculiar emphasis on the words "friends" and "associates." The picture made his implication quite obvious, especially if one kept in mind that Louise Bonner had been a prostitute. Koesler winced as the camera panned that section of the church where the working women had clustered.

In hindsight, Koesler wished he had not turned on the heat in the church. For the ladies had removed their coats, revealing clinging dresses that hugged curves and accentuated bosoms. That, plus their extravagant makeup, made it less than necessary for the reporter to get explicit about their line of business.

Koesler was just beginning to wonder how much longer it would take for . . . when the phone rang.

"Father?"

"Yes."

"I hope you realize that the founding pastor of this parish is spinning in his grave tonight. In one morning you have violated all that holy man stood for. It wasn't bad enough that you staged a funeral for a known prostitute; you had to invite all the other fallen women in the city to this travesty of a sacred rite."

"Now, wait a minute: I didn't invite anyone to this funeral. I merely agreed to bury from our church a Catholic woman who didn't have a regular parish."

"If you didn't invite them, who did? They were all there. I read about it in the *News* and now everyone is seeing it on television. This is a scandal of the highest kind. And since when has St. Anselm's been a receptacle for the refuse of society? If the woman didn't go to church, she should have been buried like a dog. At best she could have been buried from one of the inner city storefront churches."

Koesler thought he recognized the voice. "Just who is this?"

"I don't think that's any of your business."

"Well, I do. And I'm not in the habit of talking with anonymous cowards."

"How dare you!"

"Mister, you've got one distinct advantage over me: *I'm* busy." He slammed down the receiver.

Immediately, he began to regret his action. How could he have said such harsh things to such a poor misguided soul?

However, on second thought, this was not your run-of-the-mill poor misguided soul. This was the quintessential pharisee. The one whose pharisaical scandal Koesler had dismissed when he'd agreed to take on Louise Bonner's funeral. And he hadn't been unChristlike; Jesus had always reserved his harshest words and criticism for those disingenuous pharisees who fought truth and charity every step of the way.

Besides, he had been correct about one thing: He was indeed busy. There was the matter of that luscious steak. What with the phone call, Koesler had temporarily forgotten it. Now anxious, he hoped it wasn't overdone.

He quickly moved to the stove, opened the oven door, and slid the meat out for inspection. Wonder of wonders, it was hardly cooked at all. He checked the heat gauge. It was firmly set on "broil." Koesler shrugged. Instructions were instructions. And that nice lady would not have led him astray. Resigned to following this thing through to its natural conclusion, he slid the steak back into the oven and closed the door.

As it turned out, he was to have plenty of time for phone calls. For he had placed the steak in the roasting oven, which was immediately above the broiling oven. The steak was, in effect, roasting in the oven, heated by the broiler. But very s-l-o-w-l-y.

It would be hours before the steak was done to Koesler's desire. And it would be a long time before, in the course of casual conversation, he would discover how the stove had outsmarted him.

11

THE LEADERS OF THE VARIOUS HOMICIDE squads met routinely two or three times weekly with Inspector Koznicki to report on and discuss cases under investigation. It was at the conclusion of one such meeting on Friday afternoon that Koznicki asked Lieutenant Tully to remain behind.

After the others left the meeting room, Koznicki said, "I wanted to talk to you a bit more about the Culpepper case."

Tully nodded, found the information in his folder, and slid the packet across the table.

After studying it for a time, Koznicki said, "It seems to make no sense."

Tully shook his head. "Not the way it stacks up . . . although Mangiapane did a good job putting it together."

"As it stands, we have two men—what were they?—"

"Brothers-in-law."

"Brothers-in-law. Culpepper picks up Moore at his usual time. The two travel to work via the same route they take every morning. Then, out of nowhere, a motorcycle pulls up even with the car. There are two men—according to eyewitnesses—on the 'cycle. The passenger on the 'cycle opens up with automatic fire. The car is ripped open and the two men are killed instantly."

Tully nodded.

"There seems to be no motive." Koznicki looked expectantly at Tully.

"Not on the surface. Mangiapane couldn't find any connection between Culpepper and the brother-in-law—Moore—and any kind of illegal traffic. It looked like it could have been a drug or mob thing. A couple guys holdin' out or movin' in on somebody else's turf. But Mangiapane couldn't find a trace of that. Just two guys own a grocery store together. They're both straight. Neither one's makin' a bundle. Then, one morning, they buy it."

"No one got a license number for the 'cycle?"

"Too shocked. Happened too fast. People couldn't believe their eyes. We're lucky we got any description of the 'cycle guys at all. But something interesting happened today."

Koznicki raised his eyebrows.

"The widow, Mrs. Culpepper, came in. Wanted to talk to Mangiapane, but he was on the street. So I talked to her. She wanted some kind of certificate stating that she was not a suspect. I asked her why she needed it and she said that the life insurance company wanted it before they would begin payment on her claim." Tully grinned. "I told her we don't do that sort of thing."

"You think—"

"It's a motive. She profits. Suppose she gets a contract out on her husband. She's awful anxious to get to that insurance. She'd also like to get us out of her hair. It's a shot. Mangiapane is on it now. He's gonna lean on her pretty hard. She tried to be cool this afternoon but underneath she was nervous . . . plenty nervous. I think she'll crack."

"Very good. Now, then, Alonzo, what about the Bonner affair? Is anything moving on that?"

"At this moment, it's dead in the water. We've got a guy driving a black Ford and he's wearing black. Maybe he knows enough to recognize the buddy system, so he waits until El is alone on the street. He takes her to her pad and we know the rest. That's all we know about him. The problem is what he did to her. He didn't just kill her. He went way beyond that. And—and this is the big question—why?"

"I'm still going on the theory that El paid for being my snitch. Maybe the message was when he gutted her. But if there's something there, I don't know what it is. More likely, the message is in whatever it was he branded her with—that cross. And whatever those letters were he burned into her tit . . . that's probably it. If we could figure out the words. If only we could figure out the words . . ."

"The M.E. was no help?"

Tully looked away from Koznicki. "I think the guy didn't count on the contour of El's tit. He burned in only the top half of the letters. Doc Moellmann thinks there are four words to the message. Nine letters in the first word, nine in the second, two in the third, and nine in the last."

"Making twenty-nine."

"Making twenty-nine," Tully agreed. "I don't even know if there's a message in the numbers. Maybe . . ."

"And you can make out none of the words?"

Tully shook his head. "I sent enlargements over to Wayne State's Humanities Department. Some experts in languages are looking them over. So far, nothing. Every spare minute I'm not going through my files trying to find the missing link that ties El to me, I'm going over those damn pictures, trying

67

to break down the words. Most of the letters could be practically anything. It could drive you nuts."

"The case is getting old, Alonzo." Koznicki was gently suggesting that it might be time to at least put it on the back burner.

"I know, Walt. I know. In my saner moments, I know I'm not going to get any closer to it than I am now. But it's gonna bug me till my dying day. Either that or somehow, someday, I'm gonna crack it."

12

"SUNDAY, SWEET SUNDAY, WITH nothing to do . . ." Alonzo Tully was humming the tune from "Flower Drum Song." It expressed his sentiments perfectly. Today happened to be that rare Sunday when no duty called and he was determined to do nothing. But in order to fully appreciate doing nothing, one could not spend the day in bed.

So, Tully had wakened at seven and cautiously slipped out of bed, careful not to rouse Alice. She had been quite explicit in the past about not wishing to share his early-bird habit.

He had retrieved the Sunday *News* and *Free Press* from the front porch, brought them into the kitchen, brewed some coffee, made some toast, and settled himself at the table. He began skimming the papers, scanning headlines, stopping only to read the few articles that caught his interest.

One such item was the column by Pete Waldmeir in the *News*. Once again, Waldmeir was taking on the city administration in general and Detroit Mayor Maynard Cobb in particular. This, for Waldmeir, had become routine. Of all the columnists in town, no one spent more time or ink on the mayor's case than Pete Waldmeir.

Maynard Cobb was black. And that, particularly to black Detroiters, was the most important feature of the mayor. To Tully, Cobb's skin color was symbolic of Detroit's radical change.

Tully, born and raised in Detroit, easily recalled the early days, the days before any of the civil rights legislation of the sixties. But mostly, the days before Cobb enraptured and captured Detroit.

The fifties, perhaps the final decade of innocence for the United States, had been fun. A lot more fun if you were not in Korea or not one of America's minorities. Blacks in Detroit were significant numerically and distinctive in lack of clout. The white majority lived blissfully more or less unaware that they formed the cork in a bottle seething with a dark liquid. Everything boiled over during the riots of 1967 and again in the wake of the assassination of Martin Luther King, Jr.

And then came Cobb.

It was the Reverend Jesse Jackson who first pointed out to fellow blacks that no one any longer was standing in the schoolhouse door. An allusion to George Wallace's attempt to block the entrance of black students into Alabama's all-white schools.

While it was true that civil rights laws had technically removed racial obstacles to education and, to some degree, advancement, it was the election of Maynard Cobb that had opened doors and ushered blacks through them in Detroit. Then, as might be expected, patronage, appointments, and contracts began favoring minorities. And gradually, the complexion of the city's majority changed from white to black.

About nearly all of this Tully couldn't have cared less. He left politics to the politicians, business to the businessmen, and religion to the preachers. He had cut out for himself a small island called the Detroit Police Department and an even tighter plateau called the Homicide Division. As soon as someone—he didn't care who—cleared away the strictly racial impediments, he was free to rise as high in the department

69

as talent, dedication, and hard work could take him.

Now, as lieutenant in charge of one of the homicide squads, he was exactly where he wanted to be, doing exactly what he wanted to do. He answered only to Walt Koznicki, something he could easily live with. And he spent his time solving puzzles of enormous human consequence.

As a kid growing up on Detroit's near east side, he could never have dreamed he would go this far.

His parents called him Al. Only later, with the propensity adults have for nicknames, had his buddies in the department christened him "Zoo," after the last two letters in his given name, Alonzo.

Tully's father had worked on the line at Ford. He worked hard, so hard that his fellow workers finally left him alone. It was an accolade of sorts. Harassment—or worse—was the usual treatment whites gave blacks on the line. To leave a black alone to do his work was, for that era, a mark of respect.

Alonzo's mother, with eight children—he was the youngest—necessarily was a housewife and homemaker. Occasionally she would take in laundry or some other odd job or service to provide some always needed extra money.

All in all, the Tully family was a close-knit unit folding in upon itself. They—father and children—went out to work or school, each to do his or her best, only to return as if to an oasis.

As a youth, Alonzo was unsure what he wanted to do with his life. He knew he didn't want to follow his father on the assembly line. Not that it was demeaning or beneath him. It was just that he did not want to spend the major portion of his life doing precisely the same humdrum thing over and over while answering to an extensive chain of command.

It was at the suggestion of a friend that he took the test to join the police department, a test he easily passed.

In the beginning it was most discouraging. Many times he came close to quitting. The bigotry was deep-seated. But, gradually, as his father before him, he began to impress his coworkers with his skill and professionalism. In time, he became convinced that this was the life for him.

With the ascendancy of Maynard Cobb, the final barriers fell and Zoo Tully knew he had found a home, running his squad efficiently and solving puzzles.

What disturbed him right now was his inability to solve the murder of El Bonner. Several times this past week, he'd thought he was on the verge of finding the missing link, only to have the puzzle regroup and stare defiantly at him.

It was the Bonner case he was thinking about when Alice padded into the kitchen, yawning and rubbing the sleep from her eyes.

"Such deep thoughts for so early in the morning," she said.

"What early?" His furrowed brow smoothed as he smiled at her. "It's almost nine o'clock."

"A compromise. What time did you get up?"

"About seven."

"See? On Sundays I usually get up about noon. So, it's nine o'clock. A decent compromise. Anything in the papers?"

He'd been through both the *News* and the *Free Press*. But for the life of him, he could remember scarcely anything he'd read. Either there had been little of interest or he'd been too distracted. Most likely, he thought, the latter.

"There's Waldmeir's column," he remembered. "Takin' off on Cobb again."

"What else is new? I have long suspected that the mayor's secretary's job consists of cutting out Waldmeir's column before Hizzoner gets a chance to read it."

"That'll make for a happy mayor."

"A happy mayor." Alice nodded. "Detroit's most important product." She swizzled some orange juice around in her mouth, then swallowed it.

Running her hands through her hair, she padded toward the living room in near-somnambulant fashion. Tully followed. She switched on the electric fireplace. Heat began to radiate from the artificial logs. Gradually, it brought warm comfort to its immediate space.

Alice curled up on the floor before the couch directly in front of the fireplace. "This is nice."

Tully slid down beside her. He felt very much at home. Oh, yes: Sunday, sweet Sunday, with nothing to do . . .

"I can't get my eyes open." She rubbed them.

"Probably the wine you had last night. You don't need much, you know."

"The wine!" she remembered. "That's why my mouth feels like a troop of juvenile delinquents marched through it."

"J.D.s with rap sheets as long as your arm."

"Ooh." The image was disquieting. "What's on the docket today, Zoo?"

"You're kidding! You don't remember what today is?"

"Sunday."

"Uh-huh."

"There's more?"

"Uh-huh."

She concentrated. It was difficult. "The last Sunday in January."

"Uh-huh."

"There's still more? Let me think." She pondered. Finally, "Su-per Bow-l Sun-day!" She drew out each syllable to confer the proper reverence.

"I'm proud of you."

"Bob Hope! Red! Fake! Roll out! 57! 44! 40! Or fight! On 7! Hut! Hut! Hut! Hut! Hut! Hut! Hut!"

"That's eight."

"Who's counting?"

"The offensive line."

"That's what makes them offensive."

They chuckled and leaned closer together.

"Who's playing, anyway?"

"Hmmm . . . I think it's Pat Sommerall and John Madden."

"Really! I knew they were big but I didn't know they were whole teams."

"The important thing to remember is how much it costs for a thirty-second spot during the Super Bowl."

"How much?"

"More'n you and me are worth dead or alive."

"There you go, playing cop again. When does the damn thing start?"

"Who are you—Miss What? I never heard so many questions from one person. Pregame is practically all afternoon. But the kickoff won't take place till about six o'clock."

She placed her hand gently on his thigh and began tracing small circles. "What's on the docket till then?"

He felt tingling sensations and could not suppress a grin. He looked down at her. Her robe had fallen open at the neck. She wasn't wearing a nightgown. He could see the upper portion of one breast. She took a deep breath and the breast swelled provocatively. Tully had no doubt she'd staged the whole sequence. He had never met anyone as adept at seduction. He had no objections. "Whadja have in mind?"

"Have I ever told you," she said, "that you get out of bed way too early on Sundays?"

"I'm willing to be convinced."

"Come on; I'll make my case upstairs."

"Leave the fireplace on. It'll be nice and warm when we come back."

"So will we."

They did not return to the downstairs until mid-afternoon. Alice proved a prophetess: Both were feeling warm and wonderful. Tully's entire soul was silently singing, "Sunday, Sweet Sunday."

Alice went to the kitchen to begin preparations for an early supper. Nothing must interrupt the Super Bowl once it began. She also nibbled. She'd had nothing but the morning glass of orange juice.

Tully took command of the recliner chair and the TV's remote control. Festivities had reached the point of presenting highlights of past Super Bowls. It was a source of continuing amazement to Tully that the networks were able, year after year, to get so much mileage and milk so much revenue out of a simple game that should take about an hour to play. With all the hoopla, extended halftimes, and commercial time-outs, even the duration of the game itself promised to stretch nearly four hours. Only in America . . .

After a time, he became aware of sounds coming from the kitchen—homey sounds. He smiled. This was good. The thought occurred again: marriage. He was quite sure Alice was willing. But if experience was any sort of teacher, that way lay disaster.

Something happened after a marriage ceremony. He wasn't sure what to call it. Proprietorship, maybe.

Now he came and went at his discretion. So did Alice. They lived in the same house. They loved and cared for each other. But neither owned the other. There were no ugly scenes when he did not come home at the expected hour. Or, even worse, when he did not return for days at a time.

He well remembered the incessant argumentation and debates between him and his wife. The mindless accusations. He wasn't running around with anyone else. And, despite her charges, his wife knew that. Pure and simple, she was competing with his work, and she couldn't win. But she wouldn't admit it.

No, this was good. This was right. Marriage would only complicate things.

There were times when he sensed that Alice was on the verge of broaching the subject, but she always backed off. However, because he was well aware that marriage was on her mind, he knew that one day it might come to an ultimatum. He didn't want to think about that. For that could be the end of something great.

As his interest in the undiluted TV hype waned, he became more conscious of the sounds and the appetizing odors emanating from the kitchen. It was irresistible.

Tully stood in the kitchen doorway for some time savoring the scene. Alice, her back to him, was preparing a tossed salad. She seemed oblivious to all but the green pepper she was chopping. She was humming. He tried to place the tune. He knew it, but what was it? An oldie. She returned to the beginning of the chorus, and, with that, the words came to him. "We'll be close as pages in a book, my love and I."

Quietly, he approached her. She was unaware of his presence until his arms encircled her waist. She gave a startled gasp, then relaxed and leaned back into him. He kissed the top of her head while holding her. "The cook needs a kiss."

"She certainly does."

"I feel good."

"But I'll bet you couldn't leap over tall buildings in a single bound now!"

"Why would I want to do that?"

"Who's ahead?"

"In what?"

"The football game. The Super Bowl . . . what else?"

"They haven't begun to fight."

She laughed, "Well, at least this nonsense will be over until next fall."

"There's one more."

"One more!"

"The Pro Bowl."

"No!"

"Uh-huh. And we won't have to wait till fall. They'll start the exhibition season this summer."

She made a face. "At least they'll give us a couple of weeks off."

The phone rang. It startled both of them. It shouldn't have, but it did.

Tully stared at it as it rang twice more. He had a premonition. It was Mangiapane. There had been another prostitute murder. He had no basis for the presentiment. It was just there.

He picked up the receiver. "Tully."

"Mangiapane, Zoo. We got another one. A hooker."

"Was she cut?"

"Just like the other one. And branded."

"Who's with you?"

"Dominic. He's just starting the SIR."

"Uh . . . no. You do that."

"Okay, Zoo." Mangiapane felt honored. Just a rookie in

homicide and the lieutenant was picking him over a seasoned veteran to make the report.

"You're familiar with the first case. So when you start the report, I want you to pay special attention to the similarities—and differences, if there are any . . . got it?"

"Uh, okay, Zoo." Humility quickly supplanted pride. It wasn't his expertise; it was his familiarity with last week's case.

"Where are you?"

"Michigan, near Central. Wait a minute," Mangiapane glanced at his notepad, "7705 Michigan. You comin'? You can't miss it. We got units all over the place."

"I'm comin'. Get busy on that report."

"Okay, Zoo."

Tully replaced the receiver on the wall phone and, hand still on it, bowed his head.

Alice had heard only Tully's end of the conversation. Clearly, it was police business. When she heard him ask, "Was she cut?" she knew. Actually she had known without having to overhear. Intuition.

"Damn!" Tully said, fervently.

"Another one." It wasn't a question.

"If only . . . if only I could have figured it out. I've had a whole week."

"You can't solve them all . . . especially with the little you've had to go on."

"I shoulda done it. This wouldn't have happened if I'd just been a little smarter."

"You're going." Again it was not a question.

Tully nodded.

"I'll wait dinner for you."

"I don't know when I'll get back. It's gonna be late."

"It's just pork chops and salad. They'll keep."

"Better you eat now. I might not even get back."

"I'll wait. And if you don't get back, it's okay. I understand."

He gazed at her for several moments. There was sincere

76

appreciation in his eyes. "Then I'll be back. Sometime. But I'll be back."

He kissed her, then hurried upstairs to dress. Along the way, the thought occurred that he might still be married if his wife had had Al's attitude. His next thought was that he was a very lucky man indeed.

MANGIAPANE WAS ABSOLUTELY COR-
rect. There was no possible way to miss the place.

The tenement was on the south side of Michigan, a seven-lane thoroughfare at that point. It was a route that could take one from downtown Detroit all the way across the state to Lake Michigan and into Gary, Indiana.

The junction of Michigan and Central was, like so much of the city of Detroit, a mere shadow of its former self. The tenement was a case in point. It gave every indication of having been at one time a most respectable, if not fashionable, hotel. Now it was seedy. Its better days obviously were in its past.

Several blue-and-whites as well as unmarked police cars were double-parked, but in orderly fashion. And, for a chill, dark Sunday in January, with the Super Bowl about to begin, a considerable crowd had gathered.

Tully parked, got out of his car, and approached the building. As he walked, he took careful note of the crowd. Mostly neighborhood residents, he guessed. Older people, black and white, along with a significant number of hookers. He thought he recognized some. Evidently he was correct; a few returned his nod.

By no means were these women top-of-the-line whores. In effect, they were a reflection of the neighborhood.

Inside the building, uniformed officers directed him to the second floor. Again, there was no mistaking the pertinent apartment. The door was wide open, with a lot of activity going on inside as the technicians carried out their specialties.

"Zoo, over here."

Sergeant Dominic Salvia, who had been only too happy to let Mangiapane handle the report, had things well organized.

Tully crossed the room much as a skier on a giant slalom, dodging police personnel doing their jobs.

"Mangiapane told me you were comin', Zoo." Salvia, as did nearly everyone in homicide, knew of Tully's special interest in the Bonner case. So he was not at all surprised that Tully would be part of this investigation.

Tully nodded. "Is the body in the tub?"

"Yeah. Just like last week. Come on; I'll show you."

The two officers entered the bathroom. Even with several technicians crammed into the small space, Tully was able to see the victim clearly. He gasped. That surprised Salvia. In short order, homicide officers see about all there is to see. That an officer as experienced as Tully would show emotion at the sight of a victim, no matter how mutilated, was unexpected.

"Okay, Zoo, who is it?" Mangiapane stood in the doorway.

"You don't know?" Tully asked.

"We don't have an ID yet."

"Well, I don't know."

"You don't know!"

"I don't know."

"But I thought—"

"So did I." Tully jammed his hands into his overcoat pockets and shook his head. "If this doesn't blow my goddam theory all to hell and gone! Oh, I've seen her before, someplace . . . maybe even booked her sometime. But I don't know who she is. I haven't the slightest idea."

For nearly an hour, since Mangiapane's call, Tully had been mentally berating himself. If only he had been able to pick just the right file from his records, he might have found the perpetrator and prevented this murder. But, as it now turned out, his theory had obviously been based on a false premise. He did not know this victim. Thus, she did not die because of some connection with him—as had been his theory with El Bonner. So no matter what he might have done this week, this woman would still be dead.

He had been mistaken. An entire week's investigation had been wasted.

Yet, realistically, what could he have done differently? How else could he have reacted? To investigate the murder of one of your snitches . . . a murder that bore the unmistakable mark of ritual. A message had been sent; it was only natural to assume the message was addressed to him.

What a grisly coincidence!

But the message was still being sent. That much was all too obvious. Even without close inspection Tully could see the bruises on the dead woman's neck. He would be surprised if examination did not confirm that the bruises were made by the same belt. She had been gutted and the incision seemed to be the same as that inflicted on El. There was ample blood, but it was pretty well contained in the body cavity and the tub. Nothing on the walls.

She'd been dead a while before the evisceration. Just like last week. And, just like last week, the clumsy branding. He could make out the figure of a cross. But because the mark was made partially on one breast and partially on her side, it was somewhat disjoined. The impression that the mark was intended to be a cross was more evident from a short distance than close up.

Peering more intently, Tully thought he could make out the irregular marks of some sort of lettering on the horizontal bar of the cross. He wondered if this imprint would be any more clear and revelatory than last week's branding. That would be determined at tomorrow morning's autopsy by the M.E.

"Geez, Zoo, I was sure you'd know who she was." Mangiapane was crestfallen.

"Until I saw her, *I* was sure I'd know who she was."

79

Tully turned to Salvia. "Everything seems to be progressing here."

"Yeah, Zoo. The techs should be done pretty soon."

It was striking how much this apartment resembled the one in which Louise Bonner was murdered, thought Tully. Bigger —it was bigger. But it didn't have enough furniture. That was it: not enough furniture. A bed, a couple of chairs, small table, kitchenette, stove—undoubtedly here the perp heated the branding iron. The bathroom—only a few toiletries and a toothbrush and some toothpaste. Just like at El's.

Nobody lived here. This apartment, like Bonner's, was a place of work—hooker's work, but work nonetheless. Each woman lived somewhere else. This place, the one last week, just a place of work.

Odd.

"How's the canvass goin'?" Tully asked.

"Pretty good," Salvia answered. "We've pretty well covered this building. We should get a good bite out of the neighborhood before tonight."

"Zoo," Mangiapane said, "there's a couple of hookers say they know something about this. But they won't talk to anyone but you."

"Oh, great!" One of the last things Tully wanted was to be the "only" one anyone would talk to. Enough people decide there is only one person in the universe they can trust, then all you do is listen to an endless line of people. He sighed. "Okay, where are they?"

"Just down the hall. One of 'em's got a room here."

"Okay, let's go." Tully hoped the one with the nearby room might be the dead woman's buddy. It would simplify things and God knows they needed a break.

Mangiapane led Tully to the room. As soon as they entered and the two women saw Tully, their faces brightened. "Zoo!"

Tully recognized them immediately. He had never expected that his years on the vice squad would serve him so well after he transferred to homicide.

"Adelle, Ruby . . ." Mangiapane left the room, closing the door behind him. "How the hell are you, anyway?"

80

"Good."

"Fine."

"It's been a while." Tully sat at the table across from Adelle. Ruby was seated on the bed. "Which one of you gals owns this place?"

"I rent it," Adelle said. She was white. Ruby was black. "But I don't live here."

Tully looked around. Another "work" place. Easy to believe no one lived here.

"Then," he addressed Adelle, "you knew the . . . uh . . . deceased woman down the hall?"

"We were buddies." Adelle's lip trembled.

Luck knocks, thought Tully. He took out a notepad and pen and began taking notes. "What was her name?"

"Nancy Freel."

"How old was she?"

"Oh . . . wait a minute . . . I think she was . . . oh, in her late thirties, early forties, something like that."

Adelle sensed Tully's surprise. "I know she looked a lot older. She had a tough life."

She would get no argument from Tully. The figure he'd just seen in the tub looked to be well in her fifties.

Obviously, they could get most, if not all, the personal data about the victim from Adelle at any time. For now, Tully was most interested in what these women wanted to tell that they would relate to no one but him.

"The other officer told me you both had some information you wanted to give me." He looked at one, then the other.

"You go first," said Ruby.

"Yeah, I guess I should," Adelle said. "See, Zoo, it's like this: Nance and me was buddies. You know how that works."

Tully nodded.

"We been workin' together for a long time now."

Something in Tully's expression told Adelle to hurry along. She picked up the pace, but not much. "Well, this afternoon, we was workin' over by Springwells and Michigan, just a couple blocks from here. Not much doin' today. Don't know why. Maybe the weather."

Tully laid his pen on the pad. Obviously, Adelle would move at her own set speed.

"Anyway, there was this car circled the block two, maybe three times."

"What kind of car?"

"Ford, I think, all black. No whitewalls or nothin'."

So far so good.

"I guess I wouldn't have paid much attention," Adelle continued, "except there was so little traffic today." She looked at her colleague. "Why do you 'spose that was, Ruby? Even for a Sunday in January, things were really slow today."

"How 'bout that football game?" Ruby suggested.

"Oh, yeah, that Super Bowl. That must be it. Anyway," she returned her gaze to Tully, "this car was cruisin' real slow. Well, it went slow every time it got to us, anyway. So, finally, on the second or third pass—maybe it was the fourth—the guy stops and rolls down the window on the passenger side. So Nancy goes up to the car and talks business to the guy. Then she opened the door and got in. And he drove away."

"Did you get a look at the guy?"

"Well, yes and no. I can tell you he was wearin' black. All black. Hat and coat. That's how I could tell he was blond: 'cause his hair stood out against all that black."

Still on course, Tully thought. Black Ford. Guy dressed in black. For the first time, a definite indication the guy has blond hair.

"How come," Tully asked Adelle, "you didn't get a better look at him? You couldn't have been that far away."

"No, it wasn't that I was far away. It was where I was—in a doorway. I don't think the guy even knew I was there. It was so goddam cold that Nance and me took turns workin' out on the street. The rest of the time, one of us got to huddle back in the doorway. So I don't think the guy ever saw me. And I didn't get a helluva good look at him."

"Did you get the license?"

"No. Damn, I wish I hadda got it! We could nail the guy with that, couldn't we, Zoo?"

"Uh-huh; it'd help a whole lot."

82

"Most of the time, I do get the number. And Nance'd get it for me. That way we can check for each other better. But a couple of things: I was back in that doorway, like I said. By the time I got out on the sidewalk, he'd already pulled away and I couldn't make it out. And, also, I wasn't too worried. Nance and me had a signal when we thought there might be trouble. But Nance didn't give no signal at all. She just got in, like she either knew the guy or thought she could trust him. So, like a damn fool, I relaxed for a minute."

"You say she acted like maybe she knew him?"

"Yeah . . . either that or she figured she could trust him. She just hopped right into the car. Didn't hesitate at all."

So far so good in making a connection between last week and today. The guy dresses in black, drives a black car.

But why does he case the block so carefully? He circles it two, three times, maybe more. Is he looking for a specific woman? A specific kind of woman? Is he trying to make sure she doesn't have a buddy who might make him? Tully might have dismissed that last question since today the victim did indeed have a buddy—Adelle. But, according to Adelle, the guy most likely didn't see her. So, as far as the perp was concerned, Nancy Freel appeared to be alone, unprotected as well as unaccompanied.

So maybe he wants to make sure that there will be no witnesses. That makes sense. And, as far as he's concerned, neither last week nor today did his victim have any back-up protection.

But what about the other question? Was he looking for a specific hooker? A specific kind of hooker? Both the victims were white. Both were of advanced age for whores. At least both appeared to be. It was a puzzle to be solved.

And the other puzzle: Neither woman had shown the slightest hesitation in taking on the customer. Yet both were very experienced hookers. El, particularly, knew her buddy wasn't around. There must be something about this guy that instills trust or confidence. At least there certainly is nothing about him that alarmed them or caused any apprehension. Both women readily climbed into his car and rode off to their deaths. Interesting. Another puzzle to be solved.

"Okay," Tully said. "That's as much as you saw, eh, Adelle? Nancy got in the guy's car and they drove off . . . right?"

"That's it, Zoo."

"Would you recognize him? If we looked through some mug shots?"

"Geez, I don't know, Zoo. Maybe if I saw him in real life again. But I don't think I could make him with just a picture. I don't think so."

Tully sighed. You couldn't have everything.

"Maybe Ruby . . ." Adelle offered.

"Ruby!" Tully had been concentrating so intensely on Adelle, he had almost forgotten the other woman. "Ruby, where do you fit into this? Adelle saw the pickup. You saw the delivery? When they arrived here at the apartment?"

"Not exactly."

"Oh. Okay, you tell it."

"Well, I wasn't in any hurry to get out on the street today. It wasn't the kinda day there'd be many johns out shoppin'. Just a gray, cold day in January. Plus I remembered the football game. That'd keep a lot of johns home. Parties and all."

Tully sat back. He wished he could play this recital at a faster pace. But, better they recount what happened at their own pace. That way there was less chance they might omit what could prove to be important.

"So, like I said, I took my sweet ol' time gettin' out. In fact, when I left my place, it was colder out than I figured on. Bad wind—what do they call it?"

"Wind-chill factor," Adelle supplied.

"Yeah, that's it: wind-chill factor. God, it was cold enough to freeze the balls off a brass monkey. I couldn't imagine any john payin' for no blow job less'n I turned on the hot air." Ruby grinned, then continued.

"Well, anyway, since it was so cold out and I wasn't dressed all that warm, I was sort of huggin' the buildings. Two or so times I almost turned 'round and give up on this Sunday. But, for some reason or other, I decided to give it a try. But I couldn't stand that wind-chill thing for more'n a few

minutes at a time. So, like I say, I was huggin' the buildings
...you know what I mean?"

Tully nodded.

Ruby explained anyway. Evidently she thought it important
that he understand. "I mean I was stayin' close to the buildings so's I could keep out of that wind's way. Often as I could,
I'd duck into doorways, entrances, whatever, to get out of that
cold. That musta been why he didn't see me."

Tully had almost drifted off into a brown study. Her narration was so particularized and repetitive that his attention had
wandered. So he hadn't been prepared for that Hitchcockian
final statement: "...that musta been why he didn't see me."

Tully knew, without further explanation, exactly what she
was talking about. "What happened then, Ruby...I mean
when he didn't see you?"

"That's what I'm tryin' to tell you, Zoo. Here I am, makin'
my way down Michigan Avenue. And even if I'm duckin' into
any protected space I can find, I'm payin' attention to where
I'm goin'. So, when I get near Central, this building right
here, I notice this guy's head peekin' 'round the corner of the
entrance to this very building.

"Now that don't look at all right to me. Why would this
guy be peekin' 'round the doorway? Like in some spy movie
or somethin'. So I started payin' attention to this dude. I
didn't figure he could be up to no good. But with all his
peekin' 'round, I guess he just didn't see me...what with me
stayin' so close to the buildings and all. In fact, when I seen
this guy actin' so nervous and all, I just kep' myself even
closer to the buildings. Then, what with him pokin' his head
in and out, and me slippin' in and out and next to the walls, I
was almost on top of him when he finally left the building and
went out to his car."

"Where was the car?"

"Right outside the doorway. Right at the curb, right opposite the entrance to this very building."

"What kind of car?"

"Ford, a black Ford. Escort, looked to be a few years old."

"What did he do?"

"What do you mean?"

"Did he get in? Drive away?"

"Oh, no, Zoo. He just hurried out there to his car, unlocked the door, got somethin' outta the back seat, and hurried back into the building."

"Did you get a look at what he got out of the car?"

"Not to speak of. He just pulled whatever it was out of the back seat—on the floor it was, actually—and he tucked it inside his coat."

Damn! It had to be the branding instrument. So he kept it in the car. He'd strangle the victim, go get the iron, then bring it back to the room and heat it. No wonder the victims were dead so long before he cut them. "You sure you didn't get any idea at all of what the thing was that he got out of the car?"

"No, not really, Zoo. But you're keepin' me from what I 'specially wanted to tell you."

"What?"

"He was a preacher man."

"What!"

"A preacher man."

"How'd you know that?"

"When he opened his coat to hide that thing he took out of the back seat, I saw his collar for just a second."

"And?"

"It was one of them little white things preacher men stick in their collars."

"Wait a minute. Let's get this straight: The guy opened his coat—what color was it?"

"Black. Black coat, black hat, black shoes, black suit of clothes under the coat. But at the collar, this piece of white."

"And the guy was white?"

"With blond hair. I could see the sides and back under his hat."

"Did you ever see that kind of collar before?"

"Sure. Some of our preacher men wears 'em."

"But not many?"

"No, I guess not . . . leastways not out on the street."

"Ever see that collar anywhere else?"

"Hmmm. Well, yeah, on TV once in a while."

"Who wears them on TV?"

"Usually the priests. Yeah, that's right, priests."

"Catholic priests?"

"Yeah, that must be what it was . . . a white man dressed like that . . . it musta been a priest."

"Or," Tully grew more restrained and thoughtful, "somebody dressed up to look like a priest." He paused a moment. "Ruby, how good a look did you get at this guy?"

"I was almost as close to him as I am to you."

"He saw you?"

"When he was goin' back into the apartment, yeah. He seemed real surprised to see me . . . I mean, *real* surprised."

"I'll just bet he was. You'd know him if you saw him again?"

"Sure. I was so surprised when I saw him, I don't think I'll ever forget him. I thought somebody was in trouble here. Maybe dyin'. Then, when I met Adelle and told her what I saw, we started comparin' notes. Then we got real scared that somethin' bad had happened to Nance. That's when we hightailed it back here and found poor Nance. Then we called the cops."

"But," Adelle interrupted, "we didn't want to take a chance talkin' to the other cops. You know how they feel about us. Always hasslin'. We figured them other cops could make a lot of trouble for us. So when we found out you were comin', we decided we'd talk to you and nobody else." There was a determined and self-justified tilt to her chin as she concluded.

"Okay," Tully said. "You did good. Now, another officer is gonna get statements from you. It's okay to talk to him. I'll see everything is all right. We'll go down to the station. Then we'll have you look at some pictures. And you give a description of the guy to our police artists. But—and this is important—don't tell anybody else, especially the news media—the reporters—any more than we tell you to tell them. Cooperate with us, now. We gotta catch this guy. He's killin' good women."

The two seemed impressed.

Adrenaline was pumping. He was going to be on this well

into the night. Then he'd have to get to headquarters early tomorrow.

He phoned Alice. She understood, assured him that she would get something to eat, and go to bed at a decent hour whether he got home or not.

She was a good scout. He definitely did not want to ruin this relationship with marriage.

LIEUTENANT TULLY FELT AS IF HE were replaying last week's scenario.

It was just last Monday, one week ago to the day, that he was seeing Inspector Koznicki to lay claim to the case of a murdered prostitute. Tully even scheduled himself, as he had last week, to go directly to the woman's autopsy after his meeting with Koznicki.

However, there were two major differences. He was no longer working under the assumption that El Bonner was killed because of some connection with him. While that had been an interesting and most peculiar hypothesis, it had been proven false by the murder yesterday of one Nancy Freel.

Without doubt, both murders were committed by the same individual. But while Bonner had been one of Tully's snitches, he hadn't known Freel at all. So he had wasted valuable time pursuing an avenue of investigation that, in retrospect, was a predetermined dead end. He regretted the time lost, but was grateful to be on the right track now. It was much like getting rid of excess baggage. He felt freer and better able to move ahead and solve the puzzle.

The other major difference was the good fortune of chancing upon two witnesses, at least one of whom thought she could identify the perpetrator if she ever saw him again. He had sent Mangiapane off to obtain a copy of the Pictorial Directory of Detroit Priests. It was a thousand-to-one chance, he thought. Many of the directory photos were years—some, decades—old; in some cases the quality and/or the likeness was such that not even the subject's mother could have recognized him.

But one never could tell; they might just strike it lucky.

They did have a composite sketch—admittedly seldom of much practical help. By the time the police artist moved multiple-choice mouths, noses, chins, etc. around, the finished sketch could resemble any number of people, or no one. But it could have an effect on the perpetrator. It could tell him they were gaining on him, getting a little closer all the time.

And, finally, they had that singular detail of the clerical clothing. It might be a priest. It might be a minister. It might be anybody pretending to be a clergyman. But it was interesting.

It also added fuel to Tully's special, perhaps personal, pique over this case. Bonner and Freel, according to witnesses, had gone off with the killer without the slightest hesitation, even though they were very experienced women. Why not? Doubtless they had been surprised to find a clergyman john. Either or both may have served clergymen in the past. But it must have been a surprise nonetheless; it would have to be rare in any case that a cleric would be wearing his religious garb when he propositioned the women.

These thoughts ran through Tully's mind as he sat across the desk from Koznicki, who was studying reports of yesterday's new cases. He had been spending considerable time on the file of Nancy Freel.

"So," Koznicki looked up, "we were wrong about Louise Bonner."

"*I* was wrong," Tully countered.

"It was, indeed, your theory—in which I concurred completely. But, no mind; now we are on the right track."

"Yeah. One week late, but we're on the road."

"I presume you want to stay on this case even though we no longer assume that there was an association because the deceased was one of your sources."

"Uh-huh. Yeah, Walt, I want this guy. He's the same guy I was lookin' for last week. If anything, I want him more now than I did then."

"All right; the case is yours. Within reason, use as many in your squad as you need. This matter is now being treated as a media event. With all the attention focused on what we now know are serial murders, we had better conclude this as quickly as possible." Koznicki paused. Concern was evident in his expression as he returned his attention to the Freel report. "I think I do not have to tell you, it troubles me deeply that the killer is masquerading as a priest."

Tully was taken aback. But only his eyes betrayed his surprise.

Masquerade? Who said anything about a masquerade? Possible, of course, but certainly not a lead-pipe cinch. Why would Walt Koznicki assume that the killer was *masquerading* as a clergyman? Especially a seasoned officer like the inspector? He'd been around more than long enough to know that anything is possible, even a priest killer. Yeah, even a priest who mutilates as well as kills.

It became immediately apparent to Tully that this might very well become a serious obstacle in the investigation. There might very well be a reluctance on the part of investigating officers to admit the possibility that the killer could be a clergyman. And wherever that bias existed, the investigation would be crippled: Any such investigator would have excluded, without good cause, one distinctly possible solution to the crimes.

Tully resolved that once he formed his task force his first order of business would be to insist that everyone was going into this with eyes wide open, and no closed minds. They must follow the case wherever it might lead—to skid row or to a rectory. Puzzles were not solved by anyone whose mind was not open to every possibility.

But he didn't have to address Walt Koznicki's mental block immediately. Tully, not Koznicki, would be in charge of the active investigation. If the killer turned out not to be a clergyman, then Koznicki's assumption of a masquerade would be borne out. If the inspector's prejudgment was incorrect and the killer was a clergyman . . . well, time enough then for him to see the light.

As quickly as he reasonably could, Tully excused himself from Koznicki's office and commenced the brief, frigid walk to the medical examiner's office.

Tully was convinced that, in many ways, Dr. Moellmann held a vital key in this case. It was up to the M.E.'s department to confirm—or not—the conclusion tentatively reached by the police yesterday that the two prostitutes were, indeed, killed by one and the same person. Granting that, Moellmann could determine whether the killer had changed his method of murder to any extent.

It is an often erroneous belief that people who commit a series of murders are repetitious in every detail. In reality, such killers often change their methods in gradual stages, sometimes refining a technique that may improve with practice.

But in almost all cases, there is sufficient likeness that the mark of the serial killer can be recognized. And this is so because the killer wants his work to be recognized and accurately attributed. However, the change in m.o. does not always favor the criminal. Sometimes an initial carefulness deteriorates.

That very point was now being made by Dr. Wilhelm Moellmann.

"It seems our friend here has made a couple of mistakes," the medical examiner observed as he continued his measurements on the mutilated corpse before him.

"Freel?"

"No, the one who did this to . . . what's her name? . . . Nancy Freel."

"What? What mistakes?" Tully suddenly had a nervous stomach. Was it possible that Moellmann had found significant differences in the murders of the two prostitutes?

Moellmann half turned to Tully. Mildly surprised at the lieutenant's reaction, Moellmann peered over his glasses. "I refer only to this morning's papers. You did read them. You might almost have written them. This killer, he must have not been thinking, to let someone get so close to him. So close to him and yet live, that is."

It had not occurred to Tully that the murderer might be expected to kill Ruby because she had seen him at close range. Tully had not thought of this possibility because not once had he considered that he might be dealing with a mass murderer, like a Mark Essex, who killed indiscriminately from the roof of a Howard Johnson motel . . . or Charles Whitman, who did the same from the University of Texas tower.

Originally, Tully had assumed he was dealing with someone from his past who was killing a snitch in reprisal. Now it seemed clear that the killer was neither a personal enemy nor a random mass killer, but a serial murderer.

Albert De Salvo, the "Boston Strangler," preyed on defenseless women in apartments. David Berkowitz, the "Son of Sam," stalked women in parked cars.

Tully was after someone who was killing prostitutes—but apparently not indiscriminately. He was not driving down Cass or Eight Mile or Woodward at Six Mile and mowing down hookers with a machine gun . . . though God knows there were specific times of day when that could be possible.

On the contrary, he seemed to be rather carefully selecting his prey and not only killing one after another, but, with the mutilation and branding, sending some sort of message.

No; Moellmann's suggestion that Ruby was in proximate danger because she happened to stumble across him probably was unfounded. In any case, there was no point in discussing that facet of the case with Moellmann.

"Yeah," Tully said simply, "that was his mistake. A major league blunder."

"Look at this! Come see this, Lieutenant." Moellmann, studying with a magnifying glass the bruises on the neck of the deceased, beckoned to Tully.

Tully's head was almost touching Moellmann's as the two inspected the markings.

"See . . ." Moellmann pointed under the magnifying glass to the ruler that he was using to measure the width of the neck bruises. ". . . just one and seven-eighths inches. Significantly wider than the average man's belt. And exactly the width of the one used last week on what's her name . . . Bonner."

"Uh-huh."

"And then, see the incision . . ."

Tully never failed to wonder at the almost childlike enthusiasm Moellmann was able to derive from an autopsy. Particularly one with absolutely bizarre details such as these hooker murders.

"See?" Moellmann traced the incision with his index finger. "It is almost a perfect repetition of the one on the Bonner woman." There was just a touch of what might pass for admiration in his voice. Somewhat like the appreciation one surgeon might have for the work of another.

All very interesting, but, "What about the brand?" Tully asked.

"Not so good." Moellmann shook his head. It might be anyone's guess whether his reaction was regret as to the inconclusiveness of the evidence, or disapproval of the sloppy work of an artist.

"Why 'not so good'?"

"See . . ." Moellmann again used the magnifying glass, now in the area of the left breast. "I think he does not ever take into account the curvature of the breast." He shook his head rather sadly. "Evidently, he applies the brand in a . . . uh . . . sequential way. See how deep the burn mark is, here on the upper portion of the breast: He applies the iron here first, it would seem. Then, probably by pronating or flexing his wrist, he impresses the vertical mark downward. He seems to want the horizontal bar to intersect just at the nipple. Then the vertical bar continues on down the torso.

"Where he makes his mistake is just under the nipple, where the breast curves away. That's why we get the imprint of just the top portion of these letters. The bottom portion is just not sufficiently impressed. It's even worse this time. Even less of the upper portion of the lettering was imprinted. We have less to go on now than we had last week."

"Unless . . ."

"Unless what?"

"Unless," Tully said, "that's all he wants us to know."

"You mean he deliberately burns in only the upper portion of the letters?" Moellmann seemed more comfortable with the supposition that the carnal artist was deliberately giving them less than half a message rather than that he was committing an amateurish blunder.

The M.E. seemed to be enjoying a private joke as he returned to the lectern to make additional notes on the body chart. "Clever, clever, clever," he murmured. Or at least Tully thought that's what he was muttering.

It was Tully's guess that this set of serial murders would provide a chapter in the next medico-legal treatise Moellmann would edit. The way the doctor appeared to be appreciating this killer's work gave every indication that Moellmann was already mentally composing the article. The notion, true or false, amused Tully.

"So, then," Moellmann said, "are you at all close to catching this guy?"

It was an odd question from the M.E., thought Tully. Usually to all appearances, Moellmann never gave much of a damn about police progress. His interest seemed to begin and end with his practice of forensic medicine. Maybe, went Tully's reasoning, the Doc, in projecting his article on the serial murder and mutilation of prostitutes, wanted to be sure there would be a happy ending. Which, of course, would be that the crimes were solved and the killer apprehended.

"We've got some leads," Tully said.

"Better, I hope, than that composite picture in the paper today."

Moellmann's remark elicited general laughter from the doctors and technicians in the morgue area.

"Yeah, I hope." Tully went along with the joke. It was a given in the police and legal community that composite drawings usually did little more than scare the person whose likeness it was supposed to be.

Moellmann, basking in the response to his little joke, looked over the rims of his glasses at his assembled colleagues, a smile tugging at his lips. He was going to give the joke one more shove. "Why, according to the picture your police have come up with, *I* could be the killer. Or"—he looked more intently among his confreres—"maybe Dr. Rosen over there." Then, slightly more seriously, "Or, what's-his-name, Bush over there." Abruptly, the laughter died. Momentarily, Moellmann looked startled. In his Germanic subculture, when der Papa cracked a joke, all the *Kinder* laughed—whether they had gotten it or not. Thus the present silence was a bit more than ordinarily disconcerting. Moellmann tried to mask the moment by issuing several orders to a couple of the other pathologists present.

What neither Moellmann nor Tully knew was that earlier, and mostly in jest, one of the other autopsy attendants had accused Arnold Bush of resembling the picture of the killer. At which Bush had become violent and attacked the other attendant. It had taken several men to pull him off. Bush, not a technical assistant, and thus still on probation, might have been summarily dismissed by Moellmann if anyone had told the M.E. But, intimidated as they were by his strength and his temper, no one wanted to take the chance of incurring Bush's wrath.

Thus, too, no one had dared challenge Bush when he assumed complete custody of Nancy Freel's body. Just as he had done with Louise Bonner's corpse one week ago. Bush's behavior in coveting the two bodies at best was peculiar. But then, who's to say what is normal in a business whose most important product is an endless series of cadavers?

Tully picked up on Moellmann's previous question. "I got a feeling, Doc, that we're close to this guy . . . not just closer than last week. Artist's sketch or not, we do have a witness who saw him up close. Maybe the drawing that came from her description isn't a photo, but she saw him. And when we bring him in, she's gonna identify him."

"Not *if?*"

"No, Doc. *When.*"

Moellmann, again close to the body and taking more measurements, observed, "He seems to choose older women."

"Uh-huh."

"And white."

"Yup."

"And on Sunday."

"And on Sunday afternoons," Tully agreed. "All noted, Doc. And with the task force I've got, if we don't get him by week's end, we're gonna have a big surprise for him if he tries to pull something next Sunday."

"Hmmm . . ." Moellmann was so engrossed in the autopsy, he seemed not to have heard Tully's final remark.

But someone else was listening . . . intently.

Arnold Bush hung on every word. As he had learned years ago in parochial school, words were important. So important that no matter what evil you committed, all you had to do was go to confession and say the magic words: I'm sorry. And the priest would forgive you. Anything.

15

FATHER KOESLER WAS CONCERNED. HE had come again to the Burtha Fisher Home to visit Monsignor Meehan. This time, the old monsignor had decided to abandon his wheelchair and walk, though none too steadily. To complicate matters, the janitor had just washed the marble floor; signs warned of the slippery surface.

Meehan walked deliberately enough, holding onto the railing that ran the length of the corridor. Regardless, Koesler lightly grasped the monsignor's arm. The limb felt so fragile that Koesler feared that if Meehan should fall, Koesler would be left holding an arm that had simply broken off from an equally fragile trunk.

But they survived the walk and entered the visting parlor. It was one of those glorious January days where, after a night's dusting of snow, the sun shone brightly, reflecting off the unbroken white surface with an intensity that was almost painful to the eye.

"So, Bobby, it happened again, didn't it? With the murdered prostitute?" Meehan's pleasant, slightly nasal tenor was unmistakable. His shriveled body made it difficult for some familiar with his former somewhat rotund shape to now recognize him. But the voice hadn't changed. The voice alone put everything into perspective.

"You've been following the news?" Koesler never failed to be surprised anytime Meehan happened to be au courant.

The monsignor chuckled. "For your sake, I'm trying to keep up with things. And, Bobby, isn't it lucky you didn't have to make a pastoral decision about burying that poor girl . . . I mean the second prostitute."

"Indeed. That's about all I would have needed."

"A lot of flak after the first funeral?"

"A bit. Some nasty calls. A few irate parishioners."

"Anything from downtown?"

"Not a word. Blessedly. But you know how Cardinal Boyle is. He knows he carries a lot of clout, even with the secular news media. He wouldn't speak out on an issue like that unless he absolutely had to. For which I am deeply grateful."

"Oh, I didn't really think the Cardinal would give you a hard time. I wondered about the auxiliary bishops."

"I suppose with one or another of them it could have been possible. But I think in a situation like this, they take their cue from the boss."

"Well, you can never tell about these auxiliaries. Some of them can be pretty ambitious.'

"That's true. Remember our friend in Chicago—the one

97

who was running for bishop, and made it? Remember what his mother said after he'd been named bishop?"

"Wait, wait..." It was on the tip of Meehan's memory. "Yes! She was quoted as saying, 'If we'd known that he was going to go this far, we would have had his teeth straightened.'"

"That's right." Koesler was gratified at Meehan's powers of recent recollection. The Chicago incident hadn't happened all that long ago.

"Ah, mothers," Meehan said, "they surely can put you in your place. But... where were we?" Meehan searched for the conversation's drift.

"I believe you were saying something about the ambition of auxiliary bishops."

"Oh, yes... that's true, you know, Bobby. They've got to compete. Statistically, they're not all going to make it."

"Make what?"

"Ordinary—have their very own diocese to run. No, there are just so many of the poor men who will end up spending their whole episcopal lives being just mere auxiliary bishops. It's sad." They both knew he was being sardonic.

"Sad, I suppose... but still a measure of satisfaction ending up so close to the top."

"Bobby, do you remember when John Donovan and Henry Donnelly were made auxiliary bishops at the same time, here in Detroit?"

Koesler nodded. He remembered it well. The two were consecrated bishops only a few months after he had been ordained a priest in June of 1954.

Monsignor John Donovan had been Cardinal Mooney's secretary and, as such, was a logical choice for bishop. But while recognizing his devoutness, clerical wags had been at a loss to explain the selection of Henry Donnelly.

"Remember the story that was going 'round then? About their coats of arms?"

Koesler's expression betrayed his uncertainty. It was one of the more difficult tales to recount with accuracy. He'd have to

98

listen carefully and hope that Meehan would recall the details correctly.

Encouraged by Koesler's apparent puzzlement, Meehan proceeded. As long as Koesler could not remember the story clearly, it was as much fun as finding a new audience for a tried and true tale.

"You must remember that John Donovan was a shoo-in for bishop—because of his relationship with Ed Mooney... being his secretary and all. But nobody could quite figure out how Henry got in there.

"Well, as the account goes, the gentlemen picked out their episcopal rings and had only to okay their coats of arms and pick out mottoes and they'd be all set. So, according to the story..."

A good part of this tale, Koesler knew, had to be apocryphal.

"... the two bishops-to-be tried to outwait each other, each hoping to come up with the better motto." Meehan gave a Barry Fitzgerald-like chuckle. "See the competition starts even before the consecration. Anyway, finally Henry Donnelly made the first move and selected the motto, *Per Mariam*—'Through Mary.'"

That much was true, Koesler knew—and immediately wondered why Meehan had thought it necessary to translate.

"Then," Meehan continued, "when Donovan learned what Donnelly had chosen, Donovan settled on *Per Eduardum* —'Through Edward.'" If Donnelly had gotten to be bishop through the intercession of the Blessed Mother of God, then Donovan was supposed to have concluded that he'd made it through the intercession of Ed Mooney—the Cardinal.

"So, when Donnelly heard about Donovan's motto, Henry changed his to *Per Accidens*—'By Accident.'" Meehan chuckled so helplessly he began to choke.

Koesler patted him on the back—gingerly. He did not want to break the old gentleman.

Now that the story had been recounted, Koesler remembered it well. Of course, the only truth to it was Henry Donnelly's selection of *Per Mariam* as his motto. The rest was an object lesson on the infighting that goes on in the competitive world. Even inside the Church.

When Meehan had sufficiently recovered from his coughing bout, Koesler said, "Here's a brand new one for you. It just happened a short time ago."

Meehan rubbed his hands and leaned forward. It was not every day that a new and possibly memorable story came along . . . especially when one was confined in a nursing home.

"Do you know Carl Kaminski?"

Meehan shook his head. He knew very few priests under sixty. It didn't matter.

"Well," Koesler said, "this happened, as I said, just a little while ago. It seems that Carl was invited to the confirmation services at St. Hugo of the Hills—"

"Better known as St. Hugo of the Wheels," Meehan interjected, alluding to the wealth of its parishioners.

"Right," Koesler affirmed. "Anyway, as Carl told me, he went to the confirmation at the invitation of a classmate. He intended to just relax and have a good time. To ensure that, he downed two or three martinis before dinner. The fact that he couldn't remember how many he'd had was testimony that he'd had more than enough.

"Then, the fathers sat down to dinner. At which time the pastor informed Carl that he was to be chaplain to the confirming prelate."

"Don't tell me: The confirming prelate was Cardinal Boyle!"

"How did you know?"

"It had to be. It couldn't have been a mere auxiliary and still be a first-rate story. And then . . . ?"

"Then Carl knew this was not destined to be an enjoyable, relaxing evening . . . not with too many martinis and the job of accompanying the Cardinal in and out of the church. So Carl tried to eat as many potatoes and as much bread as he could get down to neutralize the gin.

"Which he did to some extent. By the time they all got to the sacristy to vest for the ceremony, Carl was feeling pretty much in control. Then he found it was his job to put the crosier together."

"The one," Meehan interrupted, "that the bishop carries with him in the case? The one in three parts that have to be screwed together?" He was beginning to anticipate.

"Exactly! Well, Carl got the bottom third and the middle third screwed together all right. But when it came to the middle and the top third, he just couldn't manage it. Actually, it turned out it wasn't his fault: The thing had just been used so frequently that the threads were stripped. No one could have gotten the crosier together. But Carl didn't know that. He wasn't sure whether it was the martinis or the instrument. So he just kept on trying.

"Meanwhile, all the kids had processed into the church, the organ was playing, and the Cardinal was vested—ready to go—and drumming his fingers on the vestment case.

"Finally, Carl gave up. He turned to the Cardinal, handed him the top third of the crosier, and said, 'Why don't you go in on your knees and pretend you're Toulouse-Lautrec?"

Meehan began laughing at the point Kaminski told the Cardinal to process into the church on his knees, so he choked out, "On his knees and what? And what?"

"'And pretend you're Toulouse-Lautrec.'"

"Oh, oh, very good, Bob. Very good." He shook his head as he wiped his eyes. "And is this true on top of everything else? Is this really true?"

"According to Kaminski, yes. And I don't think anyone could make up a story like that, do you?"

"No, not really."

"But you see, Monsignor, that while bishops—even auxiliary bishops—are upwardly mobile, I fear Carl Kaminski's ecclesiastical career has come to a screeching halt."

"Well"—Meehan was regaining self-control—"I guess that's not totally bad. After all, we got into this vocation to be parish priests. And, while God or the Pope or somebody picks some of us to go higher, it's best down here with the people as a simple parish priest."

Koesler could not have agreed more. "Yes, working in the trenches, as it were."

Meehan was silent for a few moments. Then, "Speaking of work, I've been wondering more and more frequently about Dick Kramer. For some reason, he's been on my mind a lot lately. I don't know why. It's not that he visits me—oh, maybe once or twice a year. But somehow . . . I don't know . . . have you seen Dick recently?"

"No. Just no reason to, I guess." Koesler found it strange that Meehan would bring Father Kramer up in conversation two consecutive weeks. Maybe there was some sort of ESP going on. "Are you worried about him for some reason?"

"No . . . I couldn't say worried. Concerned, perhaps. In the time we were together at St. Norbert's he was so intense. We didn't have a parochial school when he got to the parish, though we had plans for one and the archdiocese was willing to loan us the money for construction. The big thing was, we didn't have the teaching nuns.

"But once I got a commitment from the Dominicans, there was just no stopping Dick. He did all the landscaping . . . with the generous help of some of the parishioners, of course. But no one worked nearly as hard as Dick Kramer to get that school built.

"The sad thing is, Bob, he was —is—a driven man. And I worry about him at that parish of his. There comes a time when you must let something die. And that's about the state of Mother of Sorrows parish. It's dying. But Father Kramer will work it even as it sinks into the grave. The frustration of it all can take a lot out of a man . . . especially a man like Dick Kramer." Meehan looked expectantly at Koesler.

"So, Monsignor, is there something you'd like me to do about this?"

"Look in on him, if you would. I feel he needs some support. The support only another priest can give. Unless he's changed a great deal—and I don't believe he has—then he doesn't have more than few close friends. And he would never ask for help. It's just not in him to do that."

"Monsignor," Koesler protested, "I really don't have all that much time to—"

"Oh, now, Bobby, I'm not askin' you to spend a lot of time. Just look in on him once in a while. Let him know someone cares. Another priest. It'll do a lot of good. I know it will."

"Okay, Monsignor. I'll do it . . . first chance I get."

Koesler made his goodbyes. It was just 11:30 A.M. Time for Monsignor Meehan to lead the rosary in the chapel of the Little Sisters of the Poor. As usual, six or seven little old ladies and one or two little old men would join him for this daily prayer before lunch.

Before leaving, Koesler watched the pious group gather. One day, he thought, if you live long enough, this will be it: The high point of your day will be leading the rosary for a group of your peers—all of you on the shelf.

Oh well; it could be worse. Needed, for one reason or another, right to the end. There was a lot to be said for the quiet life of a simple parish priest.

In a little while he would value that quiet, simple life even more because he was about to temporarily lose it.

16

IT WAS JUST A FEW MINUTES TILL noon. Whenever she had the opportunity—and this was one of those times—Sister Mary Therese Hercher liked to spend a few quiet moments in prayer before the noon Mass.

She genuflected and entered one of the pews near the sanctuary. It was cold; she shivered as her knees touched the padded kneeler. Mother of Sorrows was a venerable parish and this edifice was a tribute to the parish's more lush days. Plenty of marble and brick, with lots of stained glass. And a huge "rose window" in the front wall above the choir loft—which these days was almost never used.

This huge structure was heated only for Sunday Masses. Through the week, particularly during January and February, it required more than ordinary dedication to visit the church for Mass or private prayer.

It would have made a lot of sense to Therese to just lock the church except for Sundays and special events. Daily Mass easily could be held in the church hall or even, comfortably, in the rectory. Only a very few people attended daily Mass. With no trouble, the small group could have assembled in the basement of the rectory and been warm and comfy. But Father Dick Kramer seemed to feel that if they were to lock the church Monday through Saturday, in no time the chancery would hear of it and they would lock it up for good and all.

That man!

Sister Mary Therese began to pray for the pastor. Stubborn, bull-headed, singleminded, dedicated, generous, caring, hard-working. She was filled with negative and positive feelings.

In the final analysis, Father Kramer had her respect and her continued commitment. If this parish was sinking slowly in the west—and she believed it was—and if the pastor was going to stay with his parish to the bitter end, then she too would stay aboard.

It was not Sister Therese's style to pray that any course of events should go on according to her lights. Rather, over the long years of a developing prayer life; through the postulancy, the novitiate, first profession, and final vows, she had fairly successfully adopted Christ's prayer in the Garden of Gethsemane—not as I will, but Thy will be done. In most instances, she had found this the most comforting and comfortable approach to God.

But not now. She was certain it was God's will that Mother of Sorrows parish should close. Well, perhaps not quite that *badly*. But she was certain that for his emotional well-being,

Father Kramer must get out of the parish and escape the impossible demands he felt the parish was making of him.

No possible way could he keep this school open. Yet he would continue to struggle until the inevitable failure occurred. And once the school, as well as several other parish services, ground to a halt, Father Kramer would be forced to leave and establish a new headquarters in a parish that more called for and could better profit from his many talents.

Then Mother of Sorrows would cease to exist as a parish. For no other priest in the archdiocese would apply for it. This had happened in quite a few city parishes. And it surely would happen here, also. So she prayed for her friend, Father Dick Kramer, that he would have the sense to admit this was a dying elephant. And that God would continue His presence among these good people even after the demise of Mother of Sorrows parish.

As she prayed, a lonely figure entered the church and walked quietly down the middle aisle. Therese recognized Sarah Taylor, the woman who just last week had lost her son in that tragic incident. The classic example of being in the wrong place at the wrong time.

Little Rudy Taylor! Therese could hardly imagine how the gang who murdered him could have mistaken this young boy for a competing drug dealer.

It had taken the police only a few days to catch Rudy's killers. The gang—boys themselves chronologically—were to be tried as adults.

What a shame! What a waste!

Either Sarah Taylor had found or was still searching for her consolation in the church. While the Taylors had been regular attendants at Sunday Mass, and while Rudy had occasionally been a Mass server during the week, Sarah had never attended daily Mass until Rudy was killed.

What could one say to someone who had suffered a loss comparable to that of Sarah Taylor's? Sister Therese had long since found mere words insufficient. But each day, during Mass, at the greeting of peace, Sister Therese had led the others in giving Sarah a little hug and a few of those inadequate words. Something seemed to be helping—probably that little hug.

Therese slid back in the pew. There was something about the hardness of the wood and the no-nonsense ninety-degree angle of the seat and backrest that argued against falling asleep in church. If that weren't enough, there was the pervading chill. All in all, at least on weekdays during the winter months, one was almost guaranteed an alert congregation.

Her gaze kept returning to Sarah Taylor. Therese remembered her early days in this parish. It was a confusing time during which she'd tried to work out existentially what the office of pastoral associate entailed, especially when occupied by a nun—technically a layperson. At the same time, she'd had to acclimatize herself to the black experience.

One of her first introductions to the differences between the black and the white culture had taken place only days after she arrived at Mother of Sorrows.

It happened when Rose Bevilaqua died. Rosè, very white and very Italian, had been a Mother of Sorrows parishioner before a single black family had ever moved into the parish. The Bevilaqua family was one of the few white families that did not participate in the exodus from that changing neighborhood. Not only did they stay put; they remained very active in the parish.

Eventually, the last of their children married and, quite naturally, moved away. Then Rose became a widow. Still she would not move. If anything, she became more involved in the parish and very popular with the children.

Then, shortly after Therese came to the parish, Rose died. Because the children loved her so much, Therese decided to take a group of them to the funeral home to pay their respects. She loaded the parish station wagon with young black girls and boys, all dressed in their very best for the solemn occasion.

It was only after they entered the funeral home that Therese learned that the kids had no idea either of what they were doing or what was expected of them.

As soon as the group entered the foyer, the children spread

out in every direction. Chased as closely as possible by Therese, the kids bolted from room to room, looking for their friend. Obviously, they did not know what it meant that she had died. Nor had they any notion of the decorum expected in a funeral home, particularly one whose clientele was nearly exclusively white.

One by one, Therese had collared and collected the children from the far reaches of the funeral home and shepherded them toward the parlor that held the mortal remains of Rose Bevilaqua.

When they reached the proper parlor, there was Rudy Taylor perched atop the casket, peering down into its open hatch. As the ragtag group entered the room, a triumphant Rudy pointed down into the casket and proudly announced, "There go Rose!"

And yet, that had by no means been Rudy's most memorable performance.

Therese recalled a confirmation ceremony only a year or so previous when Rudy unintentionally became the star of the show. The confirming bishop had been Edwin Baldwin. That was important to the memory of the event due to the fact that Bishop Baldwin, one of Detroit's auxiliaries, retained the custom of interrogating the children who were about to be confirmed. The other bishops had pretty well abandoned that practice in favor of a simple, routine, and thus usually boring, homily. However, asking leading questions of youngsters could prove hazardous, and had—many, many times.

It was Bishop Baldwin's fey habit to start almost anywhere, then allow the children's freewheeling stream of consciousness to go wherever it would.

On this evening, the bishop began at the beginning, Genesis, the Bible's first book. Various youngsters gave a quite vivid, if fanciful, description of the Garden of Paradise and that frolicsome couple, Adam and Eve. From there, they leaped over the millennia to Noah and the Flood and, eventually, to Abraham. At that point, the bishop threw the conversational ball up for a center jump, as he asked, "And who was Abraham?" Rudy Taylor waved his arm wildly, was called on, and volunteered, "Abraham Lincoln was our first president!"

At which time, the eighth grade history teacher prayed that the earth would open up and swallow her.

A commotion in the vestibule of the church brought Therese back to the present. The majority of this small congregation arrived to the sound of coughing and stamping of feet to shake snow from boots.

Therese glanced at her watch—11:59. One minute before the noon Mass. It didn't seem to matter whether it was daily or Sunday Mass, a movie, the theater, or a meeting: Most people timed their arrival for the last possible moment—or were stylishly late. Few came early—or even on time—for anything. Therese pitied those who missed coming early for Mass. There was no place more conducive to peaceful, quiet meditation than a church when no service was being conducted.

The usual ten to fifteen people scattered themselves throughout the vast church. Most huddled, almost for warmth, in the front near the altar. But there were those who did not cotton to the distinctively post-Conciliar notion of "community." These made certain that lots of space separated them from those who clustered together. In the best spirit of laissez-faire, the "community" did not force those in the farflung reaches of the church to participate in communal liturgies such as the greeting of peace.

As Father Kramer entered the sanctuary from the sacristy, he rang the bell that announced the beginning of services. There was no altar boy. A deficiency that emphasized the role of the late Rudy Taylor. Not only were priests an endangered species; now, even altar boys were on the list.

Father Kramer kissed the center of the altar, reverencing the bone-relic of the martyr saint "buried" in the altar stone. He intoned, "The grace of our Lord Jesus Christ and the love of God and the fellowship of the Holy Spirit be with you all."

"And also with you," the congregation replied.

"And also with you," said the man who had just entered the church.

108

Arnold Bush had timed his arrival carefully. He did not wish to be early and chance the others' taking note of him. On the other hand, those who came in after him would be more concerned with discovering where Father was in the Mass than taking any interest in him.

Yes, this was the perfect time. Just a few seconds late and seated quite apart from anyone else. No one would bother him. No one would extend to him the greeting of peace. He was at leisure to study the priest, Father Richard Kramer.

It was not long ago that someone—he'd forgotten who—had told him he bore a striking resemblance to Father Kramer. Until then, Arnold Bush had never heard of Father Kramer. Nor, at that time, did the possibility that he had a lookalike in the priesthood much interest him. More recently, the possibility of such a resemblance took on a much more practical significance.

So, Bush, of late, spent one or two of his lunch hours each week driving out to Mother of Sorrows church to attend noonday Mass. As a rather intense Catholic, he did not mind attending Mass more often than just Sundays. But there was much more than mere devotion involved. In fact, at these Masses he seldom said an actual prayer. He would automatically respond to the celebrant's invocations, as he just had to the opening prayer, but his mind was far from prayer and God.

Rather, he was planning his next move.

Things were falling into place rather nicely, all things considered. He needed only a little more time to tie up a few loose ends. Then, with any luck at all, his plan would be complete and ready to be put into action.

As he carefully studied the priest, Bush realized that their features were not by any means identical. Oh, they were about the same height and build; blond-haired, fair-complexioned. The likeness, such as it was, would not stand the test of close scrutiny. But to the casual passerby the similarity was enough. Yes, Arnold Bush would stake his future, his freedom, on that.

"Let us proclaim the mystery of faith," Father Kramer invited.

"Christ has died. Christ is risen. Christ will come again," the congregation responded.

Christ died for sinners, thought Bush. It was only fit and proper that sinners should die for Christ.

17

SISTER MARY THERESE OFFERED TO show Father Koesler the way to the church basement, but he assured her he was familiar with the plant and could find the way. So she told him which doors were locked and which were not. And away he went.

She was surprised but pleased that Koesler had come to visit. She wished that her presence, support, and companionship were sufficient for Dick Kramer, but she knew that wasn't so. There was just something about one priest that needed another. And Kramer did not have many priest friends, at least to the extent that any priest socialized with him, or he with any of them.

There was nothing she could do about this beyond encouraging him to give himself a break and party with the gang once in a while. He always seemed grateful for her solicitude, but he almost always begged off. Workaholism, a defect that Kramer had to a terminal degree, did not mix well with worry-free relaxation.

Thus she was happy that Koesler had come on what seemed to be a social call. Perhaps this could be the beginning of a new companionable dimension in Dick Kramer's life. God knows he could use it.

Koesler of course had no way of knowing what was on Sister Therese's mind. As far as he was concerned, this visit was the result of Monsignor Meehan's request. The next time Koesler stopped by, he wanted to be able to give the monsignor some sort of report—positive, Koesler hoped—on the state of Richard Kramer.

It was not that Koesler was in any way opposed to the possibility that this visit might blossom into a deeper friendship more frequently renewed. Such, indeed, he would welcome. But it was not in Koesler's nature to enter into another's life uninvited. In truth, there was no way he would have undertaken this visit had it not been for Meehan's concern for his former associate.

Koesler negotiated the maze of locked and unlocked doors without incident, though it was fortunate that he was familiar with Mother of Sorrows church. Otherwise, he might have become hopelessly lost and lucky to find his way back to Sister Therese for a guided tour.

As he passed through the final door leading from the boiler room to Kramer's carefully outfitted and unexpectedly complete workshop, Koesler felt a foreboding. There was nothing specific; it was just so dark and chill and deserted. He was reminded of the smokehouse where Jud Fry holed up in the musical *Oklahoma!*. Koesler shrugged; to each his own. It was not his cup of tea, but evidently it suited Dick Kramer.

Koesler would not have been able to see into this workroom had his eyes not already become accustomed to the dark. He knocked, and cleared his throat. Kramer, bent over his workbench at the opposite side of the room, whirled, clearly startled.

"Oh, sorry, Dick. I didn't mean to sneak up on you like this. There wasn't any other way of doing it."

"You startled me!" Kramer didn't seem angry, merely nettled. "What are you doing here, anyway? Where's Therese?"

"Therese is at the rectory. She gave me directions on how to find you. As to what I'm doing here: I came to visit. I expected you to be at the rectory." Koesler was aware that Kramer was tucking something into one of the workbench drawers. It appeared to be an object he had been working on, but, apparently, something he didn't want Koesler to see.

Kramer seemed to unbend. "Sorry to be so abrupt. I just wasn't expecting company. I guess I was kind of wrapped up in what I was doing. You gave me a start. What brings you here . . . I mean besides the visit?" Kramer did not get casual visitors. And he knew that everyone knew that.

"No strings, Dick . . . well, maybe one. I was visiting with Monsignor Meehan and he mentioned you. We both got to wondering how you are." Koesler paused. "So how are you?"

"Okay, I guess." Kramer fumbled in his pants pocket and extracted a crumpled half-full pack of cigarettes. He fished one out, straightened and smoothed it, then lit it from the stub that was about to expire in a nearby overflowing ashtray. "Want to go back to the rectory? We could have a drink."

Koesler waved a hand. "No . . . no; thanks just the same, but I've got enough left to do today without a midafternoon libation."

Kramer studied the other priest with a measure of abstract interest. He honestly could not fathom why one person would pay a strictly social call on another person—especially when both were busy priests—in the middle of the afternoon. "Oh. Okay, then, we can visit here, I guess. What did you want to talk about?"

Koesler didn't "want" to talk about anything in particular. When one paid a social call, especially when both parties were priests, it really wasn't necessary to announce a subject matter for conversation. One simply chewed some innocent fat for a while. Now that Kramer had suggested the need for a topic, Koesler found himself hard-pressed to come up with one. But, after a little thought, "How's Sister Therese working out?"

"Therese? Good. Fine. I really don't know what I'd do without her."

Koesler had not expected such enthusiasm, particularly from Kramer. "That's quite a testimonial! What've you got her doing to elicit all that praise?"

"Oh, Therese does a little bit of everything. She takes a special interest in the old folks . . . the ones in nursing homes and the ones shuttered up in their homes, afraid to come out even in broad daylight. Folks with bars on their doors and windows. They really need help, someone to take an interest in them . . . and Therese does."

"Nice."

"But that's not all. She takes care of the kids. Takes them out for projects, picnics, whatever. They love her. I think when they grow up, if they think kindly of the Catholic Church, it'll be Therese they're thinking of. On top of that, for all practical purposes she's the director of Religious Ed—youth and adult."

"Impressive. Everything but hearing confessions and saying Mass."

Koesler's obvious exaggeration was not lost on Kramer. "Actually, Bob," he returned the joke, "I think maybe she does hear confessions once in a while."

"Better not let the Vatican hear about that. As far as Rome is concerned, females are lucky to be allowed into church."

"Huh?"

"Well, all right, they can come in. But they'd better not get too close to the altar."

"Are you serious?"

Koesler began to wonder whether Kramer was still joking . . . or did he actually not know about the exclusion of girls from serving at the altar?

"Are *you* serious?" Koesler returned. "You do know that girls are banned from serving Mass, don't you?"

"Is that still going on?"

"You bet your sweet bippy it's still going on. You mean you're not involved in the war against altar girls?" While this was not of major concern, especially in the Detroit archdiocese, it *was* a fairly popular topic of conversation in clerical groups. But then, Koesler reminded himself, Kramer was seldom to be found in informal clerical gatherings.

Kramer shook his head. "I had no idea anyone was still concerned about that. I'm afraid we solved that question a good long while ago in this parish. Our Mass servers are coed, at best."

"Then you'd better pray you don't pull Bishop Malone for confirmations."

"What happens then?"

"Probably what happened the other week at St. Valentine's. They were all ready to go out in procession when Malone spotted some girls in the line—cassocks and surplices."

"And then?"

"And then Malone handed the pastor an ultimatum: Get rid of the girls or cancel confirmations."

Kramer whistled. "He plays hard ball, eh?"

"So it seems. You'd think a guy who grew up in Mississippi would be familiar with the evils of discrimination—but this guy doesn't appear to have learned a damn thing."

"Let's hope he doesn't come to Mother of Sorrows. *I* might be able to live with him, but Therese—never."

Ordinarily, Koesler would not have bothered counting. But he could not help noticing that, in this short visit, Kramer was already on his third cigarette. Well, to each his own poison.

"Speaking of altar servers," Koesler said, "I see by the paper you lost one of your altar boys—what was the name? ...Rudy...uh..."

"Taylor. Yeah. Nice kid. Fate is a funny thing. His mother sent him to the store for some groceries. He went, but he stopped to talk to one of his buddies. And that was it. The guys in the car were cruising the neighborhood looking for the youngster who had stung them on a drug sale. The kids were stoned out of their skulls anyhow. Plus Rudy did look a little like the guy they were after. So they shot him dead. Just like that.

"Since then, almost everybody in the parish, especially his mother, has been speculating on what if... what if... what if. What if he hadn't met his friends? What if he had just gone on to the store? He might be alive. Hell, he *would* be alive."

"Tough funeral."

"You said it."

"I had a tough one about a week ago."

Kramer's expression changed. Koesler noted it but only momentarily.

"That prostitute who was murdered," Koesler said. "You must have read about it . . . named Bonner. To this day I still can't quite figure out how I got that funeral." He shook his head. "I took a lot of heat before, but mostly after."

"The chancery?"

"No, not downtown, thank God. Some parishioners . . . some of those 'concerned Catholics.' "

"I saw some of that funeral on TV. How did you get it?"

"Funny thing: The officer who's investigating the case asked me to take it . . . and he's not even a Catholic."

"I . . . I think I saw him interviewed on that same newscast . . . the day of the funeral. What was his name?"

"Uh . . . Tuller. No. Tully. Yes, Tully. Lieutenant Tully."

"Tully." Kramer seemed to be memorizing the name.

"Then there was that second prostitute. Killed the same way, the same horrible way, the papers said."

"Yeah . . ." Kramer seemed abstracted.

"I wonder if it will happen again," Koesler said.

"What?"

"I said, I wonder if it'll happen again. The papers described them as serial murders. The reporter said the police said it could happen again. I wonder it if will. What do you think?"

"How should I know?" Kramer said, a whit testily.

Koesler sensed that he might be overstaying his welcome. After all, when one was as nearly a hermit as Kramer, visits should be kept to a minimum in time and frequency until the recluse feels comfortable with company.

"Hey, Dick," Koesler said, "I've taken up enough of your time."

He paused to allow Kramer to express the usual disclaimer of polite society. Something like, "Oh, do you have to leave already?" When it was clear that no such empty reassurance would be uttered, Koesler continued. "But it was good seeing you. We'll have to do this again. Hey, you know where St.

Anselm's is; why don't you stop by sometime? Bring Therese if you want. We can sit around for a couple of hours and solve most of the Church's problems . . . what do you say?"

"Sure, sometime."

With that, Koesler left, concentrating carefully on how he was going to escape from these ancient catacomblike buildings. He had to remember which doors had been locked and which left unbolted. His sense of direction was, for once, remarkably unerring.

As he drove away from Mother of Sorrows, Koesler rehashed his conversation with Kramer. All in all, it had not gone badly. A bit awkward at the beginning and end, but Koesler attributed that to Kramer's workaholism. The poor guy relaxed so seldom it was only natural that he would be ill at ease at the outset and, in the end, tire of the conversation.

Koesler resolved to keep this social contact with Dick Kramer open and also, at his next visit with Monsignor Meehan, to report that all seemed reasonably well with Father Kramer.

Koesler was grateful that Meehan had suggested this renewal of an old friendship. He felt that he had accomplished something this day.

18

ARNOLD BUSH NEVER WENT ON dates. Or, in the words of Sir William Schwenck Gilbert, hardly ever.

For one, he didn't know what to do about women. His upbringing had been so grossly muddled, he felt at best ambivalent about females. The time spent living in a house of ill repute—as a bygone era described it—had convinced him that women were manipulative, shallow, insincere frauds.

The archconservative Catholic school he had attended taught him that women were to be reverenced, respected, left untouched before—and pretty much after—marriage. At one extreme of his imagination stood the seductive whore; at the other the Blessed Virgin Mary. As a result, he never quite achieved any sort of realistic blending of these attitudes.

While he harbored violent tendencies toward women, he scarcely ever got close to a woman, let alone violated her. While he went well beyond Church doctrine in adoration of the Blessed Virgin and kept pictures and statues of her, these objects shared space with soft- and hard-core pornography on the walls of his apartment.

He was filled with so many varying positive and negative vectors that he hardly ever moved off square one when it came to initiating any sort of social contact with a woman, much less asked one for a date.

Enter Agnes Blondell, an attendant in the Wayne County Medical Examiner's Department. She had been increasingly attracted to Arnold over the brief time they had worked together. She couldn't put her finger on any one incident that caught her attention. It was the whole thing.

For starters, he did not come on to her the way almost every other man did. He had kept his distance. Very suave, almost continental, she thought.

Agnes was endowed with, as one of her many boyfriends had put it, a figure that would not quit. By actual measurement—and she had actually measured—38-28-40.

Her final reservation concerning Bush disintegrated when she saw a manifestation of his strength. The way he had manhandled a few of the other attendants at the morgue! The respect, if not downright fear, in which he was subsequently held! Yet he did not go out of his way to pick a fight. No; he just stood up for what he wanted. He was the strong, silent type who did not appear to be your run-of-the-mill octopus when it came to women. He certainly seemed to be Agnes Blondell's kind of guy.

So it was, late Thursday afternoon, that Agnes took the initiative. "Doin' anything tomorrow night after work, Arnie?"

He had not anticipated any such overture. Indeed, hardly anyone ever familiarized his name. He was either "Bush" or "Arnold." Thus he was uncharacteristically flustered. "After work? Tomorrow?"

"Yeah, Friday, tomorrow, after work . . . got any plans?"

If he did, he certainly could not recall any of them at this moment. "I don't know. I guess not. No, I can't think of any."

"So then, howdja like to go out somewhere? Maybe a movie or something?"

"Geez, I don't know . . . uh . . ."

"Agnes. Don't you know my name, Arnie?"

"Of course. Agnes Blondell." Bush was very much aware of Agnes Blondell as was every other still living man at the morgue. But while the others fantasized about "Jugs" Blondell, Bush had no clue as to how to relate to her.

"Call me Aggie, Arnie. All my friends do."

"But we're not friends."

"We could be. How about tomorrow night?"

"Well, sure." Why not? "What did you have in mind?"

"I dunno. A show, maybe? A movie?"

"We could go where I always go to see movies."

"Where's that?"

"The Tel-Ex Cinema at Telegraph and Ten Mile."

"Tel-Ex? I never heard of it . . . it ain't one of those Triple-X porno houses, is it?"

"No, no; no way." Not that Bush did not indulge in an occasional hard-core porno flick. But only occasionally: They were so expensive.

"This is a legit movie house. But the movies only cost one buck admission."

"All times?"

"All times."

Now, Agnes recalled seeing listings in the newspaper movie guide for the Tel-Ex. Four screens, as she recalled, with first-rate films. You just had to be patient until every other area theater had shown the movies to their satisfaction. Eventually, many of the better ones trickled down to the "Dollar Cinema." It made sense to her: Why waste all that money on a show, when, if you waited long enough, you could see it for a buck. And if it turned out to be rotten, you hadn't wasted four or five dollars. Another point in Arnie's favor: sensibly abstemious.

"Done," said Agnes. And they made their arrangements.

At 6:30 Friday evening, Arnold called for Agnes at her apartment. She appreciated promptness. She also liked the economy-consciousness of his simple black Ford Escort. Two more pluses for Arnold Bush.

They arrived comfortably early for the 7:15 screening. The movie was "Rambo VII." Agnes found irresistible the similarity between Sly Stallone on the screen and Arnold Bush seated next to her. Stallone appeared to be steroidally rounded, while Bush's strength was more muted. But, no doubt: Both were strong men. And even though Stallone was given to interminable perorations toward the wind-up of each of his movies, both he and Arnold generally let their strength speak for itself.

After the movie, they repaired to the nearby Elias Bros. Big Boy. Each ate generously from the buffet and salad bar. But then, each was a fair-sized person. After dessert there was an awkward moment. What now?

"Well," Bush said, with a tone of finality.

"Well." The word took on a little life coming from Agnes. "Well, the evening's young."

"Oh?"

"I was thinking maybe we could go to your place."

Most of the other men at the morgue would have given their severance pay for such an open-ended invitation from "Jugs." But Bush was uncertain. There were all those pictures

on his walls. What would Aggie think of that? And besides
. . . "My place ain't very much."

"I kind of figured that, Arnie. You go to economy movies.
You drive an economy car. I figured you'd live in an economy
flat. But I like that."

Well, then, to hell with the pictures! "Okay, let's go."

The drive to Bush's apartment took only about twenty minutes. When they arrived, Agnes had to admit that she hadn't
been mistaken. A lesser woman would have phrased it that her
worst fears were realized. But, somehow, Agnes was able to
view the largely deserted area as an economy neighborhood.
She said as much. Arnold was pleased.

He led the way up the rickety stairs and hesitated only a
moment before he unlocked and opened the door. He knew
this was the moment of truth—an inevitable moment.

He entered the room, turned on the single overhead light,
and stood aside. Anges entered, smiling at the room's spartan
dimensions. Then she saw the walls. "Arnie, the pictures!"
she shrieked.

"I was afraid of this."

After her initial shock, she took a closer look. "Why,
Arnie, they're the two prostitutes that we had in . . . the serial
killings."

"Uh-huh." He feared the worst.

She stepped closer to examine the pictures more carefully,
moving from wall to wall. All in all, she did not find the
pictures as distasteful as almost anyone else would have. After
all, she had seen the corpses in the flesh. If anything, she
appreciated the photographer's technical excellence. However,
one anomaly puzzled her. "Arnie, how come you got pictures
of the whores on three walls and holy pictures on the other
wall? I mean, how does the Blessed Mother figure in this?"

"Are you a Catholic?"

"No . . . why?"

"You knew it was the Blessed Mother."

"Good God, Arnie, everybody knows that."

"I suppose." That Agnes was not a Catholic was not an

earth-shattering revelation. But it would have been nice had they shared the same faith.

"So," Agnes returned, "how come you got all these pictures on your walls?"

"No special reason. Some of it is my work. And the rest of it is my religion."

"Oh." Agnes would have pursued the subject a bit further but there was a more pressing matter. She looked around. "Arnie, where's your bathroom?"

"At the end of the hall." He went to the doorway and pointed to the open door at the end of the corridor. "Nobody's using it now."

Agnes smiled valiantly and, purse in hand, traveled the short distance to the floor's one and only bathroom. She admired economy, but there was a limit. She equated separate facilities with the more primitive outhouse. She did not care for either.

Beyond responding to the call of nature, she inserted her personally prescribed diaphragm. One never knew how these evenings might end, and Agnes knew better than to trust a man to have a supply of condoms. However, what with the herpes and AIDS epidemic, she also came prepared with condoms to supply any prospective partner. Better safe than sorry, she reminded herself regularly.

She returned to the room to find Arnold standing uncertainly near the only window. He looked as if he felt trapped and was more comfortable near one of the room's two exits.

Agnes sat on the bed and patted the space next to her, an invitation to Arnold to join her.

Instead, he took one of the two straightback chairs. He did not know what to make of her. At least she did not complain about his cigarettes. He had been smoking all evening. Although she did not join in, neither did she shrink from the clouds of smoke that had permeated the atmosphere around them. There was something to be said, he thought, for a woman who did not object to another person's smoking these days.

But this invitation to join her on the bed? Confusing. All

evening he had scrupulously treated her with all the respect due a good woman. Just as he'd been taught by all those nuns and priests in Catholic schools.

Agnes did not seem upset that Arnold had disregarded her invitation. She appeared gratified with what she took to be his naiveté.

"That's nice," Agnes said.

"What's nice?"

"That you think so much of your religion . . . that you've got all these religious pictures on your wall. You don't find many men like this these days."

"I suppose. I never thought about it."

"That's another nice thing: that it comes to you so natural. You don't even have to think about it."

Bush shrugged. He was still trying to figure out what she was up to and where all this was leading.

"I also liked the way you took such special care of those two women." She indicated the photos of the two mutilated corpses.

"You did?" This genuinely surprised Bush.

"Yes. Not everybody would have done that. Oh, I heard the dirty jokes some of the guys were telling about those poor women. It turned my stomach." She indicated the turned area. Then she moved her hand up her body, accentuating the already clearly defined area of her breasts.

Bush felt sexual stirrings.

"But," Agnes continued, "you protected them, even in death. I saw how you tended to them. Wouldn't let anyone else handle them. Even fought for them! That's when I really began to wonder about you, Arnie. I'll bet you took good care of your mother, didn't you? A woman can tell that sort of thing."

"I didn't know my mother," Bush said flatly.

"Didn't know your mother! You poor thing. And yet your heart can go out to these poor creatures who were so badly treated. So brutally murdered. All that and you didn't even have a chance to know your own mother. You really are one in a million, Arnie Bush." Agnes rose from the bed and moved just behind Arnold's chair. She began to knead his shoulders.

Bush was thoroughly confused.

"They say you're not married . . . that right?"

He nodded.

"Ever been married?"

He shook his head.

"Ever had a girl?"

He shrugged.

"Any girl'd be proud to have you for her fella, Arnie."

He sat motionless.

She stopped kneading his shoulders. What was she doing? He could hear some sound but he couldn't identify it.

Suddenly she stepped in front of him. She was only inches away. She had removed her dress, revealing a black lace bra and half-slip, and a lot of body. Agnes was proud of her body. She had reason to be.

"Well, Arnie?"

Bush gasped. He was immobilized. He didn't know what to do. He was used to being in charge of things. This was one of those rare times when events seemed to be beyond his control. Obviously, the next move was up to him. But what? The evening had begun with his taking out a woman whom he reverenced as he would have the Blessed Mother. He had treated her, as far as he knew, as a gentleman should.

But there she stood, half-naked. Her dishabille was self-effected. It was a statement of some sort. The next move was up to him. The ball, as they say, was in his court. He should do something. But what?

He hit her.

Not as hard as he could, by any means. Just hard enough to topple her onto the bed.

Her eyes opened wide. She had not expected that. On the other hand, she was not displeased. This show of controlled violence excited her.

He leaped on the bed, straddling her. He grasped the bra at

the point between her breasts and yanked. The clasp gave way with a small popping sound.

Everything was hers. Truth in advertising. No falsies, no padding, no artificial uplift. Her breasts were truly magnificent.

As soon as he saw her flesh, the erect nipples, the large dark aureole, he saw not Agnes Blondell but all the whores he'd grown up among. They never cared how little clothing they wore. Lolling around the parlor, frequently their breasts were exposed. No one seemed to care.

But Arnold Bush had cared.

The whores were the antithesis of the Blessed Virgin. They were "The Enemy." But he couldn't do anything to right their wrong. Not then—he had been just a child. But now!

"Arnie! Arnie! You're hurting me! Stop! Arnie!"

He was fascinated by the white marks his fingers were making in her breasts. As he dug deeply into the unexpectedly firm flesh, the white marks quickly turned to red as bruises began to form.

"Arnie! Arnie!" Now she was frightened . . . terrified. This had gotten completely out of control and she didn't know how to put a halt to it. She could not possibly combat his strength. She knew it was fruitless to scream; she remembered thinking as they entered the building that even if anyone else lived here there was no indication anyone else was home.

His hands slid up around her throat. They began to squeeze ever more tightly.

Agnes was losing consciousnes. In a little while, she knew, she would be dead.

She summoned up every vestige of strength she had left and struck his nose with the flat of her hand.

It was as solid a blow as he'd ever felt. He shook his head and relaxed his grip on her throat. Slapping him seemed to him like the act of a virtuous woman. Again, he was confused. Was she actually a virtuous woman? Might she even be a virgin?

He removed his hands from her throat and sat back, still straddling her.

She choked and coughed and concentrated on not vomiting. With him atop her, she couldn't turn over. If she were to vomit now, she feared she might be asphyxiated by her own sickness. She massaged her injured throat.

After a few moments, she was able to moan, "Get off, Arnie. Get off."

Slowly, still confused, he dismounted.

She was grateful to be alive, and furious with him. The two emotions were not mutually exclusive. Both somehow filled her being. She glanced at her throbbing breasts. Tomorrow they would be one large painful bruise. That was the bad news. The good news was that there would be a tomorrow.

She glanced at her bra. It was beyond repair. She did not bother picking it off the floor. She slipped into her dress and buttoned it, picked up her purse, and headed for the door.

It occurred to Bush that she had no transportation. "I'll drive . . ."

She waved him off. No possible way would she spend another moment with this madman. A street mugger would be a welcome relief compared with what she had just gone through. "Taxi," she whispered, and pointed to his phone.

He called for a taxi, giving directions to his apartment. Hanging up the phone, he turned to her. "I . . ."

Again she waved him off, and left the apartment to await the taxi in the comparative security of that high-crime neighborhood.

As she rode home, she had to wonder how she could have been so mistaken. She was a careful woman. Or at least experience had made her careful. Never had she been so deceived. The strong, silent type—good-looking, too. Never made a pass at her—or at any other woman at work. A perfect gentleman on the date. The pictures on the wall, proving the special care he had taken with those poor mutilated women. And the holy pictures! What was it: You can never tell a book by its cover? Whoever first said that sure could have been thinking of Arnold Bush.

One thing was certain: She would tell the other girls at work, first thing in the morning, about her near-fatal encounter with Arnold Bush. In the ladies' room she would show them her abused breasts. It was important that none of the others ever make the mistake of getting close to this maniac. She would swear the girls to secrecy. No point in telling the men.

She was grateful to have escaped tonight's plight alive. Ordinarily not a prayerful person, now Agnes Blondell felt prayer was appropriate. Tonight—for the first time since she was a child—she would say her night prayers.

So would Arnold Bush. Except that, for Bush, prayer was a daily habit. And tonight he had a lot to talk to God about. He was confused. How could everything have become so jumbled?

His mistake—if the fault were, indeed, his—was in letting a woman into his life. He knew he never had been able to understand them. He assumed there must be good women around somewhere. There was the Blessed Virgin Mary. There were nuns. There were faithful mothers of families. But he never seemed to meet any of these good women. Why was he forever playing Adam to somebody else's Eve?

Agnes was a case in point.

She seemed to be good. They'd had a nice time this evening. The movie was entertaining. They had plenty to eat. She seemed to completely understand his picture gallery. Everything was going so smoothly. Then she had to get fresh. She had to play the harlot.

Probably it began badly when she was the one who made the overture for a date. Men were supposed to do that. Yes, he should have tumbled when she proposed they go out together. He'd have to be more careful in the future.

Well, the main thing was to put tonight behind him. He had

more important things to take care of. More important things to plan. He was inordinately proud of what he was doing. The instrument of God's justice. Of that he could be justly proud. Forget tonight. Plan the present and the future.

19

MANGIAPANE TALKED TOO MUCH—much too much. But he was a good cop. And, in time, he would make a first-rate homicide detective.

He had an inquisitive mind. That was good. And he seemed to catch on to homicide work instinctively. The whole thing was in solving the puzzle. And he liked the mysteries as opposed to the platters.

Some guys just wanted the closed folder. Some guys and *gals*—Alonzo Tully corrected himself. He mustn't overlook the women in the division. Some of them were damn good. Especially when they advanced in grade. A female sergeant or lieutenant generally was ten times as good as the equivalent man. And, as Mangiapane had pointed out not ten minutes ago, women, even women cops, smelled good.

God, surveillance was dull.

He had no one to blame but himself; it had been his idea. As a matter of fact, quite a few other cops were, at this very moment, blaming him for their being staked out in uncomfortable cars on a dreary Sunday afternoon in late January when they could have been installed in front of a nice TV set, armed with snacks and beer, watching the Pro Bowl. The last of football for this season.

But dammit, Tully didn't care. This was part of being a

cop: 98 percent going up blind alleys, only once in a while guessing right or getting an unexpected break. And that's what this afternoon was—a guess. Only time would show whether or not it was an inspired guess.

The first of the prostitute mutilation murders had taken place two weeks ago on a late Sunday afternoon. The second, one week ago on a late Sunday afternoon. Both murders had occurred in threadbare sections of the city, sections notorious for a thriving prostitution business. But sections where, due largely to the poverty of the area, there was little likelihood of finding either high-class or high-priced women. Both victims had been, for prostitutes, comparatively elderly. And both were white.

Even with the beefed-up squad Koznicki had given him, this week's investigation had turned up nothing new or helpful. There had been the usual parade of confessors—people under some weird compulsion to confess to any well-publicized crime. But each had to be checked out, even if only in a cursory manner.

Then, as a result of publicizing that composite likeness of the perp, a whole bunch of people had turned in their friends, relatives, and enemies—anyone who bore the slightest resemblance to the drawing. Those too had to be checked out. Someplace in that pile there could have been a lucky break. But there wasn't.

Adelle and Ruby had looked through police mug shots of killers, with special emphasis on those connected in any way with prostitutes. Nothing. Then, in a move Tully considered unique in the annals of the Detroit Police Department, the women were given the *Archdiocese of Detroit Pictorial Directory* to study.

That they identified no one in either collection did not surprise Tully.

Relatively few victims or witnesses correctly identify a perpetrator from mug shots. The photos, posed and dour, are frequently misleading and rarely up-to-date. Often the victim's memory plays tricks. And there is always the very real possibility that the individual's photo simply isn't there. Maybe it was the perpetrator's first crime. Maybe he had never been caught and booked. Or maybe the victim or witness was inadvertently shown the wrong book.

The priests' Pictorial Directory was another matter. It was Tully's first venture into what, in effect, were the clerical mug shots of the Archdiocese of Detroit. He had access to the most recent edition, which, having been issued in 1983, was not all that current. There were, by Tully's count, 958 priests working in the six-county archdiocese. The directory contained 763 photos. Which left 195 priests unrepresented pictorially.

A quick call to Father Koesler apprised Tully that cooperation with the directory people was not mandatory and some priests declined to have their pictures included. Tully thought this a hell of a way to run either a railroad or a diocese. But there was nothing he could do about it. Whether or not a priest was indeed the murderer, there was a fair chance his picture would not be in the directory. If it were up to criminals whether or not to have their photos in the mug book, obviously they would opt out.

So here it was, the end of the second week of the investigation. The first week had been virtually wasted under Tully's hypothesis that the first killing had been an act of retaliation against one of his prime snitches. That initial supposition had collapsed when the second victim turned out to have no connection with him.

Which brought him to today. And he knew that, realistically, Koznicki could no longer provide the luxury of a supplemented force. This, for all practical purposes, was his last chance for a big push. If he failed today—and he had to admit he well might—he would be pretty much on his own. And the possibility of solving this puzzle would diminish in direct relationship to the number of detectives working on it.

Thus, over Friday and Saturday, he and his task force had meticulously studied Detroit's many red-light districts, evaluating the neighborhoods as well as the type of prostitute to be found in each. They'd had to neglect some areas that were only marginally qualified in order to locate the sort of prostitute this perp seemed to be looking for.

Eventually, they settled on eight hooker areas, the number they had agreed on at the outset that they would be physically able to police with the number of officers and cars at their disposal.

God, surveillance was dull!

Mangiapane was driving and talking . . . driving slowly and talking fast. Tully tried to recall the beginning of the story Mangiapane was telling. If Tully could remember how it had started, he might conceivably make sense out of what Mangiapane was now saying.

Oh, yes; now he remembered. Mangiapane had gone to lunch in Greektown, where he'd bumped into Wolford and Hughes, two officers assigned to the Thirteenth Precinct. Over lunch, they talked shop, as usual. Mangiapane, with a multitude of his characteristic asides and digressions, was recounting a story the two detectives had told him.

"So," Mangiapane was saying, "they're figuring to get off their shift early, when this call comes in from this convent, the Home Visitors of Mary—great bunch of gals, do a lot of real great work—anyway, this nun calls the precinct and gets Hughes. She says there's a guy over there whose car has been swiped, and would the police send somebody over to help him.

"Well, Hughes figures this will be a great way to end the day a little early: Him and Wolford can run over to Arden Park, get the info and scoot on home.

"So they get there and there's this little guy—balding, glasses, third-rate moustache, paunchy, and very, very nervous. Somebody, he says, took his car. So the guys talk to him and one question leads to another. They ask how come he parked on this street. There ain't no businesses, all residential. Of course, there's always the chance he went into the Cathedral rectory . . . you know, Zoo, Blessed Sacrament Cathedral is just a block away, between Belmont and Boston on Woodward."

Tully of course knew the area. But he couldn't have come up with the name of the church. All he knew about churches was that there were a lot of them on Woodward and yes, he guessed some of them might be cathedrals. He would quickly defer to Mangiapane, who, as a very practicing Catholic, would know the name and location of the Catholic cathedral.

"But," Mangiapane continued, "there is a driveway off Arden Park for the Cathedral rectory. Visitors always park in that driveway. It's an obvious parking area and it's lots safer than parking on the street. So it was a logical question: Why did he park on that street?

"Well, he hems and haws for a while. Then he says he's an architect and he got out of his car so he could study the large, nice-lookin' buildings in that area . . . sort of on the spur of the moment, you know?"

Tully snorted.

"Right." Mangiapane agreed with the nonarticulate utterance. "So Hughes asks the guy for his ID. The guy hems and haws some more. Then he tells them he was robbed. And they say, 'Oh, that's interesting: You call us over here claiming somebody stole your wheels. Now you tell us that not only did somebody take your car but, oh, yeah, while I think of it, they also robbed me.

"'Just when did they do that, sir? You were walkin' up and down the street and — what was it: one or two guys?'

"The guy says, 'Two . . . it was two.'

"Wolford says, 'So, two guys take your wallet, your ID. And then they say, "Okay, while we're at it, I guess we'll take your wheels too"—that about it?'

"And the guy says, 'Yeah, that's about it.'"

"Okay." Tully was slumped in the passenger seat with his shapeless Irish tweed pulled low on his head. "What happened was this: The guy picks up a hooker on Woodward. She asks him what he wants. He says a blow job will be fine. She tells him to pull into a private driveway on Arden Park. He does. She says she's not gonna service him till she sees some green. He takes out his wallet and right then two of her friends come out of the bushes. They're armed. They force him out of his car. They take off with the wallet, the car, and the hooker.

"The driveway happens to be next to the convent. So he goes in there, tells the nuns somebody just stole his car—without bothering to mention the rest of the scenario—and

131

asks to use their phone. And the rest is history . . . right?"

Mangiapane thumped the steering wheel. "You got it, Zoo, you got it! And while the guy is telling his story to Hughes and Wolford, these nuns start cracking up and leave the room . . . 'cause they know where the guy is heading and what really happened."

"Keep at least one hand on the wheel, okay, Mangiapane?" It was ethnic, Tully thought, and he didn't usually sink to ethnic observations. But maybe there was some truth to it: that if you were to cut off an Italian's hands, he'd be struck dumb.

It certainly seemed true of Mangiapane. The gestures added zest to his storytelling. Tully couldn't conceive of Mangiapane's narrating anything about which he felt deeply without directing the movement, much as an orchestra leader would do. And, in fact, Mangiapane didn't actually need even one hand on the steering wheel. The guy was so big he could guide the car by pressing his thigh against the wheel . . . especially at the snail's pace at which they were now traveling.

Tully plucked the radio mike from beneath the dashboard and began checking with the other units spread throughout the predetermined red-light districts. Nothing. Not a nibble. And it was beginning to get late. Another hour and they would be out of the time frame in which the perp had operated on the previous Sundays.

"No luck, eh?"

Tully shook his head. Mangiapane, eyes alternately on the road and scanning the neighborhood, didn't catch Tully's response. No matter, the question had been rhetorical.

"Think we'll get home in time to see some of the Pro Bowl?" Mangiapane asked.

"Where they playin'?"

"Hawaii."

"They're about six hours behind us, aren't they?"

"About."

"And the damn game goes on forever."

"Pretty much."

"Yeah, I'd say we'll either get to see the last quarter or the late movie."

Mangiapane laughed, somewhat more heartily than was called for. He wasn't quite conscious of the fact that he was trying to ingratiate himself with Tully.

"Speaking of movies," Mangiapane was off again on one of his vignettes, ". . . you know that movie they're filming in town now?"

"Uh-huh." Everybody was painfully aware of the movie now being filmed in Detroit. The local news media, ordinarily extremely professional, lost measurable cool when it came to those rare instances when Hollywood invaded Detroit.

"Did you know that Lieutenant Horan was in charge of the squad assigned to the film crew?"

"Uh-huh."

"Well, I got this story from Hughes at lunch. He's a friend of one of the guys on that squad. And he was talkin' about the filming the other night. It was about ten o'clock. They got those whatchamacallits—klieg lights?—whatever, and they're gonna shoot right outside the Book Cadillac on Washington Boulevard.

"Anyway, they get all set up and ready to go when all of a sudden this car comes crashing through the barricades and plows into the set. Damn lucky thing nobody got hurt. Drunk driver."

"I read about it."

"Yeah, Zoo, and they had it on TV that night, too. But there was more to it than that. When they were setting up that shot, the director of the movie . . . uh . . . what's his name?"

"I don't know, but he's a major-league jerk."

"You heard this story before?"

"No, but I heard about that guy."

"Right. Well, the jerk has five, six marked cars come screechin' up to the hotel every which way. Some are parked facin' north, some south, some south-by-southwest, some east. So Lieutenant Horan, tryin' to be helpful, comes up to the director and tells him, 'You know, the police never park like that.'

"So, the jerk says, 'Get off my back, willya? This is Show Biz. This is the way the customers are used to seein' things. I'll direct the movie and you be a cop, okay?'

"Well, it's all the lieutenant can do to keep from kickin' the guy right where the sun never shines. Then this drunk comes plowin' through everything. And of course nobody can respond because everybody's radiator is kissin' everybody else's radiator.

"So then Horan comes back to the jerk and says, 'See why the cops never park that way?'"

They chuckled.

"Anyway," Mangiapane continued, "the Lieutenant got the last laugh. By the time they got everything untangled, it was too late for the shoot. So they wasted all that time and money."

"Nice when the good guys win one." Tully again reached for the mike.

If Mangiapane had been alert, he would have noticed a slight tremor in Tully's hand. It was getting late and Tully was getting anxious.

He checked with the other units. All present and accounted for. No one had sighted anything out of the ordinary.

"Gettin' late, ain't it?" Mangiapane noted.

"Uh-huh."

"There was one more."

"One more what?"

"Story. It happened to Wolford."

"That must've been some lunch you guys had."

"It was."

"Did you eat anything?"

"Sure, Zoo."

"Sounds like all you did was talk."

"No, no . . . we had, let's see . . ."

"Never mind. What was Wolford's story?"

"Yeah, well, he was in Wink's Chevy body shop. Had to get a headlight for his car. The manager's a friend of his. So while he's waiting, this lady comes in to pick up her car after repairs. But she tells the manager her radio won't work.

Which is news to the manager 'cause there was nothin' wrong with her radio in the first place. But he gets one of the guys to go out to her car with her. They're all tryin' to figure out what went wrong with the radio. Then, as she and the mechanic are goin' out the door, she says, '. . . at least I think there's something wrong with my radio: I can't turn it on . . . maybe that's because I never turned it off.'

"Can you imagine that, Zoo? She never turned her radio off! The damn thing was on when she bought it and she never turned the goddam thing off!"

Even though he did not feel like it, Tully smiled, picturing the scene. "What that lady needed was three minutes of silence." He massaged his brow. A headache was building. "And that's what we need too, Mangiapane. I got some thinkin' to do."

"Sure thing, Zoo."

And so, in silence, they continued to drive the familiar streets: Montcalm, St. Antoine, Adams, Brush, Columbia, Beaubien, Elizabeth—over and over, changing only the order.

The area was only a few blocks from headquarters. Not much was going on in that neighborhood. They passed a warehouse, storage tanks, some boarded-up structures, a few buildings still occupied—although one wondered by whom—and a couple of residences that were being used almost exclusively by prostitutes.

It might not have been much of an area but, unless Tully was badly mistaken, it contained just what the perp would be stalking.

Not many women worked these streets, nor was there much of a selection. But one thing you were quite certain to find in an area like this was that rarity—an older prostitute. And here the prostitutes came in both black and white. Low-profile, elderly white prostitutes. Little chance of any intervention from either a pimp or a hooker's buddy. Just the right kind of place.

Tully's stomach growled. Maybe it was nerves. Maybe he needed a good meal. He thought of Alice, a nice blaze in the fireplace, the football game on TV, the aroma of good food on the stove. Who needed this shit, anyway?

"Bingo."

It was the way Mangiapane said it. Unlike the way he said almost everything, this held almost a tone of reverence. The sort of tone a dedicated angler might use after waiting hours and finally getting a bite from the very fish he'd been after.

Instantly, the queasy feeling left Tully's stomach. His every sense tingled.

He glanced at Mangiapane, who was studying the rearview mirror. Tully would not turn and look. He did not need to. In his mind's eye he could see the black Ford Escort to the rear of their unmarked Pontiac.

Almost as if he could be heard by their quarry, Tully spoke just above a whisper. "Can you make the guy?"

Mangiapane hesitated. "Not quite. He ought to get his windows cleaned once in a while. From here, looks like a white guy and looks like he's wearing black. Seems like it, anyway."

Tully almost prayed, he wanted this guy so badly. He yearned to take the wheel so there wouldn't be any mistakes. But he would place his trust in Mangiapane. He had decided that at the outset when he'd told him to drive.

"He looks like he's lookin' for someplace, Zoo. He's drivin' real slow, practically stops at every street sign."

"Yeah, well, that's what we're doin' too. Right now, we're lookin' for some way to get on the Fisher Freeway from here. So cut east when we get to the Fisher and go parallel with it for a few blocks, then cut back in."

"Okay, Zoo. I think he turned in. Yeah, goin' east on either Elizabeth or Columbia . . . I can't tell from here."

"If I'm right, he's only gonna go a block or two. Make it four blocks east, then go south. We oughta be able to spot his car from there."

Tully had to admit he couldn't have done it better himself. Mangiapane paced the maneuver perfectly.

Now they were headed south. On any one of these streets,

136

any moment now, they should see—"There it is, Mangiapane, the black Escort. Let's go!"

No one was in the car. And there was only one building he could have entered—an old rundown apartment house converted from a stately ancient residence.

Mangiapane crossed to the wrong side of the street and pulled up directly in front of and facing the Escort. As the two officers sprang from their car, each drew his .38 service revolver. Mangiapane, exiting from the driver's side, was closer to the building. He paused a moment so Tully could precede him.

Just inside the door, Tully hesitated. He cocked an ear to pick up some sound that would give him a key to the next direction.

He heard it. It was muffled, but he heard it. He nodded toward the stairs, then, followed by Mangiapane, raced up them. Now it was clearer. From inside the apartment at the head of the stairs—second floor, apartment 2A—came the sound of shouting. A male and a female.

"Open up! Police!" Tully yelled. He didn't wait for a response. A well-placed kick more shattered than simply opened the door. Tully bolted in, followed, after the proper precautionary interval, by Mangiapane.

Standing at the far side of the room was a woman—white, of indeterminate age, but well worn and badly used. She was holding a knife, a large kitchen knife. She appeared to be terrified.

Just inside the door stood a white man dressed in black. Black shoes, trousers, hat, winter coat with collar turned up. He too held a knife. It appeared to be a switchblade.

"Police!" barked Tully. "Drop the knife! Both of you! Now! NOW!"

The woman dropped her knife. The man hesitated.

Tully pointed his gun directly at the man. "You got just about one more second to drop that knife."

It clattered to the floor.

"That's better."

"What the hell's goin' on here?" the woman shouted. If she

seemed frightened by the first man with a knife, she was clearly terrified by the addition of two more strangers with guns.

Not taking his eyes off the man in black, Tully displayed his badge. "I'm Lieutenant Tully. This is Police Officer Mangiapane. What's going on here?"

"That's what I'd like to know," the woman said. "I was here, mindin' my own business, when this guy walks in on me, wavin' a knife around. Well, he don't know who he's takin' on. I grabbed my knife too. Next thing I know, you two come in, wavin' guns. So that brings me back to where we started: What the hell's goin' on here?"

"Okay." Tully had not looked away from the man. "Turn around," he ordered. "Face the wall, feet apart. Then lean against the wall." The man started to speak. "Now!" Tully insisted.

The man shrugged and obeyed. Tully nodded to Mangiapane, who holstered his weapon and patted the man down. "He's clean."

"Okay," Tully said. "Turn around. Now: Who are you?"

The man reached for his wallet. He had some difficulty since his hands were shaking markedly. As he opened his coat, his roman collar was revealed.

Mangiapane gasped. "Holy shit, he's a priest!"

"That's right; I'm a priest." He sounded as if his throat and mouth were dry.

Mangiapane read from the man's driver's license. "Richard Kramer—*Father* Richard Kramer." He looked at the man. "You actually a Catholic priest?"

"Yes."

"What parish?"

"Mother of Sorrows."

"Out Grand River."

"Yes."

"Holy God!"

Tully holstered his gun and approached the priest. "Mind telling us what you're doing here?"

"Sure." Kramer licked his lips. Try as he might, he

138

couldn't seem to restore normal moistness to his mouth. "I . . . I was called here."

"Who called you?"

"I don't know. A man. He didn't identify himself. He said it was an emergency. That a woman was here. That she was in trouble. That she had to see a priest. That it was an emergency—oh, I said that."

"Why *you*? This can't be your parish area."

"I asked him. He said he'd tried other parishes, that I was the only one he'd been able to reach."

"That made sense to you? I mean, there are hundreds of parishes in this city. You the only priest home?"

"It . . . it's possible. Sunday afternoon, most priests are out of the rectory. Besides, he . . . he didn't have to call every parish in the city before he got me. We're not that far from downtown."

"So, all the other priests go out Sunday afternoon—except you?"

"I didn't. . . . I didn't say that. I said m-most priests." Kramer had never in his life stammered. Then again, he'd never been in such a situation before.

"So, you were home this afternoon . . . at the rectory?" Tully kept up the interrogation as if no one else were in the room.

"Yes."

"Anyone with you?"

"No."

"Were you also home the past two Sunday afternoons?"

Kramer pondered for several moments. "Yes."

"Alone?"

"Yes."

"Convenient."

"What . . . what's that supposed to mean?"

Tully picked up the knife the priest had dropped. "Tell me, Father . . ." there was a mocking tone when he pronounced the priest's title, "is it your usual practice to enter a room where there's somebody sick or somebody who wants to see a priest with a drawn knife?"

"I ain't sick and I didn' wanna see no goddam priest," the woman said.

The other three seemed to have forgotten her. They continued to do so.

"The knife was in my pocket when I came in here."

"That's not what the lady says."

"She . . . she's lying."

"Like hell I am!"

"Guess it's her word against yours."

"But I'm a priest!"

Tully shrugged.

Kramer found it hard to believe the officer would not honor a priest's word. Nothing more was said for a moment. Kramer fumbled for a cigarette and lit it. "Mind if I smoke?" he asked after the fact.

"Mind if I see the lighter?" Tully reached toward Kramer, who surrendered the lighter.

"Nice," Tully said. "Big."

"I smoke a lot."

"Big enough to heat, say, a small branding iron if there wasn't a hot plate handy."

"Huh? What? What's that supposed to mean?" Father Kramer's attitude became assertive. "I think it's just about time for some explanations from you. I mean, I was called out of my rectory this afternoon and asked to visit someone who needed a priest. I went way out of my way to make a sick call. I didn't break into this place. I knocked on the door. This woman invited me in. Then, for no reason, she pulled that huge knife out of the drawer. So, naturally, I drew my knife —in self-defense."

"Pretty big knife." Tully hefted the weapon. "Now why would a priest be carrying such a big, sharp knife?"

"I'm a carpenter as well as a pretty good mechanic. I always carry it with me. Frequently I'll whittle on some wood."

"Okay, go on: You say she pulled a knife, so you did too. Then . . . ?"

"That's it. I asked her to put her knife away. And she

140

started screaming at me. That's when the two of you broke down the door."

Tully turned to the woman. "What's your name?"

"Mae Dixon."

"Okay, Mae, the next time you tell your story, you're gonna be under oath. If you lie then, it's perjury. And if you change your story too many times, nobody's gonna believe you. You see Officer Mangiapane over there, taking notes, writing all this down? Well, it's part of the record. It's admissible in court.

"Now, if you change your story in court, the judge is gonna have two different accounts from you about this. What's he gonna believe? You might be tellin' the truth in court. But if they don't believe you then, that'll be perjury. And that's jail for a long, long time.

"So, how about it, Mae? You want to tell us the story the way you'd tell it in court?"

She thought this over. "Okay. I don't know how the hell he happened to come here. I wasn't expecting anyone. Just takin' the day off, like."

"You weren't 'expecting anyone'? You are then . . ."

"A hooker. God, you're gonna find that out anyway. Yeah, I'm a hooker. But I wasn't gonna screw today. Then all of a sudden, there's this knock on the door. I thought maybe it was one of my regulars."

"No appointments? You get johns just any old time?"

She cackled. "These days I'm lucky to get any tricks at all, Sonny. But it wasn't always like this. Once upon a time, a long time ago, they were waitin' for me to have time for them. But, God, that was a long time ago."

"Go on."

"Where was I?"

"You heard a knock on the door. You thought it might be one of your regulars."

"Yeah. That's right. So I just said, 'Come on in.' Hell, no use lockin' that door; all you have to do is push it . . . locked or unlocked. God! Look what you did to the goddam thing! It's in splinters."

"Okay, then what?"

"Where was I?"

Tully sighed. "Someone knocked on the door. You invited him in even though you didn't know who it was."

"You don't understand. Regulars do that. They just come on up. If I'm busy, they wait."

Tully couldn't decide whether the idea of people waiting in line for Mae was funny or was going to make him sick. "Then what happened?"

"Well, this guy, this priest, I guess, came in. He surprised me. I mean, he wasn't no regular. I never seen him before. And he's all dressed in black. Then I saw his collar. That's when I went for my knife."

"So," Tully said, "he didn't have a knife in his hand when he came in."

She worked her mouth as if chewing on her next word. "Well, no . . . not 'zactly . . . not really."

"Sure?"

"Yeah . . . but what else could it be? I saw them stories in the papers and on TV—about how this guy dressed like a clergyman was killin' us. When it happened the second time, why, hell, wasn't a hooker in town wasn't on her guard. And by damn, I wasn't goin' down without a fight. So I got my knife. Then, quick as a wink, don't he pull out that shiv and shake the blade out real professional. And that's when I started yellin'. I guess I didn't expect any help . . . not around here. But I thought if I started yellin' I might scare him off. Then you guys come stormin' in like gangbusters.

"I didn't know what the hell to think. I'll tell you, I never thought I'd be glad to see a cop!"

"Is that what this is all about?" Kramer said. "It's just a case of mistaken identity. Whoever phoned me was either a practical joker or he was confused about the address. When I came in, this lady simply confused me with someone else."

Kramer looked from one officer to the other, not sure whether it would be possible for him to just walk out.

"That's the way you see it, Kramer," Tully said, "but that's not the way I see it.

"On two consecutive Sundays, a man in black, with a clerical collar, driving a black Ford Escort, has been selecting over-the-hill white prostitutes to kill and mutilate. I had a hunch he'd do it again on the third consecutive Sunday afternoon—today. Then you drive into this red-light district in a black Ford Escort, dressed in clerical clothing and collar. You head for the apartment of a woman who fits the general description of the previous two victims. You're carrying a knife that could gut a deer. Guess who I think you are?"

"You can't..." Kramer was perspiring freely. The apartment was warm, but that had little to do with the sweat that soaked his underclothing.

"Remember last week, Kramer," Tully continued, "when you went back to your car after you killed Nancy Freel? You were going back to mutilate her. Remember just before you reentered the building, you looked to one side and maybe you saw the woman who was watching you? Well, she's our eyewitness. And she's going to identify you." Tully was almost nose to nose with Kramer.

Kramer shook his head as if denying all this was happening.

"Open your jacket, Father Kramer," Tully ordered.

Near petrified with nameless apprehension, Kramer fumbled with the single button that held the front of his jacket together. As he undid the button, the jacket fell open.

Tully smiled. "That's one of the widest belts I've seen. That belt might just hang you... Father."

"W... what...?"

"Officer Mangiapane is going to read you your rights. Listen to them carefully. Then we're gonna take a very short ride down the block to Police Headquarters."

There was the sound of footsteps running up the stairs.

For an instant, Tully wondered who it might be. Then he remembered: He had called for back-up from the other detectives on his squad who were on surveillance in other districts.

They certainly had taken their sweet time getting here. He could have been dead by now!

When he got a chance, he would read them the riot act. But for now, he felt too satisfied and fulfilled to stay angry at anybody.

20

BOB PISOR, WEEKEND ANCHOR man for Channel 4 News, opened the 11:00 P.M. report with an account of the arrest of the Cass Corridor Ripper, as he had been christened by the local news media.

"Police announced tonight," Pisor said, "that there has been an arrest in the Cass Corridor Ripper case. For the past two weeks, fear has plagued the city's ladies of the evening, as a killer who first murders, then mutilates his victims, has been on the loose.

"According to witnesses, who have provided the police with a sketch of the suspect, the man has been garbed as a clergyman. Until tonight, police had no other clues in this case. But in a surprising twist, an arrest was made late this afternoon. And, in the most astonishing development of all, the man alleged to be the murderer is, indeed, a clergyman.

"We'll go live to Police Headquarters and Channel 4 reporter Gerard Harrington right after these messages."

21

"FEEL GOOD, ZOO?"

Alice and Tully were seated on the living room couch before the glow of the well-used fireplace.

"You betcha." Tully was not paying a great deal of attention to the TV news. For him it was a rerun. He had been there for the original drama.

Tully and Alice each held a mug filled with a mixture of hot tea and rum. It would be a pleasant nightcap. At the moment, since Alice had just put the concoction together, it was too hot to drink. They warmed their hands on the mugs.

"Were you surprised?" Alice asked.

"At what?"

"That he was a real priest."

"Not much." Tully thought about the question. He was answering the woman he loved, not the news media or the guys in the squad. No need to be a smartass. "Yeah . . . I was."

"So was I. I've never been able to figure out why the guy wore a clergyman's outfit. At first, I figured he couldn't possibly be for real . . . that he must have been wearing it as some kind of disguise."

"It's been a good question all through this business. That's why I gave it little thought. I figured the same as you: It had to be somebody pretending to be a clergyman; I figured it must have been to gain the hooker's immediate trust. The two who went with him to their death probably didn't have the slightest doubt that they would be safe."

"But what would they think about a priest being a john? I mean, that has to be different."

"Listen, if hookers stay in the business long enough, they get to service just about every possible kind of guy. When they're young and fresh with tight skin, they may be screwing the chairman of the board, the corporation president, the movers and shakers. As they get used up, they move down the ladder. Then it's blue-collar, kids, old men. So if they hang in long enough, they'll probably get everybody, including priests, ministers, and rabbis.

"But the worst thing that can happen to them is when they get a weirdo. And it can happen at any level. Guy says he wants a special trick. She puts her head down and he puts a knife at her neck. Or he sticks a gun in her ear. Maybe plays Russian roulette."

"No!" Alice shuddered.

"And worse. It's the most consistent risk the hooker has to face. And she does it practically every time she turns a trick. After a while, if they learn anything—and if they survive— they get to sense who's safe and who isn't."

"But they could still get taken in by a guy who is actually dressed like a priest?"

"That's what I figured. Those two gals had been around. They'd probably seen it all. But I'd be willing to bet they didn't get many clergymen who went so far as to dress the part. If he figured he threw them off with the outfit, made them lower their guard, I guess he was right."

"So you think it didn't actually matter whether the guy was or wasn't a real clergyman? Whatever he was, he was using the uniform to quiet their apprehensions and get them to go with him without a second thought."

"I think so. So it didn't matter. I got to admit, I never actually was sure it would be a real priest. But it doesn't matter; priest or not, we got the guy."

"You're sure?"

"Sure?"

"That this priest did it."

"Huh?"

"That radio guy on WJR . . . he sort of left everything up in the air."

"What? When was that?"

"The nine o'clock news, I think it was. He gave the impression that the priest had an alibi."

"Not an alibi, but an explanation. Claims he was on a sick call or something. Person unknown calls, tells him somebody needs him. So he just 'happens' to arrive driving the car we're looking for, wearing the clothing we're expecting, going to the prime area we have under surveillance, looking just exactly the ways he's supposed to look, carrying a king-sized knife, with the right size belt holding up his pants. It's like the wolf telling Little Red Riding Hood it's just a coincidence he's waiting for her in grandmother's bed. It won't wash. It just won't wash."

Alice looked relieved. The soundness of Tully's case had been troubling her ever since the earlier radio newscast. There was only one more doubt bothering her. "But isn't your case —what do they call it—circumstantial?"

"We've been through that before, Al, in other cases. There ain't a thing wrong with a case based on circumstantial evidence. Like the rope . . . remember?"

"Uh . . . oh, yes. Now I do."

"Right. Each piece of circumstantial evidence is like a strand of rope. All by itself, each strand isn't strong enough to support the case. But if you get enough of these strands braided, you got a damn strong rope. Strong enough to hang somebody. It's not a platter case, but it is a damn strong case. We got him."

"Then you're done with it. It's all wrapped up." Alice knew well that if this case was, indeed, history as far as Tully was concerned, it meant only that he would be turning full attention to the next presented puzzle. But this case had been very special. She had never known Tully to be so absorbed in a murder case, even multiple murder. It had affected him deeply when he—as it turned out, mistakenly—assumed he was involved through the Bonner woman. But having become

147

so intimately involved, there was no turning back from that early extraordinary commitment.

She was glad it was over.

Tully rose from the couch and began pacing before the fireplace.

"What is it, Zoo? What's the matter?"

"Nothing. Nothing, really. Only that it's not completely finished. We've still got the show-up to go through. The case doesn't rise or fall on my two hookers making the priest, but it will be a bit weaker if they don't, and one hell of a lot stronger if they do."

"They will, Zoo," Alice said, conscious that she had no strong basis to have an opinion on the subject.

"Yeah, they will. Sure they will." But there was that small nagging doubt. He continued pacing.

"There's more, isn't there, Zoo?"

"The branding iron. That goddam branding iron."

"You didn't find it, eh?"

As far as Tully was concerned, Alice was the only one— outside of the authorities—who knew about the branding or exactly how the bodies had been mutilated.

"No," Tully said. "We went over the car. Nothing. We went over the path he had to take to get into the apartment. Nothing." He sipped the drink, which had barely cooled enough. "And that's the smoking gun. If we could find that, Clarence Darrow himself wouldn't be able to get him off."

"Well, the car's impounded. Our technicians are going to take it apart bolt by bolt if necessary. The damn thing could be hidden anywhere. It's just two real thin pieces of metal and maybe a small wooden handle. It could easily be in three separate pieces. They could be attached—magnetically, maybe—to the engine, the wheels, the carburetor, the tank, anywhere. I only wish to hell he'd had the goddam thing sitting on the front seat." He shook his head. "Life isn't like that." He snorted. "Not my life, anyway."

"They'll find it."

"Yeah, they'll find it." He didn't sound all that sure.

"Zoo, the news is back on. Come sit down. There's Gerald Harrington. Isn't that the lobby of Headquarters?"

"Yeah, that's what it is, all right. Sunday evenings it's the quietest place in the building."

22

A VERY SERIOUS GERALD HARrington stood before the camera and sungun. Tall, very black, with a short Afro, handsome features and a deep resonant voice, he was one of the TV reporters Detroiters tended to give credence to.

"Detroit police," Harrington said, "believe the vicious and sadistic attacks on prostitutes over the past couple of weeks are over now, with the arrest of a suspect in the case. Hard, honest, painstaking police work seems to have paid off after this area of the core city was put under surveillance this afternoon."

The camera, in a scene taped earlier, panned through the neighborhood that had been patrolled by Tully and Mangiapane.

"Not the prettiest part of our city, it was, nonetheless, the area police figured would attract the man who, for the past two Sundays, has been preying on defenseless women. And their hunch seems to have struck pay dirt."

The screen now showed the actual apartment house where the arrest had taken place. Areas surrounding the front entrance were cordoned off by distinctive protective tape. Uniformed officers were keeping gawkers, drivers, and pedestrians moving. In the background, technicians were carefully examining the terrain.

149

Harrington glanced at his notes. "Lieutenant Alonzo Tully and Officer Anthony Mangiapane were the ones who apprehended the suspect as, they allege, he was about to strike again. Here to tell us about it is Officer Mangiapane, one of the two who made the arrest."

Mangiapane blinked as the lights were turned full on him. It was not difficult to tell that he was enjoying his day in the sungun. This was fairly new to him. It was very much old hat to Tully, who did not relish talking to reporters in any case. He had given Mangiapane this assignment.

Harrington stepped close to Mangiapane. The two were about the same size, although Mangiapane's girth was slightly the larger—the effect of daily hearty doses of plentiful pasta.

"Officer Mangiapane," Harrington began, "I understand you were the one who actually made the arrest."

Technically, this was true, since he, not Tully, had Mirandaized and booked the priest. Mangiapane nodded modestly.

"Can you tell us," Harrington continued, "how you happened to be in what proved to be the right place at the right time?"

"Okay. See, it was our lieutenant—Lieutenant Tully—who got the idea. The idea was that the perp—the killer—was setting up a pattern, like multiple killers, serial killers, do. He took out his first victim two Sundays ago in the afternoon, and his second last Sunday in the afternoon—both older prostitutes. So this afternoon our squad staked out likely areas. And that was it."

"I see. So it wasn't a matter of luck, but rather good police work."

"Well . . ." Mangiapane dissolved in proud humility.

"The surprise is in the person you apprehended."

"Yes."

"And that person . . . ?"

Mangiapane appeared genuinely embarrassed. "It's a priest."

"And his name is . . . ?"

"Father Richard Kramer."

"I understand Father Kramer is pastor of Mother of Sorrows parish on Detroit's far west side."

"Yes."

"We've known for a week now that the killer was seen dressed as a clergyman. But were you thinking that you would arrest an actual clergyman?"

"No. I still can't get over it."

True. Since the arrest, Mangiapane had felt somehow unclean. It was as if he should go to confession to tell a priest that he had arrested a priest and had subjected him to all the indignities of processing.

"I see. And what's the status of the accused as of now?"

"He has been processed and he'll be in a holding cell until his arraignment."

"When will that be?"

"Tomorrow."

"I see. So Father Kramer is not being given any preferential treatment?"

"No." Although if it had been left to Mangiapane, Kramer certainly would have been accorded every possible privilege up to and possibly including the freedom to return to his rectory.

The camera moved back to Harrington in a tight close-up that eliminated Mangiapane. "So that's it from Police Headquarters." Harrington wrapped it up. "The two-week search for the person terrorizing, mutilating, killing prostitutes would seem to be over, with the alleged killer in custody at Police Headquarters.

"By far the most bizarre aspect of this bizarre case is that police are holding a Roman Catholic priest as the alleged killer.

"We're going to leave Headquarters now. But you can bet we'll be back. From what I've been told by some of the officers here, this case is far from over.

"Gerald Harrington, Channel 4 News, reporting. Back to you, Bob."

23

SISTER MARY THERESE HERCHER
sat in the only upholstered chair in her efficiency apartment.
Her mouth hung open.

This news story had become the closest she had ever had to
an addiction. Quite unaware, she had turned on the six o'clock
news, mostly to get the local weather forecast. The news that
the prostitute killer had been caught—even though the news-
people guardedly kept using the usual disclaimer words such
as alleged and accused—grabbed her attention instantly. Then
the word "priest" had been dropped, and she was riveted to
the TV set. Finally, almost reluctantly, the reporter had given
this shadowy priest a name, and Therese had used up one of
her lives. She doubted her ears. It couldn't have been Father
Kramer! Not her Father Kramer!

But how many Father Kramers could there be?

For one brief moment, she thought of finding the P. J.
Kenedy Official Catholic Directory and discovering for herself
just how many Father Kramers there were. But that and simi-
lar thoughts were the product of panic. There was only one
Father Richard Kramer in Detroit. And it was, indeed, her
Father Kramer.

Then the phone calls began. Friends torn between real concern for her emotional and physical welfare and a morbid fascination with this sordid story and the desire to be a part of it,
if only vicariously. Eventually, she removed the phone from
its plug-in outlet. She would take no more calls.

But the story went on. She followed it at every opportunity, mostly on radio, since TV would not have another newscast until eleven o'clock.

Some of the radio newscasts were more tentative than others, and she would take hope. Then a commentator would sound particularly sure of himself when he announced the charges against Father Kramer, and she would despair anew.

Mostly, it was the overwhelming feeling of powerlessness. She felt compelled to help her friend. But for the life of her she couldn't think of a single thing to do.

Briefly, she considered going down to Police Headquarters. She phoned, only to find that there was no possible way she would be allowed to see him. No one could. Not until after his arraignment tomorrow—afternoon, sometime. The officer did not know the exact time and he was far too busy to find out.

So she was reduced to following one news bulletin after another. Once Gerald Harrington signed off, she realized that would be the final substantive news of the night. Anything that followed would be a synopsis of what she already knew.

She was disconsolate, beside herself, and alone. There was no question of even an attempt at sleep. Not while Dick Kramer was probably pacing a dank cell in fear, humiliation, and solitariness.

Desperate, she turned to prayer. Not the sort of unfamiliar prayer the irreligious fall back on in moments of stress. Rather, hers was the confident prayer of one accustomed to regular conversation with God. Even in this trying time, prayer came easily. She sought God's consolation for Father Kramer, now abandoned by everyone but God. She sought light and inspiration—some practical way to help Dick Kramer.

Then, through the turmoil of her thoughts, an image began to form. It was a memory enhanced by special attributes that could be, perhaps literally, a godsend to Father Kramer. It was an awareness of the one person who was qualified in a unique way to solve this problem, if anyone could.

Father Robert Koesler.

Wasn't he a friend to Dick Kramer? Hadn't he just the other day dropped in to visit Father Kramer? It was she herself who had given Father Koesler directions on how to bypass all the locked doors in the basement of Mother of Sorrows church. Father Kramer had few friends, as far as Therese knew, at least among fellow priests. But who more than a fellow priest could better understand the predicament faced by Kramer? Priests understand priests.

Then there was the very special relationship Father Koesler had built up with Detroit's police department over the years. Some were prone to forget Koesler's many interventions. But Therese had not forgotten.

So there he was—a confrere of Dick Kramer's with friends in the police department. And now that she was considering it, she could not recall a single incident she had heard about when Koesler's involvement with investigations had not been with the Homicide Division. Perfect! Dick Kramer was accused of homicide. Certainly Father Koesler would know his way around that department.

Hope rebounded. She freely attributed her newfound solution to the power of prayer. As quickly as she found the listing of Koesler's parish in the Detroit Catholic Directory, she dialed the number.

24

THE PHONE RANG JUST AS JERRY Hodak was concluding his Channel 7 weather forecast. Father Koesler had just absorbed the informed opinion that tomorrow would be unseasonably warm. His head jerked at the first ring. Experience had taught him that usually anyone calling a rectory at this hour had trouble and it most likely was an emergency. He felt a little queasy as he answered the phone. "St Anselm's."

"Father Koesler?"

"Yes." He almost placed the voice.

"Sister Therese—at Mother of Sorrows."

"Oh, yes." That had not been his guess. "I'm sorry about Father Kramer. I just heard about it on the news. But I'm sure that . . ."

"That's what I'm calling about."

"What?"

"I've got to see you."

"Oh. Well, I have some time in the morning."

"Now."

"Now! Do you know what time it is?"

"It doesn't matter. I've got to see you."

"Are you sure we can't do this in the morning?"

"Father, if we don't talk tonight, you will be able to see me tomorrow in the psycho ward at Lafayette Clinic."

"Uh, well . . . can we do it on the phone?"

"I've got to *see* you!"

He glanced at his watch—11:32. The recap of the day's ABC network news was on. In Koesler's plan, this was to be the final conscious event of the day, to be followed by sleep. But . . . there didn't appear to be any way out. "Oh, very well. How long will it take you to get here?"

"I'm on my way. About fifteen, twenty minutes . . . and . . . thanks."

Koesler looked at his watch again. It would be almost midnight by the time she got here. Good grief.

Robert Koesler had lived almost sixty years. And, having paid attention, he knew himself pretty well. He was a creature of habit, even more of routine. Years before, he'd read one of those articles that purported to describe the differences between men and women. The example he best recalled had to do with housecleaning. Women, the article held, tend to go about cleaning a room with no particular order in mind, simply moving from one piece of furniture to the next.

Men, on the other hand, tend to make a plan before beginning, which was fine unless something interfered with or voided the plan. For example, on second thought it made more sense to clean the fireplace before cleaning the floor. At which point, the plan would be destroyed and the man would have to sit down and make up a new plan. Koesler knew he was that man.

And so it went on Sundays.

The compulsory routines on Sundays tended to drain most priests. Offering two, possibly three, Masses was not a major problem. It was the preaching. If they invested in a serious attempt to hold the congregation's attention while communicating the Gospel message, few priests had much physical or emotional stamina left by Sunday afternoon.

From afternoon on, each priest was pretty much on his own. Occasionally, there might be baptisms to perform. But usually the remainder of the day was free.

Koesler, after the morning Masses, liked to relax. Perhaps a concert or a movie or a visit with friends. Sunday evenings were for reading, listening to records, or extending the friendly visits.

As with most evenings, things wound down for Koesler about eleven o'clock at night. The routine was the news at eleven o'clock, with a mild highball or glass of wine. After local news, another fourteen minutes, perhaps, of sports or the network news, and then to bed.

Thus he could not help grousing about this upset in routine. Attired in pajamas and robe, he'd gotten almost through the news program, had taken a few sips of scotch and water, and was drifting toward sleep when the damn phone rang.

He would not have minded so much if it had been a sick call. One can't help what time one gets sick—or dies. Though, God knows, most sick people in need of spiritual ministration of a priest were in a hospital.

It wasn't that he did not sympathize with Sister Therese. He knew she was close to Dick Kramer. And there was no doubt that what had happened to the poor man was a tragedy. But did she really have to do this tonight?

His routine!

Well, there was nothing for it but to get ready. He went to the bedroom, where he slipped trousers and shirt over the pajamas. Then the clerical collar and cassock over that, muttering all the while. Thus proving that grousing can be audible even if there is no one else around to hear it.

25

THE THOUGHT HAD CROSSED FAther Koesler's mind many times before. And it occurred again as he helped Sister Therese take off her overcoat.

She was wearing a trim suit that nicely accentuated her trim figure. The only bow made to the fact that she was a religious was a small silver cross on the lapel of her jacket. The color of her suit also was a clue, but only to the practiced eye. Among the few contemporary Catholics who were able to distinguish it, the color was called IHM blue. The reference was to the distinctive dark blue that was the traditional habit of the Sisters Servants of the Immaculate Heart of Mary—the IHMs, headquartered in Monroe, Michigan, whose other claim to fame was that it had once been home to General George Armstrong Custer.

Sister Therese was a member of the IHMs. Not too many years earlier, she had worn the full traditional habit of her religious order. For most of her years as a religious, all people saw of her was a face and hands. The rest was covered by either starched linen or the IHM blue wool. Now she wore modest lay clothing, albeit usually IHM blue, and a small cross. And here he was in cassock and roman collar, a uniform that was old when America was discovered.

The first time a similar thought occurred was shortly after he'd been ordained some thirty years previous. During summer in a suburban parish, it had dawned on him, as he walked around perspiring freely under a black cassock, that he was somewhat overdressed compared with the common garb of shorts and halter worn by most of the neighborhood women.

It seemed to him that everything in the concept was reversed. It was common knowledge that, since Adam, men were stimulated by the sight of women. The more they see, the greater the stimulation. Whereas Eve and her daughters were stirred by deeper and more subtle qualities.

However.

It would not do to invite Sister Therese into one of the offices, although the thought occurred to him. She was, all things considered, a colleague. So he ushered her into the living room.

No, she would not have a drink. And yes, she was nervous and upset.

About halfway through their earlier telephone conversation, Koesler had felt he knew exactly how this meeting would develop. He would listen—which he did quite well—while she trotted out all her fears, anger, perhaps despair. After all this, she would feel better for having talked it out. And he would be able to improvise, which he despised, back into some sort of routine.

Thus he was totally unprepared when she said, "That's right, I want you to help him."

"Help him!"

"Look . . ." She leaned forward in her chair. ". . . you and I are about the only friends he's got. And I've spent hours trying to think of some way I could help him. About the only thing I've come up with is prayer."

"There's nothing wrong with prayer."

"Of course there's nothing wrong with prayer. I can supply

the *ora* but somebody else is going to have to contribute the *labora*."

"But, 'friend'? I wouldn't exactly describe myself as his friend. And I'm sure Dick probably feels the same way." Getting involved in this case was the furthest thought from his mind. The prospect of such an involvement was so overwhelming that he was reduced to fending off each and every reason she could present for his committing himself to this project.

"Father Koesler." She seemed to revert to the schoolteacher she once had been. "You know very well that Dick Kramer is a workaholic, completely dedicated to his parish. He's never had the time, or the inclination, for that matter, to pal around with his fellow priests. He has few clerical friends. No, I guess it would be fair to say he hasn't any. But you came to see him the other day."

"Yes, but—"

"You came of your own accord . . . and I can tell you he was grateful for your interest. He may not have made it evident. He isn't a very demonstrative person. But I sensed it. After you left, he came back to the rectory and he was like a new man. He was more open than I can remember seeing him in ages. He started telling me little, gossipy things. He was more relaxed than he'd been in a long, long time. And you did that for him . . . isn't that one description of what a friend is?"

"Sister, you should know that I didn't come spontaneously. I had visited Monsignor Meehan. He suggested that I visit Dick."

"Yes, after you left that afternoon, Dick mentioned Monsignor Meehan. Telling me funny stories about their days together in Inkster at . . . what parish?"

"St. Norbert's. But don't you see, if Dick has a real friend, it's Monsignor Meehan. If it weren't for him and his request, I wouldn't have visited Dick and you probably wouldn't be here now."

"From all Dick told me, I know that Monsignor is a dear man. But I also know that Monsignor is a very ancient man, in a nursing home. I surely hope that he will pray for Dick. But

159

we need somebody who can get around and do something practical for him.

"Besides, Monsignor couldn't do any more than ask you to see Dick. You didn't have to do it. All right, so somebody else suggested that you visit Dick. The fact is: You did it. And that stands for something."

"But what can I do? Dick is in jail. What he needs now is a good lawyer."

"And we'll see that he gets one."

"I'm sure that's true. That brings us back to praying, which is what the rest of us could best do for him."

"Most of the rest of us. But not you."

"I don't understand."

"You are just about the only priest in this archdiocese who has an easy entrée with the police."

"That's not so. That's just not so. For one thing, there's the police chaplain."

"I know there's a police chaplain. But he mingles with the police on a professional basis. Counseling, visiting them, conducting services for them."

"Well? So?"

"So, he has not worked with them on murder cases." Her body language emphasized that this was the heart of the matter, the point she most wanted to make.

It took Koesler a moment to absorb her implication. Then he laughed. He couldn't help himself. "You've got this all out of proportion."

"Have I." It was more a statement than a question.

"Indeed. I assume you're alluding to the fact that I happen to be a friend of Inspector Koznicki, who happens to head the Homicide Department. Well, that's no secret."

"It's also no secret that you've been in on a few investigations too."

"It's a fairly good secret. But, even knowing about that, it's obvious that you don't know how I got involved in those cases. And since it seems relevant, let me explain.

"You seem to think that I'm some sort of latter-day Father Brown, dreamed up by G. K. Chesterton. I'm no detective,

Sister. Granted, over the past several years I have gotten involved in a few investigations because I happened to be in the wrong place at the wrong time. But whichever way you care to look at it, I've never volunteered to assist in an investigation. That would be presumptuous, to say the least. I have no training in police work . . . not even an inclination to be a detective. It's just that every once in a while a crime takes place and I seem to be in the middle of things.

"But that's certainly not the case here. This time, crimes have been committed—a couple of extremely heinous murders—and I am not involved in any way. For a change, I'm peacefully minding my own business in my—for the moment, anyway—peaceful little parish."

"But you—"

"If you'll let me finish, Sister, I think I may speak to the question I think you have in mind.

"There is nothing particularly 'religious,' let alone Catholic, in the murder and mutilation of prostitutes. It's true that your friend and my brother priest has been arrested as a suspect in the case. And that is tragic. We all ought to pray and do whatever we can to help Dick. But I am no more equipped to intervene in this case—even if the police would tolerate such an intrusion—than any other priest. Monsignor Meehan, for instance.

"In the past, don't you see, I have been drawn into some homicide cases by some accident, some quirk of fate, through no voluntary act on my part. But that's not true here. I'm not involved in this in any way. So your appeal to things that have happened to me in the past doesn't apply here. It's apples and oranges. I'm sorry."

Koesler fervently hoped she would not cry. He never quite knew what to do when women cried. Often he felt drawn to offer a shoulder. But he never could get beyond his position as a priest to do anything even that innocently physical. At this moment, Sister Therese did seem so perilously close to tears that he felt like putting her on his lap and just holding her. But he could not.

Fortunately, the tears did not appear. She merely grew re-

161

flective, gazing at her hands folded in her lap. When she finally spoke, it was without looking up. "I can't argue with anything you've said. And I know it's getting late."

It *is* late, he thought.

"I just want to say one more thing, and then I'll go," she stated. "Father Kramer has no one really close to him."

That's not exactly true, thought Koesler. This lady is as close as anyone will ever get to Dick Kramer. Probably she loves him. In all likelihood, he will never know. For all of that, she will never admit it, even to herself.

For some reason, Koesler suddenly thought this to be overwhelmingly sad. Once again, given the present status of celibacy and chastity, to which at least all three of them subscribed, there was nothing to be done about it.

"And Dick needs somebody now," she went on. "He desperately needs someone. For what reason I cannot possibly imagine, this good man has been accused of . . . of murder." She shook her head. "I still can't get myself to put the two together in the same sentence—Dick Kramer and murder. But the police have somehow put them together. And as long as this charge hangs over him—whether he is in jail or we are able to get him out on bond—he will be helpless in the face of this shame and embarrassment. I know him well enough to know this is true.

"That's why, Father Koesler, he needs someone. Not just anybody, but someone who can be an alter ego for him. Dick Kramer will be powerless to come to his own defense in the sense of proving himself innocent. He needs someone to do just that; someone who will take on this accusation as if it were leveled against himself.

"It's as if Dick will be locked up inside himself whether he's locked inside a cell or not. He needs someone who will care enough to exert the same amount of concern and total dedication to proving him innocent that Dick would do for himself it he were able.

"Father Koesler, I don't know where he's going to find such a person—other than you. You are about the closest person—the only person—he has to be such a friend. You at least know your way around in a situation like this. But I suppose it is silly of me to put those two qualifications together and come up with someone who would work as hard to clear Dick's name as Dick himself would, were he able."

It was, Koesler thought, an eloquent plea. In its face, all he could do was to try to reassure her that he would do all he could, and that, with all the prayers that would be said, God surely would not let any permanent harm come to Dick Kramer. Maybe, Koesler told Therese, as he bade goodbye, this would prove to be a beneficial experience for Dick and for all of them.

The words were lame. Koesler knew it and he was aware that Therese knew it. One of those things, he thought. What could anyone do at a time like this?

Removing cassock and collar, he was once again in pajamas, over which he drew his robe.

His routine had been destroyed, utterly destroyed. He checked his ever-present watch. After 1:00 A.M. He wasn't the least bit sleepy now—but it would be one more time when the faithful few who attended daily morning Mass would have to excuse an overly tired priest without even knowing why they were excusing him.

At this hour, he dared not return to his highball. He made a cup of instant decaffeinated coffee. As he sipped the steaming brew, which seemed perfectly fine to him, he wondered why it was that no one else seemed to appreciate his coffee.

As he sat in the silent living room, trying to slow everything down toward sleep, he could not help but reflect on his conversation with Sister Therese.

He realized that his rejection of her final argument was totally a reflex action. He was not in any way involved in this matter. For a change, he would have the luxury of sitting on the sidelines and rooting for the good guys. All that he had told her about the difference between this situation and the cases he had been connected with in the past—it was all true.

And yet . . . and yet . . .

He felt compelled, for some reason, to consider her words absent his automatic dismissal.

He imagined himself imprisoned for a crime, a capital crime. In this invention, he had been condemned to death. He had a month to live, at the end of which he would be hanged.

This was not, by any means, getting him closer to sleep. Nevertheless, having begun, he had to press on to whatever end might follow.

Of course he was innocent of the crime for which he had been condemned. But what could he do? He was locked away with but one short month of life remaining. There was no possible way he could clear himself. Of course if he had been able to leave his jail cell, he would devote his every moment to proving his innocence. He would not eat or sleep, except as absolutely required for life and strength. If he were to lose this battle to clear himself, he would lose life itself. Nothing that had ever happened to him or would ever happen to him was as crucial as this quest.

But, in this daydream, he could not leave his cell.

The scenario had become so real to Koesler that he actually began to feel the confinement of prison as well as the helplessness of his situation.

His one chance, his only chance, was to find someone on the outside who would act for him. This person, whoever it might be, would have to become as totally and thoroughly involved as Koesler, the jailed man, himself. This alter ego would have to at very least take a leave of absence from work —from family and everything else, for that matter—and devote every hour of every day for that final month as if his own life depended on it.

That was it! That was what would distinguish this alter ego from every other conceivable friend. This person, alone among everyone the accused knew, would be the only one who would work to prove innocence as if his own life depended on it.

Koesler, in all his many flights of fancy, had never before invented a conundrum like this. He became fascinated with the prospect. If he himself were to actually be in a situation such as this, whom could he call on? Who could be depended upon to abandon all else and work on this case as if his very own life depended on it?

One by one, he considered all those who came to mind, beginning with all his priest friends. One by one, quite reluctantly, but quite realistically, he dismissed one after another. Oh, they would be distressed, no doubt about that. They would offer prayers. They would express genuine concern. But, he realized, each would beg off—just as he had done only a few minutes ago when Sister Therese had pleaded with him for help.

Devote your time, energies, concentration, persona to the cause as if your own life depended on it. . . . Was there anyone?

Finally, Koesler focused on the one person who might do it. A friend he had made many years earlier. A married man with three children now grown and on their own. A man who had worked up from the assembly line to a white-collar position at Ford Motor Company. Yes, Chuck would do it. The one and only friend of all the many people Koesler had known who would give all.

If this man was so outstanding, why, Koesler wondered, had he not thought of him sooner? He had not come to mind earlier, Koesler concluded, because they were not really that close. Then why could Koesler suppose Chuck might do it? Why could he be depended upon to work as if his very own life depended on it?

It wasn't the friendship that turned the scale, Koesler decided; it was, indeed, the man himself. A Christian—that rare individual who actually put the Gospel teachings into practice in his life. A Christian. Would only a Christian do it? No. Certainly not. How parochial! But it would have to be someone correspondingly selfless. In his context, in his work, such a person would probably be a Christian. And one of the very highest order.

Koesler felt shame. What sort of Christian was he? What

sort of Christian was he trying to be? Sister Therese had handed him a challenge to his Christianity—an opportunity—and he had handed it back to her with appropriate bureaucratic gobbledygook. He was not involved. Of course he would pray. But he could not get involved. He had never before been involved in quite that way.

He knew what he must do. He looked up Sister Therese's phone number and dialed. "Sister, I hope I'm not disturbing you."

"Father Koesler?" Her tone revealed surprise. "No . . . no; sleep is not high on my agenda."

"I just wanted to apologize. And to tell you that I'm going to get into this thing. I don't know exactly how I'm going to get into it or what I'm going to do after I'm in. But I'm going to do everything I can to clear Dick Kramer."

"You mean it?" In a split second she went from one of the low points of her life to an exhilarating high. "You've made me so happy. Thank you. Oh, thank you!"

"No thank *you*. In your own quiet way, you taught me a very important lesson about being a Christian. I hope to God I never get too old to learn. Thanks for teaching."

"I didn't . . ."

"You did. Good night."

He was sure she would sleep well now.

His coffee? Only a small lukewarm amount remained. He didn't need it. He was ready for sleep. There was something very satisfying as well as relaxing in having settled on a course of action. He felt very good.

He was all wrapped up in the abstract. He was going to get into the case of the State of Michigan vs. Father Richard Kramer. And Koesler would exonerate his brother priest.

Fortunately, he could drift into a peaceful sleep without for a moment considering the concrete, real questions: How was he going to clear Kramer? What obstacles might he have to face? How strong was the case against Kramer?

If these questions had occurred to Koesler, he would have had to confess that he hadn't the slightest clue as to their answers. Not only did he not know the answers, fortunately he was not even aware of the questions. Neither was Sister Therese. So, in their separate bungalows, each had a very good night's sleep.

26

SOME DETROITERS WERE FOND of complaining that Michigan did not know how to have a winter. During an average season, the elements came at Detroit from every imaginable direction.

Ordinarily, future weather marched in a stately line from west to east—at least most people supposed that was nature's plan. So one was accustomed to watch high and lower pressure systems enter the continent in Washington and Oregon, and proceed through the Dakotas and Minnesota, on to Chicago and into Detroit.

Frequently frustrating this orderly progression, however, was the jet stream that plummeted Arctic air in from Canada or pumped unseasonably warm weather from the south. Most puzzling were the occasional winds from the east that threatened the impressive homes along Lakes St. Clair and Erie with flooding.

So, while unexpected for a Monday late in January, a springlike day was a welcome change. Commuting Detroiters, in elephantine procession toward downtown via the Lodge or Ford Freeway or one of the main thoroughfares, generally were more patient with near gridlock conditions. Natives understood this was a lull, and that snow, ice, and bitter winds would return. But this *was* nice.

Lieutenant Zoo Tully did not need special help from the weather to feel ebullient.

He had solved a puzzle, a particularly personal puzzle. He always felt good after having solved a case, but this was exceptional. Even though he was not as personally involved with the killer of Louise Bonner as he had initially assumed, the connection never quite faded from his mind nor did his approach to the case alter. For no sheerly rational reason, from the beginning he had considered this his private preserve.

As he turned the corner on the fifth floor leading to homicide, he was a tad late. For him, par for the course. Plus, on this day, it was a small personal reward.

Walking down the corridor, he encountered several other homicide detectives. They knew, of course, about yesterday's arrest. To a person, they congratulated him. Yet some seemed somewhat reserved. Or was it his imagination? Much more of this hedging, and it just might take the edge off his day.

There was only one officer, Mangiapane, in his squad room. The rest would be occupied with interviews, other cases, old and new.

Mangiapane was bent low over his desk, laboriously suffering through paperwork. Tully correctly assumed that Mangiapane was preparing the complaint against Father Kramer. Reports, records—anything to do with paperwork—was not Mangiapane's forte. Which had little to do with being a cop —Sherlock Holmes didn't have to fill out complaints to the satisfaction of some prosecutor or judge. While he may not have been a Holmes—who was?—Mangiapane was a good cop. And he would get better.

"How's it goin'?" Tully poured coffee into his mug, grateful that some earlier arrival had bothered to brew it.

"Oh, hi, Zoo." Mangiapane had been concentrating so diligently he hadn't heard Tully come in. "Okay. Slow."

"When's the arraignment?"

"Two this afternoon."

"You got time."

"Yeah; looks like I'll need it."

"Well, move it as fast as you can. We got stuff to do."

168

"Yeah, okay." Pause. "The inspector wants to see you."

"Mmmm. Okay." Something was up. This was not the usual response from Mangiapane. Ordinarily, he would jump at any interruption to put aside and, for at least the time being, block out all thought of paperwork. Tully had expected him to turn his chair away from the desk, maybe get a cup of coffee. Anything but pursue the report. Mangiapane had scarcely lifted his nose from the paper.

"Somethin' wrong?" Tully asked.

"Huh? No, nuthin', Zoo."

But something was wrong. Not only with Mangiapane, but with the other cops. There seemed to be an ineffable chill in the atmosphere. Well, Tully wouldn't push it. In time he'd find out. "I'll be with Walt."

"Right, Zoo."

He carried his coffee down the hall to Koznicki's office. This time he paid no attention to anyone he passed in the corridor.

Koznicki, alone in his office, was studying the contents of a folder. Tully knocked perfunctorily. Koznicki looked up and nodded. Tully entered.

"Just one moment, Alonzo." Koznicki returned to the file he was perusing.

Tully sat in the chair opposite Koznicki's desk. As with everyone he had met so far today at headquarters, Tully had more than half expected Koznicki to be at least congratulatory. After all, he and his team had cracked a major homicide case involving that most dangerous of perpetrators, a multiple murderer. He had expected commendation, especially from Koznicki. Tully sipped his coffee and studied the inspector.

Of course! That had to be it! Tully recalled a previous conversation in this very office. Koznicki had referred to the clerical garb worn by the suspect as a "masquerade." No way was this dyed-in-the-wool Catholic ready to believe that an actual priest was the mutilating slayer of prostitutes. That would also explain the chilly reception Tully had gotten from some of the other officers this morning.

And that certainly was what was bugging Mangiapane. Not

only had Tully trapped and arrested a priest, but he had obliged Mangiapane to process the suspect and, to top it off, to face the news media.

They were trying to make him feel guilty. He'd be damned if they'd succeed.

"So"—Koznicki put the file aside, looked across at Tully and smiled—"you made the arrest." There seemed no genuine warmth in the smile.

"Uh-huh."

"It was a clever plan you had. It seems to have paid off."

"Seems?"

"You made an arrest."

"Walt, let's get right to it. I got the guy."

"How sure are you?"

"How well do you know me?"

Koznicki seemed somewhat taken aback. "How well do I know you?"

"I don't play games. You know that."

"What do you mean?"

"I didn't grab Richard Kramer just to make an arrest, close a big case."

Koznicki was extremely grave. "I . . . I know that."

"Then why am I being treated like some kind of leper?"

"Leper?"

"It's not just you, Walt. And I'm not saying it's everybody in the division. But for once, in January it's warmer outside than it is in here."

Koznicki fixed Tully with a steady gaze. "There are some problems."

"Oh?"

"Catholics have a difficult time with the fact that we have a priest in custody." Tully was about to respond, but Koznicki held up one very large hand. "Particularly this priest. The Archdiocese of Detroit has been very cooperative. Their director of information sent over Father Kramer's record."

The inspector indicated the file he had been studying when Tully entered the office. Koznicki didn't mention that the file had been released to the police not through any spirit of cooperation on the part of the information office, but due to a direct order from Cardinal Boyle. From many previous professional contacts, Koznicki and Boyle knew and respected each other. By no means was everyone able even to get through to the Cardinal. Koznicki was one of the few who had access.

"Not only do we have his record," Koznicki continued, "but there have been many calls regarding Father Kramer." He indicated an impressive stack of messages. "It seems that Father Kramer is a most respected priest . . . indeed, one of the most diligent priests in the archdiocese."

"The Son of Sam was a hard-working mailman. The guy who blew away a dozen or so in the McDonald's in California didn't have any record either."

"We are not talking about your average worker. This is a priest!"

"Where's the surprise? For the past couple of Sundays he's been dressing the part."

"Alonzo, anyone can purchase clerical garb . . . at a religious goods store or even through the mail."

"Okay, Walt, anybody can do it. It could have been a guy pretending to be a priest. Or it could have been a priest. And this is the God's honest truth: I was willing to go with it either way. I didn't give a damn which way it went. But now, after the kind of reaction that's goin' on, I wish to hell it'd been some nut dressed up like a priest."

Koznicki raised an eyebrow.

Tully went on as if answering an unspoken question. "At least there wouldn't be this knee-jerk reaction to arresting a priest."

The statement was rather strong coming from a subordinate. It was by no means the first time Tully and Koznicki had crossed swords. One of the things Tully liked best about his boss was that Koznicki was a most self-secure person who never felt threatened or became defensive. Tully never felt he had to hold back any honest opinion. If anything, Koznicki was the one who, despite his enormous bulk, felt constrained to tiptoe over metaphorical eggshells.

171

Besides, Tully was forced to admit, Koznicki usually was right. This time, however, he was wrong!

Koznicki had by no means completed his challenge. "Father Kramer claims he was summoned on a sick call, a mission of mercy."

"So he claims."

"Might it not be so?"

"No."

"Just 'no'?"

"Who would have called him?"

Koznicki shrugged. "Someone who wished to set him up. Make him a sitting duck. The real perpetrator."

"The real perpetrator..." Tully's tone dripped incredulity. "Walt, how could 'the real perpetrator' arrange to have Kramer resemble the guy whose description we already had? How could he make him drive a black Escort? How about the oversized belt? And," Tully emphasized, "how about that knife? It's not a little pocketknife on a chain with a miniature flashlight. That's an honest-to-God switchblade that you could skin a bear with. If somebody—anybody—set him up, how did the guy arrange every one of even the most insignificant details to correspond with all we know about the real killer? Coincidence? Walt, *coincidence!*"

Koznicki was silent.

Tully continued. "Walt, like I said, I didn't give a damn who it was, as long as we got him. If you push me into a corner, I wish it hadn't been a priest. But if it is, it is."

"There is, of course, one thing more."

It was Tully's turn to lift an eyebrow.

"The iron...the branding iron."

"I know." Tully bit his lip. It was a weak point. Perhaps the only weakness in the entire case. Not, he thought, a fatal flaw, but definitely a loose end he wanted tied.

"You did not find it."

Tully shook his head. "We went over the car as thoroughly as we could. Over every inch of ground around the building. We didn't find it. But it's somewhere. We've got the techs taking that car apart piece by piece. From the one woman who

172

saw him close up, his M.O. seems to be that he accompanies the pro to her pad. Then he kills her. Then he goes back to his car to get the iron. Then he brands and guts her. But . . . I don't know. One guess is that he assembles the iron. In which case he could have one piece of it attached, magnetically maybe, inside the engine and another piece someplace in the chassis. The handle? Anywhere."

"It is the smoking gun."

"I know. I'd give . . . a lot to find the damn thing. But even without it, we've got a good solid case. Especially if my two witnesses can make him in the show-up."

"When is that?"

"Tomorrow morning."

"But first, the arraignment."

Tully glanced at his watch. "In just a couple of hours."

"Who is the judge?"

Tully shrugged as he rose to leave. "Who cares? That's another world. But it would be nice if, whoever the judge is, he wouldn't start out by presuming that no priest could have committed these crimes."

27

ONE THING WAS CERTAIN: FA-ther Kramer could not possibly have committed these crimes. Father Koesler decided to pass this thought on to his companion. "There is one thing for sure," Koesler said, "no priest could have committed these crimes. And if you knew Father Kramer, you'd know that he, of all people, couldn't have done it."

Inspector Koznicki could not help smiling. "That is precisely what Lieutenant Tully fears."

"What's that?"

"That people will presume that no priest in general and Father Kramer in particular, could possibly be responsible for such brutal murders. I assure you I cast no aspersion on Father Kramer when I say that Lieutenant Tully is one of our best officers. He has an enviable record of convictions as a result of his arrests."

Koesler turned to look directly at his friend. "You don't mean to say that you think Father Kramer could be guilty?"

Koznicki tipped his head slightly to the side. "I hope he is not guilty, I must admit. But the verdict is not in. In point of fact, the trial has not begun. This is only the arraignment."

Tully had no sooner left Koznicki's office earlier in the day when Father Koesler had called. He told Koznicki of his interest in the Kramer case. He did so apologetically, admitting that he really had no business getting involved, particularly in volunteering involvement. But, after a soul-searching self-analysis, he'd had no option but to do what he could for his brother priest.

While he did not tell Koesler so, Koznicki had expected the call. Indeed, mindful of their past collaborations, he would have been surprised, even disappointed, if Koesler had not called.

Koznicki did not consider Koesler to be any sort of para-expert in police work. But the inspector had come to appreciate the priest's keen analytical mind. He would not have wanted, nor even permitted Koesler to become involved in just any investigation. Nor, he knew, would the priest presume to do so.

But when it came to homicide investigations that included any sort of Catholic element, Koesler had been helpful in the past. And in the present instance, Koznicki was quietly pleased that Koesler was aboard. The odds seemed stacked against Father Kramer. He could use someone like Koesler in his corner. It might even make Lieutenant Tully at least re-evaluate some of his conclusions.

Father Koesler had wanted, at the outset, to attend the arraignment. Koznicki offered to accompany him. So they had met at headquarters, had a somewhat late, light lunch, then walked over to the Thirty-sixth District Court. Koznicki was easily able to get them both into the courtroom before the general public was admitted.

In the courtroom with them at the moment were several uniformed Wayne County Sheriff's deputies, a few Detroit police officers—including Tully and Mangiapane—defense and prosecuting attorneys, and a most healthy representation of the local news media. No cameras, still or TV, were permitted in the courtroom; a couple of artists seated in the otherwise empty jury box were already sketching the scene.

Several sheriff's deputies gathered at the doors, which were then opened. Outside, in the hall, a considerable crowd had gathered. The spectators would have surged into the court had not the deputies halted each for individual checking with portable metal detectors. Consequently it was possible for the already seated Koesler to study each one.

There were, by Koesler's count, seven priests, in addition to himself, in attendance. Most, like Koesler, were in clerical garb. The brethren were gathering to support one of their own.

For only a few brief moments, Koesler caught sight of Sister Therese. She passed very quickly through the metal detector and was immediately lost in the crowd. She was wearing her order's modified habit clearly denoting that she was a nun. Koesler could not recall ever having seen her in a habit—even modified.

Once the benches were filled, the doors were closed. It was not unlike church in that the crowd spoke in whispers and the only ones who seemed completely at home—like priests in church—were the court officers.

"Where are the lawyers?" Koesler whispered.

"At the tables just in front of the judge's bench," Koznicki replied. "The rather nice-looking woman on the left in the

beige suit is Dava Howell, the prosecuting attorney. The tall
black man on the right . . ."

". . . is Bill Johnson. I recognize him from his pictures.
Used to be on the Detroit Common Council." Koesler was
impressed. Bill Johnson's professional skill was such that he
now accepted only the most challenging cases. His success
ratio was impressive.

Koesler had read a lot about Dava Howell. Although she
was young, her conviction percentage almost matched Johnson's acquittal record. Koesler wondered if she had been selected from the prosecutor's staff because the murder victims
were women. Newspaper photos did not do Dava Howell justice. She was much more attractive in person.

A hush fell over the crowd as a door near the bench opened
and the defendant, escorted by several burly uniformed police-
men, was led into court and seated at the end of the table at
the right, next to Johnson, who immediately leaned over and
said something to him.

Koesler was jolted. This was not the same Dick Kramer of
just the other day. Already he seemed a changed person. He
was wearing a black suit, undoubtedly the same one he had
worn yesterday when he was arrested. It looked rumpled, as if
he had slept in it, which was probably so. He was not wearing
the roman collar, just a white shirt open at the neck.

From the moment he entered the room he looked at no one.
He went straightway to his place and proceeded to stare at the
floor.

"All rise," a deputy announced loudly and banged a gavel.

Still like church, thought Koesler. The priest processes in,
the congregation stands.

"The Thirty-sixth District Court for the County of Wayne
in the State of Michigan is now in session. The Honorable
John Bowmont presiding." The deputy concluded his introduction and everyone sat again.

Koesler was prepared for a rather lengthy session. But it
was over in a fraction of the time he'd thought it would take.
In effect, the judge read the charges to the defendant—crimi-

176

nal charges brought by the State of Michigan. Defense attorney Johnson informed the court that his client would stand mute to the charges. The judge then entered a plea of not guilty. Johnson motioned for bond to be set. Bond was denied. And Father Kramer was taken from the court to the nearly always crowded Wayne County Jail.

The judge, having called a recess, was gone. The defendant was gone. The attorneys were packing up their briefcases. The doors opened. The crowd filed out. In the corridor, print, TV, and radio reporters were trying to approach and interview anyone who looked as if he or she might have a relevant comment. The hallway was illuminated with the unreal light of the TV sunguns.

"That's it?" Koesler couldn't get over the speed of it.

"Earlier, the judge issued the warrant," Koznicki explained. "And we have just witnessed the arraignment. In effect, this legitimizes the continued holding of Father Kramer in jail."

"What now?"

"As far as the trial is concerned, the judge has set the preliminary examination for this Thursday morning. At that time, the prosecution must make a case strong enough for the judge to decide that a trial is necessary. Otherwise the charges will be dropped."

"Thursday!" Koesler thought about that. "Three days. Isn't that a rather long time to wait?"

Koznicki smiled. "On the contrary, Father. It is rather soon. There is much to be done between the arraignment and the preliminary examination. It was less than twenty-four hours ago that the arrest was made. The police have convinced the prosecutor's office that the complaint is justified, and the judge has issued a warrant.

"Now the police and the prosecutor must build their case. And I can assure you, in this instance, they still have a long way to go on that.

"Then too, the defense has a right to what is called 'discovery.' The defense has a right to know what sort of 'proof' the prosecution has. Believe me, Father, three days is a rather brief period in a case such as this."

With the exception of a couple of deputies, Koznicki and Koesler were alone in the courtroom. They retrieved their coats and hats from the rack.

"Where to now, Father?"

"Well, if I'm going to try to help him, I guess I'd better go see if I can talk to Father Kramer."

Koznicki touched Koesler's arm, causing him to pause before leaving the courtroom. "If I may offer a suggestion, Father."

"Of course."

"Hold off your visit until tomorrow afternoon."

"If you say so . . . ?"

"Something very important is scheduled for tomorrow morning. It is called a show-up, wherein a couple of witnesses will try to identify the man they saw last week entering the victim's apartment building."

"Oh, you mean like the line-up they have in movies?"

"Yes, a line-up. We call it the show-up. The case against Father Kramer will neither stand nor fall on the result of the show-up, but it will be very important nonetheless."

"And if the witnesses cannot identify Dick?"

"That will be one bit of circumstantial evidence the prosecution will not have."

"And if they do?"

"It will be a very important bit of circumstantial evidence favoring the prosecution. You see, Father, we have here neither a perpetrator caught in the act, nor an accused person who has pleaded guilty. All the evidence against Father Kramer is circumstantial. Which does not mean it is weak evidence; almost all evidence in such trials is circumstantial. The more such evidence mounts, the better it is for the prosecution. In this, you see, Father, quantity adds up into quality."

"Then you feel it would be better if I delayed visiting Dick until after the, uh . . . show-up."

"We will know so much more then, Father. By that time,

he may need your presence more. I sincerely hope not. But it is possible."

"Then tomorrow afternoon it is."

"Good. I shall arrange special visiting privileges for you tomorrow. Say, two o'clock?"

"Two o'clock it is then."

28

"THE SECOND DAY IN A ROW WE have a promise of temperature in the forties," Inspector Koznicki said. "If this continues all the snow will be gone."

"Yeah," Tully responded, "forty degrees. That's Detroit's plan for snow removal."

Koznicki sensed the pressure Tully was under. The two sipped coffee as they stood looking out a window in Tully's squad room. There was nothing of great interest to see from that vantage. A brick wall and, if one craned far enough, a tiny slice of what Detroiters liked to call Bricktown.

But they weren't standing there to enjoy a breathtaking vista. Tully was marking time until the show-up. Koznicki was keeping him company.

Without success, the inspector was trying to recall a time during their association when Tully had been this nervous. Nor was this anxiety easily explainable. This morning's procedure, following yesterday's arraignment, was one both officers had gone through at very frequent intervals over the years. To Tully, it should have been almost second nature. Yet for the past hour, he had restlessly checked the details over and over. "What time you got, Walt?"

"Eight . . . 8:40."

"It's getting late."

"You have twenty minutes until the show-up. Plenty of time. Who's picking up the witnesses?"

"Mangiapane."

"Good. And the subjects in the show-up?"

"Salvia."

"Both reliable officers. You have nothing to worry about."

"I'm not—" The phone on Tully's desk rang. He grabbed it. "He's here already? Okay, stay with him. Get him some coffee." He hung up and turned to Koznicki. "Johnson's here . . . Kramer's lawyer."

"Good."

"He's early."

"He will be able to talk to his client before the show-up. Just about perfect."

"What if Mangiapane gets here late? Johnson could leave. Then we'd have to reschedule the goddam show-up—"

"Alonzo, please. Johnson is one of the best, a true professional. He will want to get this over once and for all as badly as anyone else. But then you too are a professional. One of the best. It is unlike you to be so worked up."

Hearing it helped. Tully's taut muscles seemed to relax. "You're right, Walt. I don't really know what it is. I don't know why I want Kramer so bad. But I do. If this show-up works, it'll be another nail in his coffin. God, I'm even beginning to care what happens to him in court. One thing for damn sure: He's not gonna walk because of some screwup over here."

"Do you have anything more?"

"The knife. Way down deep next to the handle the techs found a smidgen of blood. The rest of the thing was completely clean."

"The blood type?"

"O positive."

Koznicki shrugged. "The most common type."

"It's Kramer's type."

"Oh?"

180

"And Nancy Freel's."

Although for all purposes Koznicki was trying to be supportive, had anyone probed he would have had to admit he was disquieted by Tully's single-minded pursuit of Kramer.

Koznicki was well aware that a policeman must have a restrictive attitude toward crime and criminals. An officer could not afford to be judgmental. The policeman's lot was to make an arrest for good cause and to present a solid case supported by firm evidence to the prosecutor. While mindful of this, still Koznicki found himself at odds with Tully over this case.

Quite beyond his conscious control, Koznicki found himself judging Father Kramer and finding him innocent. And the inspector was just as certain that Tully had judged the priest and found him guilty. "So," Koznicki said, "both Father Kramer and the woman have the same blood type. That could mean the blood found on the knife was, indeed, Father Kramer's."

"Maybe. But Kramer has no cut marks on his body. And for the blood to have clotted where it did, there should have been a rather serious cut . . . like, maybe, an incision all the way down a woman's torso."

Koznicki could not deny that the circumstantial evidence was piling up. "One more nail?"

"You got it."

"And the iron—the branding iron?"

Tully shook his head. "Not yet. They're still taking the car apart."

"They have not completed the operation yet?"

"As far as I'm concerned, they'll never get done as long as there's one piece of metal attached to another. On top of that, one of the guys is getting a search warrant for the home— what do you call it?—the rectory . . . and the church too."

"That is the smoking gun, you know."

"Uh-huh. And it may be a little tough to convince a judge or a jury of what you and I both know: that it is not unusual for killers—even serial killers—to change their M.O.

"That branding had to be a cumbersome thing to pull off.

He'd have to get the thing red-hot over a hot plate or, failing that, with a lighter. And after he got done, he'd have to cool the thing before he could pack it away. After two tries, he could have figured it just wasn't worth it. If he gutted the victim, maybe carved something on her body, we'd still know it was the same guy. It's happened before . . . I mean a killer changing his M.O."

"That is true."

"But I sure as hell would like to find that thing." Tully's knuckle tapped the desk.

"The smoking gun."

"Yeah."

The phone jingled. Tully had the receiver in his hand before the first ring was completed.

After a few words exchanged, Tully hung up and turned to Koznicki with a sense of finality. "Mangiapane's up on nine. He's got the witnesses. Time to get started."

As he turned to leave, Koznicki patted him on the back. He could not force himself to wish good luck.

At the door of the squadroom, Tully turned back, winked, and said, "One more nail."

29

WHEN TULLY REACHED THE ninth floor of headquarters, he first looked in on Adelle and Ruby, made sure they were as comfortable as possible, and introduced them to Johnson, who was, as usual, impeccably dressed.

Next, Tully went backstage, as it were, to where Sergeant

Dominic Salvia had assembled the required seven people who would participate in the show-up. As was the practice, Tully brought Johnson along. It was the attorney's prerogative to suggest any minor changes he might want in the subjects presented or their positions in the show-up. Afterward, the attorney was to sign the show-up form acknowledging that everything had been conducted fairly.

Johnson knew Salvia, so no introductions were necessary.

"Who you got?" Tully asked.

Salvia enumerated the seven. Four were police officers, two were maintenance employees; the seventh, of course, was Father Kramer. Each man wore a black overcoat and black hat. Four were blond. The other three had gray hair that, under the hat, more or less appeared blond. All were roughly the same size, but were facially quite different, with the exception of one policeman named Harmon, whose features closely resembled Kramer's.

"How do you want them placed?" Salvia asked.

"Oh," Tully said, "how about we make Kramer fourth and Harmon fifth. Put the others anywhere you like." Tully glanced inquiringly at Johnson, who nodded agreement.

"Okay," Tully said to Salvia, "I'll get the witnesses ready and we'll go."

Tully and Johnson returned to the lounge, where Tully explained the procedure to the two women. "You both know Mr. Johnson. He's gonna be in the show-up room with us. He's not gonna say anything. He's just here to observe.

"We're gonna take you in the room one at a time. There's gonna be seven men standing on an elevated platform. There'll be one-way glass between you and the men, and there'll be bright lights shining on them. So all they'll be able to see is their own reflection. There's no way they can see you. But they can hear you if you speak loudly. So speak softly only to me or Officer Mangiapane. We'll want Mr. Johnson to hear what you say, too.

"The seven men are all wearing black coats and hats like the guy you both saw a week ago Sunday. That guy didn't say anything. So none of these guys will speak.

"Now, I gotta tell you this because it's very important: Just because we got seven guys in there for you to look at don't necessarily mean that one of them is the guy you saw. Maybe he's there and maybe he isn't. You just go in there with an open mind. If you see the guy, you tell us. And one more thing: Take your time. There ain't no hurry. Okay?"

The two women nodded. Evidently, they were impressed, and not a little apprehensive.

"Okay," Tully said. "You first, Adelle."

Adelle, Johnson, Mangiapane, and Tully filed into the show-up room, leaving Ruby alone behind.

It was a rather impressive sight, particularly for someone —such as Adelle—new to it. Seven men looking straight ahead, seeing nothing but a pane of glass only a few feet in front of them. The bright lights focused on them made it impossible for them to see beyond the glass. With the black coats and hats, they looked so very much alike it was almost comical. Almost—except that one of them might be an exceptionally vicious murderer.

Adelle seemed overwhelmed by it all.

"Take your time," Tully cautioned.

"I don't know."

"Take your time."

"I just don't know."

"They look too much alike," Mangiapane complained.

"That's the idea," Tully responded.

"They look so much alike," Adelle said.

"That's what I said," said Mangiapane.

"Easy," Tully cautioned.

From behind the glass, Salvia had the men turn full-circle, pausing at each quarter-turn.

"That ain't no help, Zoo," Adelle said. "The guy I seen talkin' to Nancy was sittin' in the front seat of a car. And he turned to face her. So what I seen of him I seen head on."

"Leave 'em facin' front, Salvia," Tully called out.

"Okay, Zoo."

Adelle studied the men for a few moments. Then she said, "Can I get up real close to them, Zoo?"

"Close as you want, Adelle. They can't see you."

Adelle walked up to the glass so close she was almost touching it. Then she walked slowly along the line, pausing before each man, some for a longer period of time than others. Finally, she backed away from the glass and stood by Tully. From that distance, she studied each of the seven men one more time.

Finally, she shook her head and shrugged. "I don't know, Zoo. I didn't get that good a look at the guy. But from what I remember of him, I'd say there are three guys in that line-up who could be him."

"Which three, Adelle?" Tully moved aside to make sure that Johnson could hear her reply.

"Well, there's number one, and number four, and number five."

"Okay, Adelle. Can you get it down any closer than that?"

Adelle looked over the three she had selected once again and shrugged. "One, four, and five. That's the best I can do, Zoo. I didn't get all that good a look at the guy. Maybe Ruby can do better."

"Okay, Adelle. Thanks."

Mangiapane escorted Adelle back to the lounge and returned with Ruby.

Ruby waited until she adjusted to the room and its peculiar lighting. Then she approached the men and studied them, one after another. Unlike Adelle, Ruby had been through this routine before—from both sides of the glass. She knew what to expect.

She asked Tully to have the men turn. He gave the order to Salvia, who transmitted it. Once again, the men turned in a complete circle, pausing at each quarter-turn. Ruby watched the process closely.

"Zoo," she said, "when I saw the guy, he was walkin' up the stairs and he stopped for just a second when he saw me. So I saw him from the side and he had his head turned. So he was lookin' sort of over his right shoulder. Could I see 'em like that?"

"Sure, Ruby." Tully spoke to Salvia, who had the men

make a quarter-turn to the left and, from that position, face the glass. "That about it, Ruby?"

"Yeah, that's it, Zoo." She returned to the glass and once more studied each man carefully. After the seventh man, she came back to number four and spent several moments before him, then moved on to number five. Several times she alternated between numbers four and five.

Tully, Mangiapane, and Johnson barely breathed.

"That's it, Zoo. That's the guy."

"Which one, Ruby?"

"Number four."

"Are you certain sure?"

"Oh, yeah, Zoo. That's the guy. Ain't no doubt about it. For a while, I couldn't make up my mind between four and five. You did a good job on them, Zoo. They's almost twins. But it's number four."

"Okay, Ruby," Tully said, "we got just a little bit of paperwork to do and you'll be all done."

"Did I get the right one, Zoo?"

"Yup."

"Praise the Lord."

As they left the show-up room, Johnson turned to Ruby. "If you don't mind my asking, how were you able to make up your mind between four and five?"

"The eyes."

"The eyes!" Johnson seemed surprised. "Vicious?"

Ruby shook her head. "Gentle."

Mangiapane snorted. He could hardly wait to tell Police Officer Harmon he was lucky he didn't have nice eyes. Otherwise he would have been fingered for murder.

30

AT EXACTLY 2:00 P.M., FATHER Koesler arrived at the Wayne County Jail, which was located across the street from Detroit Police Headquarters. He embarked on the red-tape procedures required for a visit with Father Richard Kramer. Due to the intervention of Inspector Koznicki, the two priests would be able to visit in the relative comfort of a private room rather than in the stark partitioned visitors' room.

A deputy sheriff ushered Koesler into the room. As the officer left to get Father Kramer, there was a sharp snap as the door locked automatically.

This was not Koesler's first visit to the county jail, as well as some of the state's other places of incarceration. Common to each and every one was this suffocating sense of locked doors. No door was ever unlocked before the prior door was locked.

Never having been jailed himself, Koesler had to project what the experience must be like. Particularly with his slight tendency toward claustrophobia, he was sure the worst part of this bad situation would be the locked doors. So, as they traveled through the building, the unending series of doors clicking locked was particularly unnerving to him.

A key turned in the door and Father Dick Kramer entered.

Koesler had assumed Kramer would be dressed as he had been yesterday at his arraignment. So it came as a surprise to see him wearing a prison uniform—though not a completely unpleasant surprise. For some reason, Kramer looked a bit more at ease in prison grays than he had in that rumpled,

187

slept-in black suit. Yesterday, he had resembled a homeless bum fresh, and literally, off skid row. Now he looked as if he had been interrupted from work in his machine shop.

They greeted each other rather awkwardly.

"I brought you a carton of cigarettes," Koesler said, "but the guard took them."

"I guess I'm not allowed to have the full carton." Kramer smiled briefly. "I wouldn't have anywhere to put it anyway. I guess they allow you a pack at a time—as long as the supply lasts. I'm not too conversant with all the rules and regulations."

"I hope you never get to be."

"Amen."

Koesler sat down and, as he did so, so did the other priest.

"Dick," Koesler said, "I've been trying to put myself in your place. And, as near as I can come to how you must feel, I suppose you're wondering whether anything is going on out there. I just wanted to assure you that a lot of people, myself included, are doing all we can to help."

Kramer nodded. "You're right about one thing. I've been wondering if there is a real world out there. Mine seems to have toppled over. I . . . I don't know what's happened. It's like a long nightmare I can't wake up from."

In all the years Koesler had known Kramer, he'd never known him to be so open about his innermost feelings. Undoubtedly, this was an indication of how deeply and radically Kramer had been affected by this tragedy. It also seemed an added indication that Kramer had somehow become the innocent victim of a classic case of mistaken identity.

"I talked to Therese," Kramer said.

"You did?" Koesler was not surprised.

"I called her. I'm not allowed to receive any calls."

"I'm glad you talked to her."

"So am I." Kramer plucked a cigarette from his shirt pocket. Before striking the kitchen match the guard had provided, Kramer looked inquiringly at Koesler. "Mind?"

Koesler shook his head. He was not in the habit of denying

smokers their opportunities. He certainly would not deny this beleaguered priest one of his few remaining pleasures.

"She told me about the conversation the two of you had last Sunday night." Kramer inhaled deeply; his words were punctuated by wisps of smoke.

"She's a very persuasive lady."

"I know. She's been able to get me to do just about everything she wanted me to do. Except, maybe, to give up these." Kramer held up the smoldering cigarette.

Koesler nodded. A former smoker, he had a firsthand appreciation of the addiction.

"Anyway," Kramer said, "I want to thank you."

"Just yet there's no particular reason to; I haven't done anything."

"You were at the arraignment. You're here. You're with me. I appreciate it. I really do. Besides, I agree with Therese: Your contacts in the police department may prove helpful. I don't exactly know how. But I'm willing to believe. One thing is for certain: I have to get out of here."

Koesler looked concerned. "It must be pretty bad."

"Very bad."

"Good God, has there been any . . . abuse?"

"Oh, you mean from the other guys, the other . . . prisoners. Oh, no; nothing like that. Actually, they've treated me rather well. But I've got to get back to the parish. The longer I'm gone, the more likely it's going to be that the chancery will take it away from me."

Koesler thought it inappropriate to suggest that it was extremely unlikely that the chancery would remove Kramer as pastor of Mother of Sorrows. Nobody was standing in line waiting for the parish. Nobody else wanted it.

But Koesler was relieved that Kramer had suffered no abuse from the other prisoners. One could never be sure of what might happen within a prison.

"I really don't think you've got anything to worry about as far as the chancery is concerned. I'm pretty sure Cardinal Boyle would not let that happen. But, as for getting out: How about bail?"

"Not yet. Our next chance is Thursday when I have my preliminary examination."

"Not till then? Isn't there a chance they will simply drop the charges?"

"I don't think so. Not now. One of their witnesses identified me in the line-up this morning."

"No!" Koesler was deeply shocked. "How could that be!"

"I don't know." Kramer lit a fresh cigarette from the one he was discarding. "I just don't know. My attorney tells me it happens. The cops have to warn witnesses that the person they're looking for may not be in the line-up. And the cops did this morning, my lawyer said. But then he said most of the time the warning doesn't do any good. The witnesses are psyched-up to pick out somebody. Mistakes happen. But for the guy they single out, it is one pretty damn big mistake."

"Good grief! I can't believe it! Somebody actually picked you out of a line-up. Incredible!"

"I really doubt my lawyer would kid about a thing like that."

"Well, if I'm going to try to help, I'd better know what's going on. Have they got anything else?"

"My knife."

"Your knife. You mean the big one."

"Yeah."

"But you've had that for years. God, all the way back to the seminary. I could testify—any of the guys could testify—you've had that thing for ages. We used to sit around and watch you carve things. There's nothing wrong about that knife."

"They found some blood on it."

"Blood!"

"Mine. About a week ago, I cut myself. It wasn't a bad cut, but it bled pretty good. I thought I cleaned it up. I must've missed a drop or two up near the shaft."

"But it would be your blood type."

"It is. It's also the blood type of one of the victims."

"No! This is truly incredible."

190

"And my cut was so minor, my wound is all healed. So they won't believe the blood came from me."

"It's like some fiendish conspiracy. Obviously someone set you up last Sunday to be found by the police. Is it possible the same guy concocted all the rest of this so-called evidence?"

"I haven't got it figured out. I don't even know whether I *can* figure it out. I keep trying to put it together, but it doesn't go together for me. It's like trying to do a jigsaw puzzle with several missing pieces."

"Let's try to put it together. I guess if I'm good at any of this, it's assembling things in some sort of logical order. Game?"

Kramer nodded and coughed rackingly several times, eventually bringing up sputum. Koesler recalled his own years of addiction; each morning had begun with coughing up his insides.

Everything was better without tobacco. But everyone had to discover that for oneself.

Koesler waited for Kramer to finish clearing the blocked passages, then said, "Okay, let's start with two days ago . . . Sunday." With more than thirty years as a priest, and relating to another priest only a few years younger than himself, Koesler could visualize a typical Sunday as if it were happening to himself. "You finish with morning Masses. How many do you have?"

"Two. Ten and twelve noon."

"Right. So you're tired and unwinding. Then the phone rings. What time was that?"

"About 2:30, 3:00. I wouldn't have fixed the time so easily except that I've gone over it with my lawyer."

"Sorry to go over the same material. But maybe I can understand and appreciate it even better than your attorney."

Kramer knew that was true.

"Was anyone with you when the call came?"

"No one."

Koesler tilted his head to one side. "Too bad. It would have been a tremendous help if someone had been there to corroborate the call. It's also too bad that so few people will appreciate how small the odds are that there would have been anyone else around, especially on a Sunday afternoon. That's about the only time a priest has to himself, whether he wants to be alone or not."

"Absolutely."

"So the call comes. A sick call?"

"Yeah. The guy who called—"

"It was a man? You're sure?"

"He didn't seem to be disguising his voice at all."

"You recognized the voice?"

"No."

"Then?"

"He said there was this lady who was real sick and needed a priest. And he gave the address."

"Which was way out of your parish. But it didn't matter because it was pretty close to downtown and there wouldn't be many priests around that area, especially on a Sunday afternoon."

"Exactly." Kramer was buoyed by the simple fact that Koesler seemed to understand so much more readily than the attorney. Both Johnson and Koesler were on his side. But Koesler understood completely and immediately.

"Then?"

"The rest of it is part of the record. I got there expecting to find a woman on her deathbed. I figured I'd have to call a doctor for her. I tried to get the guy who called to do that, but he hung up before I could do it. And I thought I had better at least take a look before I did it. So I went.

"When I knocked on the door I was surprised that she could invite me in with such a strong voice . . . I mean for a dying woman. Then when I entered the apartment, she let out a scream and pulled this huge knife. I didn't know what the hell was happening but I didn't want to get all carved up for my trouble. So I got my knife out . . . to sort of establish a Mexican standoff, you know.

"There was a lot of yelling. We were both yelling at each other. Then the cops busted in . . . actually it would have been sort of comical if it hadn't turned out to be so tragic."

Koesler, who had been nodding his understanding and agreement throughout Kramer's narration, said, "Okay, you were set up for this. There's no doubt about that. But how?"

"I don't know. I just don't know." Kramer chain-lit another cigarette and coughed.

"Whoever did it knew, or guessed, that the police had certain areas of the city under surveillance. Or maybe he actually saw the police patrolling that area. Somebody who had it in for you. Anybody come to mind?"

Kramer gave the question only a moment's thought. "No . . . nobody . . . not anybody vindictive enough to go to all the trouble."

"A good point. That *was* a lot of trouble to go to. Anybody who felt he had some score to settle with you could have found a helluva lot of easier ways to do it."

Koesler paused and rubbed his chin. "But then why didn't the police buy your story? It seems perfectly logical to me."

"They kept saying it was too impossible to be a coincidence."

"What was?"

"That I was dressed as a priest. And, as we know from the papers, so was the killer."

"So? Priests are not supposed to wear their uniform because some criminal decides to dress like us?"

"No, it was more than that. I drive a black Ford Escort. So did the killer."

Koesler was about to interject a thought, but Kramer continued. "Then, there was my knife. Again, the papers said that the prostitutes had been stabbed."

"But a knife! Lots of people carry—"

"They were most persistent about the size of the knife. I'm not sure why. Then there was something about my belt . . . its size, its width. I don't know what that was all about. I asked them. But they seemed determined to wait until I tell them. And I don't know what the hell I'm supposed to tell them."

"Isn't there any way of finding out?"

"Tomorrow, I think. My lawyer spends tomorrow, or part of it, with the prosecutor. He described the legal process. I think it's called discovery. He gets to find out what they think they have against me. We have a right to that information before the preliminary examination on Thursday."

"This is all happening so fast."

"Maybe. Or not so fast. There's no way I can get out of here too soon."

Kramer reached for another cigarette, then thought better of it and tapped it back into the package. Koesler visualized Kramer's lungs begging for mercy.

"Let's see what we've got." Koesler wished he had a pad. Evaluating a situation like this seemed to work better when one could write out the possibilities. "It's obvious somebody framed you. That you were set up last Sunday is patent. It didn't take too much imagination to figure that you would respond to that sick call. Or that you would be wearing your clericals. Maybe one of the younger priests would show up in a turtleneck and jeans. But our vintage would come in roman collar.

"The guy—whoever it is—knows you drive a black Escort. He knows you ordinarily carry a knife—but then, you always have. He knows something about your belt, which, for some reason that we are likely to discover tomorrow, is important to the police.

"Okay, all of that information is not all that hard to come by. It's easily available to anyone who knows you even in the slightest way.

"Who would do this to you? It's got to be obvious: the real killer. For two consecutive Sundays he went about killing defenseless women and setting you up at the same time.

"All this guy had to do was know just a little bit about you—things he could find out merely by observing you. Then he could dress like a priest, drive a black Escort, carry a knife—with which he could kill—and do whatever he did with a belt like yours. It wasn't all that hard." Koesler felt the exhilaration of having solved the puzzle. Or at least part of the puzzle.

"That's got to be it. That's really got to be it." Kramer, in that distracted automatic manner of a smoker, selected another

194

cigarette and lit it, using the second and final match the guard had provided.

"That leaves the big question . . ." Koesler seemed deep in thought. "Who is it? Who did it? And, now that I think of it, how did he know that a witness—and he always took the chance of being seen by somebody—how could he know that a witness would confuse the two of you? How could he guess that a witness might identify you as the one who did it? Luck? That seems improbable. Coincidence? I don't know."

"Wouldn't all he'd have to know," Kramer suggested, "is what my lawyer told me: that witnesses are likely to go into a line-up already programmed to identify somebody? They had all of us—there were seven—dress totally in black. Right away that makes us look an awful lot alike. And the woman who identified me seemed to spend a God-awful amount of time doing it . . . or at least it seemed that an awful lot of time elapsed. Maybe the killer was counting on the witnesses acting or reacting like witnesses usually do. Or maybe it was blind luck . . . or just a coincidence. After all, how could the killer know there would be witnesses?"

"I don't know. I just don't know. That's the only piece that doesn't seem to fit with the puzzle. Did he know, did he have any reason to guess, that this might happen? That someone would mistake you for him? I don't know. It bothers me."

"Well, anyhow, I feel better. Just going through this with you has lifted a weight off my shoulders, Bob. You know, I know—we both know—I couldn't have done it."

"Yes. But realistically, Dick, that may not be enough. I know in our form of law in this country, an accused person is innocent until proven guilty. But in our case, we may have to find the guilty party before—" Koesler stopped in midsentence and looked intently at Kramer. "What did you just say?"

Kramer seemed confused. He could not remember. Few people pay close enough attention to remarks they make to have a verbatim recollection. "I don't know . . . something about our both knowing that I didn't do it."

"No; you didn't say you didn't do it; you said you *couldn't* have done it."

"Same thing." Kramer drew nervously on his cigarette.

"Not exactly. If I were considering you and your being accused of a crime, I'd think of you as a priest—and a good one. And I would find it inconceivable that you could have committed the crime. And I'd say of you that you couldn't have done it. If I were speaking for myself accused of a crime, I'd say I didn't do it."

Kramer stubbed out the cigarette without lighting another. "So?"

"So, what were you doing the two Sunday afternoons before this past one?"

"What I was doing day before yesterday: nothing."

"No one phoned? No one stopped in for a copy of a record —marriage, baptism, confirmation, death—nothing? Two consecutive Sundays and the phone didn't ring even once? I know you're in a quiet parish, Dick. But I've been in quiet parishes too. And as restful as you would like Sunday afternoons and evenings to be, it would be something to write home about if nothing at all happened for that length of time."

"I told the cops I was at the rectory alone and nothing happened."

"I don't know whether they believe you. But I'm a priest, and I find it very difficult to believe. Nothing? Nothing at all happened? Come on, Dick: Are you trying to protect someone? If you are, let me assure you: It isn't worth it."

Kramer selected another cigarette and tapped it against the table, compressing the tobacco. He remembered he had no more matches and replaced it in the pack. Koesler wished he would hurry along. Their allotted time had almost expired.

"If anything had happened, I wouldn't have known about it," Kramer finally said softly.

"You wouldn't have known about it? You weren't there?"

"I was there, all right. Unconscious. Dead drunk."

"Drunk!" The statement had taken Koesler by surprise.

"Every Sunday. Every Sunday for months. More than a year. It's the only time they let me alone."

"They? The parishioners?"

"They. Everybody. Everything. The pressures. The drive.

The concern. There's nothing I can do about keeping the school open, paying the bills, teaching classes, giving convert instructions, fighting off the chancery. Sundays—the only day I can find any peace. Two Masses, homilies, liturgies. You know that, Bob. Wiped out."

Koesler nodded. He knew it well. The laity probably couldn't guess how much it took out of their priest to offer multiple Masses and really try to deliver an interesting and meaningful homily two, perhaps three times a day. It was draining—emotionally and physically.

"So," Kramer continued, "by early to midafternoon, I am exhausted and faced with the one and only time in the week when no one is likely to bug me. And I won't bug myself."

"So you drink?" Koesler easily perceived how difficult this admission was for Kramer.

"It started well over a year ago. Just something to help unwind. A light scotch, maybe. Then, more . . . into oblivion. After months of this, it took more and more to reach oblivion."

"You were building a tolerance."

"I didn't admit it at first. But then it became inescapable. And then, after a while, I wasn't getting any real rest in the way of sleep. But it didn't matter. I needed that escape. And no one was being hurt by it. Except possibly me. And I didn't touch a drop the rest of the week. Just Sundays."

Kramer was an alcoholic. Koesler knew enough about the disease to recognize that. But why drop the concept on the poor man? Kramer had enough trouble as it was. Time enough to get treatment for him after extricating him from this mess.

"Well, then, if you were completely out of it on those Sunday afternoons, you couldn't have committed those murders."

Kramer shrugged. "Bob, what difference does it make to the police? I have no one to testify that I spent the time inside my rectory, drunk or sober. What they demand—and I need —is someone to say, 'He couldn't have done it. He was home. I was with him.' And there isn't any such person.

"So you see, as far as this problem is concerned, it doesn't

197

matter whether I was drunk or sober. I have no witness one way or the other.

"But I guess that's what I meant when I said I couldn't have done it. That was rather clever of you to pick up on that."

"Clever or not, we're back on square one." Koesler grimaced. "It would help a lot if we could find the one who did it."

"Are you good at miracles?"

Despite the gravity of the situation, Koesler smiled. "No, 'fraid not." His smile grew more reassuring. "But I do feel I've accomplished something. Now we know there's somebody out there who has been watching you pretty carefully and possibly even knows about your Sunday routine. That would make it quite perfect, wouldn't it? Suppose the guy knew you were virtually unconscious and necessarily alone every late Sunday afternoon and early evening. Then he would know that as he went about framing you, you would have no alibi.

"And how would he know?" Koesler now seemed to be musing out loud. "Simple surveillance would tell him you never leave the rectory on Sundays. But what are you doing? He phones. But you don't answer. Maybe he tries looking in a window. Or," triumphantly, "the garbage! Very popular now, I hear. He rummages through the garbage and finds empty booze bottles on Mondays." He looked at Kramer. "It wouldn't be that hard."

Koesler was now ascending the emotional high that accompanied the solving of another puzzle. "I'm beginning to get a sense of the person we're looking for. I really think this visit has been a help."

"For me, too," Kramer said. "By God, I think there may be light at the end of this tunnel."

The guard opened the door. "Time's up."

Kramer rose. "And, Bob: Thanks for the cigarettes."

The door slammed and clicked locked behind Kramer. Then Koesler was ushered out of the building through the repetitive precaution of the locking of the door behind before the opening of the door in front. When he finally reached the street, Koesler experienced a rush of relief similar to that which he always felt after visiting a hospital. In both instances he was glad to get out and grateful he was neither a patient nor an inmate.

He retrieved his car after paying what he considered an exorbitant parking fee. Once again he fantasized that if he were mayor of Detroit the first thing he would do would be to take control of all the lots and allow free parking everywhere. Short of a good mass transit system, which the city had badly needed for decades, Detroit needed free parking to compete with the free parking amply available throughout the suburbs.

Koesler did not look forward to the drive home. He would be immersed in the ceaseless stop-and-go of rush-hour traffic. It was at times like this he questioned his choice of a stickshift model. Oh, well; at least the long slow drive would give him time to think.

Quite naturally, his thoughts revolved around Father Kramer.

Dick Kramer was a sick man. And the poor soul, in all likelihood, didn't realize how sick he was.

There was the smoking, of course. That would take its toll as it did with all serious smokers. No one who knew Kramer was a stranger to his chain-smoking and the accompanying racking cough.

The drinking was another dimension. Koesler could readily understand how Kramer could rationalize away the drinking problem. Kramer himself had said it: He did not touch a drop Monday through Saturday. So how could someone who confined his drinking to one day a week be an addict?

The answer of course was in the compulsion and mostly in the inability to quit. Each Sunday as soon as he was alone and, for all practical purposes, abandoned for the remainder of the day, he would begin drinking. At that point, it was a repetition of the old truism: One drink was not enough and two was too many. He could not stop until he passed out. Unconsciousness was nature's way of cutting off the irresistible urge.

Then the self-deception begins. Koesler had known so many alcoholics. Generally, they had some rules of thumb that convinced them they had no problem. Classic was the person who would abstain from alcohol until noon each day. And each day at noon he would proceed to get loaded. He didn't have a problem because he could wait until noon. He had things under control. And Dick Kramer could wait until Sunday. He too had things under control.

But he didn't. He himself described the situation best. It started innocently enough with a mild drink to help unwind after hard work. Then the tolerance grew until he was putting away probably a fifth or more at one sitting.

With any luck, Father Kramer had a sojourn at Guest House in his future. There, as had been the case with hundreds of priests, he could become a recovering alcoholic.

It was the unique approach of Guest House, conceived by its founder Austin Ripley, that a priest is not likely to make it in the standard Alcoholics Anonymous program. The reason had everything to do with the position accorded a priest in the Catholic community. Catholics tend to put their priests on pedestals. When a priest falls from that pedestal into an illness such as, say, alcoholism, he falls farther than the average person.

Guest House—the original located in the Detroit suburb of Lake Orion—he knew, had as its prime goal the restoration of the priest's sense of dignity. Next it offered the very best of physical, psychological, and religious therapy. And it seemed to work outstandingly well.

If anyone needed the solicitous ministrations of Guest House, it certainly was Dick Kramer. Not only was he suffering from alcoholism, but, even though he had been convicted of nothing, he now was an inmate in a prison system. His sense of self-dignity was undoubtedly at rock bottom.

So, as Father Koesler turned off Ford Road onto West Outer Drive, he had formed two sequential resolutions: He would clear Dick Kramer of the charge of murder. Then he would make sure that Kramer had the benefit of the success-prone Guest House.

Koesler did not often make such ambitious resolutions. By far the more momentous of the two resolves was getting

200

Kramer exonerated. But after this afternoon's consultations with Kramer, Koesler felt some indefinable link with the real killer . . . the man who had set Kramer up.

Was it a premonition that he and the killer would soon meet and that, somehow, Koesler would recognize the man?

After parking his car, Koesler decided to visit the church before going to the rectory. He had a lot to ponder. And, to date, he had never found a better place to think than in an empty church.

31

MONSIGNOR MEEHAN HAD SEEN THE television reports, he'd heard of it on the radio broadcasts, and he'd read about it in the local papers. Indeed, he could have gotten the word almost anywhere in the world.

That a Catholic priest had been accused of murder was news of the first order. That a Catholic priest had been accused of the ritual mutilation-murder of two prostitutes was news almost anywhere. And so almost every news agency carried it.

Meehan of course followed the story anxiously. After all, he and Father Kramer had lived and worked together in the same parish years ago and since then the Monsignor had always considered Kramer a friend. But the coverage, no matter how thorough, could never be as comprehensive as a first-hand report. This is why Meehan was paying such close attention to Father Koesler's words. Koesler had been there.

Ordinarily, during his visits with Monsignor Meehan, Koesler aimed to keep his side of the conversation brief. Meehan's attention span was not all that it had been. Some time back, Koesler had noticed that when he was telling a particularly long story or making a lengthy explanation, Meehan's eyes would begin wandering as his attention waned.

None of that today, however.

Yesterday, as part of a packed courtroom, Koesler, accompanied once again by Inspector Koznicki, had attended the preliminary examination of Father Kramer. Now he was recounting that event to Monsignor Meehan. And he had the monsignor's attention.

"How'd he look to you?" Clearly Meehan was concerned and worried about Kramer.

"Okay, I guess. But I had visited with him a few days ago. And I saw him at the arraignment a day before that. So maybe I've come to expect that sort of bewildered expression he's wearing. It's as if Dick suddenly found himself on a different planet where everything is strange and foreign. Fortunately, they don't allow any cameras in the courtroom. But there are these artists sitting in the area normally reserved for the jury. And they're sketching away furiously.

"The courtroom was packed. There were sheriff's deputies and police officers. In the middle of all this hubbub, Dick was just there in a sort of passive way . . . like an inert piece somebody placed on a chessboard."

Meehan slowly shook his head. "Poor man. The poor man."

Koesler thought about that for a moment. "Yeah, I guess he is a poor man, in one sense of the word. But in another sense he's rich. His Church is backing him up. There were quite a few priests in the courtroom. Most of them, even the younger guys, were in clericals. Several nuns, too . . . although not all of them were in even a modified habit. But they were there, and you could tell."

"Oh, that's good. That's good. How about the Cardinal?"

"He's behind the scenes, as usual. You probably read the statement he released: that Father Kramer enjoys the presumption of innocence, as would each of us in a court of law. And that he's sure that when all the facts are in, Father will be vindicated. And, finally, that he requests the prayers of all Catholics in the archdiocese to support Father Kramer in his hour of need."

"Yes, I read it, Bobby. Cardinal Boyle certainly has a knack for taking the hysteria out of an event and replacing it with sheer logic."

"But I think that's mostly for popular consumption. I'm sure he feels this whole messy episode very deeply. The word is that he's the one who got Johnson to defend Dick."

"Is that so? I wondered how that happened. If I recall correctly, Johnson doesn't try that many cases anymore. He's more a corporate lawyer now, isn't he. Where all the money is?"

Koesler nodded.

"But," Meehan continued, "he's one of the best."

"*The* best. Actually, it was sort of fifty-fifty . . . or maybe even sixty-forty. After he was approached by Sister Therese, he was reportedly sort of interested in the novelty of the case. Then—or so the story goes—came an invitation to dine with the Cardinal. And that did it."

"I should think so. You ever get an invite to sup with the Cardinal?"

"Never."

"Nor I. But it was good of him to go out of his way like that for Dick.

"Well, then, go on with it: How was the—what do you call it?—the preliminary examination?"

"Uh . . . well, you must have read about it."

"Yes, certainly. But you were there. I want to hear it from you."

"Well, it was much more brief than I had expected. Inspector Koznicki said the lawyers call it a 'minitrial.'"

"What happened?"

"It's very simple, really. The whole idea is to establish—or not, depending on whether you're the prosecution or the defense—that a crime has been committed. And then, whether or not there's probable cause that the crime was committed by the accused. So that's what they argued.

"The prosecution's case seems to center on the fact that Dick wears the same kind of clothing we do—and which the murderer is supposed to have worn. And that Dick drives the same make and color of car the murderer did. And that Dick carries a knife. And that he fell into the trap they set for the murderer.

"Oh, and there's something about his belt . . . but they didn't bring that up. Inspector Koznicki said that the prosecution doesn't usually play all its cards at a preliminary examination. They present just enough to have the judge agree that there is 'probable cause' to hold the defendant over for trial.

"Which is just what happened."

"Well, I know I wasn't there . . . but to me their case seems pretty flimsy."

"I've got to say that the prosecution did better than I portrayed its doing. That prosecuting attorney is really good. I suppose to someone who could be objective about this, it could be and probably is one of the more fascinating trials in memory. But you and I don't fit into that objective category."

"Most certainly not."

"On top of it all, the prosecution didn't bring in those eyewitnesses who identified Dick. And the inspector says their testimony may prove to be the most damaging evidence of all. But even without them, the ruling was that Dick was to be held over for trial in circuit court."

"That's the one that puzzles me. How could they do that? How could they possibly identify Dick—I mean, when the man certainly wasn't there?"

"Dick's attorney told him it does happen. Even when the police don't influence them, sometimes witnesses so expect to see a particular person in a lineup that they find somebody to identify even if the guilty party isn't there.

"Anyway, Dick said his attorney was quite sure he would be able to break their testimony in cross-examination."

"I fervently hope and pray so."

"Interesting, though; through the inspector, I met a young detective named Mangiapane."

"A good Italian Catholic lad?"

"Absolutely. He was at the lineup. He told me all about the proceedings and—off the record, unfortunately—that he thought it was possible, just possible, that the women could have made a mistake. I think he's on our side."

"We can use all the help we can get."

"You said it. Especially with that Lieutenant Tully. He is so dead sure that Dick is guilty that it's frightening. And the inspector claims that Tully is the best homicide detective on the force."

"Everybody's entitled to one major mistake. And this is Lieutenant Tully's. So..." Meehan tapped his cane against the floor. "...what happens now? How do we get poor Dick out of that godforsaken jail?"

"Well, he has to go to trial first."

"Before that. Isn't there a bail?"

"Yes. As a matter of fact there is ... although the prosecution argued strenuously against it."

"They want their pound of flesh, do they?"

"They argued that Dick is charged with a most serious crime and that he poses a danger to the community."

"Horsefeathers!" Which was about as vulgar as Monsignor Meehan ever became.

"That's what the defense said: that Dick has an unblemished record and is an upstanding and, in fact, leading member of the community.

"So then the judge said that while the prosecution had met its burden to prove probable cause, he didn't believe the evidence was compelling enough to prohibit setting a bond."

Meehan grinned. "I bet then they wished they'd trotted out all their 'evidence.'"

"Probably. But there really wasn't anything more they could do at that point. So the bond was set at..." Koesler paused as if unwilling to pronounce the figure. "...at one hundred thousand dollars."

Meehan dropped his cane. "One hundred thousand dollars!"

"That means coming up with 10 percent of that total—ten thousand dollars."

"Ten thousand? Cold cash? Who's got that kind of money?"

"Nobody I know. The priests have started a collection with the idea that if the total never gets to ten thousand, whatever has been donated will be returned. There's not a lot of hope. At least not in the immediate future. And the chancery does not involve itself in such matters."

"Meanwhile, poor Father Kramer rots in jail for no good reason." Meehan shook his head. Then, as if forcing himself, he brightened. "Well, anyway, Bobby, we've got you on our side."

Koesler tilted his head to one side. "What do you mean?"

"I did a little callin' around myself. And I talked to Sister Therese."

"Oh."

"She told me you were going to help Dick."

"I'm praying for him."

"That and more. She said you were going to get involved."

"Getting involved doesn't mean any miracles are going to happen."

"You've done it before, Bobby."

"Miracles!"

"Maybe not. But you've helped the police before. It's common knowledge."

"I don't know how common the knowledge is. But you've got the right verb. I've helped a few times. And I'm only involving myself in this case because the murderer had the gall to wear our uniform when he was committing his crimes. You and I—and all priests, for that matter—know that no one knows what it's like to be a priest except another priest. So if this murderer wants to pretend to be a priest, like as not he's going to make some mistakes that a real priest will be able to recognize.

"I guess my advantage over any other priest who might get actively involved in helping Dick is that I already have a bit of an entrée to the police department through Inspector Koznicki. But please, Monsignor: no miracles."

206

Meehan chuckled. "All right then, Bobby: no miracles. But we're counting on you all the same."

Koesler grew more serious. "I just wish I had more confidence. I feel that I'm limping."

"Oh?" Meehan matched Koesler's somber demeanor. "What is it then?"

"I don't know exactly. It's . . . it's like the real killer knows Dick better than I do."

"How can that be?"

"Well, quite obviously, the real murderer has been stalking Father Kramer for some time—and very painstakingly. He knows Dick's routine better than almost anyone else." Koesler would not mention Kramer's drinking problem and his consequent lost Sundays. He did not consider Kramer's confidence protected by the seal of confession, or even as a professional secret. But there was no point in mentioning it to others. Time enough to address that problem after Kramer was cleared of these charges.

"He knows," Koesler continued, "what kind of car Dick drives, that he habitually carries a knife, what his schedule is. Even what size belt he wears."

"He knows that much! He knows all that!"

"Yes. And I know so little. Outside of that visit I paid him—after you mentioned it would be a good idea—I rarely see him. We don't travel in the same circles. Matter of fact, he doesn't travel in any circles. A loner, now and even in the seminary.

"Dick was only a couple of years behind me in the seminary. But I—we—hardly ever saw him. Always working—studying, reading, busy in the boiler room, the machine shop, with the carpenter—always working.

"And it hasn't changed since ordination. None of us ever sees him. Why, when I visited him this latest time, he was busy in his workshop. And if he hadn't been there, he would have been out in his parish ringing doorbells or in the school or repairing the church or something like that.

"The problem, Monsignor, is that the real killer knows him and I don't. That's why I feel as if I'm limping. If I'm going

207

to be able to find out where the killer made his mistake, the one that will trip him up and expose him, I've got to know Dick at least as well as the killer does." He shook his head. "But I don't."

The two were silent for several moments.

"I see," said Meehan finally. "Well, I suppose I was about as close to Dick Kramer as anyone in the archdiocese. What is it you need to know? Maybe I could be of some help."

"Maybe you could." Koesler brightened. "Maybe you could.

"Well, then, the obvious question is: What makes Dick Kramer run? His most overriding characteristic is that he's a workaholic, and has been for as long as I've known him. Which goes back to our earliest days in the seminary. From the very beginning, he's been wrapped up in busy-ness. Why? Any ideas?"

Meehan hesitated as if he knew the answer but was unsure whether to reveal the information.

"I think I can shed some light on that question," he said at length. "It's not for certain. But I've had a pet theory for a long, long time. Maybe I'm dabblin' in pop psychology without a license, but I'm pretty sure it all fits together."

"Anything is better than what I've got, which is no clue at all. What have you got on it, Monsignor?"

"Well, see, Bobby, it all began when Dick Kramer applied for entrance to Sacred Heart Seminary in the ninth grade. He applied and took the entrance exam, just as all of you did, in July, a couple of months before school began in September. That was in '44 or '45, I forget which. The thing of it is, he was turned down."

"Oh, no. I'm afraid you're mistaken there, Monsignor. Dick was admitted. I remember him as a freshman. He was admitted."

"So everyone thinks. But they're not quite correct. Oh, he passed the entrance exam okay. A bright lad. But there was a complication."

Meehan's hesitation suggested he might not continue.

"A complication?" Koesler prompted.

"He . . . Dick was illegitimate."

"He was!"

"Oh, not in civil lar. His parents were married. But by a judge, not by a priest. His father had been married previously. One of those cases canon law couldn't touch. His father, a Catholic, had married a Catholic—before a priest, two witnesses, the whole thing. There weren't any impediments to the marriage. It just didn't work out. So they were divorced in civil law.

"Later Dick's father met the girl who would become Dick's mother. They fell in love, deeply in love." He looked at Koesler almost challengingly. "By God, they lived together very happily for some thirty years. But because of that previous marriage, they couldn't get married in the Church. So when Dick was born, as far as Church law was concerned, he was illegitimate.

"There was only one way that this technicality would have any effect at all on Dick and that was if he were to try to become a priest. Church law prohibited illegitimates from the priesthood. As you know, that particular law was not common knowledge as far as the laity in general was concerned. Ordinarily, they learned about it only if they bumped into it headfirst."

"Not only was it not popularly known," Koesler interjected, "it was not universally enforced. You could get a dispensation from it."

"I'm coming to that," Meehan said. "You may remember, back in those days, that along with taking an entrance exam, you also had to bring copies of your baptismal and confirmation certificates as well as a copy of your parents' marriage certificate.

"Well, Richard came with the whole package and presented it to the rector of the seminary. Of course the marriage certificate was of the civil ceremony, since they hadn't had a religious ceremony. And on the copy of his baptismal certificate was the notation, *filius illegitimus*, signifying that he was, indeed, as far as the Church was concerned, illegitimate. So

209

the rector then had to explain to him why he could not be admitted to the seminary.

"It was the first that Richard had ever known about his technical status in the Church. He didn't even know what illegitimacy meant.

"It was a fantastic shock to Richard. All he wanted in life was to be a priest. Now he was given to believe he would never have a chance. Not through anything he had done or was responsible for, but because of something his parents had done.

"Well, it just tore him to shreds. All of a sudden, he understood why, although his parents went to Mass with him every week without fail, they never went to Communion. At first, he had been too embarrassed to ask them why they didn't receive Communion. Then when he got nerve enough to ask, their answer was very vague. So he hadn't asked again. And he tried to stop wondering.

"Then, all at once, when he was just thirteen, at what should have been one of the happiest moments of his life—being accepted as a student for the priesthood—he learns the whole truth. Can you imagine what that did to him?"

"I sure can." Koesler found himself emotionally wounded right along with the young Richard Kramer. "But what happened? Something must have happened. I can remember Dick as a freshman in the seminary. Mostly I can remember how damn hard he worked."

"Intervention, that's what happened. His pastor went to bat for him. Old Father Lotito."

"I remember him."

"Well, he was Dick's pastor. And he knew what a grand priest Dick would make. So Father Lotito, as soon as he heard what they'd done to Dick, got right over to the seminary. Raised holy hell with them." He smiled. "You could do that in those days only if you were quite fearless. And Father Lotito was certainly that.

"So they made an exception for Dick and accepted him. That's why your recollection of Dick's being in the freshman class at Sacred Heart is correct. But it was also flawed. They let him into the seminary but, I fear the damage was done."

"The poor guy. The poor kid! What a thing to happen to a young boy. Sometimes, I swear, the Church can have a heart as cold as stone."

"Anyway, that's my theory of why Dick Kramer works so exceptionally hard. Once I had occasion to talk to his parents —they're both gone now, you know. They said that he was never like that when he was growing up. He used to play and even, every once in a while, get into minor scrapes—nothing serious—just like any other youngster. But he changed at exactly the time he entered the seminary. And Father Lotito said the same.

"What happened, I think, is that being turned down by the seminary made him feel like a second-class student. So he set about to prove that he was not only as good as anybody else, but that he was better than he needed to be.

"So, his life, since the day he discovered his illegitimacy and was admitted to the seminary only by way of exception, has been filled with competitiveness. Mostly he's been competing with himself to prove that he was good enough to be a seminarian. Good enough to be a priest.

"And that's the way it went, Bobby. When Dick got to the end of his studies in theology and was about to be ordained, the seminary authorities had to petition Rome for the necessary dispensation. It was the final indignity for Richard.

"That's why, you see, so much depends on getting him free and clear of this ridiculous charge against him. His self-concept isn't all that strong to begin with. Can you imagine what this is doing to him as he finds himself locked up in a jail with criminals? Treated like a criminal himself?

"That's why we've got to do everything we can to clear his name and get him out of there just as soon as possible. That's why we're counting on you to help . . . from the inside, as it were."

As Monsignor Meehan concluded his story, Koesler felt an increased and intensified sense of urgency. Up to this moment, he had been devoting practically 100 percent of every possible moment to clearing Kramer of the charges against him. But what was it they said in sports: From now on, he would give 110 percent.

During his drive home, Koesler reflected that for the first time in memory, he and Meehan had visited without telling each other a single anecdote. That seemed to emphasize the gravity of Kramer's plight.

When, finally, he returned to his rectory, he looked it up. Sure enough, in the current Code of Canon Law, A.D. 1983, there was no mention of illegitimacy as an impediment to ordination. But in the old Code, A.D. 1917, there it was: Canon 984 noted that among the "irregularities" prohibiting ordination was illegitimacy, unless one were subsequently legitimized.

There was no doubt about it: Sometimes the Church had a heart of stone.

32

IT HAD BEEN A VERY GOOD DAY. Sundays, particularly Sundays that he didn't have to work, were Tully's favorites.

This day had begun with the relatively recent routine with which he was becoming very comfortable. He had wakened, retrieved the papers, started coffee and breakfast. Later, Alice joined him, rubbing sleep from her eyes and shuffling around the kitchen in soft, warm slippers.

They ate a leisurely breakfast, wading through the papers, reading aloud items from stories or columns that particularly interested them, conversing about implications.

Afterward, Tully lit the fireplace in the living room where, to a background of Ed Ames and Sinatra records, they made love.

It was well after noon before they began the process of considering what to do with the rest of the day. It was a testament to Alice's persuasive powers that she talked him into going down to the ice-skating rink in Hart Plaza adjacent to the Renaissance Center. It was an outdoor rink and Tully liked neither the out-of-doors during winter nor ice-skating. Alice, on the other hand, was an excellent skater and loved the brisk beauty of a rigorous winter.

Skating—or in Tully's case, slipping, sliding, and falling —was followed by a relaxed dinner at Carl's Chop House, one of downtown's few quality restaurants open on Sundays.

Now they were on their way home. Tully decided to skip life in the fast lane of the freeway in favor of laid-back Livernois—once far more appealing than it had become.

"You're a good sport, Zoo." Alice had abandoned the passenger seat to cuddle against Tully, her head resting firmly on his shoulder.

"If I was such a good sport, I wouldn't have been cleaning off the ice all afternoon."

"So you're not one of the Red Wings. You try."

"Actually, it's easier with both ankles flat on the ice . . . more like roller skating that way."

She chuckled. "I meant you are a good sport for humoring me in the first place. I know you're not nuts about the cold. And there's no place in town colder than where the wind whips right off the river."

"Don't remind me. This afternoon you almost saw a black guy turn into a white guy . . . come to think of it, that way I might be more acceptable to your Nordic parents."

"Stop worrying about my Nordic parents. I am no longer subject to their approval. This isn't *Guess Who's Coming to Dinner*. Besides, if we ever find ourselves in Minnesota, my father and mother will be nice to you. Right after I tell them that you pack a rod."

"Al, you've been watching too many Edward G. Robinson

movies. It's a gun. It's okay to call it a gun. And I don't pack it; I wear it."

"Whatever."

"Feelin' pretty high, aren'tcha?"

She smiled and snuggled closer. "Yeah."

"And with good reason. You saved that kid just about single-handed. What was his name again?"

"M'Zulu."

"I don't know how you keep those African names straight." It was Tully's turn to smile.

His sally sailed right over her head. "Actually, I didn't come to his rescue; Kronk Recreation did."

"You know about Kronk Recreation? Until now, I figured you thought Everlast was an eternal reward in the hereafter!"

"Actually, somebody told me about Kronk and I took the kid there. It was kind of an accident. But it made sense, don't you think? I mean, the kid was fighting all the time anyway —sort of nonprofessionally. The trouble was, he was winning all the time. Police very seldom run in the losers."

"They've suffered enough."

"Anyway, Mr. Steward thinks he has a great future."

"Another Tommy Hearns?"

"Who's Tommy Hearns?"

"You may be right, Al. Maybe M'Zulu's getting tied up with Kronk *was* a bit of an accident."

"That's what I said."

"Uh-huh. What weight's he gonna fight at?"

"What what?"

"It *was* an accident. Is he gonna be a flyweight, middleweight, welterweight? What?"

"Oh, that. Mr. Steward says with some decent food and dedicated conditioning he can become a very good heavyweight."

Tully whistled. "Another Joe Louis!" Pause. "You do know who Joe Louis was?"

"Of course, silly. He's the guy they built the monument to—the fist—on Jefferson."

"That's it—the Brown Bomber. Well, Al, if Steward is

214

right—and he usually is—in a few years M'Zulu will be able to buy and sell us."

"Really! There's that much money in it?"

"If a guy really makes it, more than basketball."

"Wow."

"Indeed! It's times like this I kind of envy you, Al."

"How so?"

"You really work at rehabilitating people. We can joke about it but M'Zulu was on a direct approach toward my department. He's already got an impressive record: assault, battery, B&E, car theft. He was one step from getting in over his head in drugs. And after that it was almost sure that he would either kill or be killed.

"But you reached him, got him into Kronk. Now if Steward stays on his case, the kid'll stay clean. That's not bad for a day's work, Al."

"That's nice, Zoo . . . good words. But you shouldn't put yourself down. Take M'Zulu, for instance. Supposing he hadn't gotten into Kronk. Supposing his life had gone the way you just outlined it. Once he got a gun and maybe killed somebody, where would he stop? He'd be a killer and one more threat to innocent lives in this city. You'd be the one to stop him. You'd solve one of your 'puzzles,' as you like to call them, and get him off the streets."

"Yeah, get 'im off the streets." They passed the University of Detroit campus—almost home. "Get 'im off the streets. Like I got Kramer off the streets."

"That was different, Zoo. You haven't closed that case yet . . . I mean, in your own mind you haven't closed it."

"Sure I have. He's locked up. We got our man. That's all she wrote."

Alice hesitated. "You mentioned him in your sleep the other night."

"Huh?"

"You said his name while you were sleeping."

Tully grinned. "Alice, do you realize I wouldn't know that I talk in my sleep if it weren't for you."

"You don't."

"But you just said—"

"That's why it was so out of the ordinary: You don't talk in your sleep. At least I've never heard you. Until the other night when you said his name."

"What else did I say?"

"Nothing . . . just his name."

"I'll be damned!"

"You told me that once the puzzle was solved you didn't think about the case anymore. It made sense to me. The thing about how the courts can screw everything up so you don't put any faith in that system . . . that your interest stops when you solve the puzzle."

Tully seemed lost in thought. "You're right on both counts, Al. Ordinarily, I leave the case on the prosecutor's doorstep and never think about it again. If I testify in court, so be it. But I don't give a damn." He frowned. "For some reason, this one's different."

"Is it because the first woman was your snitch and you thought there was a link? That that might be the reason she was killed?"

"Partly, I guess. That's definitely what got me into this thing on a personal basis. Yeah, I guess that's part of it.

"But then the fact that this guy was either a preacher or pretending to be one really reached me. It's like when you find a bad cop. Who you gonna turn to when it's a cop who's muggin' or rapin' you? A preacher or a priest is the same thing. Your instinct is to trust a preacher man. The ladies who went with Kramer were confident—in a line of work where there can be little confidence, where there is plenty of danger. He tricked them. He lulled them. Then he killed them. And then, as if that wasn't enough, he gutted them and branded them like cows.

"He really reached me. I'm gonna follow him right through circuit court, right up to the goddam Supreme Court, if it goes that far. I want to nail that guy."

Alice sensed the cold chill of Tully's anger.

"Will it hurt . . . I mean, will it weaken the case that the branding iron hasn't been found?"

"Who knows? No telling what a judge or jury will do. We got enough evidence without the damn iron. But once it gets to court . . . who knows?"

"Still looking for it?"

"Promise you won't tell?"

"What?"

"If Walt knew how many people I got lookin' for that iron, he'd piss kielbasa. Fortunately, in the past few days we've had a bunch of platter cases . . . just paperwork, no puzzles. So we've been able to fudge a bit and keep lookin' for the iron. Took the car to pieces and put it back together again. And the hell of it is, it might still be in there. There are so many places to hide a couple of real thin metallic rods in a car. The guys combed it, but—nothin'."

"Maybe it just isn't in there."

"Always a possibility. That's why I got every spare on the squad goin' through the rectory and the church. But you know, in the church basement Kramer's got a workroom with everything you'd need to make an iron like that. Oh, it's somewhere, all right. But where? I'd sure as hell like to turn it up before the trial. Like I said, we don't need it. But it sure would help to have it. The final nail in the coffin."

"Do you have to put it just that way?"

"Tender? Don't tell me you can't believe a priest would do this."

"Well, I'd prefer to think a priest didn't do it. But if it's believing in Father Kramer or you, you know whose team I'm on."

"That's better."

Tully backed the Pontiac into the side drive so, should the necessity arise, he could get out in a hurry.

Before leaving the house, he had turned the thermostat down. The first thing he did on reentering was to readjust it upward to sixty-eight degrees. "God, this has been a cold day! First the ice rink, now the house."

Alice came up from behind and threw her arms about his waist. "I'll warm things up for you, lover. Besides, for being such a good sport today, you deserve a good long back rub."

"I'd hate to tell you what part of my back needs the rub."

"I know. I watched you fall on it this afternoon."

The phone rang.

As Tully reached for the receiver, he said, "If this call's for me, I got a hunch I'm gonna need a rain check on the back rub . . . dammit." He had made it crystal-clear to his squad that when he was off duty he was to be contacted only for puzzles, not for platters.

"Zoo? Mangiapane."

"Uh-huh." Tully had recognized his voice.

"Zoo, all hell broke loose this afternoon."

Tully said nothing. Someplace down the line he would have to program Mangiapane to get right to the point.

The silence told Mangiapane there would be no response. So he proceeded. "He did it again, Zoo. Kramer."

"What?"

"Kramer did it again. This afternoon. Just like the other ones."

"That's impossible. Kramer's locked up."

"No he ain't, Zoo. Somebody sent bail for him yesterday."

"Jesus! I didn't know."

"You weren't here yesterday."

"Who put up the cash?"

"Guy named Murphy . . . the one with the Cadillac dealership."

"I know who Murphy is. Now, take it slow, from the top."

"Okay, Zoo. Dom Salvia took the call about six this evening. Some broad calling in a homicide. Friend of hers. Part of their routine is they check on each other. They're both hookers, Zoo. So when she checks she finds the other hooker dead in a bathtub."

"Witnesses?"

"We haven't found any yet. We're still canvassing the neighborhood."

"How'd you make Kramer?"

"Same M.O., Zoo. Exactly the same."

"Everything?"

"Strangled, gutted, and branded."

"Same brand?"

"Looks like it."

Damn! thought Tully. Where the hell does he keep the goddam thing? "Who's the victim?"

"This you ain't gonna believe. One Mae Dixon."

"Mae Dixon." Pause. "Isn't . . . isn't that the broad from last Sunday?"

"That's the one, Zoo. The same broad and the same place where we found Kramer last week."

"Son . . . of . . . a . . . bitch," Tully breathed with fervor. "What chutzpah! Same broad, same place. Well, that ties it. Let's go get him."

"Already have, Zoo. He's right back where he was yesterday. We got the judge to revoke bail."

"Good, good. Good! This time you got the goddam branding iron?"

"Negative, Zoo. We couldn't find it. And, just like last week, when we read him his rights and told him he could remain silent, damned if he didn't go that route again. He hasn't said a word, let alone tell us where the iron is."

"Then start over. Get the techs to go over the car again. Maybe this time he left it in there."

"Right, Zoo."

"I'll be right down." Tully hung up and turned to Alice.

"I could tell from your end of the conversation. Kramer did it again?"

"Uh-huh."

"How come you didn't know he got out on bail?"

"I probably would've heard about it if I'd been in yesterday or today. Too bad. I sure as hell would've put a tail on him. We'd have got him bare-naked. But that's okay; we got him now." Tully was struggling into his overcoat.

"You're going down to headquarters?"

"Uh-huh."

"From the look on your face, you're going to enjoy this as much as you would've liked the back rub."

"Apples and oranges, honey. But this ain't gonna take all night. I'll be back in a while. Maybe I'll still have a chance to cash in that rain check."

"I'll be waiting."

"We got him, Al." Tully opened the front door and paused a moment before leaving. "Iron or no iron, this is the final nail in the coffin."

He fairly levitated as he left the house.

33

FATHER KOESLER COULD NOT help feeling uncomfortable. He was not the type to impose on anyone. Yet here he was waiting to see Inspector Koznicki on a busy Monday morning.

Koesler would not have dreamed of calling for an appointment had it not been for last night's jolting news. For the third Sunday this month, the top story on radio and television had been the brutal murder of a Detroit prostitute. And for the second consecutive Sunday, Father Richard Kramer was accused of the crime.

Koesler had reached Koznicki rather late last night. The inspector had been his usual courtly self and graciously agreed to meet with Koesler at headquarters at ten o'clock the next morning.

After setting up the appointment with Koznicki, Koesler had phoned Sister Therese. As he had anticipated, she was devastated. She had seen Kramer only briefly after his release on bond. She had wanted him to go into seclusion somewhere to regain his energy and to avoid any further notoriety.

But he wouldn't hear of it. Over her strenuous objections he had returned to Mother of Sorrows, even though the chancery had sent another priest to perform the weekend liturgies. Kramer had gone into his own form of seclusion, unfortunately right into the heart of the maelstrom. Even though he put himself in the exact spot where anyone who wanted to could find him, he wanted to be alone. So she had complied and hadn't heard from or about him again until Sunday night when all hell had broken loose.

Koesler had talked to her at length, reassuring her and, finally, convincing her to stay at least temporarily with her parents, who lived in the far suburban community of Waterford Township. With Sister Therese safely tucked away, Koesler could turn full attention to the considerable mess in which Dick Kramer was mired.

As he waited for Inspector Koznicki—he was early for his appointment—he wondered again at the relatively small office space allotted to the head of a division as vital as homicide. Koznicki's bulk made the office seem even smaller than it was. On the other hand, Walt Koznicki was not the type to stand on ceremony, demand perks, or expect obeisance. He was an extremely hard worker, who, if not in love with his work, respected its significance.

The door to Koznicki's office opened and a detective Koesler had never met stepped into the hall. Noticing the priest, he greeted him with a smile that hadn't been there previously. Koesler was used to the automatic deference frequently accorded the clergy.

"Father . . ." Koznicki created the impression he had nothing more important to do this busy Monday morning than give valuable time to the priest. "Sorry to keep you waiting."

"I'm early." He knew Koznicki knew he was always early.

"Well, come in." Koznicki stood aside so the priest could

enter. They were both large men, though Koznicki out-weighed Koesler by forty or fifty pounds.

Koesler took a chair near the desk. It was warm. Must have been used by the detective who had just exited. When Koznicki crossed behind the desk and was seated, the room seemed so crowded Koesler thought a disinterested third party might find the scene ludicrous. He decided from here on he would have greater empathy with sardines.

"Tragic, tragic." Koznicki folded his ham hands on the desktop and studied Koesler with great evident concern.

"According to this morning's paper, Father Kramer is back in jail . . . is that true, Inspector?"

"Yes, sad to say, it is. We had to ask the judge to revoke bond. He really had no alternative."

"I didn't even know he was out of jail."

"Understandable. It was approximately two days after bond was set that the bail was made. In a situation such as that, usually there is little publicity. Notoriety generally is attached to extremely public events like an arraignment or a preliminary examination, as happened in the case of Father Kramer. But unless Father Kramer, or someone else who happened to know, told you, more than likely, as happened here, you would have no way of knowing.

"By the way, Father, something that has been puzzling us is the intervention of Mr. Murphy in posting the bond for Father Kramer. None of us can make the connection. And Murphy is saying nothing, particularly after yesterday's events. Do you have any notion as to why?"

"As a matter of fact, yes. Jim Murphy is a friend of Monsignor Meehan's."

Koznicki's raised eyebrows asked about that connection.

"You see," Koesler explained, "Monsignor Meehan was once Father Kramer's pastor and, at another time, he was mine. For the past few years, Monsignor's been in nursing care at the Little Sisters of the Poor. I visit him pretty regularly. We've talked about Father Kramer, especially lately with all the trouble. Monsignor wanted Father out of jail very, very much. And the Monsignor has been a priest for more than fifty years. He knows so many people, from the very wealthy to the poorest of the poor. I know he is a friend of Jim Murphy's. Without even calling Monsignor, I'm positive that's how the bail was made. But if it's important, I could easily check."

Koznicki waved a hand. "It was only a matter of interest."

It happened with great infrequency these days, but just now Koesler wanted a cigarette. "How bad is it, Inspector?"

"It could scarcely be worse. Everything was exactly the same as in the previous two homicides. But we have not recovered the knife that was used. Since the original has been retained as evidence, the supposition is that the weapon used yesterday was discarded afterwards."

"How can they be sure Father Kramer did it?" It was a foolish desperate question.

"Because they are sure Father committed the first two murders. Because the judge found probable cause to hold him over for trial for the first two murders. And because the modus operandi yesterday was identical to the others. If only the murder had been committed while he was still in custody. But . . ." Koznicki turned palms up in a gesture of hopelessness.

"But couldn't someone else . . . ?"

"No one knows all of the details of the other murders. We have held back many of the particulars from the media so that only we and the killer would know the whole story, as it were. Thus, should someone other than the real murderer attempt what we call a copycat crime we would recognize the difference. But yesterday, every detail of the previous two was observed." Koznicki paused. "Do you intend to continue your . . . special interest in this case?"

"He didn't do it. Of that I am certain."

"Not too long ago, I would have tended to agree with you."

"But now you don't?"

Koznicki shook his head. "However, I would not attempt to deter you."

"Will you help me?"

"In whatever way I can. But I can offer you no hope."

"I need a lot of help. At this point I don't even know where to begin."

Koznicki considered several possible suggestions. "I think it might be good for you to talk with our medical examiner, Dr. Moellmann. Have you ever met him?"

Koesler shook his head. "No, but I certainly have read about him. Extremely interesting person, as far as I can tell."

"After you speak with him, you may change your mind about pursuing this case. And it is possible that would not be undesirable. Supposing I send Officer Mangiapane over with you, and while you are on your way, I will call and prepare Dr. Moellmann to talk with you. He would not feel free to discuss the details of this case with you unless he has authorization from me.

"In fact, Lieutenant Tully is presently there." Koznicki glanced at his watch. "They should be finishing the autopsy on the Dixon woman about now. This would be a most appropriate time."

Koesler got up to leave, then paused. "One more thing, Inspector. I have the impression"—he did not think he needed to mention that Sister Therese was his informant—"that Father Kramer intended to spend the weekend at his rectory. I suppose there was no witness to confirm this."

"There was a priest sent by the chancery to say Mass, since no one thought Father Kramer would be available to do so. But the substitute priest left immediately after the last Mass early Sunday afternoon."

"But Father Kramer did stay at his rectory? That's where he was arrested?"

"Yes." Pause. "There is one more thing." Koznicki seemed ill at ease. "He was intoxicated."

Koesler's initial reaction was dismay. Clearly it was a measure of Kramer's dependency on alcohol that he would drink yesterday of all days. Koesler was dismayed and depressed at how much Father Kramer needed treatment, specifically the treatment to be found only at Guest House. And how very remote was the possibility of that happening now. First, Father

Kramer would have to be cleared of these charges of murder. And after yesterday, that task had been complicated enormously.

It was Koesler's secondary reaction that caused him to object strenuously: "But if Father Kramer was intoxicated, he couldn't possibly have committed that murder!"

From what Kramer had described as a Sunday routine of drinking until stupefied, Koesler's concept was of a man so drunk he would lie wherever he dropped. And he could not understand why Inspector Koznicki couldn't immediately understand this.

"Oh, no, Father," Koznicki insisted, "such is by no means always the case. People who are intoxicated can and do perform all sorts of actions. They drive—often successfully; sometimes, tragically, not. They work through an afternoon and evening after drinking too much at lunch. It goes on and on. Intoxicated people are, simply, unpredictable. Some collapse and sleep it off. Others go on with daily activity, sometimes impaired, sometimes more keenly. In fact, one might argue that, not infrequently, drink takes away natural inhibitions. Thus, if Father Kramer were intent on committing such a heinous crime, alcohol might repress his conscience."

Koesler considered this. And, in the end, rejected it. There was, of course, truth in what the inspector said. But none of what he said fit Dick Kramer. The impossibility was that Kramer ever would be more "intent" on murdering someone. Not even possibly.

"Well," Koesler said, "if I'm going to begin, I'd better get over to the medical examiner's office. And . . . thanks for your time and direction."

As Koesler left his office, Koznicki prepared to make calls —first Mangiapane as an escort, then Moellmann to prepare him for the visit. He watched as his priest-friend disappeared around a corner, and wondered what it would take before Koesler would be forced to abandon his quest—which, at this point, really was an impossible dream.

34

THIS WAS FATHER KOESLER'S
first visit to the Wayne County Morgue. As familiar as he was
with downtown Detroit he had never paid any attention to the
squat square building tucked in between Bricktown and
Greektown. Nor had he ever adverted to the grisly procedures
that were the regular course of business there. Now that officer Mangiapane had ushered him into the vast gray interior
of the main floor, consideration of what was going on downstairs was inevitable. And creepy.

Mangiapane introduced Koesler to the receptionist, who
gave him a genuine, if surprised, smile. Priests were not frequent visitors at the morgue. Once in a long while, one might
come in to identify a corpse. But even with some dispute
among Catholic theologians as to when the soul departs the
body, all would agree that the morgue was beyond the purview
of the Sacrament of the Sick.

"Inspector Koznicki just phoned, Father," the receptionist
said. "I sent the message down to Dr. Moellmann. He should
be up here any minute now. He was just about done."

As she finished speaking, the sound of voices entered the
lobby. Two men and a woman appeared. The woman and one
of the men wore white coats. Koesler presumed, correctly,
that the two were pathologists and that one had to be Dr.
Wilhelm Moellmann. The man in plainclothes Koesler already
knew to be Lieutenant Tully.

Mangiapane's introduction of Koesler to Tully was interrupted. "We've met," said Tully. "Sorry to run off, Father, but

226

I've got lots of work to do." With that, he was gone.

Shortly, the woman, too, was gone, leaving Koesler and Moellmann standing alone together.

Moellmann scrutinized Koesler. "So," he said (it came out "tzo"), "so this is *the* Father Koesler. I've heard about your work with the police." Emphasizing the article made Koesler sound like an instant celebrity. If the tactic was intended to disconcert and put the priest on the defensive, it worked, at least to some degree. For a moment, Koesler was speechless. Then, "Someone's pulling your leg, Doctor. I don't work with the police."

"One keeps one's ear to the ground, one hears things."

To Koesler, Moellmann seemed to be translating from a more familiar German even as he spoke. But Koesler had heard of Moellmann, too. He was, according to popular reputation, one who jokingly pulled legs unmercifully. But, at the core, he was one of the very best pathologists in the business.

Moellmann led the way up the marble steps toward the second floor and his office. "Tell me, Father Koesler..." The "oe" of Koesler's name became an umlaut; somehow it pleased the priest. "...what is your interest in this case? What brings a priest, of all people, to get involved in a murder so messy?"

"A priest is accused of these 'messy' murders."

"So?"

"So I don't think he did them."

Moellmann's face expressed more surprise than Koesler's statement merited. That, thought Koesler, must be part of the performance.

"Lieutenant Tully thinks the priest is guilty," the M.E. stated.

"I don't." It was said a bit more forcefully than was Koesler's habit. Perhaps he was playing along with Moellmann.

"And you don't!" Moellmann's wonderment seemed unfeigned. "Lieutenant Tully is an excellent detective. I have never known him to be this convinced and not be correct."

"Every rule has its exception. But if I'm going to help my

friend, Father Kramer, I'll need all the help I can get—particularly since, as you say, Lieutenant Tully is so convinced he's guilty. That's why Inspector Koznicki sent me to you." Koesler hoped the implication was obvious. From Moellmann, Koesler needed information, not discouragement.

"Very well." Moellmann led the way into his inner office. He proceeded to go through his file cabinets, extracting rather full manila folders, to which he added the one he had carried from the basement. He put all of them on the desk between himself and Koesler. "There, that's it. The current 'Case of the Mutilated Prostitutes.'" He then proceeded to arrange photos and charts on the desk.

Koesler looked about as if searching for some specific something.

"What is it, Father? What are you looking for?"

"The tapes."

"The tapes? What tapes?"

"Don't you tape-record your autopsies?"

"Tape—? Oh, you mean like Quincy and all those medical examiners you see on the television?"

"Well, yes."

Moellmann grinned. "No. No, I have a body chart at each body and I make all notations on that chart. Then when I come up, I fill in all the details while they are still fresh in my mind. Each person works according to his upbringing. You know? In Goethe's *Faust*, it says someplace in there . . . eh . . . 'The way he coughs, the way he spits'—in German it rhymes—'he has copied the boss.' So no one here—all eight doctors here—no one dictates. Everybody does the same as I do."

Koesler nodded understanding as he tried to absorb the enormity of the violence depicted in these pictures.

Moellmann watched Koesler intently. The priest didn't realize it, but he was undergoing a test. He could stomach studying these pictures—or he might become physically ill. Moellmann would continue his help only if Koesler was not upset at the horror exhibited.

Koesler was surprising himself in keeping everything down and quiet.

"You see," Moellmann said, "I have the police make sure that I get a set of the scene pictures because I want the whole file, the whole case all together."

"These are all pictures the police have taken, then?"

"No, no. I have our photographer take more pictures. You see, I take more interest in these bodies than in all the others—arteriosclerosis and stabbings and shootings. Because these are a ritual and they are more interesting, I spend more time with these. Make very definitive diagrams, drawings, and be very explicit so I don't lose anything in translation. And I make sure that they are photographed very adequately. Not only for documentation, but also for purposes of teaching. Because you don't see this often."

Koesler wondered whether, in this instance, familiarity bred tranquility. He was getting more used to the pictures and, as a consequence, was able to study them more intently. "Did you use the word 'ritual,' Doctor?"

"Yah. I've not seen people ripped open like this after death."

"That happened after the women were dead?"

"Yah, after death. That immediately makes it a ritual."

"You mean the evisceration?"

"No, the whole thing. The strangulation, the cross, the evisceration. This combination—that is what makes it a ritual."

"And you've never seen anything like this before."

"Well, not exactly. I've seen people with tic-tac-toe on them."

Koesler's mouth dropped open. "Tic-tac-toe? You mean with X's and O's? Somebody played tic-tac-toe on a person's skin?"

"Yah. With a sharp object. A knife, a screwdriver, something like that. People do strange things."

"I should say."

"Sometime back, maybe you remember, we had a series of prostitutes who were murdered on Cass Corridor. He used—I don't recall what it was—but it was something plaited, about this wide. . . ." Moellmann raised his right hand, fingers indicating a span of a couple of inches. "It was black . . ." He tried to recall how it was he knew the color. ". . . because I had it eventually. He left it—I don't know—or they found it on somebody. Maybe somebody came in and caught him and he just ran and left the victim with this thing. But all the other victims had this plaited imprint on the skin and we would see the body and we would say, 'Oh, that's another one of those.' There were four or five of those.

"But you see, that's what I would say when they brought in one of these. The first body, I knew it was a ritual. And I knew there would be more."

"You did?"

"Of course. There was no reason to perform such an elaborate ritual just once. I knew I would see it again. The only question was, how many times. If Lieutenant Tully is correct and if . . . uh . . . Kramer stays in jail, this will be all."

Koesler prayed the murders were finished. He rejected the hypothesis that they were over because Kramer was locked up. But he had to admit that among all those close to the investigation, he stood virtually alone in believing in Kramer's innocence.

But believe he did. So he had to get on with it.

"Then, these marks, Doctor . . ." Koesler directed Moellmann's attention to one of the photos. ". . . around the neck of the victim. These are marks of a plaited object?"

"No. No, that was the weapon in the other cases I just told you about."

Koesler surmised that patience was not Moellmann's long suit. He was fleetingly thankful that he'd never had the doctor as a teacher.

"See?" Moellmann continued. "There are the marks of a belt, though not a very ordinary belt. See, the indentations— there, on the skin. I'll show you. Press your fingers against your wrist. Hard, a lot of pressure. See, it is blanched. If you do it hard enough, it will stay. See what I'm talking about? See how fast it goes away now when you take your fingers away. That's because the blood goes back in. But if the person is deceased and the belt stays on the neck—he doesn't remove it; he leaves it on there—then, when I remove the belt, it will be pale all around. I'll be able to tell you the width of the belt because the upper and lower edges of the belt will scrape the skin. As you can see, the instrument used here—the belt—is rather wider than the ordinary belt."

Koesler, looking carefully, could detect nothing outstandingly unusual about the mark on the victim's neck. On the other hand, this was the first time he had ever studied the body of a strangled person. He decided to give the benefit of any doubt to Dr. Moellmann's expertise.

He looked away from the photo to find Moellmann studying him. "Are these pictures disturbing you, Father?"

"Well, I couldn't say they qualify as light morning viewing. And I may pay with a few nightmares. But, all in all, no; I'm all right."

"Good." Was it Koesler's imagination, or did Moellmann seem disappointed? "This, here, the branding mark, should be the final thing that interests you." He began rummaging through the photos, in search of blow-ups of each victim. He found them and set them side-by-side before the priest. "See, these are shots of the left breast of each of the women—magnified, of course. You can see clearly the form of a cross burned into the flesh."

"This happened after they were dead?"

"Oh, yes, of course."

Thank God, Koesler breathed.

"Now, you see, these are the first two victims. There is some form of lettering on the horizontal bar of the cross. Here is a closeup of just the lettering. Here is a magnifying glass. Look."

Koesler looked. The marks meant nothing to him.

"They don't mean much, do they?"

"No."

"For a time—well, for the first couple of weeks—we thought the marks might be the top part of some letters. And that the reason the bottom part of the letters was not imprinted was because of the natural curvature of the breast. See, the top of the vertical bar is the strongest, deepest imprint. So, what the guy did was start there at the top and sort of rolled the iron downward. See, the bottom of the vertical bar is the weakest imprint. We reasoned he was not putting as much pressure on the iron as he rolled it down the woman's breast. Maybe a difficult angle or something.

"But then, with the third victim, we were in luck. This time he was able to exert pretty much equal pressure during the whole process. See, now on the third one, the marks don't fade out at the bottom. They are etched clearly and definitively. But, sad to say," Moellmann turned both palms up, "they still seem to mean nothing. Just gibberish."

Koesler studied most intently the brand on the third victim.

Without doubt, there was a greater clarity. Still he could not glean any meaning from them. The longer Koesler studied the marks, the more certain he was that they were letters—the topmost portion of letters. The hypothesis, after the first two murders, that this was some sort of truncated lettering, certainly seemed accurate. But the branding of the third victim contradicted that theory. There was no gradual fade-out of the letters nor of the bottom of the vertical beam. The marks were crisp and clean. But why would someone go to all that trouble just to leave a mark that was impossible to fathom? Was it some sort of code? There must be some explanation of all this. But what could it be?

As he drifted back to the present, Koesler noticed that Moellmann was gathering the photos, notes, and charts and returning each to its proper folder. The show was over; the time Moellmann had allocated for this exhibition was up.

Koesler rose and gathered his coat and hat. "Thank you very much, Doctor. It was very kind of you to give me so much time."

"This came to you through the courtesy of Inspector Koznicki. And now, Father, you know about as much as the police. Much of what I showed you is very confidential." The statement was delivered as a warning.

"I'm good at keeping secrets, Doctor."

"You know, don't you, that Father Kramer has a workbench with appropriate tools so that he could easily have fashioned this branding iron?"

"Yes, I know that, Doctor."

"And still you think he is innocent?"

"Yes."

Moellmann shook his head. "One last thing: Did those markings mean anything at all to you?"

"Not really. Although the longer I reflect on it, the more they remind me of something. But I can't think what. It may come to me—probably in the middle of Mass or a shower, or shoveling snow."

"Well, if it comes, don't keep that a secret."

35

FATHER KOESLER'S MIND WAS reeling as he descended the stairs to the morgue's street floor. If it was possible to learn too much in a brief period, he'd just done so.

On reflection, it was not so much the sheer weight of new knowledge as the fact that he expected himself to utilize it. He was beginning to wonder whom he was kidding. Dr. Moellmann was a highly respected pathologist—among the best, if not *the* best, of the country's medical examiners. And he had no argument with Father Kramer's guilt in these murders.

Inspector Koznicki: one of Koesler's better friends. The priest knew the inspector to be a cautious man, rich in experience in police work, particularly in homicides.

Originally, Koznicki had been on the side of the angels. Indeed, until this very morning, Koesler had been sure he could count on the inspector's active support. Now even Walt

Koznicki had lost confidence in Kramer's innocence. Though he would continue to give counsel, it was obvious he held out no hope. Koznicki was going through the motions out of friendship rather than conviction.

And both Dr. Moellmann and Inspector Koznicki, as the foundation for their opinion, cited Lieutenant Tully.

Through Koesler's several adventures in the realm of homicide, he had never before encountered Tully personally. Although he had been vaguely aware of the lieutenant's reputation, this was the first time they had figuratively crossed swords. Apparently, Tully was something more than merely good. Reputedly, he possessed some sixth sense when it came to homicide. A sense that his fellow professionals respected.

Koesler could not help thinking that if Tully had been a woman and operated on an intuitive hunch that Kramer was guilty, he would have been derided as an hysterical female. But as a macho man, his sixth sense was revered. Yet, in the final analysis, it was no more than a highly formed, experientially proven intuition.

And to cap the climax, Dick Kramer seemed to be on their side. Why in God's name had Kramer not spent yesterday in the credible company of someone—anyone? At the very least, he might have taken steps to guard against his inclination toward alcoholism. He knew Sundays were his Achilles' heel. He had confessed as much to his attorney as well as to Koesler.

Why hadn't Kramer managed to stay sober one single Sunday? The Sunday for which he would most need an alibi?

Finally, what was there about the mark of the branding iron? The whole thing was so ugly, so perverted. But, at least as far as Father Koesler was concerned, the mark of the cross and its accompanying inscription was a puzzle that needed an insight and then a solution. He could not say the answer was on the tip of his tongue. It was buried far more deeply than that. Knowing himself, he realized that no amount of concentration would bring this solution to the fore. It would come, if it came at all, spontaneously. And there was nothing he could do but wait for that moment and hope it would come.

He was pulling up the collar of his overcoat preparatory to

leaving the building, when he heard an insistent voice behind him. "Father! Yoo-hoo! Priest! Wait a minute! Please!"

Koesler turned. It was a woman in the uniform of one of the morgue's technical assistants. A tall, blonde, not unattractive woman. Koesler searched his memory, but could not recall ever having met her. This was a constantly recurring nightmare. He had been a priest so long and had served in so many parishes and met so many people that he simply could not remember everyone from his past. Yet almost everyone expected to be remembered. His acquaintances had it so much easier than he. All they had to do was call him "Father" and they were home free. Whereas he had to come up with a name. One of the tricks of the trade was to postpone for as long as possible using any name at all. Perhaps it would come to him. Or the individual might volunteer the name.

So Koesler merely remained in a half-turn and watched, as the woman closed the distance between them. "Father?"

"Yes."

"You are a Catholic priest, aren't you?"

"Yes." If she wasn't sure whether he was a priest, she was not from his past. So she was in his present and perhaps his future.

"One can't tell these days. But you looked like you were a priest."

"And you are . . . ?"

"Agnes Blondell. *Ms*. Blondell."

"How do you do, Ms. Blondell. I was just about to—" He never got the opportunity to explain that he had a very busy schedule. Much to Koesler's surprise, the woman took his elbow quite firmly and began leading him downstairs toward the autopsy area.

It was the element of surprise that worked for her. Before he knew what hit him, Koesler was down the stairs and into an area that reminded him of a many-celled dungeon. Out of the corner of one eye, he caught sight of the large metal trays on which bodies were undoubtedly placed for dissection and autopsy. Fortunately for him, none of the trays was occupied. The crew was nearing lunch break.

All the while, the woman kept chattering. As best as he could grasp, Ms. Blondell was concerned about the eternal welfare of one of her fellow workers who claimed to be Catholic but she wasn't so sure about that. His behavior vis-à-vis women—apparently unless they were dead—fell considerably short of white knights of old. The man needed to consult a priest. Maybe go to confession or whatever it is Catholics do when they need a priest.

Koesler was embarrassed and growing more so by the moment. At the outset, he had not actively resisted her high-handed tactics because he had mistakenly assumed there was a medical emergency that required the spiritual ministrations of a priest. Now it seemed nothing more than a marital spat without benefit of marriage.

"This," Ms. Blondell announced in a righteous tone, "is Arnold Bush. He's the one I've been telling you about."

The man reminded Koesler of a creature who was dangerous only because he had been forced into an inescapable corner. Bush looked at Koesler. Bush obviously was annoyed. Bush looked at Agnes. Clearly he was furious.

Koesler glanced around the room. The rest of the attendants and technicians seemed amused, although not in any overt way. And they were decidedly keeping their distance. Koesler surmised that the others had some reason to fear Bush. But, at least at this moment, that fear was not shared by Agnes Blondell.

This scene that Koesler found himself a part of was by no means unique. However, it had been a long while since he'd been in a like situation.

Usually it happened on those infrequent occasions when a wife would bring her husband to the rectory so that the priest could impose "the pledge" on the man, who, at that point, was usually close to delirium tremens. Thus coerced, the victim would pledge to abstain from booze forever. In a lifetime, some men took the pledge dozens of times. It is said you can lead a horse to water but you can't make it drink. In Koesler's experience, you could lead a man to sobriety, but you couldn't guarantee he'd be sober next week.

236

Such, obviously, was the case here. Ms. Blondell seemed determined that Father Koesler effect some sort of reformation. Mr. Bush did not appear to share her conviction of the need for reform. Thus, if anything was going to happen here—and Koesler had no clue as to what Agnes intended to happen—it would depend entirely on Bush's undergoing a massive change in attitude.

Whatever might ensue, this was the antithesis of Koesler's method of operation. And he deeply resented the woman's forcing this situation on him. "Ms. . . . ." Koesler had forgotten her name.

"Blondell."

"Ms. Blondell, would you mind very much leaving me alone with Mr. . . . ."

"Bush."

". . . with Mr. Bush here?"

Her expression said she was not all that eager to leave, but if the priest insisted . . . "Well, all right. I suppose you need privacy to do whatever it is you Catholics do." She left and joined some of the female onlookers waiting to learn the outcome of this scene. Conspiratorially, they left together to conjecture on Bush's fate now that he'd been turned over to his priest.

Bush and Koesler regarded each other silently for a few moments. Finally, Bush tossed his head in the direction of the departed Agnes Blondell. "She's a bitch."

Koesler could not debate the point.

On reflection, Bush concluded that this priest had nothing to do with the present humiliation. It was entirely Blondell's fault. No use blaming the priest. "I don't know your name."

"Koesler. Father Koesler."

"Is that K-E-S-S-L-E-R?"

"No; K-O-E-S-L-E-R."

"German?"

"Yes." Though he was half Irish, Koesler rarely acknowledged that fact. To a casual acquaintance, the explanation was not worth the time it took.

"I'm sorry you got mixed up in this. It's none of your

affair. But then, it's none of her business either."

"Granted."

Bush looked at his watch. "We got a break now. You want to go to lunch? We could get a salad in one of the Greek places."

Koesler briefly considered the invitation. "Okay." He felt too sorry for Bush to refuse him.

As usual around midday in Greektown, auto traffic was perilously close to gridlock and the sidewalks were clogged with pedestrians. Partly because he wanted to get this engagement over with as quickly as possible and partly because it was so cold, Koesler walked rapidly. With his longer stride, the much taller Koesler unconsciously forced Bush to almost run just to keep up. When they reached the Laikon Café, Koesler felt invigorated. Bush was panting.

"Do you always walk this fast?" Bush gasped.

"Only when it's cold," Koesler answered as he looked over the early luncheon crowd, found a space, and headed for a table for two not far from a window.

They each ordered salad. The coffee was poured immediately.

Their conversation had barely begun when Koesler sensed lunch would be destroyed if Bush were allowed to explain his work. Without doubt someone had to assist in autopsies, but Koesler knew he would be happier if he never heard a graphic description of the work. So he steered the talk in this and that direction until they chanced on Bush's avocation of handiwork and his fascination with machines, both human and constructed.

So pleased was Koesler to have stumbled on this neutral subject, it did not occur to him that Arnold Bush and Father Kramer had identical hobbies.

By the time their salads were delivered, the subject of Bush's pastime was pretty well exhausted. Through the salad course and more coffee, Koesler coaxed Bush into giving an account, albeit abbreviated, of his life. It was a knack Koesler had, springing from his genuine interest in people, that caused others, oftentimes even strangers like Bush, to open up.

238

Bush, however, was not about to reveal all. He had been wounded too often to bare himself completely. His carefully edited personal narrative skipped over such items as the time he had spent living in a bordello. But, testing the waters, he did throw in a few controversial facts such as his on-again/off-again practice of Catholicism.

When Koesler rejected the bait, neither greeting the news with widened eyes nor berating him for his backsliding, Bush found himself warming to the priest somewhat. He was indeed sorry to have the lunch end. But the priest, though gracious enough, appeared to be in a hurry. So, too soon for Bush, the luncheon was over. And, wonder of wonders, the priest picked up the tab. If Bush needed another reason to trust this priest, the fact that he would pay for lunch was it. For one used to having the flow of money go from the laity to the clergy, this was a unique experience.

Koesler left the restaurant and leaned into the cold damp gale that gusted in from the Detroit River and twisted through the canyons of downtown. Fortunately, his car was parked only a few blocks away. He hurried into the vehicle, shivering, but grateful to be protected from the biting wind-chill.

Before starting the car, he cleaned the mist from his glasses and thought about this unexpectedly busy, if not as productive as he had wished, morning.

He had been disheartened by Inspector Koznicki's loss of faith in Father Kramer. And yet, it had not been a complete surprise. A police officer such as the inspector had to rely on his vast experience, together with all available evidence. In the end, no one could understand a priest like another priest could. In this case, Koesler was willing to wager his knowledge and experience in the priesthood against even the vastly superior experience in criminal behavior and homicide of his friend, Inspector Koznicki.

Then there was Dr. Moellmann, a most provocative man. Due to his patient explanation, Koesler now knew exactly what had happened to those poor women. The necessary restraint of the news media couldn't do justice to the violence of those deaths. The word "mutilation" was inadequate to describe the obscenity of that horrible evisceration, not to mention the branding. And what could those marks mean?

What irritated Koesler most was that those branding marks did mean something to him. But what? There was some clue buried just outside his conscious mind that promised to open a door to this mystery. But he couldn't find the key. And there was the further discouragement stemming from Dr. Moellmann's implicit confidence in the certitude of Lieutenant Tully. Koesler had to admit that any disinterested third party would consider it foolhardy for him to continue to stand in opposition to the combined expertise of Koznicki and Tully. But there Koesler stood. With his faith in Father Kramer, he could do no less.

Finally, this morning, there was Arnold Bush.

In retrospect, their meeting had been sheerly ludicrous. Koesler knew that he would forevermore smile at the memory of Agnes Blondell's leading him around the mortuary. And yet, there was something vaguely unsettling about Arnold Bush and . . . Koesler could not quite put his finger on it. Something Bush had said. What was it? At the time, it had slipped by Koesler and it was still evading him.

Then there was the disquieting thought that somewhere, somehow he and Bush had met previously. There was just something familiar about the man. But Koesler had been assigned to so many parishes over the years, been on so many committees, done business with so many people, that it was not uncommon for him to meet someone for the first time who would remind him of someone else he knew.

Koesler was tempted to dismiss the entire Bush episode. But something prevented him. After this business of clearing the good name of Father Kramer was over and finished, Arnold Bush merited another look.

But, for the moment, Koesler was running late. And two witnesses who had identified Father Kramer as the killer were waiting for an interview that had been set up by Inspector Koznicki.

God bless Inspector Koznicki.

36

FATHER KOESLER WAS SOME-
what shocked and slightly surprised at the appearance of Sister
Therese Hercher.

She was not disheveled. Her IHM blue suit was as clean
and neatly pressed as ever. No, the difference was in her face,
especially her eyes. If eyes were indeed the mirror of the soul,
then her soul was hurt and in deep pain.

"Are you getting enough sleep, Sister?"

"Yes. No. Not really. This thing has been a living nightmare.
And it's getting worse. It seems that everytime I get close to
sleep I think of Dick locked up like a common criminal and I
can't make it. I can't relax enough to sleep, at least not often."

Koesler had offered her coffee, which she refused. Was it
that she did not want to put any block in the way of sleep? Or
was it his coffee?

It was a little after ten o'clock Monday night. Earlier in the
evening, Sister had phoned Koesler, who, detecting the mental turmoil in her voice, invited her to visit him at St. Anselm's rectory.

"Maybe you should see a doctor, Sister. Maybe he could
give you something to relax you . . . help you get to sleep."

She waved away the suggestion. "I want to experience
what he must be going through. That way I won't let up in
trying to get him out of there."

She looked intently at Koesler. She was squinting. He attributed that to her underlying need for rest. "How did it go
with you today? Any progress?"

He bowed his head looking at the floor beneath them. "Not much. All in all, it was pretty discouraging. According to three rather well informed people, we—you and I—are about the only ones still convinced that Father Kramer is innocent."

"Oh?" Her tone was combative. "Who?"

"Inspector Koznicki, Lieutenant Tully, and Dr. Moellmann, the medical examiner."

"We're not the only ones." She seemed to take resolution from the one-sided odds. "All his parishioners are praying for him. It's even greater than that. I get a sense from the whole community, the city, the archdiocese, that the people—the vast majority—don't believe for an instant that he's guilty."

Koesler suspected she was right, though his grounds likely were different from hers. Those who actually knew Dick Kramer knew that he could not have committed these crimes. As for the others in that "vast majority" cited by Sister, Koesler guessed that even without knowing Kramer most people simply found it impossible to believe that a priest could be capable of such depravity.

"Though I've got to admit," she reflected, "that you're right: The police seem convinced that he is guilty. And they're working overtime to stack up evidence against him. Do you know what they did today? They searched the rectory, and even the church!"

"You were there?"

"They served the search warrant on me!"

While normally Koesler's prime sympathies lay with the police and the legal system protected by the Constitution, this, he thought, was going a bit far. Not only had they arrested a priest and charged him with unspeakable crimes, now they were serving search warrants on nuns. What next?

"Do you know what they were looking for?" Koesler was quite sure they were after the branding iron. But since he had been informed of the details of these murders in confidentiality, he was not about to reveal what he knew.

"Specifically? I haven't the slightest idea. I suppose they were on—what do they call it?—a fishing expedition. Anything that might implicate Dick."

"Did they appear to find anything? I mean, anything that you noticed?"

"I couldn't be everywhere. One bunch was searching the rectory, the other went to the church. I went with the ones in the church. They never would have found their way around that place without a guide."

"And?"

"I don't know. They paid the most attention to Dick's workshop. That's the place they asked specifically to see. They went over it with a fine-toothed comb. I tried to listen to what they were saying. But obviously they didn't want me to learn anything. At one point I know they were looking for some sort of knife. I don't know why; they've got Dick's knife. They took it from him last week when they arrested him the first time. And they're holding it as evidence now, aren't they?"

"That's right. But there's a knife missing. The one that was used yesterday on that poor woman . . . Mae Dixon. Naturally, if they think Dick Kramer committed the crime, then he had to have the knife that cut her open. It's true they have his knife. But as far as they're concerned there's no reason he couldn't have another one. Or he could have replaced it. Of course we know they'll never find another knife because he didn't do it. But it won't stop them from looking.

"But that was it—the knife? They weren't looking for anything else?"

"I couldn't say. They weren't exactly confiding in me. I did hear mention of some kind of brand. I took it to mean the kind or brand of knife they were looking for."

"But they didn't find anything."

"Not that I could tell. They looked pretty glum when they left.

"But how about you? Didn't you tell me you were going to have a chance to talk to those women who identified Dick as the killer?"

Koesler nodded. "I talked with both of them."

"And?"

"They're nice people. At least they were very open with

me. I think that was because Lieutenant Tully asked them to cooperate with me."

"But you couldn't shake them—their stories?"

"One of them—the one called Adelle—is not too certain. She's the one who was standing in a doorway several yards from the car that picked up her friend. She 'Fathered' me to death. I think because I'm a priest she was doing her best to tell the truth, the whole truth, and nothing but the truth."

Therese was thoughtful. "Just as she will have to do on the stand . . . when she's under oath."

"Exactly. So I would think that a sharp attorney like Mr. Bill Johnson shouldn't have a difficult time discrediting her testimony."

"And the other one?"

"Ruby. Not so good. She was only a few feet from the man. Of course she saw him for only a few seconds. He was moving, reentering the apartment building. He looked in her direction and seemed startled to see anybody up that close. Seemingly, he had looked around very carefully before going to his car, and then when he was sure no one was around— that no one could see him—had dashed out to the car."

"Then why didn't he see her if she was so close?"

"It was bitter cold. She was moving from one sheltered spot to another . . . sort of going from one doorway to another."

"So she was moving toward the building just as he returned to it."

"Right. As he hurried up the steps, he glanced in her direction. He was surprised to see her and he paused only a second or two and then hurried in."

"That's it? That was all there was to it? A couple of seconds?"

"That's it. But she seems so positive. So very, very positive."

"She's wrong!"

"Yes, she's wrong. But she's also lucky."

"Lucky!"

"A detective named Mangiapane told me all about the show-up. He said that among the men they had joining Dick was a detective who was almost his clone." Koesler hesitated. Something was trying to get through to his conscious mind. But it wouldn't come. "Anyway, both Adelle and Ruby had a lot of trouble sorting out the detective from Dick. Ruby definitively did it—she didn't have any doubts."

"So she's not apt to break on the stand."

"I don't think so. Though I'm sure Mr. Johnson will lean heavily on the infinitesimal seconds she had to make such a crucial identification. But, having met Ruby today, I'd say she won't budge an inch." Koesler glanced at his ever-present watch. It was nearing eleven o'clock. According to his schedule, he was only a few minutes from the late news, a nightcap, and bedtime. While he had every intention of giving Sister Therese all the time she wanted, he held hope that his routine would not be too severely fractured. "Sure you don't want some coffee? Or maybe a drink?"

"No, nothing. Thanks."

"Mind if I have something?"

"Of course not."

Koesler went to the kitchen, put a few ice cubes in a tall glass, poured in a couple of fingers of scotch, and filled the glass with water—the nightcap. Now if Sister did not stay beyond another half-hour, only the late news would be missing from his routine. He could live with that.

He returned to the living room, sat again across from Sister, and gently rattled the ice against the sides of his glass. He liked the sound. "And how about you? Weren't you going to check some of your contacts?"

"Yes. I went to see a friend, a Sister Helen, who runs a halfway house for women who want to get out of the life—the profession, she calls it. She knows more about prostitution and prostitutes than just about anybody. Over the past couple of weeks she's been checking things out for me. Today she had four women who regularly work the areas where all three of the victims were picked up. Or, with Mae Dixon, where she lived and worked."

"And?"

"And nothing, really. None of them was aware—before

245

these murders, that is—of anything like some john dressed as a priest. All of them said that something like that would have been noised about. And none of them had seen anything like that, nor had there been any word on the street about it. All of them said that if Adelle and Ruby say they saw the guy, they probably saw him . . . that they weren't the kind who would give false information—especially to Lieutenant Tully."

"So . . ." Another discouraging word.

"But," Sister added, "that doesn't mean that Adelle and even Ruby couldn't be mistaken in their identification of Dick as the man they saw."

"Of course."

The phone rang—11:10. Just what I need, thought Koesler: a late-night sick call. He excused himself and took the call in his office. "St. Anselm's."

"Father?"

"Yes."

"Father Koesler?"

"Yes." It didn't sound like a sick call.

"This is Arnold Bush."

Arnold Bush . . . now, there was a familiar name. But after all these years, all the people he'd met, and the lateness of the hour, nothing clicked.

Spurred on by the silence, "Arnold Bush . . . from the examiner's office. We had lunch today."

"Of course."

"I hope this isn't too late to call."

"No . . . no." Depending on why he was calling, this could easily be too late for a call.

"I want to invite you over for dinner."

It was too late for a call. "That's very kind of you, Arnold, but I'm pretty busy just now. Maybe in a month or so . . ." Koesler recognized that this was the type of invitation that would eventually have to be accepted. He had the feeling that Arnold Bush was determined.

"But I need you now."

"What's the matter, Arnold?"

"I can't tell you over the phone. I got to see you."

246

"And it's really urgent?"

"Yeah, really."

Koesler consulted the calendar on the desk before him. "Well, if it's really an emergency..." There was a parish council meeting tomorrow evening. Under the circumstances, he could be late for it and probably not miss a thing of great importance. "How would tomorrow evening be?"

"That would be perfect."

"Six-thirty be all right?"

"Fine."

Bush gave Koesler the address and offered directions. Even though the street name was not familiar, Koesler knew the general area and knew he could find it.

When he returned to the living room, Sister Therese was putting on her coat. The remainder of tonight's schedule, at least, would remain intact.

At the door, they promised to keep in touch in their all-out effort to clear Dick Kramer.

Koesler finished his drink and got into bed. His last conscious thought was about Arnold Bush. What could be so important that it demanded a face-to-face meeting? After all, they had just met today. He couldn't imagine what it might be. So he put it out of his mind.

Still, there was something—as yet indefinable—about Arnold Bush. Something that nagged at Koesler. But he couldn't put his finger on it. That troubled him. Maybe at the meeting tomorrow night. Maybe then.

37

THE NEIGHBORHOOD WAS FAMIL-
iar enough. But Koesler could not recall ever having been
there socially.

The area was best known for its principal structure, the
massive Masonic Temple, which had once housed the annual
week-long visit of the Metropolitan Opera. Now the Met no
longer played in Detroit and not that many other events were
booked in the overly large auditorium. Just down the street, at
the opposite end of Cass Park, stood Cass Tech, easily Detroit's premier public high school.

Father Koesler recalled many memorable occasions at the
Masonic Temple. Among them were concerts by outstanding
artists; operatic performances, including his first experience,
Carmen; a superlative *Porgy and Bess*; Yul Brynner's *The
King and I*.

None of that was going on tonight. The neighborhood was
shrouded in snow, and bitterly cold. The streets were practically deserted. He searched carefully for a parking space that
would be in a well-lit area and at the same time not too far
from his destination—an apartment building at the corner of
Fourth and Temple.

He found a near ideal spot. Its only drawback, common to
much of the city, was the number of drifts that had piled up
over many snowstorms and, short of a warm spell, would not
be removed. He slid into the tracks of previous cars and offered a silent prayer that he would be able to extricate himself
when the time came.

The time of departure was essential to his strategy for the

248

evening. He intended to return to his rectory for at least some of the parish council meeting. On the one hand, he really ought to at least make an appearance at part of that meeting and on the other, he did feel somewhat queasy about this dinner invitation.

One thing, and one thing alone, had brought him to this point: his too often indulged inability to say no. It had been an element of Koesler's personality so long as to be immemorial. And it was so ingrained that he knew it was foolishly futile to resolve to change.

This invitation had come without warning. And it wasn't that this evening had actually been free of any other engagement. There *was* the council meeting. Also, he wanted to devote every possible moment to the cause of freeing Father Kramer. Besides, he would much rather have had his routine meal at the rectory—a little wine and no surprises.

But here he was at the desolate corner of Fourth and Temple on the mostly uninhabitable fringe of downtown Detroit. And here was the apartment building, down-at-the-heels as expected, that housed Arnold Bush, Koesler's host for the evening.

There was no difficulty in entering the building. It had no security system whatsoever. Koesler had no reason to expect any guard. But if he'd had his druthers, he would have been extremely grateful for at least a semblance of security.

He climbed the rickety stairs to the second floor and easily located Bush's apartment. In addition to having the number on the door, it alone among the second-floor apartments had a thin line of light shining out from beneath the door. Additionally there was the pungent odor of cabbage cooking.

Koesler braced himself and knocked on the door. It was opened almost immediately. A smiling Arnold Bush greeted him, took hat and coat, and draped them over the single shaft of ancient wood that served as a clothes tree. Koesler had brought no wine or other gift. Priests, as a singular class, generally considered their presence gift enough.

"Thank you for coming. Thank you very much." Bush—for Bush—was effusive.

"Not at all." Koesler was not sure what he had expected,

but it certainly was not this one-room efficiency. A table, two straightback chairs, a bed—more a cot, actually—and a hot plate that appeared to have four burners, two of which were being used to cook dinner. The unmistakable odor promised cabbage and something. The odor, strong as it was, was unable to mask the pervasive nicotine smell that seemed to have permeated everything in the room. Several strategically placed ashtrays were full to overflowing.

But by far the most outstanding feature was the walls. All four walls were filled with pictures. One, the wall next to the bed, held a series of syrupy religious art. The other three walls were covered with photos that appeared to be the same as or similar to the horrors he had viewed yesterday at the medical examiner's office.

Bush noticed Koesler's observance of the photos. "Interesting pictures," Bush remarked.

Koesler managed to close his mouth. "To say the least." Outside of Moellmann's office, he'd never seen anything comparable, and was uncertain how to react. The only safe avenue, he decided, was to focus on the religious art. He stepped close to the wall next to the bed and appeared to study those pictures. There wasn't one he hadn't seen previously at one time or another. Nor was there one he didn't dislike.

"Did you notice, I got one of the Sacred Heart of Jesus and one of the Immaculate Heart of Mary." There was a touch of pride in Bush's voice.

Koesler quickly scanned the wall and located the cited works near the center of the collection. "So you do." Jesus was portrayed as a wimp, Mary as a bland woman who'd never had either a thought or a human experience. Each was gesturing toward a heart-shaped organ, such as one might find on a valentine, which was positioned roughly where one would expect to find a human heart, but outside the body.

"You don't find pictures like that much nowadays," Bush opined. "Well, certainly not this many." Koesler guessed that Bush had not been in many traditional, or even nontraditional Catholic homes lately. A multitude of Sacred Heart, Infant of Prague, and the like, were still venerated in many Catholic homes. Taken one at a time, they could at best be tolerated, at worst ignored. In this number, they were overwhelming.

Bush gave Koesler a few more minutes to savor the religious spirit that these pictures could generate. "The other pictures"—Bush indicated the remaining three walls—"are from my work. At the morgue," he added needlessly.

Without getting too close to them, Koesler looked just long enough to confirm that they were the after-death photos of those three poor women. Short of a more intense study, he couldn't tell whether these were the same as the pictures Dr. Moellmann had showed him yesterday morning. But they seemed at a glance to be duplicates.

It was commendable, Koesler supposed, to take a certain measure of pride in one's work. But really! "Where did you get all these pictures, Mr. Bush? Are they the same as the ones in the medical examiner's office?"

"Arnold," Bush insisted. "Yeah, they're mostly the same. The tech is a friend of mine. I got them from him." Bush neglected to specify that the technician didn't *give* the photos. He sold them. Nor did Bush intend to confess that he had removed porno magazine shots from one wall just to put up the photos of Mae Dixon.

While trying to block out the content of the pictures themselves, Koesler did observe that each picture, clinical as well as religious, was framed. And each frame appeared to be formed by a similar or identical mold.

"Interesting frames, Arnold. Where did you manage to get so many different sizes in the same design?"

"Made them myself," with evident pride.

"Yourself?" Koesler looked around the room, the unspoken question obvious.

"Oh, not here. There's a bump shop a little north of here. I know the owner. I work there two, three nights a week. Help him some. Do some work on my own. He's got all the tools, everything."

Oh, yes; Koesler recalled that Bush had mentioned his hobby at lunch yesterday. It hadn't occurred to Koesler then, but now it did: Bush and Father Kramer had the same hobby.

And both had easy access to a supply of professional tools. Interesting coincidence.

"But, dinner is ready," said Bush. "Come on; sit down."

Bush obviously had done his best to prepare what, for him, was an outstanding meal. He served Mogen David wine. Koesler was at the opposite end of the spectrum from a sommelier, but with one sip he knew this was more a garden variety grape juice than a choice wine.

His worst fears were realized when he discovered that the companion to the cabbage that was being cooked over the other burner was corned beef. The latter ranked near the bottom of the few foods not relished by Koesler. This would not stand up as a gastronomically memorable evening, except in a negative way. But he would sip the wine, nibble at the corned beef, and fill up on cabbage.

Koesler, at Bush's invitation, offered a traditional prayer before the meal. As they prepared to eat, Koesler said, "By the way, Arnold, last night on the phone you said that this was an urgent matter. You haven't mentioned just what this emergency is."

"I didn't say urgent. *You* said urgent. It was your word."

Koesler tried to recall the conversation in detail, but he couldn't. However, he'd had the definite impression that this was a matter of urgency, no matter who had used the word. "You seem to remember our conversation better than I, Arnold. What was it that was said?"

"I told you I needed you. Now. You were the one used the word 'urgent.'"

"You needed me now." Koesler required only a moment to consider the implications. "Sounds like an urgent matter to me."

"Maybe. But I didn't say it."

This was a strange one . . . possibly the strangest person he'd ever met. The literal-mindedness. And the pictures! "Very well, Arnold; you needed me. For what?"

"It's hard to say."

"Try. Think: You said you needed me . . . what made you think you needed me?"

"Because you didn't get mad at me."

252

"Get mad at you?"

"In the restaurant. After what that bitch, Agnes Blondell, said about me. Well, I was kind of testing you when we had lunch afterward. I told you some of the bad things I did during my life. And you didn't get mad. Like priests do. You want some more corned beef?"

"No, no, thanks. Maybe a little more cabbage . . . that is, if you've got any extra."

"Sure thing, Father." Arnold heaped more cabbage on Koesler's plate, quite burying the slice of corned beef that the priest had barely touched.

Maybe, thought Koesler, it was the quality or grade of corned beef to which he'd been exposed; but tonight's offering certainly ranked with the worst he'd ever tried. It was heavily marbled. And as far as he could recall, that was the sort of corned beef he'd always been served. Perhaps there was a far leaner beef that might make the difference.

In any case, he would have no struggle making do with the cabbage. There was almost no way he knew of spoiling cabbage.

"Have you had all that much trouble, Arnold? I mean with priests who get mad at you?"

Bush nodded. He had a mouthful of food, which he chewed and swallowed before speaking. Koesler was grateful.

"In confession, mostly. But sometimes I'd go in the priests' house and try to talk to one of them. And sooner or later they'd get mad and start yelling at me."

Koesler shook his head. "You've had spectacularly bad luck, Arnold. Most priests aren't like that." Even as he spoke, Koesler could recall a whole string of priests he'd known while growing up who'd been exactly like that. He liked to think the ranks of the hellfire-and-brimstone gang had been thinned by now.

"Well, the ones I've met were. You were the first one who seemed sort of understanding. And I didn't even tell you the worst of it."

Koesler toyed with a small slice of corned beef. "But you're going to now, aren't you Arnold."

"Well, if you don't mind."

"That's what you had in mind when you said you needed me . . . right?"

"Yeah. Is it okay? I mean, if you get mad, it will be all right. It'll just mean I made a mistake and you're like all the rest."

"Shoot."

"Okay. I wasn't confirmed."

"That's it?!"

"See, I thought you'd get mad."

"Arnold, I'm not angry. Just very surprised. What's so horrible about not having been confirmed? Besides, you can be confirmed any time."

"That's just the beginning."

"Oh." Koesler poured more Mogen David into his glass. Maybe he could get to like the stuff.

"See, I didn't get confirmed because I didn't have any real home. See, I was an orphan. At least that's what they told me. But I did a little checking on my own. I got no idea at all who my father was. He was gone right after he got my mother pregnant. She was a Catholic. That's why she had me baptized. But then she dumped me."

"She abandoned you?"

"She put me in an orphan asylum. A Catholic place, because she was a Catholic. Then I went into a series of foster homes. Mostly Catholic because the agency who had charge of me was Catholic . . . or at least knew I was a Catholic. That's why I got to make my First Holy Communion. But when it came time to get confirmed I was in another foster home and they didn't let me get confirmed because you had to have a new suit. And there wasn't no way they was going to buy me a new suit."

"They wouldn't enroll you in a confirmation class because—well, that's outrageous. I don't know whether it was worse for them to keep you out of the class or worse for the parish to require new clothing. What did they dress you in, for God's sake?"

"Well, every once in a while we'd go down to the St. Vincent de Paul clothing store and get second- or third-hand clothes for just some change. Sometimes for free. But—now, this is the bad part—this couple I was living with then, they had to hit the road. The law was after them for bad checks.

"So they took the kids—I mean the ones who were their real kids—and left the state. But there was no way they was gonna take me with them. They had enough to handle with their three."

"So she turned you over to the agency again?"

"No. And it's okay if you get mad now. The woman turned me over to her sister who ran a cathouse."

"A cathouse? A house of prostitution. What happened to the agency?"

"I sort of slipped between the cracks."

"How old were you then?"

"Twelve."

"You poor kid."

"Are you mad?"

"At you? No. Maybe at the system. Maybe at your foster mother. But certainly not at you."

"See, I was right: You don't get mad. But now that bad stuff starts."

Bush launched into a monologue, an autobiographical sketch of life in a brothel as seen through the eyes of a growing boy going through an extremely painful and unusual adolescence.

Koesler listened. He listened so intently his mouth became dry from hanging open. As he listened he found himself comparing his boyhood to the aberration that was forced upon a hitherto innocent youth.

Bush had begun bordello life as a curiosity. Chances are there might have been in that house the traditional hooker with a heart of gold—some kind woman who might have protected and mothered him. But Bush bucked odds all his life. Instead of being sheltered and protected, he was treated as a joke. Upon arrival at the house, he was introduced to each and every fact of life by a series of the inhabitants. He was encouraged to—or at least no one seemed to mind if he did—surreptitiously watch from hiding places as the girls plied their trade. He knew what a condom was before he was able to spell the word.

While the parents of other children his age were insisting on the completion of homework, Arnold was running errands for the women as well as for their customers. As a final obscenity, Arnold was taught how to satisfy clients who preferred boys as sexual partners. He was allowed to keep a small percentage of what he earned.

At a comparable age and at almost the same time, Koesler was a seventh grader in a parochial school. He had loving parents who lavished attention on him. He had older sisters who included him in their lives. He lived in a protective cocoon.

At about the time Bush was learning how to turn a trick with a john, Koesler was in a seminary, further insulated from the world, the flesh, and the devil.

As his narration continued, Bush congratulated himself on his judgment of character. This priest was exactly what Bush had hoped him to be. No yelling, no table-pounding, no widened eyes, no fingerwagging. He just sat and listened. Perfect. Maybe, you never know—and at this point it could go either way—but, maybe he could tell this priest the whole thing. Get it all off his mind.

Koesler, for his part, was all but spellbound by the tale. He'd read of lives like this. But he had never actually known anyone who had spent his tenderest formative years in a milieu where immorality was so pervasive it became merely amoral. As the priest listened, he tried to imagine what effect such an upbringing might have on a person. What sort of adult would develop from so bizarre a background? What moral values could possibly endure the immoral soil in which this grew? What sort of attitude would such a person harbor toward women in general, when the women among whom he grew up used and abused him so shamefully?

As Bush continued his story about a life that had taken every possible wrong turn, Koesler, not pressed to respond, started to see something develop in Bush. It was not sharply at first. But then it began to take shape. A likeness. To whom? If one were to put . . . a collar . . . a roman collar . . . a clerical vest, on Bush, he would look very much like—no, he would look exactly like—Dick Kramer.

Odd that it had not occurred to him before. Both men were blond. Both were of stocky build. But most of all, facially they were so alike.

Then his mind took another turn. Something had been bothering him. A question. How . . . how something—oh, yes—how was it possible for two eyewitnesses . . . Who were they again? Adelle and Ruby . . . His train of thought leapfrogged. Adelle had seen the killer from a distance of several yards. Ruby had seen him from only a few feet away. Both women had identified Father Kramer in the show-up. Ruby, who'd had the best vantage, had been the more certain of the two. They both had identified Kramer. And they were both wrong. But—and this had been his problem—how could they have been so mistaken? That policeman, Mangiapane, had told Koesler about the police officer lookalike in the show-up. The women had had some difficulty making the identification because of him.

How well would they have done, Koesler wondered, if Arnold Bush had been in that show-up? Could they have told the difference between a similarly dressed Bush and Kramer? And would they have been so sure of themselves? Koesler thought not. He wondered if there were any possibility of repeating the show-up with Arnold entered in the sweepstakes. It might be worth inquiring into.

Now, nearing the end of his account, Bush decided to include the episode in this very room with Agnes Blondell.

Mention of the Blondell woman wrenched Koesler from his distraction.

Bush confided how confused he had been when Agnes had taken the initiative and arranged the date. How he'd tried to be a perfect gentleman. Even when she had come up to his apartment, he'd had no intention of taking advantage of her. Then, out of the blue, she had come on to him. And when he responded, she had gotten on her high horse and left. Only to spread cruel and vicious rumors about him. And it had been her fault entirely. He'd had nothing to do with it. Merely responded.

And that, Bush concluded, is how he had come to meet Koesler. Which, as far as Bush was concerned, proved that good could come out of bad.

As he spoke, Koesler could well imagine how, with his history, Bush might have reacted to a woman who was foolish enough to toy with his emotions. It might well have been, thought Koesler, very lucky for Agnes Blondell that she had escaped from that encounter. And that thought led to another. But again, Koesler was not quite able to bring the new concept into focus. Possibly he might have, had Bush not interrupted his thinking process by addressing him with a direct question: "You haven't eaten all your corned beef. Didn't you like it?"

Koesler started. "Oh, too much cabbage, I guess. That happens. Especially when you like cabbage as much as I do."

"Well, then, all done?"

"Yes. Yes, indeed." Koesler glanced at his watch. It was almost time to leave if he was going to catch at least part of the parish council meeting.

"Just some dessert then."

"Oh, I couldn't. I really must go." Koesler was convinced he had paid his dues this evening. Bush had said he needed Koesler—"now." And he'd had him. Koesler was sure all Bush had wanted or needed was to talk this out—tell someone. Now, thought Koesler, it was over.

"Just some Jell-O," Bush fairly pleaded. "I made it myself."

How else, Koesler wondered, would one get Jell-O without making it oneself. "Well, okay. They say there's always room for Jell-O. I guess there must always be time for it, too."

With a satisfied look, Bush cleared the few dishes from the small table. Then he went to his small, portable fridge to get the Jell-O. Things were such, and space so limited, that it appeared that Bush was going to require a few minutes to get the Jell-O on the table.

Koesler, filled with cabbage at least, felt the urge to stand and stretch a bit. There wasn't much space in which to walk nor was there much to capture one's attention. Except the pictures.

Koesler, perhaps instinctively, went to the "religious" art. Arguably, in this assemblage there wasn't much from which to choose. If only because he'd seen these saccharine monstrosities too often, he turned to the photos taken by Bush's technician friend.

He went rather rapidly from one to the next. He recognized some of the prints from the medical examiner's files, though he had to admit he had not spent that much time looking at them yesterday morning in Dr. Moellmann's office.

Once again, Koesler puzzled over the sheer brutality of these attacks, the violence done to the bodies of the victims.

"Dessert's ready."

Just as well. He'd had quite enough of Bush's version of Pictures at an Exhibition. Koesler could not help but think of Spiro Agnew's aristocratic comment when scheduled to tour a slum: "If you've seen one slum you've seen them all." Overwhelmed by these pictures, Koesler was about to paraphrase Agnew: When you've seen one mutilated prostitute, you've seen them all.

Of course this was not true, unless one were dealing with this specific case where each victim had been brutalized in identical ways. The bruised neck, the evisceration, the branding.

He returned to the series of framed pictures and stood staring at them.

Bush looked up from his chair at the table. "Is something wrong?"

There was no response. Bush tried again. "Is something the matter?"

"Something is wrong," Koesler said slowly. "Something is very, very, very wrong."

Bush joined Koesler. "What is it?"

"These pictures here." Koesler pointed to a series of prints, the latest additions to the gallery. "These are photos of the latest victim, Mae Dixon, aren't they?"

Bush did not need to study the pictures. He knew them well. "Yes, Mae Dixon. So?"

"There's a progression to these photos. The first ones—these, up higher here—were taken in the apartment. Of her in the bathtub, I suppose."

"Yes."

"And the later ones, down here, one row lower: These were taken at the mortuary."

"So?"

"There are two photos that were not taken by the technician."

Bush began to perspire.

"Those two photos were taken by the killer."

Koesler waited, but Bush said nothing.

Koesler continued. "I had to look very closely because the angle is different from the other photos. But if you check carefully, there's something missing. In these two pictures, Mae Dixon has not yet been branded. The picture seems to be taken from a higher angle, almost overhead. But it does show enough of the poor woman's breast so you can see that the brand mark should be there. Right here." Koesler touched the photo. "But it isn't. Mae Dixon, at this time, at the time this photo was taken, was dead. She'd been strangled. And she'd been cut open. But she had not been branded. The other photos show that she was, indeed, branded. But not now, not when this picture was taken. There's only one explanation: The murderer took this picture between the time he strangled and cut her and the time that he branded her."

Koesler looked long at Bush, who remained silent. "You did this, Arnold. You strangled her. You cut her open. You took this picture. And then you branded her."

Bush took his seat again at the table. He took a pack of cigarettes from his shirt pocket. He removed a cigarette and dropped the pack on the table. He tapped the cigarette several times on the tabletop. He placed the cigarette at the edge of his lips and lit it. He inhaled deeply, then let the smoke escape slowly through his nostrils. It was a most reflexive routine. Every action indicated that he was carefully considering his response to Koesler's charge.

"What if I didn't take those two pictures?" he said finally.

"Then who took them? Who did you get them from, Arnold? Whoever took them murdered Mae Dixon."

Bush pinched off another deep drag on his cigarette. Who? Who could he have gotten them from? No matter who he

260

named they would, of course, check. And they would find that the accusation was false. There was no one to blame—no one but himself.

"Stupid," Bush murmured. "Stupid. I wanted my own pictures. Everything else was mine. The plan. It was a good plan. It was maybe a perfect plan. Everything else. The tools. Everything was mine. I wanted my own picture. Stupid!" He spat out the final word.

Koesler waited, but Bush added nothing more. "Not only that," Koesler picked up, "but you involved an innocent man and a priest besides. You set him up, didn't you, Arnold? Poor Father Kramer has been publicly humiliated and imprisoned because of you. He could have been convicted. He would have spent a great number of years—maybe the rest of his life—in prison. Arnold, how could you have done this?"

But Bush was no longer listening. He was retracing in his memory the painstaking preparations he'd made. How carefully he had plotted the whole thing. And for what? For what?

Father Koesler was numb. He would not have expected to be. He would have expected to be delighted, triumphant. There was never a doubt in his mind that Dick Kramer was innocent of these crimes. But, from time to time, Koesler had doubted that he or anyone else would be able to set the record straight and clear the priest. Never had this depression been more deep than just yesterday when he had learned that not only did Lieutenant Tully believe Kramer guilty, but that this opinion was shared by Dr. Moellmann and even Inspector Koznicki. Now this was all changed. It was nothing less than Divine Providence that had come to his aid. A miracle of sorts.

Meeting Arnold Bush. What a spectacular accident! Agnes Blondell, out of nowhere, leading him almost by the nose to the basement of the morgue, where he had been introduced to Arnold Bush. Lunch in Greektown. All Arnold had been looking for was a nonjudgmental priest. Not that impossible to find, especially in this day and age.

So he'd listened to Bush. Then the call late last night. His strong inclination to postpone the dinner invitation into infinity. But Bush had been insistent—and there was Koesler's reluctance to refuse anyone. Then, dinner tonight. One last look at the photo study of the mutilated prostitutes. The very last second glance at those pictures and spotting the fatal flaw.

Especially that he, Father Koesler, should spot the final clue. He who had always been so poor at paying attention to detail.

Yes, if it was not a miracle in the technical sense, surely in a more popular sense it was miraculous.

At any point, this easily might not have happened. Had he been in the lobby of the morgue seconds earlier or later, Agnes Blondell would have missed him. Had he firmly refused Arnold's dinner invitation, he never would have suspected, let alone stumbled upon, the telltale pictures.

And if none of this had happened, like as not the doomsday predictions of almost everyone else would have come to pass. Father Kramer probably would have been convicted.

So why didn't he feel better? Why was there no ebullience?

Koesler was not sure. Maybe because he was forced to trade one soul for another. What had Bush become that had not been programmed beyond his power to control? What a painfully shameful way to treat a child! Shuffled from home to home, ending in a brothel. How much genuine responsibility did Arnold Bush have to shoulder for his crimes? How guilty was he in the eyes of God, the most understanding judge of all?

It was, any way it could be considered, a tragedy.

Perhaps that was why there was neither relief nor joy in Koesler's heart. He had simply traded one tragedy for another.

Meanwhile three innocent women had become homicide victims. The time had come to pay the price.

Bush lit another cigarette. All evening, at great personal discomfort, he had abstained from smoking for the sake of his party for the priest. It no longer mattered. In a short while his life of freedom, such as it was, would be at an end. The police would be here. Called by the priest.

Called by the priest?

Bush had killed before. Could he not do it again? With this priest out of the way he would be free.

It was a consideration.

But, in the end, no more than a consideration. It was one thing to snuff out a whore. Whores had snuffed out his youth often enough. It was quite another thing to kill a priest. No, he was deeply enough into this without descending further.

Whether he had picked up the vibration of Bush's thoughts or not, Koesler hastily moved to the phone. He thought briefly of dialing 911, the emergency number. He dialed the home of Inspector Koznicki.

38

IT HAD BEEN A FRENZIED EVEning. All in all, a memorable night.

Inspector Koznicki had arrived at the Bush apartment within a half-hour of Father Koesler's call. However, the first to arrive had been the uniformed police Koznicki had sent to secure the scene and begin the necessary procedures of arrest and the gathering of evidence. Then it had become a chain reaction. Koznicki had been followed by Lieutenant Tully, whom the inspector had called. Then came Officer Mangiapane whom Tully had summoned.

The Miranda Warning was given and a now sullen Arnold Bush interrogated. He waived his right to have an attorney present. Still, he was less than cooperative. Most questions were answered with monosyllabic grunts.

When the police technicians arrived, Koesler and Koznicki left. By mutual agreement, they regrouped at Norman's Eton Street Station, a converted early railroad station managed by James McIntyre, one of Koesler's parishioners. Besides being a good restaurant, Norman's afforded Koesler undisturbed seclusion. The manager saw to that. Before leaving Bush's apartment, Koznicki invited both Tully and Mangiapane to join them at Norman's once the statement had been taken and the booking and processing had been completed at headquarters.

Mangiapane had been flattered by the invitation. Tully would much have preferred to skip the engagement, but, from long association, he could tell when one of Koznicki's courtly invitations was, in reality, a command performance.

As yet alone, Koesler and Koznicki had been seated at a balcony table. Most of that section had been vacated by that hour of the evening. Koesler nursed a glass of Chablis while Koznicki sipped a port.

"What will happen now?" Koesler asked. "I mean, to Arnold Bush?"

"To Bush? I assume he will be charged with murder in the first degree. Three counts. It seemed that he was ready to confess to that charge when we were at his apartment, although he said too little for us to know what the outcome will be." Koznicki glanced at his watch. "They should have taken his statement by now."

"And Father Kramer?"

Koznicki brightened. "He should be freed tomorrow morning. One of two things could happen: His attorney could request a writ of habeas corpus, a move he could make tonight. But I doubt he will do that either tonight or tomorrow. More probably, he will wait for our recommendation, after which the prosecutor's office will move to dismiss the charges against Father Kramer."

"And then he will be free?"

"And then he will be free." Koznicki looked intently at the priest. "I must say I find your reaction to all this somewhat surprising, Father. You discovered the evidence that will clear Father Kramer. His freedom has been your goal from the outset. And now to be the instrument that accomplishes that goal . . . well, I should think you would be extremely happy. But I must say you are not the picture of joy."

Koesler smiled. "Sorry, Inspector. You're right: I should be happier than I am. And I don't know whether I can even explain. I guess I just don't do very well in the abstract."

264

"The abstract?"

"I didn't realize it all these years, but my notion of jail and imprisonment was an abstract perception. I've seen jails in movies and on TV. I've read about people being imprisoned by rightful authority and by tyrants and terrorists. I've visited people in prison. But it wasn't until I visited Dick Kramer in jail that the reality hit me. I think I might be able to adjust to almost everything about prison life except the essence of it all—being locked away. Lacking the freedom to . . . be free.

"Now in a very brief time, I've come to know Arnold Bush. To know how he became what he is. I guess I just can't be happy about a human being I know and understand being locked up, probably for the rest of his life."

"But Father," Koznicki spread his hands open-palmed on the tabletop, "this Arnold Bush has murdered three women!"

"He says one."

Lieutenant Tully had arrived.

"One?" Koznicki was clearly startled.

Tully and Mangiapane seated themselves.

"That's what Bush claims," said Tully. "He admits to the murder of Mae Dixon, but not the other two."

"How could that be? How could that possibly be?" Koesler spoke more loudly than he intended. The intensity of his tone drew a waiter to the table.

Tully ordered a light beer, Mangiapane a regular. Neither Koesler nor Koznicki reordered.

Mangiapane scratched his head. "I don't know. I can't figure it out. We got him. We got the pictures he took. We got the knife. We got the belt. And, best of all, we found the branding iron."

Koznicki seemed especially pleased. "You found the iron."

"Yes, sir." Mangiapane was far from being on a first-name basis with the boss. "We got it. But he claims he can't tell us what the inscription means. Said he copied it. And he still won't admit to more than the last murder."

"If he will not admit to the first two murders," Koznicki said, "does he have an alibi for the first two Sundays?"

265

Tully shook his head. "He lives alone and he is a loner. Same as Kramer," he added.

Koznicki looked sharply at Tully.

"But why?" Koesler asked. "Why would he not admit he killed *all* the women?"

Koznicki cocked his head to one side. "There is a possible reason. There was no way he could deny responsibility for the murder of Mae Dixon. The evidence speaks for itself. However, he may be considering some sort of plea such as temporary insanity—some plea that would be difficult to sustain over a full pretrial period.

"That would seem to jibe with his attitude when we arrived at the apartment tonight. It is somewhat rare that a suspect will waive his right to have an attorney present and then be as uncooperative as Bush was. It was almost as if there actually was an attorney present advising him as to when to speak and when to remain silent."

"That—or he really didn't commit those first two murders," Tully murmured.

"Didn't do them!" Koesler exclaimed. "If he didn't kill the first two women as well as the third, who did?"

"We got a guy locked up for that," said Tully dispassionately.

"Lieutenant!" Koesler said, "you can't still believe that Father Kramer did it!"

"I always did believe it."

Koznicki was about to intervene, but thought better of it. The battle lines had been drawn. It was between Father Koesler and Tully. It might be revealing one way or the other to let them go at it.

"What about a week ago Sunday?" Koesler pressed. "There can be no doubt that Bush set up Father Kramer. And you arrested him."

"Bush doesn't admit that."

"He doesn't admit to it!"

"No. And without a confession there is no evidence that he made a call that would bring Kramer to the Dixon apartment. So maybe there was no call. Maybe, as is alleged, Kramer came to

266

the apartment to kill Dixon just as he killed the other two."

"Lieutenant, that makes no sense. Not in the light of what we've learned tonight." So intent was he in his debate with Tully that Koesler was virtually oblivious to the presence of Koznicki and Mangiapane.

"On the contrary, Kramer looks as guilty now as he did before you came up with Bush."

"What about the iron—the branding iron, Lieutenant? When you arrested Father Kramer you were unable to find the branding iron. And in the previous two murders, the killer returned to his car to get the brand after strangling the victim. You didn't find the iron either on Father Kramer's person or in his car. In fact, you've never found a branding iron that belonged to Father Kramer!"

Tully sighed. "Anytime you're working with human behavior, you're going to find variables and atypical situations you don't and can't expect. I don't deny it would help to find that iron. But the mere fact that Kramer didn't have it when we got him doesn't mean he didn't have it at one time. He may have made his statement. He may have found it too clumsy an instrument. Even in serial murders, perps change their M.O. They can go from guns to knives to ropes. As long as they can leave a telltale calling card. And in this case the identical cutting and gutting would be enough."

"But Lieutenant, you've got the branding iron! Detective Mangiapane just said you found it tonight, at Bush's apartment. Never mind his desperate claim that he doesn't know anything about the inscription. That's it. What do you need with another one?"

"We got *a* branding iron tonight. Not necessarily *the* branding iron."

"But I assume it conforms with the marks left on the victim's bodies."

"It appears to. We'll see."

"And if it does . . . ?"

"Bush could have made a duplicate. He saw the bodies. He handled them. He had blown-up photos of the brand. He

267

worked in a tool shop. He could have made his own instrument."

"That's stretching things pretty far, don't you think?"

"Not if you're a professional in police work." Tully finally got the chip off his shoulder. "They call them copycat murders. It happens. We try to avoid that kind of thing by keeping details of murders—particularly serial killings—out of the media. Otherwise we'd be flooded by wackos duplicating weird murders to the last detail. Usually when there is a copycat murder, the killer messes up badly on one or another detail because he's not totally informed. But in this case there was no avoiding it. Not when the copycat works in the M.E.'s office. He knows as much as the police, the M.E., the original killer. He knows as much as anybody."

Koesler considered ordering another glass of wine, but immediately dismissed the notion. He was in an argument with a most worthy adversary, the result of which argument might well mean the release of Father Kramer. At least temporarily.

If Tully's reasoning were to convince Inspector Koznicki, it seemed possible that the police department would actively oppose the release of Father Kramer.

"One final point then, Lieutenant: The two of them—Arnold Bush and Father Kramer—look enough alike to be blood relatives. What would you think of this scenario? Supposing Arnold Bush kills two prostitutes. The newspapers tell him that the police recognize these as a series of killings by one and the same person. He knows the police will be closing in on these crimes. He also knows that he has a lookalike who is a priest. Easy enough for him to know that. Priests are very public people. They take part regularly in public liturgical functions. Besides, Father Kramer's picture has been in the *Detroit Catholic* newspaper any number of times.

"So, the third consecutive Sunday, he phones Father Kramer and dupes him into going on what appears to be a sick call. He knows that Father Kramer drives a black Escort—as does Bush, of course. The trap springs and Father Kramer is arrested. The following weekend Father Kramer is released on bail. Bush, in the M.E.'s office, would be aware of the scuttlebutt from Police

Headquarters just down the street. No great trick, I think, for him to learn about Father Kramer's release on bail. And this allows Bush to commit the third murder, again creating the impression that Father Kramer has struck again.

"He failed only because, by accident, I happened to discern pictures on Bush's wall that could have been taken only by the killer.

"So it is inescapable: Bush killed the third woman. It follows that he also killed the first two. But, for a reason yet to be discovered, he doesn't want to admit that just yet." Koesler concluded with the trace of a verbal flourish.

Tully smiled. "Not bad, Father. But how about the following premise: Suppose Kramer killed Louise Bonner and Nancy Freel. He tries to kill Mae Dixon, but we grab him. He's booked and his picture appears in the papers. Bush sees the picture and the resemblance. He knows all the details of the killing from his job at the morgue. He also knows the identity of the third intended victim. So he decides on a copycat murder.

"We think Kramer pulled off the third one too, but that is disproved when you latch onto those photos. So we've got the killer of the first two women in jail already. And now, thanks to you, we've got the killer of the last one—the copycat—in jail too. Besides how could Bush possibly know that we were planning a blanket surveillance on that third Sunday?"

Tully was conveniently overlooking the fact that he had discussed just such a surveillance with Dr. Moellmann, within earshot of Arnold Bush.

Koesler shrugged. "Lieutenant, our arguments are hypothetical. You suppose one thing, I suppose another. You think you know for sure; I think I know for sure." He looked to Koznicki. "Inspector?"

Koznicki said with a sense of assurance, "We must, finally, weigh the sum of circumstantial evidence. The weight falls on the shoulders of Arnold Bush. There is no shadow of a doubt he is guilty of the murder of Mae Dixon. The presumption must be that he is guilty of the first two murders. Tomorrow we will recommend to the prosecuting attorney that she move to dismiss the charges against Father Kramer."

Koesler breathed a sigh of relief.

Officer Mangiapane finished the beer and wiped his lips with the back of his hand. "Can I tell them about the mothers, Zoo?"

Lieutenant Tully said nothing.

"Mothers?" From Inspector Koznicki came part question and part command.

Mangiapane, now conscious of everyone's eyes upon him, wondered whether he'd drunk the beer too quickly. Perhaps it would have been better not to have brought up the mothers. That was the clear message he was picking up from Tully. But now he felt obliged to continue.

"Uh ... mothers ... Well, see, me and Zoo were on surveillance, on this very case, and he told me about his theory about mothers. Uh ... sorry, Zoo, if you didn't want me to bring it up ..."

Still Tully said nothing.

"Well, anyway, Zoo said that in cases like this where you have a multiple murderer or a serial murderer or a woman killer, nine times outta ten you're looking for somebody who had problems with his mama."

"Oh?" said Koznicki, to whom the theory was not unfamiliar.

"Yes, sir," Mangiapane affirmed. "Usually, he said, you got an orphan or a bastard or somebody who was institutionalized. And what he's doin' is he's killin' mama over and over again. Because he's convinced that all his troubles started with his relationship—or lack of one—with his mother.

"Zoo had a whole list of multiple murderers who fit the profile. I could remember only a few of 'em ... like John Bianchi, Dave Berkowitz, Ted Bundy, Al Fish, Ed Kamper, Albert De Salvo, Richard Speck, Norman Collins, Charles Starkweather ... I forget ... there were quite a few others." He looked brightly at Tully. "Why don't you tell 'em, Zoo? It's your theory."

Tully was turning his glass slowly, meditatively. He did not look up. "It's not *my* theory. It's been pretty well documented. It's in their records. It's in their own statements.

270

"Bundy complained that because he'd been a bastard, he'd been robbed of a past. He was bitter about that. So were all the rest. When Kemper killed he was acting out the rage he felt toward his mother. De Salvo—the 'Boston Strangler'—was dominated by his mother. He hated her for it. But it was taboo to get *her* for what she was doing to him so he killed woman after woman.

"Berkowitz—who was the 'Son of Sam'—was another bastard, who gave that as his reason for shooting women. He himself said that he was an accident: 'My birth was either out of spite or an accident.'

"It keeps on going like that."

"Anyway," Mangiapane said, "I thought that after the inspector said we were going to move to dismiss, that it would be okay to talk about the mother thing. Because . . . because . . ."

"Because," said Tully, "I told Mangiapane at headquarters after we booked Bush that at least we finally had a suspect who fit the profile. How could it be better? A bastard who spent his youth in a whorehouse."

"He said it was better than Kramer," Mangiapane added.

"Actually, it wasn't that much. Everybody who has—or thinks he has—reason to hate mama doesn't become a killer. Nor is each and every mass murderer illegitimate. But I must admit, now that the decision has been made, it was the one and only chink I ever saw in the case against Kramer. At least he had a normal childhood."

"Oh, but—" Koesler blurted.

Tully looked pointedly at the priest. "But what?"

"Uh . . . nothing."

Quietly and deeply Koesler was in turmoil. Should he bring it up or not? There was no possible way Tully could know that Dick Kramer qualified as an ecclesiastical bastard. If Tully had checked—and probably he had—he would have found records attesting to the fact that Richard Kramer was the legitimate son of Robert Kramer and Mary (née O'Loughlin) Kramer. There would be no grounds for Tully to check a baptismal record— which would reveal that Robert and Mary had not been married

271

in the Church and that, therefore, he was—for ecclesiastical purposes only—illegitimate. Koesler himself would have been unaware of this fact had he not been told by Monsignor Meehan.

But why bring it up? This was no more than a theoretical argument that now was over and finished. Besides, Koesler was only too conscious that he was foreign in this field and that Tully was the expert. Better leave well enough alone.

"Well," Koesler observed, "it's getting late. And my parish council met tonight without benefit of my presence. I'd better get back and see if they sold the parish out from under me."

Koesler, preparing to leave, noticed that Tully was still looking intently at him.

Koznicki, tugging at his French cuffs, glanced at his watch. "It is late and we have much to do tomorrow. Good night, gentlemen."

That was it. Everybody prepared to leave. Three police officers looked in vain for the bill. Father Koesler's parishioner, the manager of this restaurant, had delivered another freebie to the priest.

Father Koesler considered Koznicki's dictum. Koesler tried to consider what *he* had to do tomorrow. Nothing outstanding.

He had no way of knowing how busy he would be.

39

SLEEP ELUDED FATHER KOESLER. It had been well past his bedtime when he'd arrived at the rectory. That alone was enough to ruin the routine.

Taking into account the glass of wine at Eton Street, he had decided against his usual mild nightcap. Again the violation of routine.

He tried reading—sitting first in a chair and then in bed—but it didn't put him to sleep. If anything, he was so distracted that he found himself rereading paragraphs two and three times.

Partly, he decided, he was charged up from all the excitement this evening—Arnold Bush and the police and his animated argument with Lieutenant Tully. But it wasn't just the stimulation of the argument with Tully that was keeping the priest from his much desired sleep. It was more the questions the lieutenant kept raising that continued to plague the priest.

Drat that stubborn man! Bullheaded is all it was. He had been that way from the beginning. Convinced that Dick Kramer was guilty. Doing everything in his power to prove Kramer guilty. And even now, with proof that Arnold Bush was the real killer, Tully refused to accept the fact that he was—had been—wrong. Still asking questions. Did the man believe himself infallible? Good grief! Even the Papacy had only one uncontested infallible statement on record in the slightly more than 100 years since the doctrine of infallibility had been defined. And as far as he knew, no one had claimed even a tiny fraction of inerrancy for the police department.

But those questions—and some that occurred to Koesler even though they had not been asked by Tully—continued to nag.

That point that Tully had raised about troubled youth—institutionalized, adopted, illegitimate. How deep was Dick Kramer's resentment over his ecclesial illegitimacy? Did he blame his mother for marrying out of the Church? The knowledge of his awkward status had not come to Kramer until he was about to enter the ninth grade. A little late, wasn't it, for the early sort of self-conflict to which Tully referred? Yet it *had* radically changed Kramer's attitude, making him compete with a mirage of legitimate peers. He had forced himself to do as well or better, in every field, than those who had had the good fortune to be born legitimate.

Then there was the fact that the prostitute-victims were

older women. Did that have anything to do with a "mother figure"? Or was it more a commentary on Bush's predilection? After all, there was little question of Bush's resentment of his mother. She had given him away, deserted him, thus initiating his hurt-filled youth. Whereas Kramer's relationship with his mother was a matter of pure conjecture.

A good case could be made for Kramer to blame either or both of his parents for their canonically invalid marriage. After all, it was his father's prior marriage that prevented their wedding in the Church. On the other hand, it was Kramer's mother who held the key. The invalid marriage hinged on her assent or refusal. And even if somewhat archaic, still it was customary for men to blame women for whatever went wrong.

At the bottom of all this rationalization and questioning was what bothered Koesler most of all. While it was true that Lieutenant Tully had scarcely considered that anyone but Dick Kramer might be the guilty party, it was equally true that Koesler had dismissed the possibility of Kramer's culpability from the outset.

Now, despairing of sleep this night, Koesler decided that to be totally objective, he ought to at least consider the possibility that Kramer might be the killer. He would play devil's advocate; if nothing else it would satisfy his sense of fair play.

Koesler was already aware of a plausible, if remote, motivation for the murders: Kramer's illegitimacy, at least in the eyes of the Church. What else might conceivably fit?

Well, Kramer had no idea of what was going on when the crimes were committed. He was drunk. On the other hand, according to Inspector Koznicki, people could—have been known to—do things while in a drunken state. There were, of course, drunk drivers. But could an alcoholic go through such an elaborate performance as ritual murder while in a stupor? Especially when such an action would be entirely incompatible with one's normal nature?

Then, there was the gibberish of that branding iron. On the first two victims, it looked for all the world as if there was some sort of coherent message there. As if it was the curvature of the breast that prevented the entire message from being impressed on the victim's skin.

However, as Dr. Moellmann had pointed out, with the third victim the brand clearly broke off sharply at the furthest point of the previous two markings. Meaning that there was no coherent message. Meaning that it didn't mean anything.

Or did it?

Bush claimed he had nothing to do with the first two murders. If that were true, he would know no more about the brand marks than the police or the morgue would. So if he were to make a branding iron—for the copycat theory that Tully favored—he could go no further than the "incomplete" marks on the previous two victims. And that also would explain why the marks on the first two seemed to fade out and why the marks on the third were definitive.

Kramer, Kramer, Kramer. He could have constructed the branding iron in his workshop. No doubt about that. But why?

At birth, he was branded a bastard—uh, there's that word again. But it's true. He was branded illegitimate from conception actually. Not by society at large, but by the church alone. Yet nothing would happen as a result of that ecclesial designation. There was little chance he would even know about it. It would matter only if he were to try to enter a seminary toward a vocation to the priesthood. And once he did, at least as far as his psyche was concerned, all hell broke loose.

Like so many things in life, it had been an accident of timing as much as anything else.

There was a cartoon—old now—about Catholics eating meat on Friday. For centuries Church law had prohibited Catholics from eating meat on Friday. The object was the fostering of a penitential spirit, as well as the commemoration of Christ's death on Good Friday. The obligation bound Catholics under pain of serious sin. Theoretically, then, Catholics could be—and maybe were—condemned to hell for eating a succulent slice of prime rib, or even a hot dog, on Friday.

Then, seemingly out of nowhere, in 1966, the ban on Friday meat-eating was lifted. Overnight, it was no longer a sin.

The cartoon depicted a typical scene in hell, wherein one devil says to another devil, "What are we going to do with all the people who are here for eating meat on Friday?"

To some extent, that was the situation in which people like Dick Kramer found themselves.

If, between 1917 and 1983—the lifetime of the first Code of Canon Law—a child was born to parents at least one of whom was Catholic but whose marriage was considered, for whatever canonical reason, invalid, that child was illegitimate in the eyes of the Church. The only practical sanction was in being barred from the priesthood. After 1983, on promulgation of the new Code, such an illegitimate child was home free.

A man such as Dick Kramer could conceivably build up quite an anger over that sort of seemingly cavalier treatment.

He would be angry . . . an idea was coming; it was knocking on Koesler's mind . . . he would be angry . . . of course! He would be as angry with his parents—with his mother—as he would be with the Church. But not as long as Church law remained unchanged.

However, what if the Church were to simply change the law? What if, after all those years of feeling inadequate, soiled, unclean; what if, after all those years, the Church simply said, "Oh, it doesn't matter anymore"?

The first time Dr. Moellmann showed Koesler the mark of the branding iron, something, some glimmering from the past tried to enter his consciousness. He knew the memory would get there eventually. He just didn't know when.

Now.

Father Koesler needed to do some checking. And it could not begin until the workday began. But already he felt that deep sense of relief that comes from breaking through to the ultimate clue.

It was the middle of the night. There was nothing to do but wait. Koesler decided to read again. But so relaxed was he now that after a few paragraphs, he drifted into a sound if not untroubled sleep.

40

SHORTLY AFTER THE DOORS were unlocked at the chancery, Father Koesler arrived.

He'd been in this building many times in the past. At least to the clergy of the Roman Catholic Archdiocese of Detroit, 1234 Washington Boulevard was a familiar address. The ancient building housed St. Aloysius Church, a three-tiered structure that was unique, at least to Detroit.

In the same building above the church were residence rooms for priests assigned to downtown functions, as well as for visiting clergy. In addition, there were offices for the archbishop, the tribunal, and the chancery, among other departments. Hidden away here—appropriately, some might say—were the archives of the archdiocese.

While Koesler had on occasion visited almost every other department in the building at one time or another, he had never, until this morning, called on the archives. Even before the chancery opened this snowy morning, he had phoned Sister Clotilde of the Sisters, Servants of the Immaculate Heart of Mary to make certain she could and would accommodate him this morning. She could and would, but she did little to hide her surprise that he would call her. They knew each other only in passing and, to her knowledge, he had never before visited the archives. And her sharp memory covered a great number of years.

She sat him at a large table and fixed him with a quizzical smile. "Now, what can I do for you, young man?"

It was his turn to smile. He was in his late fifties, and she couldn't have been much older. Age, he thought, like so many other things in life, was relative. "I'm interested in the mottoes of Popes."

She inclined her head slightly to one side. "You are, are you?" There was something tantalizing about her tone. But she said nothing more that might clarify the remark and Koesler didn't pursue it.

"I'd like to start back around the turn of this century. In which case, each Pope, before becoming Pope, had been a bishop and then a Cardinal. And as bishop, each one had a motto as part of his coat of arms. That's what I'd like to see."

She whistled noiselessly. "A tall order, young man. But let's see what we can find."

Koesler started to rise but Sister Clotilde waved him back in his chair. "You stay put," she ordered. "I'll bring things to you. It's easier that way."

The first item she brought was a mug of steaming coffee, for which he was duly grateful. Next, she brought a chronological list of Popes. "Maybe," she said, "this will help you tell me exactly who you're interested in."

"Absolutely. Very good. Okay, let's see..." Koesler ran his finger down the list. "Let's try Pope Benedict XV, who was Pope from, uh...1914 to 1922."

She returned loaded down with books, several of which she pushed toward him. "You start with these and I'll take the rest."

There followed the quiet turning of pages, then exchanges, one book for another.

Koesler said, "I think this is it, Sister, doesn't this look like the motto for Cardinal Giacomo della Chiesa?"

"It sure does. And he became Pope Benedict XV. Is that what you're looking for?"

"I don't know. Wait a minute."

Koesler checked the motto against the drawing he'd brought with him—a reproduction of the marks left by the branding iron. "No, that's not it. It doesn't fit."

"What doesn't fit? Maybe it'd help if you told me what we're looking for."

278

"It's just too complicated to explain just now, Sister. I do need your help though."

Clotilde sighed. "Very well. Somebody else you want to look up?"

Koesler ran his finger down the list. "Let's see . . . yes: Pope Pius XI—1922 to 1939."

"I guess I should be grateful for small favors." Sister Clotilde shuffled back into the archives, arms burdened with the books just used and being returned to their shelves. "At least you're picking on fairly recent popes." Though no longer in view, she could be heard talking to herself. "Dear, dear, dear; where are you, Achille Cardinal Ratti? Ah, here!"

She reentered the reading room, again laden with books. "Here we go again." She divided the volumes between them.

After several minutes of searching, Sister Clotilde said, "Ah, here it is. This is it: the coat of arms for Cardinal Ratti, soon to become Pope Pius XI."

Koesler almost snatched the book from her hands.

"Well, for the love of Pete," she chided. "Take your time, Father Koesler. Moderation. In all things moderation."

"Sorry." He quickly but thoroughly checked the motto against the marks that had been burned into the flesh of three murder victims. It did not match. His expression told the tale.

"No go, eh?"

"Not yet."

"There's more?"

"One more."

"Who?"

"Pius XII."

"I don't know why, but I had a feeling we were headed toward him." She was gone for a few moments, then returned with more books. "You're sure now . . . no more?"

"No more. This has got to be it."

"I think I can find this one." Clotilde selected a volume and paged through it. "Here you go: the motto on the coat of arms of Eugenio Cardinal Pacelli. *Opus Justitiae Pax*—'Peace, the Fruit of Justice.'"

Koesler began to shake his head, but took the volume from

her anyway. He tried to work the motto into the upper half of letters that the brand had made. It was not even close to fitting.

He sat back with wildly conflicting emotions.

He was wrong. His theory, which had seemed so promising last night, went nowhere this morning. Definitely out of character for him. He was by no stretch of the imagination a "morning person." But, to the extent he had been so sure of himself, he now felt a rather deep depression.

On the other hand, his groundless theory was one more indication that Father Kramer was innocent. Koesler had given it his best shot. Usually when he reached a conclusion such as this, it proved to be well founded. And, as devil's advocate, for the first time in this investigation he had thrown aside the presumption of innocence for Kramer.

Accepting Lieutenant Tully's challenge to look at the facts with complete objectivity, Koesler had tried to tie the murders to Kramer and had failed.

Yes, definitely mixed emotions. But, if anything, the predominant feeling was one of relief that Kramer had come out of this clean. The next order of business would be to get Dick Kramer out to Guest House so he could get a handle on his alcoholism before it got completely out of control.

So deep in thought was Koesler that he had to fight his way back to reality and focus on what Sister Clotilde was saying.

"I said, there's more to this, you know."

"More? What do you mean?"

"I mean that the mottoes don't stand pat when a Cardinal becomes Pope."

"What?"

"The coat of arms automatically changes when one becomes a Pope. And so, it seems, does the man's motto."

"What?"

"You're repeating yourself. Here . . ." She handed him an impressive tome.

He studied the book, somewhat bewildered as to its relevance. It was *Acta Apostolicae Sedis—The Acts of the Apostolic See*—Volume XXXXII (1950). A slip of paper marked a specific place in the book. Koesler paged to it.

It was a document entitled *Munificentissimus Deus*—"The Most Gracious God."

He could not guess why Sister Clotilde had given this to him, nor why she had marked this section. He flipped several pages and came to the end of the document. It was signed, *Ego Pius, Catholicae Ecclesiae Episcopus, ita definiendo subscripsi*—"I, Pius, Bishop of the Catholic Church, identify this with my signature." Then came the seal:

"You see," Clotilde said, "Eugenio Pacelli took another motto once he became Pope. *Veritatem Facientes in Caritate* —'Accomplishing Truth in Charity.'"

Koesler stared at the motto for several moments. Then, slowly, he began to trace the words into the brand markings. They fit. Perfectly. It was a premonition come true. He stared at them.

After several moments, Sister Clotilde spoke. "That what you were looking for?"

Koesler nodded.

"When we got down to Pius XII and were still looking for mottoes, I thought that's what you might be looking for. Something came to mind and I thought that might be it." She paused. "Don't you want to know how I guessed?"

He looked at her wordlessly.

"I remembered that a few weeks ago, one of your confreres

was in here looking for exactly the same thing. But not the motto for Eugenio Pacelli; the one after he became Pius XII." Another pause. "Want to know who it was?"

Barely audibly, he said, "Father Kramer."

"How did you know?"

"Bingo." But there was no joy in it.

41

THEY SAT AROUND THE SMALL DINing room table in St. Anselm's rectory. With three large men, the table seemed smaller than usual.

Mrs. Mary O'Connor, parish secretary and wide-ranging factotum, had made a generous supply of coffee. Inspector Walter Koznicki, for one, was most grateful that Mrs. O'Connor, and not Father Koesler, had attended to the coffee.

Koesler was clearly a wreck. His hands were trembling slightly but noticeably, particularly perceptible to the trained eye of a psychologist.

Koesler's state was the principal reason Dr. Rudy Scholl had decided not to return to his office. He wanted to make certain that Koesler would be all right before leaving him. It had been a stress-filled afternoon for everyone, but especially for Father Koesler.

Nor had Koesler's condition been overlooked by Inspector Koznicki. He thought it might be helpful to keep the priest talking. So Koznicki had asked a series of questions. As, now, "Tell me, Father, how were you able to make sense of those markings left by the branding iron? That really turned out to be the linchpin in this case."

Koesler's smile was self-deprecating. "It was last night. I

couldn't sleep. Among the things on my mind were those meaningless marks on the victims. You see, it had never seriously crossed my mind that Father Kramer could possibly have been responsible for these murders. But last night, I finally decided to take Lieutenant Tully's suggestion and at least consider the possibility.

"One thing I knew that none of the rest of you did was that Dick Kramer was technically illegitimate, at least in the eyes of the Church. The significance of that popped into my mind last night when Lieutenant Tully was talking about his—I guess—well-founded theory on the importance that illegitimacy plays in the eventual crimes committed by quite a few multiple murderers.

"The total impact of illegitimacy hit Dick Kramer just as he became a teenager and applied for entrance in the seminary. I suppose this knowledge would affect different boys in dissimilar ways. Apparently, it devastated Dick and had its effect from that time on.

"All this I knew from talking to an older priest friend of mine who also is a friend of Dick's.

"So from that point, I asked myself: Supposing just for a moment that Father Kramer could have committed murder—what might motivate him to do the unspeakable? Could he have harbored a grudging resentment, even subconsciously, against his mother? In a mind too tired and stressed to think clearly, Dick might have held his unfortunate mother responsible for his distinctively second-class Church citizenship. After all, traditionally, the man proposes marriage, while the woman accepts or rejects. So perhaps Dick thought that since his father had been married previously and thus was excluded from a Church wedding, his mother should have turned him down. But she didn't. They were married by a justice of the peace and when Dick came along, he was considered by the Church to be a bastard. And, without special dispensation, he would be barred from the priesthood.

"Then, each of the victims was an older woman. Could that mean that someone—Dick?—was striking out at a mother figure?"

"Very interesting, Father," Koznicki said. "True, we did not know of the special character of Father Kramer's irregularity. How could we have known? How were we to guess?"

Dr. Scholl shrugged, responding only because Inspector Koznicki happened to be looking in his direction. Essentially, he continued to study Father Koesler, who now seemed somewhat more self-possessed. Silently, he endorsed Koznicki's ploy of encouraging Koesler to talk and get outside himself.

Koesler, for his part, was experiencing another of his recidivist urges. He wanted a cigarette. Fortunately none was at hand.

"Now," Koznicki continued, "how in the world did you come up with the motto that completed the branding marks?"

"I don't really know. I guess it was some kind of fluke . . . a combination of things, as I recall. What triggered my thinking was that I remembered that illegitimacy is no longer an impediment to the priesthood."

"It is not?" Koznicki was never sure what the new Church would or would not do. He considered for a moment. "That may be a step in the right direction."

"Oh, I agree," Koesler said. "But I wondered what that might do to a man like Dick Kramer. Imagine having your whole life turned topsy-turvy by a Church law. To have that law overshadow everything you do. Then, when the Church finally gets around to revising its law for the very first time since it was first codified in 1917, there isn't even a mention of the previous impediment!

"I thought it very possible that Dick—again, maybe subconsciously—now might be angry not only at his own mother, but also maybe in a more repressed way at Holy Mother Church.

"Then something else happened. You know that older priest I mentioned? His name is Monsignor Meehan. I visit him pretty regularly at the Burtha Fisher Home. I guess it does us both good. We just keep telling each other the same old stories over and over.

"One of the old stories, which I hadn't heard for a number

284

of years, concerned the selection of mottoes for a couple of Detroit's auxiliary bishops.

"You know, the first time I saw a picture of those branding marks at the medical examiner's office, something was knocking at my mind. It couldn't get in then, but I knew eventually it would.

"It happened last night. And it happened in a simultaneous way.

"At almost the same time as I was recalling Monsignor Meehan's story about a squabble over mottoes for coats of arms, I was also thinking about how angry Dick Kramer might well be over the Church's flip-flop attitude on illegitimacy. The two thoughts seemed to converge. Obviously, there was a change of leadership in the Church to bring about such a 180-degree switch in attitude. So someone in Dick's shoes could project his anger on one or another Church leader who ruled at a significant time. And that leader, now dead, would be personified by the motto he chose to symbolize his life.

"That's why I visited the archdiocesan archives this morning: to check out this theory. The first possibility, according to my hypothesis, was Pope Benedict XV, who was pope during the time the first Code of Canon Law was written and published. The second guess was Pius XI, who was Pope when Dick Kramer was born.

"Neither of their mottoes fit the incomplete markings on the victims.

"But the third guess hit pay dirt. Pius XII was Pope when Dick was at first rejected, then accepted by the seminary. This was the time when the enormity of Dick's situation hit him like a ton of bricks. And Pius XII's Papal motto fit perfectly in the puzzle the killer left.

"I suppose that would have been enough by itself. But when Sister Clotilde, the archivist, mentioned that Father Kramer had looked up the identical information sometime earlier, well . . ."

"Yes," Koznicki agreed, "that was a rather neat package."

Dr. Scholl noted that the tremor in Koesler's hands increased at this point. The priest began toying with a toothpick in an apparent effort to ease his agitation.

Koesler continued. "The evidence against Dick seemed incontrovertible. And yet I still couldn't believe that good man could possibly have done it. There had to be something deeply, radically wrong. Some terrible psychological aberration that caused this.

"That's when I called Dr. Scholl. I've referred so many troubled people to him, we've come to know each other quite well. Anyway, the doctor was kind enough to take all this time away from his schedule to help." He looked directly at Scholl. "For all you've done today, I will be forever grateful. Especially for, in effect, breaking this to Father Kramer."

Scholl simply nodded.

"Since Inspector Koznicki didn't join us until we got to Mother of Sorrows to confront Father Kramer," Koesler said, "maybe you could now explain your diagnosis to him, Doctor?"

"Well, it's hardly a full-blown diagnosis at this stage," Scholl said. "And I'm sure the inspector is familiar with a dissociative reaction."

Koznicki was indeed familiar with that specific variety of abnormal behavior. Forensic psychiatrists had alleged it often enough in court to elicit an immediate negative reaction from both police and prosecutors. But even without this doctor's expert testimony, Koznicki was very much prone to agree with this diagnosis. His nod, more for Koesler's benefit than his own, encouraged Dr. Scholl to expound.

"Briefly," Scholl proceeded, "it's based on very normal behavior—just as is every abnormality. Fear of heights, for instance, is quite common. But when the fear becomes so intense that it immobilizes a person, when it becomes beyond control, when it is irrational, it too becomes an abnormality, a pathology.

"So it is with a dissociative reaction. Perfectly normal people go on vacations to get away from the demands of everyday life. The housewife appreciates getting away from the house, from cooking, cleaning, grocery shopping, and the like. The businessman may prefer a wilderness where there are no demands to

286

shave, dress according to Molloy, attend meetings, and so forth.

"The dissociative reaction raises this natural desire to escape to a pathological level. It can take the form of massive amnesia, or a fugue—flight—or even multiple personalities. And I would not be surprised if we have all three of those manifestations in the case of Father Kramer.

"In Father's case, it would seem at least that he has been holding in an enormous amount of pressure and stress over a great number of years—starting at age thirteen when he was rejected by a seminary and discovered he was considered illegitimate. He seems to have compensated by attempting a constant overachievement.

"Frankly, carrying all that emotional baggage, I'm surprised he lasted as long as he did without a breakdown."

"It was the drinking that threw me off the track in the beginning." Koesler was addressing Koznicki. "I figured that if Dick was, by his own word, drunk pretty regularly on Sunday afternoons, and specifically on the two Sundays when the murders were committed, he couldn't possibly have done them. But the doctor assured me it is possible."

"Not only possible," Scholl completed the thought, "but I've seen it in my own practice any number of times. People go through elaborate functions and have no recollection of them whatsoever. What probably happened here was that Father Kramer did not drink as much as he thought he had. Or that he had built up a pretty good tolerance for a considerable amount of alcohol. In any case, the relaxing effect of the drink helped him slip into the reaction. As much as anything else, it was a matter of duration. I think Father suppressed this pressure for as long as he possibly could, and then he reacted."

"And he wouldn't know? He wouldn't have the slightest notion of where he'd been or what he'd done?" Koesler, still in a sense of near-disbelief, asked.

Scholl nodded. "A person must present a difficult report at work on Monday morning. A report for which he is completely unprepared. On Sunday he travels to Chicago. He is still there on Monday morning rather than in Detroit where he's supposed to be. He has experienced a fugue, a flight. He has no memory at all of having traveled to Chicago. He doesn't know how he got there or why he went. Only that he could not face that meeting. Then his defense mechanism took over.

"You saw earlier when I mentioned to Father Kramer the incident of his having gone to the archdiocesan archives to find the motto of Pope Pius XII, he remembered rather vaguely having done so. But he was unclear as to why he'd done it. Many dissociates can remember events that led to a fugue without any memory of the flight itself.

"What happens then—and, specifically, what happened in Father Kramer's case—was that his personality began to disintegrate. One Sunday, operating under a completely distinct personality, he forged and made the branding iron he would later use. He hid it and when the fugue was over, forgot it entirely.

"But he was ready. He was ready to throw off all that pressure and stress.

"And so the tragedy took place. On two consecutive Sundays, Father Kramer—or, rather, a distinct other person within Father Kramer—stalked a likely victim. His subconscious mind had been feeding for years on the notion that his mother, having given birth to an illegitimate son, was a whore. So he went looking for an older prostitute. He accompanied her to a place of assignation. Then he killed her, ripped out her reproductive organs, and branded her.

"As he returned to his normal self, he had lost a good deal of his subconscious hostility, but could not possibly face what he had done—or, rather, what his other personality had done. So he made a sweeping denial of the tragedy and of his participation in it. Then he made a sweeping repression of all he had denied. In other words, first he denied it happened, then he repressed the denial. As a result, he made all of his actions inaccessible and unconscious."

Dr. Scholl paused, satisfied that he had adequately explained Father Kramer's pathological reaction to intolerable stress. And indeed he had, particularly as far as Inspector Koznicki was concerned. Koznicki was certain that Scholl would testify for the defense along with a parade of expert witnesses. And, from his vast experience, Koznicki knew their testimony would be

288

effectual, particularly in Father Kramer's case. It was almost the only possible explanation for what had happened.

"Finally," Scholl concluded, "you both saw Father Kramer's reaction earlier this afternoon when I, in effect, talked him through the whole scenario. At first, he seemed a bemused listener. After all, he had just been released from prison. Another man—Bush—had been indicted for all three murders. And Father was back in the safety of his rectory with no memory of what he had actually done.

"But, as my explication of what really had happened continued, Father changed. First, in an incredulous reaction. Finally, there was a radical change as the truth began to seep into his conscious mind and the inaccessible began to become accessible."

Koesler would never forget it. Indelibly etched in his memory was the naked horror on Dick Kramer's face when he first began to comprehend what had happened. Koesler knew he would forever remember Kramer's cry of utter despair when faced with reality. That long, tortured wail, "Nooooo!" And, at that point, Kramer had only begun to get the first dark glimpse of the hell he would have to enter.

Fortunately, they had been able to get Father Kramer admitted to the psychiatric ward of the hospital under arrest and watch. He had been heavily sedated. He had a long, long way to go.

Father Koesler seemed more calm and self-possessed than he had even a few minutes before. Dr. Scholl decided everything was under control here and that it was more than time for him to get back to work. He made his farewells and departed.

Koznicki seemed undecided about leaving. "How about one more cup of coffee, Inspector?"

"Well, very good." Seeing it was not Koesler's coffee. "One more then."

"What now?" Koesler asked as he poured coffee in both cups. "Now?"

"The disposition of these cases. Like they used to do on the TV 'Dragnet' series. What's going to happen?"

Koznicki rarely indulged in speculation. He firmly believed that police work ended in the courtroom. From that point on, it was up to the justice system. However, he couldn't help but have an opinion based on years of experience. He could not bring himself to withhold that opinion when his friend asked for it.

"Arnold Bush," Koznicki said. "I do not see any way for him to avoid murder in the first degree. If that is the verdict, there is a mandatory sentence of life in prison with no possible parole. The only way out, short of death, would be a pardon by the governor."

"And Father Kramer?"

"Ah, yes, Father Kramer. That is another question. I believe we have just heard the totality of his defense in Dr. Scholl's explanation of a dissociative reaction. Father is blessed with one of the finest defense attorneys possible. But even with a far lesser lawyer, I feel Father's plea would be 'not guilty by reason of insanity.' And I believe that will be the verdict."

"Then what will happen to him?"

"If that is indeed the verdict, Father will be sent to Ypsilanti for sixty days, to be examined and evaluated by forensic psychiatrists. Then, dependent on their findings, he would be committed to a state facility until he is pronounced cured."

Koesler pondered for a moment. "Then there is a chance he will be free someday?"

Koznicki nodded as he blew over the surface of his hot coffee and tasted it. He wondered if there were any diplomatic way of suggesting that Father Koesler take a lesson or two in coffee-making from Mrs. O'Connor. Or from anyone, for that matter.

"And then what?" It was Koznicki's turn to ask.

"Then?"

"If and when Father Kramer is pronounced cured and released from custody, what will happen to him then? What will the Church do?"

"A good question." Koesler sipped the coffee. He could not tell the difference between Koesler-brewed coffee and anyone else's. "I'm not sure. I think it would be impossible for him to return to a ministry here. Not with all the notoriety of this case."

"But Father, the publicity has been nationwide. For all practical purposes, worldwide!"

"You're right. It has. So then what? A missionary to the backwoods of some Third World country where there hasn't been any news of anything? Something hidden away in one of the chancery offices? I don't know. This sort of thing scarcely happens. Only once in my lifetime—and this is it."

They were silent for a time. Koesler picked up one of the cookies Mrs. O'Connor had thoughtfully put out. He nibbled as he mused. Suddenly he brightened. "I think I have a solution, Inspector. But you're going to accuse me of having watched too many soap operas."

"I would never do that to you, Father. Your solution?"

"A good part of Dick Kramer's treatment, rehabilitation, what-have-you, will consist in coming to terms with himself—and with his priesthood. It is distinctly possible that in the time he is in therapy he may evolve a whole new outlook on life—life in general, his personal life, his life in the priesthood.

"I could well imagine that when he walks away from prison he may walk away from the priesthood as well."

"You really can?"

"Uh-huh. It would solve a lot of problems—for himself and for the Church. The Church really has no place to put him. And he must learn to live with what he's done. He'll have his hands full just doing that.

"Which leads me to my final thought for Dick Kramer: Call it a wish or a prayer—but I hope he will marry Sister Therese Hercher."

Shock passed over Koznicki's face.

"With his most peculiar set of circumstances," Koesler continued, "I expect he could get one of those rare laicization decrees that would enable him to marry in the Church. Therese could comparatively easily be released from her vows. It certainly would not be the first time in modern history that a priest and a nun would marry. She fairly worships him—a fact that has been evident to nearly everyone but him. And he will need her. He will desperately need her.

"And that, Inspector, is as close as I can come to a happy

291

ending. And it's a long way off with plenty of 'ifs' all around it."

Koznicki touched napkin to his lips. Koesler helped him into his coat and accompanied him to the door.

"Giving it some thought," Koznicki said, turning back at the doorway, "I very much like your scenario for Father Kramer. And I join you in your prayer. But one final question, Father. Before you found the motto of Pope Pius, did it never even once enter your mind that Father Kramer might be guilty?"

Koesler smiled. "Just once. Officer Mangiapane told me about the show-up when that eyewitness identified Father Kramer. I was sure she was mistaken. Then, when it seemed certain that Arnold Bush had committed all three murders, I had to wonder. The witness said the man she saw on those front steps had 'kind eyes.' Bush's eyes are hard, even cruel. Father Kramer has the gentle eyes."

They bade goodbye.

As Koesler closed the door, he realized he had to add one plea to his prayer for Father Kramer. That one day he might be able to forgive himself.

42

IN THE BACKGROUND, ON TV, the Red Wings were playing the Black Hawks. As with any time a Detroit team played a Chicago team—football, basketball, baseball, or in this case, hockey—there were no holds barred.

Neither Alonzo Tully nor Alice Balcom were paying much attention to the game. Each worked very intensely at very difficult jobs and whenever possible they spent quiet times together.

Tonight they were intertwined at one end of the couch. Tully was massaging Alice's shoulders and neck. Alice emitted periodic sighs of pleasure and unwinding.

"It's all over, isn't it, Zoo?"

"Over? Not hardly; the Wings are down by only two goals."

"Not the hockey game, Zoo; the case. The Cass Corridor Slasher."

Tully snorted. "Goddam, I'm not sure. Everytime it looks like we've got a lock on it, something else develops." He paused. "Forget it. You're right. It's dead now. It's over."

"And Kramer is guilty of the first two?"

"Pleading insanity."

"Will it stick?"

After hesitation: "Probably."

"Are you sure?"

Pause. "No. That's up to the court. We got the guy."

"And the third was a copycat."

"Yeah. Bush. Arnold Bush."

"One thing I can't figure. The other guy—Bush—he set up Kramer, didn't he?"

"Uh-huh."

"But how did he know Kramer did the first two?"

"Blast Yzerman! Can you beat that! Gets a penalty while we're two goals down and five minutes left in the game! . . . What? How did he know? He *didn't* know. What he knew was we released an artist's sketch of the killer. Bush knew the sketch resembled him. He also knew he looked like Kramer. The killer dressed like a priest, drove a black Ford, looked very much like both himself and Kramer. After that it didn't much matter.

"As far as Bush was concerned it didn't make much difference whether Kramer was the guilty one or not. Though the possibility there was a third look-alike out there dressing like a priest, et cetera, was pretty slim.

"Bush, of course, knew the killer's M.O. He saw the results of it in the morgue. His plan was to set Kramer up, have him arrested. If Kramer actually was guilty, so much the better. If he wasn't, like as not the real killer would lay low for a while and see what happened to Kramer—who might just take the fall.

Then, as soon as Kramer is out on bail, Bush had one free copycat murder at his disposal, which would satisfy his need for revenge on whores and which could be dumped on Kramer.

"It worked pretty good until that priest spotted that photo in Bush's apartment."

"'That priest,'" Alice reminded, "was more help than you thought he'd be."

Tully chuckled. "You ain't gonna let me forget that, are you? If Koesler hadn't been so goddam stubborn about Kramer bein' innocent, God knows what woulda happened. Kramer was up for Murder One—two counts—until Koesler found Bush. Then Bush was up for Murder One—three counts—until Koesler found the key to the puzzle. Now Kramer will probably walk when the shrinks say he's cured. And Bush'll rot for his copycat crime."

"A little lower, Zoo. Right there between the shoulder . . . ahhh. So, like I said, the priest was more help than you thought he'd be."

"There were times when I thought he was more of a hindrance than a help. But when he located the branding iron Kramer used, I had to admit you were right."

Alice sat bolt upright. "He found the iron!"

"Yup. That hasn't got to the news yet."

"And you didn't tell me!"

"I been busy.

"Actually, he didn't find the thing; he told us where to look. He said he got the idea from talking to some old priest in a nursing home. It was some kind of joke about a guy who flunked his priest test when he said they should burn down a church and throw the ashes in a sacrarium."

"A suck-what?"

"Somebody—Mangiapane probably—was talkin' to Koesler about how we'd looked everywhere for the iron. We practically took Kramer's car and the rectory and the church apart lookin' for that iron. So Koesler ups and says how Kramer probably considered the iron a sacred instrument in what Doc Moellmann said was a ritual. And when they're done with sacred items, priests are supposed to dispose of them so they won't be desecrated by us human beings. And the traditional place to do that is the sacrarium."

"The suck-what?"

"Babe, I'm gonna end up knowin' so many Catholic words I'll be able to teach catechism. In the sacristy—where the priest gets dressed for Mass—there's a sink they call the sacrarium. It don't lead to the sewer system. It goes straight into the ground. We dug out the sacrarium in Mother of Sorrows church and—voila!—the branding iron. And with all the letters on it . . . just like Koesler found in that Pope's motto."

"Your turn," Alice announced.

He did not object as they traded places and she began to knead the tension from his shoulders.

"Well, that pretty well wraps it up." She paused. "You know, you could feel pretty sorry for that Father Kramer."

Tully was in deadly earnest. "I could feel lots sorrier for him if I didn't feel so bad about three ladies who would be alive today if it weren't for him."

ABOUT THE AUTHOR

William X. Kienzle, author of the highly acclaimed *The Rosary Murders* and *Death Wears a Red Hat*, was ordained into the priesthood in 1954 and spent twenty years as a parish priest. For more than twelve of those years he was editor-in-chief of the *Michigan Catholic*. After leaving the priesthood, he became editor of *MPLS Magazine* in Minneapolis and later moved to Texas, where he was director of the Center for Contemplative Studies at the University of Dallas. Kienzle and his wife Javan presently live in Detroit, the setting for all three of his novels, where he enjoys playing the piano and organ and participating in sports as diversions from his writing.